LEAGUE OF SHADOWS

Also by Ron Terpening

Fiction

IN LIGHT'S DELAY

STORM TRACK

THE TURNING

Literary Criticism

CHARON AND THE CROSSING:
ANCIENT, MEDIEVAL, AND RENAISSANCE
TRANSFORMATIONS OF A MYTH

LODOVICO DOLCE, RENAISSANCE MAN OF LETTERS

BEAUTIFUL ITALY, BELOVED SHORES:
AN ILLUSTRATED CULTURAL HISTORY OF ITALY

ANTHOLOGY OF ITALIAN LITERATURE:
MIDDLE AGES AND RENAISSANCE

LEAGUE

OF

SHADOWS

RON TERPENING

Stuyvesant & Hoagland
New York

2/05

Publisher's Cataloging-in-Publication
(Provided by Quality Books, Inc.)

Terpening, Ron.
    League of shadows / Ron Terpening. — 1st trade ed.
    p. cm.
    ISBN 0-9755761-0-0
    1. Fascism—Fiction. 2. Ovra (Organization : Italy)—Fiction.
3. Mussolini, Benito, 1883-1945—Fiction. 4. Italy—History—1922-
1945—Fiction. 5. United States. Office of Strategic Services—
Fiction. 6. World War, 1939-1945—Underground movements—
Italy. 7. Historical fiction. I. Title.
PS3570.E6767L36 2005   813'.54
                                QB133-2036

Cover design by Robert Aulicino

Printed in the United States of America by Sheridan Books, Inc., on acid-free paper

For Vicki
with love

CONTENTS

PRELUDE

CHAPTER 1

Friday, August 9, Zanderij airport, Parimaribo, Suriname

The first burst, fired from directly below the craft, tore through the starboard wing of the single-engine Norseman. Machine-gun fire. The throaty roar of the engine drowned out the sound of the bullets ripping through the plane's ancient fabric. The pilot, as if unaware of the danger below, took no evasive action. Moments later, announced by a terrible explosion, the second burst, streaming up from a hill in the plane's flight path, shattered the forward windscreen, killing the pilot. The plane, which had just passed through three hundred meters on its ascent out of Zanderij airport, shuddered and lost speed. Strips of tattered fabric ripped away. The starboard wing dipped and began to flap violently.

In the cabin, strapped into a seat in front of the freight compartment, the plane's owner, a Dutchman named Theunis Kloos, struggled to free himself from his safety harness. Blinded by the rushing wind, he screamed for help over the engine's roar, but the pilot, a Bush Negro in his employ for the last eight years, failed to respond. Blood from the man's lacerated head splattered back through the cabin, striking Kloos in the face with the force of hard-driven rain. Panic seized the Dutchman. The quick release handles of the rear exit hatch were within reach, tempting him to jump. A chute! If only he'd worn a chute!

But the plane was still flying, had righted itself as if on autopilot.

Ja hoor! He had a chance!

The aircraft, a demilitarized C-64A transport, built by Noorduyn to ferry freight and passengers in World War II, had seen postwar service from the Canadian bush in the North to the jungles of Suriname on the coast of South America. For the past ten years in Suriname, Kloos had utilized the plane for transport between the capital city of Paramaribo and his plantations deep in the interior. It had suffered its bad days, including a crash landing at Nieuw Nickerie, but Kloos had lovingly restored it, and the original Pratt and Whitney engine, a 600-horsepower Wasp, had not missed a beat.

God bless the old beast! They were both too rugged to die.

With the strength of a man twenty years younger, Kloos freed himself from his seat and staggered to the cockpit. Shielding his eyes from the wind, he looked at the dials on the instrument panel. Fuel flow normal. Temps and RPMs okay. Oil and hydraulic pressure steady. Kloos lowered the lifeless body of the pilot to the floor and then slipped behind the stick. The plane had swung slowly to the west, into the afternoon sun. To the north, out the right window, Kloos could see the aquamarine of the Atlantic shelf merging in a blur with an aqueous sky. The polders along the fluvial coastal plains, joined by silvery lines, *leidings*, narrow canals for the runoff, reflected the afternoon sun like shiny mirrors, and in mid-distance, patches of savannah rose to meet the undulating hills and the rain forests that lay to the south. With the skill of a man who had flown for much of his life, Kloos brought the plane, juddering violently now, around on its original heading. The landing strip at Brokopondo would be the closest. He could already make out the shimmer of the reservoir behind the dam. Below him slithered the wide Suriname River, dark with tannic acid, winding its way through the tropical jungle like a fat water snake. An easy direction marker. And at worst he could bring the plane down into its meandering current.

His briefcase with the files . . . He looked over his shoulder, straining to see. What had he done with it? Five minutes ago, he'd been clutching it in his lap. And then, before he could turn around, the plane started to come apart. One corner of the V-shaped strut that anchored the starboard wing to the central frame broke loose, and pieces of fuselage started to flake away.

The plane began a slow spiral to the right, toward the jungle. Kloos fought to bring it around, to land in the shallow river bed, but the controls were dead.

The Norseman lost height quickly then, plunging down into the thick mass of jungle. Before the undercarriage touched the tree tops, the starboard wing ripped off and the plane began to disintegrate. Kloos lost all sense of perspective, the only sensations those of thunderous sound and darkness.

He woke to a horrible scream that seemed to last forever. When he realized it was his own voice, he tried to stop but the agony in his back was unbearable. Somehow, in the crash landing, he had been turned around in the cockpit and a jagged edge of the control panel had gouged a seam along his spine. When his scream finally diminished to a prolonged moan, he heard shrill voices in the distance. Shouted commands. The sharp, ringing notes filtered with clarity through the still-silent forest. The guerrillas would soon arrive.

Overhead, the plane's canopy had been stripped back and laid bare. The engine cowling was nowhere to be seen. Like the cords of a collapsing parachute, vines rose into the dim expanse stretching above him, hanging loosely from immense trees whose tops were lost in leafy darkness. He reached up and tugged on a vine. The gnarled liana straightened, held his weight. The voices were closer now. Excited calls growing louder as men hacked their way through the jungle's dense undergrowth. Kloos knew who they were. Guerrillas. Hailing each other in Taki-Taki, a pidgin mixture of English and Dutch. Men who hated him. They had lain in wait for his flight. Twice now, they had tried to kill him, angry at his support for the government in power. When they found him, they would torture and then kill him.

With sinewy arms knotted in strain, he pulled himself out of the cockpit and perched on the mangled frame. Each movement sent a stab of pain up his spine. Gritting his teeth, he slowly worked his way to the ground, landing in soggy soil choked with jungle vegetation. What remained of the plane was suspended in a tangled net of lianas, poised three meters above the ground. With a frightened glance around him, Kloos plunged into a swampy morass, moving quickly away from the crash site. Buttress roots, thorny palms, razor grass—a mass of tangled undergrowth impeded his progress. A kingfisher shrieked a challenge, jumping from branch to branch above his head. The murky water rose to his chest. Its putrid smell stung his nostrils and the back of his throat. Strands and clumps of rotting vegetable matter swirled around him. Dusk would rob the land of all light within a matter of hours. To survive, he would have to spend the night in the forest, with poisonous insects, spiny rats, and capybaras, with jaguars, crocodile-like caimans, and twenty-foot anaconda, with the dreaded bushmaster snake.

Suddenly he halted. The guerrillas had reached the plane. He could hear their excited cries barely fifty meters away. It would take the men only a few minutes to search the plane. *The case!* He'd forgotten to look for it in his mad scramble from the smashed cockpit. Better for it to have been lost in the jungle as the plane disintegrated in its mad plunge to earth. If the guerrillas found it . . . He didn't want to think about that. The case contained files that were his livelihood, damaging evidence of past crimes of men in power. Men and women were willing to pay to keep secret what the files disclosed.

He had to go back. Soon. In the darkness of night, the plane would be impossible to find. When the men left, he would come out of hiding and wait for daylight to search the surrounding jungle. Finding the case was all that mattered. He moved toward higher ground, crawled up a muddy bank and crouched under the tangled roots of a manioc tree, searing off through force of will the pain in his spine. Moving slowly, skirting the edge of the swamp, ready to slip into its depths if necessary, he approached the crash site. From thirty meters away, he counted the guerrillas. Eight of them, all heavily armed. They had cut the net of tangled lianas. What remained of the plane lay flat on the trampled vegetation. And then he heard the words and his heart froze.

Hier is het pak! De koffer!

They'd found the case.

A man emerged from the cabin with the leather satchel in one hand. He raised it above his head and shouted in triumph.

Kloos felt his stomach cramp, overcome by a sickness that

dizzied him, left him feeling weak as if he'd been suddenly and savagely emasculated. The adrenaline that had propelled him away from the downed plane dissipated like mist in a dry wind. In despair, he put his face down in the mud, his fingers clawing the ground, the pain in his back, which he had succeeded in beating down, now overwhelming. It would have been better had he died in the crash.

He lay on the ground, unable to move, while the men made a desultory search of the area and then disappeared into the undergrowth, their voices slowly waning. Kloos dreaded the thought of what remained to him now—nothing short of open, gut-wrenching war. *They'd taken his livelihood.* No longer would he be able to work from behind the scenes. No longer would others, in fear, jump to his commands. The powerful would no longer automatically heed his call. He choked down the madness that threatened to engulf him. Control, he thought. *Control!* His jaw grew rigid with the strain. He'd gone it alone before, he could do it again. *That was simply the way it had to be . . . .*

CHAPTER 2

Sunday, August 11, the Virginia countryside near Washington, D.C.

At night, the manor house rose like an apparition from the crest of a gentle hill, its darkened, westward-facing windows overlooking an Italian garden that lay spread out below it like the pleated skirt of a woman at rest, her knees two small knolls around which wound a long unpaved ribbon of a driveway. The guards had completed one circuit of the estate with their leashed attack dogs and were now watching TV in a caretaker's cottage near the southern wall of the property. The dogs were in a nearby run. They were not allowed to roam, for they had fallen into the habit of chasing and killing the miniature deer that ranged the walled, fifteen-acre estate.

Flood lights bathed the exterior of the imposing Victorian manse, and occasionally a starburst of sparks flitted from one of the massive chimneys and then died in the moist night air. Unseasonably cool for summer. The fire came from the master den, one of the colder rooms with its floor-to-ceiling windows that faced the east and were soonest in shade.

The owner of the mansion was in the den, sitting in a luxurious teal-blue wing chair ten feet from the hearthstone, feet stretched out toward the crackling pine fire, back to the door that led into the second-floor hallway. As was his habit at this late hour, he was sipping a cherry brandy while reading a leather-bound volume from his magnificent library, a work of history, which he took up and put down as the spirit moved him.

Major industrialist, international gadfly, close friend and confidant of the President, he was a vigorous man of medium height with dark brown hair and an unlined face that belied his seventy-some years. Among other things, he was founder and former chief executive officer of S & A Amalgamated, a conglomerate of steel and aluminum companies with subsidiaries and affiliates worldwide.

Deep in thought, he stared vacantly at the pine logs, his ears deaf to the splutter and pop of the resin that oozed out along the ax cuts, grew brittle in the heat, then exploded against the metal screen. Above the marble mantelpiece hung a row of framed ribbons holding medals won in the Second World War. The old man's eyes settled on the medals, so familiar as to be unseen. To him, they were all meaningless, at best ornaments to impress his guests. The only medal that mattered was one he could never display, awarded to him in a secret ceremony in Switzerland, late in 1943.

The war years . . . the undercover missions . . . the treachery and betrayals. So long ago now, and yet so close.

A noise outside drew his attention to the French doors to his right. The tall glass panes gave out on the dark countryside and reflected his solemn countenance. He picked up a gun lying on the lamp stand to his right and pointed it at the reflection. A lesser man—or one given to symbolic acts—might have pulled the trigger, shattering the window and erasing the worried vision that stared back at him. A face frightened by the possibility of imminent failure.

The old man laid down the gun and laughed dryly. He was not a man of symbolic acts or vain gestures. When he pulled the trigger—or, rather, when his men did it for him—someone else would be in the gun's sights, someone else would die. His ruthless ambition would chew up the opposition like mud under tank tracks. There were three men he feared. Three men from the past who knew they'd been betrayed, but not by whom. Only now, after all this time, it seemed one of them had stumbled onto the secret. Had he told the others? Probably. If so, each one would die—until there was no one left who knew, no one except himself, and then the legacy of the past would finally cease to haunt him.

He glanced at his Patek Philippe pocket watch. Ten minutes yet before his man Akkad arrived for a final briefing. And then maybe he could get some sleep.

He shook his head. Why now? The Washington Post lay on the floor beside his chair, open to the page where he'd seen the short article on guerrilla activity in Suriname. An old Norseman shot down by leftist guerrillas, the *bosneger* pilot killed, on board the owner of the plane, a man named Theunis Kloos, whose body had not yet been found.

The Dutchman had already blackmailed him once. But Kloos was in South America, a right-wing, would-be dictator whose man in Paramaribo, currently in charge of the government, was as corrupt as he. The old man in the States had let himself be blackmailed, buying with his contribution to the Dutchman's cause not only protection for S & A's bauxite mines in Suriname but silence. And now this . . . A plane shot down in the jungle. The body not found. A hint that certain files were missing . . . maybe in the hands of the guerrillas.

Who would have thought Kloos would wind up in Suriname? Sure, it was a former Dutch colony, and Kloos came from Holland, but still . . . a stroke of bad luck that. The only one of the three who had ever seen him face to face. And that by accident— passing in the halls of the Vatican. And then a second time, over forty years later, in Suriname of all places, the two had met. Now, the old man's intelligence sources had informed him that the Dutchman, for some reason, was in touch with a Mafia don, ensconced in his villa in the Sonoran desert south of Tucson. That made no sense—until they told him the mafioso was a man named Beppe Aprico.

It was then that the old man had begun to worry. Beppe Aprico was a dangerous man, head of the Southwest's largest drug syndicate, protected in his younger days by the CIA because he had often provided the agency with illicit funds for covert political action. If Kloos had gotten to Aprico, that meant Thomas Gage would be next. The three of them had served together in northern Italy, late in the war. Aprico and Kloos had disappeared soon after, but Gage had gone on to a twenty-year career in intelligence. They were dangerous men, despite their age, and the old man had acquired a dossier on each.

• • •

Vasco Akkad listened intently as his boss talked. Half-Italian, half-Lebanese, raised and educated by an English nanny in one of the nicer suburbs of Rome while his parents, actors both, cavorted around the globe, Akkad began his career as a mercenary trained in a Libyan terrorist camp, working deep cover—or so he claimed later—for SISMI, the Italian military intelligence service. But to the men who hired him in the years that followed, the details of Akkad's background were of little concern; what mattered were the results he promised—and then delivered; he was a master of dirty tricks, not the least of which was murder.

He listened while his boss told him about the three men— about the plane that had been downed in Suriname—and then about the grandson of one of the men, a kid who was an undercover cop with a narcotics squad.

The old man tugged on the loose folds of skin at his neck. "I'd like you to start with Gage. Ex-CIA but he'll be the easiest. He lives by himself in a cabin in the mountains outside Durango. Ever been to Colorado?"

Akkad shook his head.

"Well, he'll be miles from help and shouldn't be much of a problem. Best of all, I don't think the others will learn about it in time to react before you get to them."

"I like to do the tough ones first—*il padrone* and *l'Olandese*, the mob guy and the Dutchman, then the easy one."

"It's a question of geography. Take care of Gage first. Aprico second. The mafioso's holed up in a villa in the desert surrounded by men for protection. And the Dutchman isn't going to be easy either. He's got his own army in the jungle. A plantation up the Commewijne river in Suriname. The CIA says the whole country's up in arms, so when you get down there you'll be dropping into what may turn out to be a war zone."

"What about the kid?"

"The kid?" The old man paused and stroked his jaw. Gage's grandson was an unknown factor. "I've been thinking about him."

"I don't like undercover cops."

"Yeah, he won't like you either." He pursed his lips. "It's a problem. He's been using his grandfather's connections with Aprico to infiltrate the family. Aprico thinks the kid's an accountant."

"This kid, what's his name?"

"Nick Ferron. Gage is his maternal grandfather. Ferron wouldn't even be a narc if it wasn't for Gage. The old man pulled a few strings in Washington."

"Why'd he have to do that?"

The man crossed his legs and sighed. "It's a long, complicated story."

"Skip it, then."

"No, it doesn't hurt to know the connections." He reached for his snifter, swirled the cherry brandy, then set the glass down without drinking. "Ever hear of the Grand Coulee Dam murder?"

Akkad shook his head.

"It was before your time. A famous case back in '66. Frank Ferron, this is the cop's father, Franco Ferroni I guess they called him then, came here from Italy to work on the dam. He wound up marrying Thomas Gage's daughter, a girl named Irene. Anyway, the guy went crazy—some kind of jealous fit—and wound up killing his wife for talking to the neighbor. They'd had two kids by then and he almost got both of them—Nick and a younger sister. They testified against him in court."

"The father in prison now?"

The old man snorted. "Frank was sent to the Federal pen in Washington. About two years later one of Aprico's hoods stabbed him to death. The Feds couldn't prove it, but it looked like Gage called in a favor from his old buddy. Got the guy that killed his daughter. I don't think the kids ever knew. The boy was only ten when it happened. Gage raised the kids. Retired from the CIA and moved out west with his wife. She died a couple years later. He ran an insurance agency until the kids were old enough to be out on their own."

Akkad sat forward in his chair. "It sounds like I should do the kid, too." He shrugged. "Raised by his grandfather, you know, they gotta be close. You don't want any loose threads."

The old man nodded. "Just remember, the kid's a cop. You sure you can handle this?"

"What's he know—a little ka-ra-te?" Akkad waved his hand as if brushing at a fly. "Maybe I can use the cop against the *mafioso*—especially if the kid is already inside." He tapped the tips of his fingers together for a moment, then looked up. "I could set up a drug bust."

"Don't complicate the simple. I don't want Aprico busted. I want him dead." The old man's voice had risen a notch.

Akkad raised both hands in a placating gesture. "No problem. I'll get in touch with some friends in the DEA." Thinking it out as he spoke. "They can set up the bust, take this cop Ferron out at the same time. Make it look like, you know, he went in with *il padrone*." Akkad lay one finger over the other. "Like they're together in bed."

The old man waited a moment, then spoke. "I don't need to know how you're going to do it. Just take care of it. And one other thing. When you're finished up here, when you're down in Suriname and Kloos is out of the picture—"

"Yeah?"

"Find his files and destroy them."

Akkad grinned. "That's all? For free maybe I take out the guerrillas too."

The old man frowned. Akkad was doing his James Bond impression and his flippancy grated on the old man's nerves. "Just do what you're told. I don't want any papers left. The same goes for the guys in this country. If you find anything that connects them, letters, papers, whatever, destroy them."

"I'll use the *corolla di ombre*. That'll take care of the problem."

"Now what the hell is that?"

"The little pieces of a flower." Akkad made a plucking motion with his hands. "Shadows. My men are like petals."

The old man shook his head. "The corolla of shadows—will you forget the fancy names, for Christ's sake. Keep it simple and get it done. That's all I'm asking."

"You got it," Akkad said. He counted out the targets on the fingers of one hand. "Gage . . . Aprico . . . the kid if he gets in the way . . . Kloos . . . the files." And then, unable to resist, he unsheathed a twelve-inch, serrated combat knife, kissed the blade, and added, "See you one week from now."

PART ONE

THE UNKNOWN FACTOR

"There is always an unknown factor. That is the umbra."
—Benito Mussolini, after sketching a figure
throwing a cone of shadow

BOOK ONE

THE ADVENT

"Certainly virtue is like precious odors, most fragrant when they are incensed or crushed; for prosperity doth best discover vice, but adversity doth best discover virtue."
                    —Sir Francis Bacon

CHAPTER 1

Tuesday, August 20, Sonoran desert near Tucson, Arizona

Hector Torres leaned back against the wall of the ranch house. "Know what the don did when I whacked his bodyguard? Splattered the guy's brains all over the don's new suit?"

Nick Ferron shook his head.

Torres snorted. "Shit his pants. Stench was terrible, man. He eyeballs me and then he says, 'You mind if I go to the toilet?' And I go, 'It looks like you already have.' 'Yeah,' he says, 'only I can't flush my shoes.'"

Ferron laughed.

Torres stroked the stubble on his chin. They'd been in the house five days now. "Fucking guy figures he's next, still has a sense of humor."

"That's Chicago for you," Ferron said. "Out here, they come to the desert, their balls dry up. Like those little round onions."

"Fuck that shit. Don't never retire, man. Put you out of action."

"Yeah, except for Aprico. He's different. He's got *coglioni* down to here."

"You mean *cojones*, dude. You ain't been around my sister enough."

"I haven't been around your sister at all, Torres."

"Yeah, well you need a little Chicana pussy, man. Forget that Italian shit. Sound like you a mafioso or something."

Ferron shrugged. Hey, that was how he'd done it. But no use telling Torres. None of the guys knew he'd been undercover, that he was the source.

What he'd told the chief was that for the last two months Aprico had been shacked up with one of the Columbian mules. A girl who couldn't have been older than sixteen. Living in his desert hideout where the medicine chests in the bathroom held more pillboxes of coke than of aspirin.

Not long now, if the weather forecast was right for once.

Five days they'd waited. Seventeen men in the squad. Too damn many. Packed into the abandoned ranch's bunkhouse and a small adobe casa. The adobe had a ceiling of vigas and saguaro ribs, with a foot of dirt packed on top of that, but no air conditioning. It should have been cool, but after a summer of relentless heat, the mud walls and ceiling were like the sides of an oven, and the bunkhouse was worse. Only one archaic shower, with almost no water pressure. A quick shower every other day, the captain had said, to which someone had grumbled, "Fucking going to smell us coming a mile off."

The members of the MANTIS assault team were waiting in the abandoned ranch for a monsoon storm that would be severe enough to cover their entry into Beppe Aprico's desert compound. They needed a lightning storm to explain the sudden loss of power, a storm strong enough to last into the evening when darkness would cover their movements. Any advance warning of the raid and invaluable documents would be destroyed by the men around Aprico. Once the monsoon season's first storm broke and the captain radioed the go command, an agent would throw a switch at the substation south of Tucson, at which point the compound's electrified outer fences and the alarm system for the villa itself would fail. Ferron had reported that the portable emergency generator ran only the interior lights. He'd seen to it that the main backup generator had malfunctioned; it was now in Los Angeles for repair.

Five days, while the forecasters kept saying the monsoon storms would arrive that afternoon. Unbearable heat, the stench of sweat, lousy food, general discomfort—a fugue state that reminded him of a gloomy Futurist painting he'd seen once in one of his grandfather's Italian books. What was the title? *Those*

Who Wait. He couldn't remember the artist, just the vision of ghostly shadows in green and gray waiting to be carried off.

One of the Senior Agents provided by the DEA had told them they could use the time to get to know each other better. That was a laugh. Ferron had no interest in baring his soul to strangers— especially cops. He had no friends on the force—not even Hector Torres—and didn't want any. The job had cost him his wife. Made him feel sorry for himself and that made him angry. Hadn't he always hated cops when he was a kid? They hadn't done anything to stop his father.

And what made him think MANTIS would be any different? He'd joined the undercover squad because it allowed him to work alone. And now he'd been ordered to take part in a major raid. He worked intelligence, not assault, he'd told the chief. "And, besides, I've just cracked the surface. We wait and we can round up the whole ring. We got suppliers outside the country. We got mules that transport the drugs. There's gotta be somebody who oversees the transaction at the other end. Shoot, we won't even be coming close to the distributors in the West and Southwest."

The chief had listened, but in the end, what with pressure from higher up, there'd been no choice. Aprico was too important—a big name—a supposedly retired Mafia don. Congress and the newspapers would love the news. Senator Sprague would be out in a flash, his mug on the evening news. One more *capo* brought to justice. But with Aprico out of the picture, Ferron said, someone else would step in to fill the breach. At most, MANTIS would gain a month or two of leeway. The chief shrugged. The decision had already been made.

Something was going on. Too much interference—agents from the DEA, FBI, Customs Service, and the Border Patrol, Federal and State prosecutors, an officer from the Criminal Investigation Bureau of the State Police, IRS investigative accountants, and a woman from the Federal Organized Crime Drug Enforcement Task Force. And Senator Sprague would take credit for everything. His men were hovering in the background, making sure the Senator would be available for any photo ops. The MANTIS agents were beginning to feel like the ugly kid sister, along for the ride but stuck in the trunk.

So the five days had passed like blood dripping through a clepsydra.

For a while, to pass the time, the guys told jokes. When those ran dry, they traded horror stories, each one trying to outdo the others. Nick could have told his own—from his childhood—but no one would have understood.

He'd thrown a rock and hit his younger sister on the head, and now his dad was beating him. They stood in the kitchen, face to face, the boy with his arms crossed in front of his chest, protecting his stomach while his father slapped him back and forth. The blows stung, but he was afraid to raise his hands higher for fear his father would slug him in the belly and knock the wind out of him. He was asthmatic and if he lost his breath, the panic would start. So he protected his stomach while his dad taunted him in his strong Italian accent, told him he would teach him to pick on someone smaller than him, asking him see what it's like?

Blood began to spurt from his nostrils. His head swung with the blows and the blood splattered the white kitchen walls to each side. His father asked him why he didn't protect his face, but the boy said nothing in response. He avoided the angry eyes, just stared at the massive, hairy arms, at the thick fingers of the hands that struck him. Waiting it out. The blows stopped after a while, and finally his father left the room, shaking his head in disgust. The kid stood there silently, unable to move, blood dripping down his lips and onto his shirt. And then instead of words came silent tears.

He tuned out after a while, thinking about his dog. He hoped the high school kid he'd hired to feed and walk Rowdy was doing his job. After Sharon had packed up and returned to her folks in L.A., divorce papers in hand, the golden retriever was the only one left he could talk to. And the nice thing was, the dog never talked back. Just gave him that quizzical grin with one side of his upper lip stuck on his gums.

Sharon was another matter. She'd called again a week ago, wanting to rehash the past, trying to get him to talk when he didn't feel like it. *It was over!* He was tired of talking. Hell, he was tired of being manipulated. That's when she'd exploded. Tried to blame everything on *his* past. His *dad* had fucked him up, she said, not her. What could you say to that? Maybe it was true. He hated what his dad had been—a vile beast: wife beater, child abuser, murderer. Hated him more when he recognized the same anger in himself—only he'd never taken it out on others, just turned it in on himself. But most of all, he hated not being able to kill a man who was already dead.

Sharon's call wasn't the only one he'd received last week. The day before the squad was locked up in the ranch, incommunicado, his sister had telephoned from Durango. Barbara had told him that Wolf, their grandfather's Australian shepherd, had turned up in town without him. She was worried.

"How long's Gran Babbo been at the cabin?" he asked. Gran Babbo was an affectionate term for their grandfather. In the early years, when they were still young and Thomas Gage was the only dad they had (forget the monster locked up in prison), no matter how often he told them Gran Babbo was incorrect Italian, that they should call him "nonno," the name stuck. "Great Daddy." That said it all. He was the only man Ferron had ever loved.

"He's only been there a few days," Barbara said, "but I think I'll send Richard up this weekend. Make sure everything's all right. Did I tell you Gran Babbo spent a week in Washington, D.C.?"

"You're kidding. The way he talks I didn't think he'd ever go back."

"He said he'd got a letter from someone in South America. He didn't want to explain, just said something about it putting him back on track."

"On track for what?"

"He wouldn't say. And he left for the cabin once he got back. Said he'd spent the week in the National Archives. He didn't look happy."

"I wish he'd talk more about what's bothering him. It's like he's still trying to protect us."

Barbara didn't say anything for a moment. She took a deep breath. "I'm worried he might have had a heart attack."

Ferron heard the quaver in her voice. "He's too strong for that."

"Nick, he's seventy-four."

"I've never seen a healthier guy for his age. He'll be tramping up the hills for another twenty years." He paused. "Any snow in the mountains yet?"

"No, and you know Gran Babbo can handle snow. He's got enough food up there to last a month."

"Then what's the big worry? Wolf probably just wandered off. He's more used to the house in town than the cabin."

She was silent for a moment, a low hum on the telephone line. "Two men came by to see him," she finally said. "I told them where the cabin was." Sensing his displeasure, she hurried on. "They said they were acquaintances. Friends of his former comrades in the OSS."

He didn't like that. The cabin was private. Family only. Not even for old wartime buddies or their friends. "Have they come back?"

"Not that I know of," she said.

"Well then, if anything's gone wrong, they'll help him."

But the more he thought about it, the more it bothered him. Three weeks before the raid, in a telephone conversation, his grandfather had told him to contact a man in Durango if anything strange were to happen to him. Ferron had tried to press him for information, wondering if his grandfather was worried about repercussions from Aprico, but Gage had just joked about his paranoia resurfacing. A sign of senility, he'd said. At the time, Ferron had dismissed his grandfather's fear. They hadn't even raided the compound yet. Aprico was no threat. But perhaps his grandfather had been thinking about someone else. Ferron didn't know anybody who called themselves "former comrades in the OSS" and he'd been to several of the reunions in Switzerland with his grandfather. Were those just his sister's words? And the letter from South America bothered him. As far as Ferron knew, Gran Babbo had never mentioned having friends south of the border. All his old pals were in Europe. It was Beppe Aprico who had the contacts with South American drug cartels.

Five days now to think about what his sister had said. Five days with no news. *Fucking weather! When in hell was it going to rain?*

CHAPTER 2

Saturday, February 13, 1943, Rome, Italy

In his imagination the first thing he saw was the Tiber, turbid and slow in the dusky haze of a summer evening. The plane trees on the embankment towered into the sky in full leaf, their trunks mottled by the play of light and shadow. Along the Trastevere, the windows of the apartment houses were open to catch the evening breezes, and white muslin curtains wafted inward, bearing the scent of flowering wisteria. At one casement a woman leaned out to greet him, her hair floating in the breeze like silk strands in an underwater paradise.

But it was just a dream . . . a summer fantasy . . . an idyll.

Instead, in the harsh light of reality, on a winter day, what he noticed first were the boots and the black shirts, and the vision that came to mind was a memory of marching. Not the *passo romano*—the Italian version of the goose-step, instituted in '38 to impress il Duce. No, what he remembered was the clomping of the Blackshirts in their knee-high boots during the march on Rome in 1922. Five years old, perched on his father's shoulders outside the Embassy on the Via Veneto, watching the ragged hordes pour into the city in jubilation. Against his will he thought of the moment now, in the washed-out light of a late afternoon in February, as the car drew near the Ponte Salaria on the outskirts of Rome. At the access to the bridge, four jackbooted members of the Blackshirt militia, armed with carbines and revolvers, were stopping traffic and asking for papers.

The sight caused his heart to flutter, its pace quickening despite the deep breaths he took. His name was Thomas Gage and he was twenty-six years old, but that was not what his papers said. His papers said he was Alberto Griglia, thirty-two, a season veteran. Though not new to war, Gage had the looks of a teenager—hair cut close to the scalp, with a cowlick jutting over his forehead, a finely chiseled face that at the moment, with his gaunt cheeks and thin lips, tended to the haggard, and a wiry body that only hinted at his strength. It would not pay to look young and scared.

The car was a ten-year-old Bianchi Torpedo, a four-seater with folding seats. The driver, a short, heavy-set man named Antonio, bald-headed but with a thick black mustache, had papers allowing the vehicle to be driven from Genoa to Rome on business. A tag in the window showed him to be a member of the *Partito Nazionale Fascista*, the PNF. In the buttonhole of his suitcoat, he wore the PNF pin. When he had rendezvoused with Gage at a farmhouse near the coast just south of Civitavecchia, he had pointed to the pin and joked about the letters. *"Per necessità familiare,"* he said. Out of family necessity.

Please, no foul-ups, would be more like it, thought Gage.

His papers had been cobbled together two weeks earlier—at least the first set he would show, not those hidden in the lining of his coat, which were artful forgeries identifying him as an Austrian aristocrat. The papers in his hand, a booklet he had not expected to use, were those of a solder, his own photo attached in place of the original. Alberto Griglia, a *caporale* in the Italian 35th Army Corps, former *Ardito*, a member of the Death's Head Brigade, in reality a prisoner-of-war captured at El Quattara in the battle for El Alamein. The last line in the papers, followed by a military stamp, had been altered to show him on leave to attend to family business in Milan. Under il Duce, family business came before all else; those who had prepared the papers knew enough to take advantage of any chinks in the armor of fascism.

Gage was dressed in a soiled tweed suit, a dark felt slouch hat at his side. Beneath his feet was a dilapidated cardboard suitcase. The false bottom, only a quarter-inch thick, hid five hundred in Gold Seal dollars. Around his waist, in a thick money belt, he had another two thousand in lire.

Please let us through, he thought. If they let us through, I will— I will what? A grin appeared despite the tension. Another memory . . . his father had taken him into the basement of the university library when he was ten. Standing at the urinals in the men's room, he read the graffiti left by the students. *If I pass biology, I will return and kiss this urinal.* And then by another hand: *If I pass anatomy, I will go to the train station and kiss the dirtiest of the shitholes there.* And finally, in small block print: *If I fail physiology, I will kill Benito Mussolini.* And enough people had tried. Four in 1926 alone. Too bad no one had succeeded.

The Blackshirts were beating a boy they had dragged from a three-wheeled truck at the head of the bridge, just four vehicles away now. Two of them carried the limp body to a troop transport parked nearby and tossed the boy into the back. In a few minutes, the Bianchi Torpedo was first in line. The fascist militiamen surrounded the car and suddenly a layer of cold sweat broke out on Gage's body. He brushed the moisture off his upper lip, then rolled down the window.

"Papers." The voice was gruff.

He reached into the inside pocket of his suit coat and handed the man his booklet.

The militiaman was of medium height with rough-shaven cheeks, crooked teeth, and a scar on his forehead. He flipped to the last page and read the most recent annotation. "What was the nature of your family business?" he asked, bending down to look into the car. His breath smelled of garlic.

"My mother's funeral. I'm an only son."

"Is your father living?"

Gage shook his head. "He died in the last war."

"Where's your uniform?"

"I left it in Rome with my cousin. I'll pick it up there before I report back."

"What's in the suitcase?"

"A change of clothes . . . and some books."

"What do you need the books for?"

"They were my mother's . . . Some of D'Annunzio's poetry. It's all I have left of her."

"Step out of the car, please."

Damn! He turned to look at the driver. Antonio shrugged. His papers had already been returned to him.

Gage opened the door and stepped out. "What's the problem?" he asked, shutting the door behind him.

"Just a moment," the militiaman said. He walked around the car and over to a civilian standing by the truck.

What now? Antonio was still sitting in the car. Gage looked around, gauging his chances of escape if he should need to make a break for it.

Not good.

But this was what he had asked for, wasn't it? A chance to work undercover in Rome. Bill Donovan had been scouring the prisoner-of-war camps for Italians sympathetic to the Allied cause. He'd looked in the States for Italian-Americans. He'd talked to General Clark at the training center in Port-aux-Poules, near Oran, where the newly constituted Fifth Army was practicing the new invasion techniques. The OSS now had the authority to operate in sabotage and guerilla operations. And what had Gage done? Convinced his boss that he was the best man for the job. His Italian was as good as a native's. He knew the country well.

A graduate of Yale University, he had been raised from the age of four in Rome, where his father, a former professor of international law, had been an attaché in the U. S. Embassy. Fluent in Italian, German, and English, with a smattering of classical Greek, some Latin, and passable French, Gage had been recruited by the British Special Operations Executive in the summer of 1940. Following his training at Camp X, located in Canadian bushland on the northern shore of Lake Ontario, he had been sent to Greece, where he worked with remnants of the Venizelist party, organizing an intelligence network that reported on the Italian military situation in Albania. When the British were finally forced to withdraw from Greece, he was posted to Cairo, where he interrogated Italian and German prisoners captured during the British counterattack in Cyrenaica. In December of '41, he returned to Washington, D.C., to be with his wife and three-year-old daughter. From the SOE, it was a simple matter to pass to the new intelligence service set up by Colonel Donovan in January of '42. And from a desk to action, first in North Africa—at the glorified rank of Major, now in Italy.

Only his job wasn't sabotage. General Clark had other ideas for him, all now in jeopardy. The two men at the truck were joined by a third, who was slowly flipping through Gage's papers. In a moment, one of the men came over and said, "Which suitcase is yours?"

He pointed to the cardboard case in the car.

The man opened the passenger door, retrieved the case and took it around to the others. From where Gage was standing, he couldn't hear what the men were saying. Suddenly, one of the Blackshirts motioned to the driver. "*Avanti!*"

Gage opened the door to get in and said, "What about my suitcase and papers?"

"Not you," the man said. "You stay."

"I need to get to Rome. My cousin's expecting me. I still have a week of leave."

"Not any more," the man said. "Change in orders. You're needed at the front immediately."

He watched in dismay as Antonio shrugged, then put the car in gear and drove slowly across the bridge. To protest was to court disaster.

"Wait here." The militiaman joined his comrades.

What was wrong with the papers? He recognized the fear creeping over him. He had seen it often enough in the eyes of prisoners captured in Africa. At least *they* had fellow soldiers in camp for moral support. *He* was alone—his own identity, everything he relied on from the past, lost to him. He thought of the mission that had brought him back to Italy. Two weeks ago he had met Colonel Donovan at General Clark's temporary headquarters in Port-aux-Poules. Already it seemed a lifetime ago . . .

CHAPTER 3

Saturday, January 30, 1943, Port-aux-Poules, Algeria

The camp was located in a grove of pine trees and the pungent scent of resin merging with an odor of kerosine had produced a queasy feeling in his stomach, not helped by the foul-tasting concoction that passed for coffee. Outside—with the sun blazing down, igniting the desert sand and the sea—he had seen a dozen jerry-cans with WATER FOR DRINKING painted in white on their sides. That accounted for the taste of tin in his coffee. And the heat was unbearable—it should have been winter and it felt like summer.

He had listened while the two men talked about sending agents behind the lines, recruiting informers, organizing *coup de main* groups, and searching out leaders to be subsidized. It was then that Donovan turned to him. "Tom, we're going to be sending you to Rome." Gage couldn't help grinning. "We'd like you to cultivate the friendship of antifascist leaders in the area. And we need more information on Italy's war status, someone to verify the activities of the SS."

Gage had straightened in his chair. "The SS, sir?"

"That's right." Donovan paused and wiped his brow. He was an unassuming man who spoke in a soft, slow voice. "We know they're now under orders to operate directly in Italy."

General Clark rested his elbows on his desk. In contrast to Donovan, who had round cheeks grooved by deep lines running from his nose to the corners of his mouth, Clark was a tall, slim man, neat in manner and efficient in action. At forty-six, he was the youngest lieutenant general in the history of the Army.

"Have you heard of the OVRA, Major?"

"Certainly, sir. Mussolini's secret police."

"Good." The general pounded the desktop. "I can't get the slackers in G-2 to tell me what the damn acronym means."

Gage repressed a grin. "Even the Italians don't know, sir. Some say it stands for *Opera Vigilanza Repressione Antifascismo* or *Organizzazione Vigilanza Reati Antistatali.*"

The general frowned. "Translate those terms for me, Major."

"The first means something like the 'League of Vigilance for the Repression of Antifascism' and the second refers to an 'Organization of Vigilance for Crimes against the State.' I don't think the meaning matters, sir. I've talked to some people who say the whole thing's a psychological ploy—that the initials mean nothing. Just a trick of Mussolini's. Adds to the fear, they say."

The general rubbed his cheeks. "I ask, Major, because there's one other thing I'd like you to do in addition to what Bill has outlined. Ike is concerned about the fascist government destroying documents before we can get there to save them. We'd like to see if you can't get in touch with someone in the OVRA willing to work with us—to save his own skin. If we can keep them from destroying their files, we'll have dossiers on the activities of every Fascist of importance."

"That's a difficult task, sir. The agents of the OVRA wear civilian clothes. No one knows who they are."

"We know where their headquarters are located, right?"

"That's true, sir. In the Viminal. Along with the Ministry of the Interior."

"Then I suggest you start with a clerk in the Ministry—or a police official. Bill tells me you have contacts in Rome . . . with antifascists. Perhaps they know people opposed to the regime. Someone serving in an official capacity. Mount an operation to steal the files if you can. Have a team ready to assault the Viminal when and if the invasion occurs."

"You mentioned stealing the files, sir. I've heard estimates that they number more than two hundred thousand."

"Damn. That many?"

"I'm afraid so, sir."

Donovan raised a finger to get their attention. "If you find someone with access to the files, Tom, they might concentrate on the fascist hierarchs. We can provide a list of over thirty ministers, past and present. I assume the files are organized alphabetically."

"That's just it, sir. No one really knows, do they?"

The general's brow furrowed. "Do your best, Major, that's all anyone is asking. These bastards deserve to be punished."

"One other item, Tom," Donovan said, as Gage nodded toward General Clark. "I picked you not only because of your contacts in Italy and your command of the language. The Brits have been vetoing some of our proposals for infiltrating the mainland—their sphere of influence and all that. I figured since you served with the SOE before coming with me, they might take kindlier to helping you out."

"Am I going in alone?"

Donovan nodded. "At the start."

"I'm going to need a pianist in Rome."

"That's been arranged. We've already dropped a wireless in to the team that will pick you up. *Radio Fenice*, they call it."

Radio Phoenix. At the time, he had imagined the W/T man huddled in a nest somewhere in Rome, in a small room at the top of an apartment building, cold ashes coming to life, wings poised, waiting to be reborn. Finally . . .

After that, they had talked of his mode of entry. They couldn't risk a parachute drop. The Germans had intensified their A-A batteries around Rome. So they'd sent him by submarine to a point off Sardinia and then by motor torpedo boat to the coast just south of Civitavecchia. That was where Antonio had picked him up.

Antonio had got him this far. Now it was up to him to do the rest . . .

The Blackshirts had finished talking, all but one moving down to the next cars in line. The militiaman with his papers, a middle-aged guy with a swarthy complexion, motioned to Gage. The American walked over to the truck, eyeing his suitcase at the man's feet.

"Your mother lives in Milan?"

He looked up and nodded, his eyes tightening.

"Then why do you speak in *Romanesco*?"

He tried to swallow, his mouth suddenly dry. He knew his Italian was perfect, but the accent was Roman. He hadn't thought about that. But he'd told them he had cousins in Rome, that he still had a week of leave. He cleared his throat. "After my father died, I was raised in Rome with my cousins."

The man stared at him. "When did your father die?"

"At Caporetto. In 1915."

"What division?"

The questions struck him with a physical force that left him gasping for air between responses. The cover story he'd memorized drifted in and out of his mind. "The 19th . . . I think."

"You think?"

"I was just a baby. I never really knew my father."

The militiaman tapped Gage's papers in the palm of his hand. "What do you think about the Germans?"

He frowned. "The Germans?"

The militiaman nodded.

Gage shrugged. "They're our allies—"

"But they killed your father."

"In the last war . . . yes."

The militiaman smiled. "And now we fight with the swine, right? I fought against General Stein in the Battle of the Isonzo. In the IV Corps just like your father. Only I was in the 46th Division. The 19th was annihilated. Caught between Stein's 50th Austrian and the German 12th Division. They never had a chance."

Gage nodded numbly. "I was too young to remember it."

The Blackshirt closed the booklet and handed it to him. "For you, we make an exception. Get your uniform and report before curfew tonight. You're needed at the front by tomorrow. Sorry about the car. You'll have to walk." He straightened and tossed off a salute. "May you fight as gloriously as your father."

CHAPTER 4

Tuesday, August 20, Sonoran desert near Tucson, Arizona

The coyote had lain in the hot dust all day while the monsoon storm clouds piled up from the south, anvil heads billowing angrily skyward and streaking north, growing darker as the hours advanced. Sheets of flash lightning flared on the horizon.

The coyote had seen the rabbit just after dawn that morning, had given chase, a quick jump, a cut to the left, a rush through chiltepin bushes and shrubby hackberries, until suddenly the rabbit disappeared down a rocky hole. The coyote, a female with three hungry pups waiting for her, began to dig but soon encountered a jumble of boulders. She stuck her nose into a small crevice, smelled the musky scent of her prey, and began to paw frantically, clawing at the rock to no avail.

She withdrew to a thicket of stubby mesquite and waited as the sun rose and the heat grew, searing the desert terrain until shimmering heat waves distorted vision. That summer's drought had made food scarce, until even her mate had crossed the highway and disappeared into the outskirts of the city, from where he had not returned. The chance for a rabbit was not to be missed. The coyote had already lost a wood rat to a red-tailed hawk that morning.

Her pups would wait out the day in the shade of the den, afraid to venture far from its safety. She could not return without food. And so she waited through the scorching hours of midday.

Finally, late in the afternoon, after the sky had turned dark from one stretch of the horizon to the other, and splotchy, hot rain began to splatter in the dust, the rabbit appeared at its hole. The creature sniffed the air, which was just beginning to stir with the coming storm, then hopped a few feet away from safety, hiding in a clump of dry desert grass.

The high-pitched mechanical whine of the cicadas drowned out all other sounds, stunning the ears of prey and predator alike. The coyote waited, crouched on her belly, legs stretched taut beneath her body, ready to attack when the rabbit moved to open desert. Soon, heavy drops of rain pelted the coyote's head, but she lay motionless, her eyes intent on her prey, one drop of moisture appearing on her nose in anticipation of the kill. Lightning flickered to the south, its rumble almost continuous now but still muted and distant.

The rabbit hopped away from the dead grass and stopped below the graceful branches of a wispy paloverde, the tree's brown seedpods rasping in the breeze. The rain was beginning to increase in intensity, cooling the air, and the rabbit shook its body and hopped toward an open stretch of gravelly desert. And that was when the coyote streaked out of her hiding place, savage hunger coursing through every relentless motion. She caught the rabbit after it made two quick, frantic leaps, and broke its neck before the powerful hind legs could claw at her face. She ate the entrails quickly, hot intestines steaming in the rain. Lightning blasts crackled ominously in the air, suddenly closer now, as the storm rushed over the parched land. With the remains of the stringy rabbit clenched firmly between her jaws, the coyote set off for her den, a small cave cut into an outcropping by high water the summer before. She was hurrying now in the heavily falling rain, her maternal instinct strong. Three pups were waiting.

Ferron was dozing when Torres nudged him with his foot. "Hit the deck, Nick. Cows of heaven finally let fly. Pissing up a real storm. Just what the chief's been praying for."

Ferron rubbed his eyes. He stifled a yawn, atmospheric pressure weighing down on his head like a nightmare. "About time." He got to his feet and brushed the seat of his pants.

"Where're the rest of the guys?"

"In the van and ready, man. Captain's called for you twice."

"Gotta speak up," he grumbled. "We ain't all clairvoyant."

Torres grinned and opened the casa's heavy plank door. Outside, they could hear the motors of the vehicles as the drivers warmed them up. Dust swirled around the vans, the storm's lead winds sweeping over them. Heavy drops of rain thunked into the metal roof panels and streaked down the windshields. Ferron could smell the ozone in the air.

Okay, let it begin.

No need to go over the plan. They knew it inside and out by now. The men were divided into four squads. Two would hit the outlying buildings where Beppe Aprico housed his staff and operations men. One squad would take the hangar and seize Aprico's private jet and anything else coming in. The fourth squad, including Ferron, Torres, and six other men, one a chemical agent specialist, were to attack the villa itself, entering the compound from different directions. Two men were assigned to breach the guard house at the main gate, two would come over the fence near a tower to the south, two from the west, and Ferron and Torres were to cut through the perimeter fence where it crossed an open wash just north of the compound. The assault on the villa was coordinated to begin at 2030 hours, which gave the teams roughly twenty minutes to get in place outside the compound and ten minutes for the penetration itself. The power to the compound would be cut at 2015 hours. No electrified fence to worry about, but plenty of armed guards. If they resisted, silenced weapons were to be used on them.

Yeah, but that didn't mean they wouldn't shoot back. And their shots would sound the alarm for Aprico. Ferron didn't like that.

He'd be the first man in.

As the coyote ran, her paws struck the water, which creased the desert in tiny rivulets and puddled in the depressions. She crossed one wash that was already beginning to flow with liquid mud and hurried across the desert lowlands where the water was beginning to form broad sheets, corrugated and pockmarked by the downpour. Ignoring the rain, the coyote moved steadily toward the low-lying bluff where her den was located, an oval sand island held together by roots of greasewood and sage, its shape delineated by two branches of a wash that ran toward what was usually a dry riverbed. As she dropped down a gentle slope and approached the sandy outcropping, flood waters were already lapping at her belly, tugging on the rabbit which hung from her mouth. She lifted her head and struggled through the water. She could see the island now, the den flooded. Her three pups were running back and forth on the narrow strip of land, as clumps of sand collapsed into the stream on either side and were swirled away in the muddy onrush of the deluge.

Without hesitation, the coyote entered the wash and began swimming toward the island. The current swept her along, carried her beyond the clump of land, rolled her over once before she washed up against a shrub and righted herself. When she finally crawled out of the torrent, with the rabbit still clutched firmly in her mouth, the island was behind her.

On higher ground, she dropped the rabbit where she knew she could find it later, and began to trot back along the bank of the wash toward the island that was rapidly disappearing. When she drew abreast of the pups, she barked twice to let them know she was there, and then once more entered the muddy current, now a churning maelstrom that swept along, destroying everything in its path.

The white panel truck with U.S. Government plates raced across the little-used desert track that was already covered by a sheet of water that made the driving treacherous. The rain had begun falling steadily and gave no sign of letting up. The downpour thundered into the roof panels like an unending fusillade of high-powered weapons, drowning out thought itself and rattling the nerves. The vehicle traveled without lights, the driver relying on night-vision goggles provided by the commander of the Western Army National Guard at Pinal Air Park. The goggles had a restricted field of vision, encompassing only forty degrees, and provided little depth perception, but they sharpened the driver's vision from a normal nighttime range of 20/200 to a much improved 20/50.

The men sitting in darkness in the back of the van were

wearing Nomex fatigues, gloves, and belaclavas that protected them from flash fires. They were armed with an assortment of weapons, including some seized in earlier raids under the state's RICO statutes. A few carried their service revolvers, others .45 caliber semiautomatics. In addition, some were armed with submachine guns, H&K sniper rifles and Bennilli autoloading assault shotguns. Ferron's partner, Hector Torres, a Vietnam vet and former fire-team leader, carried a .357 Magnum revolver and a Mossberg 500 combat shotgun. He had a Tac II double-edged knife strapped to his leg sheath and a coil of rope at his waist. Ferron's sidearm, silenced for the initial assault, was a 9mm SIG-Sauer P226 pistol with a fifteen-round magazine, which he carried now with a round chambered. Slung on a strap over his shoulder was an H&K MP5 submachine gun of SWAT team issue.

He shook his head. Enough weaponry to start World War III.

The communications van, which functioned as the tactical operations center, would take its position on a bluff about five miles from the compound. Each man on the entry team was equipped with radios and earphones, operating on a special frequency that most scanners could not pick up. Nevertheless, their orders specified they were not to be used except in emergencies.

"Here we are, guys," the man sitting next to the driver said. "Torres and Ferron. Hit the dirt."

The two men slipped out the back of the van and crouched in the rain. A tremendous explosion split the air. Ferron gritted his teeth and flinched involuntarily. *Fucking lightning!* They'd been dropped off a hundred yards short of the compound's fence and they watched as the van disappeared rapidly into the darkness, skirting the fence as it headed to the south. In the heavy rain, neither one had yet slipped on his hood. Ferron wore an Oakland A's baseball cap and Torres a Boonie that made him look like he'd just stepped out of the jungle in Vietnam. He unleathered his combat knife and nodded. "Let's take 'em, man."

They were less than two hundred feet from the fence, lightning blasts tearing through the air around them, when Ferron stopped and grabbed Torres by the arm. "See that," he whispered, pointing toward the wash that surged along to their left.

Torres went into a crouch, the shotgun in his left hand swiveling in the direction indicated by his partner. "What?"

"There's a damn dog out there."

"Where?"

"On that island."

A flash of lightning snapped overhead and struck the ground not more than two hundred yards away. Ferron saw a blaze of light as if a bush had exploded into flame, and then thunder rippled over them with a ground-shaking roar.

"Jesus," Torres gasped. "Too fucking close!"

"Did you see it?" he asked. "There's a dog out there in the wash."

Torres shook his head. "That's not a dog, man. That's a coyote." He spit off to the side. "It's a goner. Sand's caving away. Pups don't have a chance."

"Pups? I thought those were rocks. You saw some pups?"

"Come on, man. We got less than ten minutes now."

Ferron moved toward the edge of the wash, where the rushing water was sucking at the banks. Lightning flickered again, over the compound now, reflecting in the clouds above them. He braced himself for the shock wave—a blast of thunder that rattled his teeth.

"Damn," he said. "You see that? Fucking island's disappearing."

Torres moved away from him. "Come on, man. We got to cut through the fence, take care of the guards, and get inside."

In the dim light provided by lighter spaces in the clouds, the sun already below the horizon, but the night not yet completely dark, Ferron saw the ground crumble beneath one of the island's shrubs, as the angry waves snatched the roots and twisted the plant free. A single mesquite tree held together the island's last scrap of earth. Another flash, a zig-zag in the sky from one cloud to another.

He said, "Get back here, Torres, and give me that rope."

"You're crazy, man. What you going to do with a rope? Lasso 'em?"

"I'm going out there." He took off his jacket, wrapped it around the submachine gun, and placed it on the muddy ground.

Torres swore. "I can't hold you in this current, Nick. Wash you away like a leaf. We don't got time now. We're gonna get our ass kicked, we fuck up everything."

"Forget the damn timetable. The others'll wait till we get there. I go in first, right? Let them sit on their duffers a minute."

"I can't believe this shit, man." Torres unhooked the coil of rope from his belt. "You know what the Buddha said, right?"

"No, I don't." Ferron took the rope and tied one end around his waist. "What did the Buddha say?"

Torres snorted. "Get real, man."

Ferron tossed him the other end of the rope. "The Buddha said, 'Get real, man'? I'm sure."

"Or words to that effect."

"I'm going in, Hector. Just hang onto the damn rope, okay? I'll start out upstream and try to swim out. You keep me from going too fast downstream, got that?"

"Come on, Ferron. You can't do this. You're crazy, man."

"Wrap your end of the rope around that mesquite if you have to." He pointed upstream to a stocky tree not far from the edge of the wash.

"And if the fucking tree's uprooted?"

Ferron grinned. "Send it on down and I'll ride it over."

"Yeah, sure, man. You gonna fucking get your ass fired for this."

Ferron was already knee deep in water, the current tugging against his legs. He stumbled, dropped one hand into the water, and caught himself. "Hector, shut up and dig in your heels. You're giving me too much slack."

When he was waist deep, the force of the current knocked him off his feet. It was impossible to stand in the raging flood. He let the current carry him then, the rope cutting into his waist, swimming as hard as he could toward the small clump of land in the middle of the wash. The island was barely visible now above the lapping waves. His arms were like canons flailing through mud. He hadn't removed his military boots, thinking he could walk most of the way with the rope helping him to keep his balance, but now he realized he was badly mistaken. He was tiring too quickly. Hector was going to have to pull him back to safety even if he made it to the island, which he could barely make out about forty feet away. What was out there? Three pups and an adult? Probably the mother. Unwilling to leave the litter behind.

Twenty feet away, he felt the rope grow taut. The water sucked at his body as he struggled to keep his head above water. What in hell was Torres doing? Was that the limit of the rope? Suddenly his stomach sank as the rope seemed to come loose and the waves carried him fifty feet, tumbling him like a barrel before he could feel the tug on the line and struggle to the surface, coughing muddy water from his lungs.

Torres had left the safety of the mesquite and was running along the bank, one end of the rope wrapped around his back, his heels skidding along in the mud. It had taken him a while to check the stream's impetus, his arms bulging as he tried to relieve some of the strain on his back.

The current swung Ferron closer to the island and he grasped for the branches of a bush that had collapsed but whose roots had not yet pulled free.

The coyote growled then, shrinking away from him, pups silent, crouched in fear. He could see she was a female, still nursing.

"That's okay, girl," he said as he lurched to his feet. The current swirled around his legs like a churning river around the pylons of a bridge about to collapse.

The coyote bared its teeth.

Forget the mother. She'd have to make it on her own. But would she let him get close enough to grab the pups? And if he made it to shore and she didn't, what then? Three pups abandoned to die a slow death. Maybe drowning was better. But goddamn it, he hadn't come this far to turn around and leave without trying.

He opened his mouth and snarled, the back of his throat vibrating. The coyote raised its hackles as Ferron stumbled through the crumbling desert soil toward the pups. The mother was in the water then, one pup following her. Ferron grabbed for the pup as it floated past, caught it by one leg and lifted it out of the water. The other two pups began to whine as their mother disappeared into the darkness, carried away by the raging storm.

He tucked the one pup under his left arm, grabbed for

another, added it, and then swore as the third jumped into the water. He had to push off from the island and went under before he could grab the thing. But he saw it trying to swim and he kicked back as the island crumbled away, flailing with his free arm, adding his own momentum to that of the river. He caught the pup with his right hand just as the current was sucking it down and then felt all of them go under.

Hang on, damn it. He'd come too far to lose any now. Yeah, and what about his own life? He couldn't hold his breath much longer. With his right hand, he tried to stroke, tried to right himself, no longer aware that he was clutching one of the pups in that hand. And then he felt the rope tighten, realized Hector had seen them in the flash of a lightning bolt and was pulling in the slack. The rush of the water increased but he was able to turn on his back and float with his head upstream, gasping for breath and hearing the pups coughing and doing likewise.

One of the pups was starting to slip from under his left arm. It took all his strength to keep it clenched against his body. He was afraid if he squeezed any tighter he'd crush the life out of them.

Shit. He was going to lose one.

He gasped in a lungful of air, brought the pup in his right hand up to his mouth and sank his teeth into the soaked fur at the nape of the neck, and then with his right hand free, he grabbed the pup just as it slipped from under his left arm. The pup in his mouth hung as if lifeless, and he wondered if it was dead, but then briefly he could feel its breath on his face, the pup relaxed and submissive as if he were being carried by his mother or father. For a moment, his legs caught in some debris, and then the river pulled it away and he was free, his feet finding the bottom of the wash as Torres pulled him toward shore, his buddy's powerful biceps bulging with the strain.

Ferron was on his feet then, trying to grin, a pup clenched in his teeth and one in each hand. The current had lost its grip and he was struggling free. He'd made it! Feeling like a madman who'd just saved the queen, he lifted both hands in a sign of triumph. Doggone! Couldn't have done much better if he were a Golden Retriever. Rowdy'd be proud of him.

• • •

"Do you realize what the fuck time it is?" Torres said. The two men were crouched over the three pups.

Ferron laughed. "Have you ever seen a more pathetic sight?"

The pups looked like scrawny little rats, shivering with cold and hacking the water out of their lungs, huddled together in fear.

Torres leaned over him and helped him to his feet. "The fucking captain's been on the radio for the last five minutes."

"Watch out!" Ferron said, and Torres jumped back a foot as a creature materialized out of the darkness. The mother coyote looked the worse for wear, her coat tangled and dripping mud, but she was alive.

"I'll be damned," Ferron said. "She made it. Step away from the pups, Hector. That's the mother come back."

In a minute, the coyote and her pups had slunk away into the desert. Torres found his knife and sliced the coil of rope around Ferron's waist. "Did you hear what I said about the captain calling?"

Ferron grinned at him. "Are we ready or what?"

"Ready?" Torres swore. "Fuckin' team went in without us." He shook his head, then sheathed the knife. "Shit, man, they probably think we're dead."

CHAPTER 5

Saturday, February 13, 1943, Rome, Italy

Two hours before blackout, the clouds piling up over Rome were suffused with a soft haze of golden light, the fallen sun tinging the farthest reaches with thin tracings of pink that slowly faded into gray satin. It was a delightful evening for February—the hour of the *passeggiata*—and Gage was surprised to see so few people on the streets. He glanced at his watch. He'd finished his ersatz cappuccino a half-hour earlier and now the waiter was hovering nearby.

"*Altro, signore?*" The white-jacketed waiter was at his elbow, a fascist stickpin clearly visible in the man's lapel.

"No, *grazie*. Not just yet. I'm waiting for a friend." He was seated outside the Caffè Aragno on Corso Umberto. The Fascist Foreign Office was located nearby and the *caffè* was frequented by foreign service employees, secretaries, and fascist deputies.

Now the waiter looked at his own watch. Gage knew what he was thinking. A stranger, a meeting just before the blackout. If the waiter was a police agent and asked to see papers, he would find an ordinary police identification card issued by the German gauleiter in Vienna, with a pass for travel to Italy stamped by the *Reale Questura Centrale* of Milan. And in the inside breast pocket of his suit, Gage carried a letter typed on the stationery of a men's clothing store in Vienna owned by his uncle, Count Neumann, attesting to his *bona fides* and confirming that he was in Rome to handle his uncle's business interests. Both had been removed from the lining of his coat after Gage had destroyed his first set of papers. He was no longer *caporale* Alberto Griglia.

Ten minutes later, he signaled the waiter, who was hovering nearby, and ordered a glass of Aurum. At the far end of the square, a squad of Blackshirts marched toward the southern end of Corso Umberto, led by a young kid carrying the fascist standard. The marchers were all in their early teens—the *Balilla*, he thought, one of the youth groups founded by Mussolini. Named after a kid in Genoa who threw a rock at a group of Austrian soldiers a century ago, starting an uprising that drove the Austrians from the region. The members each wore a dagger, and those in the front row carried a *manganello*—the cudgel that their elders had made famous in the twenties when the fascists first came to power.

As he sipped his drink, he thought of what the fascists had done to his teacher when he was only eight and still attending the public *scuola media*. 1925. The fascists were strengthening their control of the country. Gage's teacher had expressed her disagreement with some of the changes to the school system the fascists were just beginning to propose. The next day, a band of Blackshirts stormed the school, held the classroom hostage, and forced the teacher, a single woman in her early twenties, to drink a glass of castor oil. Then, in front of the class, they lifted her skirt, made her bend over, and smeared bootblack on each buttock. But that was not the end of the indignities. At gunpoint, they forced the woman, tears streaming down her cheeks, to jump up and down on her desk in front of the class until her bowels loosened. And then the fascists hooted insults and disappeared.

The hatred that Gage's father had tried to instill in him for everything fascist was solidified in that one day of terror and humiliation. And the shock intensified when he learned that one of his friends had turned the teacher in. The boy belonged to the *Figli della Lupa*, the Sons of the Wolf, the fascist youth group for boys from six to eight in age. At first Gage had been jealous, but after the incident with his teacher, his jealousy had changed to fear. His friend had proudly shown Thomas his *libretto personale*, a blue service book in which every detail of his record was inscribed, including merit points for having reported the teacher.

• • •

He felt a tap on his shoulder and turned to find a young woman—a girl really, with thick black hair that fell in waves to her shoulders. She was wearing a burgundy sweater over a white blouse and gray skirt. Her face was pale and she wore no lipstick, but her eyes glowed and the serious look on her face seemed ready to change to a smile. "Uncle Antonio told me I'd find you here," she said, her hands touching the chair opposite him.

He smiled to put her at ease, then exchanged the code phrases expected of him.

The girl, no more than sixteen or seventeen he guessed, sat down and clasped her hands. "*Un caffè macchiato,*" she said to the approaching waiter, tossing her dark hair over her shoulder. When he turned away, she reached out and touched Gage on the arm. "Uncle Antonio asked me to invite you over for dinner," she said, "but I imagine you'd like to get settled in first."

He nodded. Good, she was going to accompany him to the apartment. He knew they would walk along a route that would be cleared for them by Antonio's agents. A series of stores, businesses with two exits, twisting alleys, somehow they would make sure he wasn't followed when he went to Count Neumann's apartment building. Once there, he would introduce himself to the building's warden as the count's nephew, Thomas Karl Ludwig, show his identity card and key, and take possession of the apartment. Each *palazzo* in Rome had its warden, quite often the janitor or the *portiere*, and every street its leader, every quarter its district secretary. The warden would report his arrival to the appropriate authorities and that report would be sent to district headquarters and then forwarded to the National Directorate of the Fascist Party on Corso Vittorio Emanuele. If they sent someone to check him out, he could show a used railway ticket from Vienna to Milan and on to Rome, in addition to the other pocket litter that Bill Donovan had provided.

"I'm Carla Ceruti," the girl said after the waiter had served her coffee, which, due to the shortage of the real thing, was a *miscela*—a mixture of roast corn and chicory. "Antonio's niece. We'll be working together once you're settled into the apartment."

He was pleased with her confidence. She spoke in a firm voice that attested to her maturity—the war forced one to grow up quickly, though he had always found Italian girls more mature than their American counterparts.

In the distance the Vatican bells began to toll the Angelus. He finished his Aurum, leaned forward and placed his empty glass on the table. "Are we being watched?"

"Two men at least . . . Did you notice the newspapers posted behind the windows in the arcade?"

He nodded. He'd seen them earlier—a copy of *Regime Fascista* from Bologna and the local fascist paper, *Il Giornale d'Italia.*

"There's a man standing there with his back to us, but he can see our table in the reflection on the window, and then there's a fellow smoking a cigarette near the column. I surveyed the square before I approached you. He signaled to the man reading the newspapers. And there may be others. You ready?"

In the distance, he heard a siren that seemed to grow in volume and then was suddenly cut off. A field-gray Opel with German military plates passed them on Corso Umberto, heading toward Piazza Venezia, followed by a wood-burning bus that belched clouds of black smoke. He watched both vehicles until they disappeared in the distance, then left twenty lire on the table, enough to cover the bill and a tip, and picked up his suitcase. "It's now or never," he said. "Let's go."

Chapter 6

February-March, 1943, Rome, Italy

Every day, at hours determined by code the prior day, an airplane took off from Tangiers, overflew Sicily and the German anti-aircraft batteries dug in there, received the radio signal, then returned to its base in North Africa. For five minutes, the maximum amount of time they could risk because of possible attempts by the Italian or German authorities to triangulate their position, Radio Fenice tapped out coded messages relayed by informants in the Roman resistance.

Gage spent his time in the apartment abbreviating and then encoding messages passed to him by either Antonio or Carla. When he had nothing else to do, he either slept or read books taken from Count Neumann's library. The apartment, on the third floor of a building on Via dell'Arancio in the vicinity of the Ponte Cavour, was musty with disuse but elegant in its furnishings. The living room contained a seventeenth-century Gobelin tapestry on the wall opposite a large fireplace, and huge French windows to one side led out to a small terrace overlooking Piazza Monte d'Oro. The dining room was furnished with baroque chairs and a rectangular wood table from a cloister refectory. Off the dining room, there was a small smoking room and library decorated in an old English style, with glass-enclosed bookshelves and black leather furniture. The count's pipe rack stood next to a comfortable wing chair, and two chrome and glass lamp stands added a modern touch. The bedroom held a floor-to-ceiling *armadio* and a huge marriage bed.

Only once during the first two weeks did he leave the apartment and that was at Carla's insistence. Late February, a Thursday afternoon, Carla's eighteenth birthday. He went with her family for a celebration at Rampoldi's Bar near the Piazza di Spagna. They drank a bottle of Strega and toasted Carla's future, while the bells of the church of Trinità dei Monti pealed out the hours. He talked to Carla's younger sister, Nina, and afterwards, he and Carla took a drive in the family's Topolino. First down Via Sistina, past the Hotel de la Ville, where German officers were billeted. Then down Via del Babuino, past the Hotel de Russie, with its warm, red facade and its exotic gardens stretching up to the Pincio. It, too, had been taken over by the Germans. The streets around the two hotels were saturated with police officers—both those in full uniform, with their polished boots and revolvers, and the auxiliary policemen, who wore red-and-yellow arm bands.

Behind the wheel, Carla said, "A friend of mine works as a clerk for the police. She says the Questura has on file a detailed report of every hotel, pension, or office building in Rome occupied by the Germans—their headquarters, command posts, car parks, food depots, hospitals, and psychiatric wards. I tried to see if she could get a copy but it wasn't possible."

He looked over at her and nodded. She was going to be a resourceful person. Soon, using her contacts, they would begin to insert themselves into the upper levels of fascist society, people his "uncle" the Count would have socialized with prior to the war. In the meantime, he would have to learn more about Carla. His life was in her hands.

By March, he found it difficult to stay inside the apartment. He wandered from his apartment to Piazza della Repubblica near the train station and then back. He strolled down the Corso Umberto from Piazza di Spagna to the river. He crossed the Ponte Sant'Angelo to the castle and hoofed it up to the Vatican and back. He stopped by a bottega on the Via Ripetta, not far from the Piazza del Popolo, a shoe store in which Count Neumann held a controlling interest. He met the manager, an effete man who overdid his *savoir faire*. Gage assured him that he was in the city merely to ascertain that all was going well, and that he intended to remain through the spring and summer. He could tell the manager considered him another playboy in the manner of his uncle the Count—and that was fine; it would help explain his recourse to the more frivolous appanages of his uncle's rank— late brunches in the city's more popular gathering spots, afternoon coffees along the Via Veneto, soirees to the opera, and the late-night parties of the highest levels of fascist society, bacchic revelries that lasted till dawn. They would all provide opportunities for the collection of useful bits of intelligence.

A few days later, when he was sure no one had followed him, he began a systematic survey of the twelve major roads that led in and out of Rome. He noted the placement of ack-ack batteries, the tank defenses, the storage depots, the armored cars of the PAI— the Italian African Police, known for their exploits in Ethiopia and Libya. The PAI guards wore an MM shoulder insignia, which stood for Mussolini's Militia. They were proud of it now, he thought, but let the Allies take Rome and see how they felt. The PAI would be the first to beg their compatriots for the five-pointed *stellette* of the regular Italian Army.

He counted the columns of German vehicles, noted the number of uniformed German soldiers in the streets and the SS men with their short Sten guns. He would have liked to have surveilled Rome's airports—Ciampino, which was close to Frascati and under German control, Littoria, Centocelle, and farther out, the airfields of Guidonia to the northeast, and Cerveteri to the northwest, but access to all was strictly controlled.

One day he wandered the streets around the Regina Coeli jail and stopped at a local *caffè* for a snack and glass of Otard brandy. On one wall, under a banner reading *Credere, Obbedire, Combattere*—Believe, Obey, Fight—hung pictures of Mussolini and Victor Emmanuel III, the steel-helmeted King doing his best to look of military mien. He had once seen the man up close and knew he was a diminutive figure with a Napoleonic complex, a diffident man whose fragile ego was bolstered when the Duce offered him the crowns of conquered Ethiopia and Albania, thus flattering the little man with the title of Emperor-King.

Before he could leave, having sniffed the air and found its

fascist aroma not to his liking, two German officers stepped out of a Fiat 1100, with a German Embassy tag prominently displayed in the windshield. They joined three Italian PAI guards at an outdoor table. Over a fifth of Haig, ordered by the Germans, they traded toasts, growing more and more boisterous. One of the Italian officers passed around a pack of Macedonias and the Germans were forced to accept the foul-tasting cigarettes. Gage had seen other German officers, especially those who frequented the Birreria Lowenbrau on Via Nazionale, with seidels of imported beer and packs of Chesterfields and Lucky Strikes.

He sat in the *caffè* for over an hour, watching the men outside, before they left and he felt safe enough to come out. If the PAI guards had asked for his papers for some reason, the Germans might attempt to speak to him in their native language. His German was good, had gotten much better, in fact, after his marriage to Olga, but still it was not like that of a native Austrian.

One evening in the third week of March Carla Ceruti stopped by after work, with a cut of black-market veal in her handbag and a bottle of Lacrimae Christi. Carla worked as a sales clerk in a furriers on Via del Babuino, a shop much frequented not only by those of ancient Roman nobility but by the parvenu wives of the Fascist Party hierarchs and others with pretensions to nobility. Some customers attempted to flatter the owners with black-market goods, which were sometimes distributed to the staff.

"I will cook dinner for us," Carla said, glancing at her watch. Each household in Rome was limited to one half-hour of rationed gas per day. "First a plate of spaghetti and then *vitello arrosto* with potatoes and peas."

"You're making my mouth water already," he said. He had lost weight since his arrival in Rome. That morning, shaving in the Count's private bathroom, he had noticed how cavernous his cheeks had become.

At the kitchen sink, filling a pot with water, Carla said, "I have an invitation for myself and a guest for a party this Friday. Interested?"

"It's about time." He was setting the small table in the kitchen; the dining room was too large for just the two of them.

"Who's doing the inviting?"

She set the pot on the stove, lit a match and ignited the gas jet. "Do you know the Maison Venturi in Via Condotti?" He didn't recall it. "Edda Ciano buys her gowns there. One of her designers is giving a party at his villa in Ostia. We can go by electric train." She paused and glanced over her shoulder. "I didn't tell you— my father lost his pass from the War Office for the Topolino. No more driving for us. Only official cars on the streets now."

"Will Ciano's wife be at the party?" Edda Ciano was Mussolini's daughter, the wife of Count Galeazzo Ciano. Ciano, former Minister of Foreign Affairs, had recently been assigned— demoted most people said—as ambassador to the Holy See. Antonio had shown Gage the article in an evening edition of *Il Giornale d'Italia*.

She shrugged. "Who knows?" She dropped the pasta into the boiling water, added a drop of oil and some salt, and then bent over to adjust the control knob for the oven, where the veal was roasting. "If she is, do you want me to introduce you?"

"You've met her?"

Carla turned away from the stove and put her hand on her hip. "Certainly. No one in the resistance has my contacts." Her voice mocked the haughty tone of an aristocrat. "This Friday, I will present you to signor Elio Pavan, an official of the OVRA."

"Of the OVRA?" he repeated in marvel.

"That's what you wanted, wasn't it?"

In his exuberance, he strode over to her, grabbed her arms and kissed her on both cheeks. She blushed and turned back to the pot of spaghetti.

"How did you get involved in this? Risking your life. Most people your age have been indoctrinated by now."

"Not all of us." She turned to look at him, hesitating. "My brother . . ." Her eyes filled suddenly with tears. She brushed at her face angrily and then turned back to the stove.

He said nothing. He stood near the table, waiting for her to regain her composure.

"I was only eleven when my brother died. Fredi believed every word that came out of the Duce's mouth—all the talk about a second Roman Empire."

He saw her tremble. He walked behind her and put his hands

on her shoulders. "That's okay, you don't have to talk about it."

She shook her head and wiped at her eyes again. "I thought I was over this." She cleared her throat, which had grown husky. "I haven't talked about him for a long time. Fredi fought with General Badoglio in Ethiopia in '36. He used to write us about the battles, trying to impress us with how easy it was—how there was very little danger. At night the men would sing 'Santa Lucia' and 'Funiculi, Funicula' and their regimental songs . . . Everyone was happy. Morale was high. They had artillery, airplanes, machine guns, and hand grenades—and the natives had spears and single-shot rifles and outmoded trench mortars. The Negus had no chance, Fredi said. One day General Badoglio would sit on his throne in Addis Ababa."

She paused and took a shaky breath.

"But here we read in the papers how the natives would smear their white *shammas* with mud and sneak into our encampments at night under the cover of darkness . . ." She swallowed hard, then bit her lower lip to keep from crying. "The Ethiopians would kill our soldiers and then castrate them with their hooked knives . . . and our men weren't much better. Fredi told us about General Graziani, why he was called the 'breaker of natives.' He would take dissident chieftains up in airplanes and drop them on tribal encampments. And the fascist militia would pour wet concrete down the throats of captured natives during interrogation. Graziani was moving north from Italian Somaliland. He wanted to beat General Badoglio to Addis Ababa. Everyone wanted to be the first to capture Haile Selassie. Fredi was with the infantry troops that took Amba Aradam for Badoglio. He said they were going to beat Graziani to the prize. But he didn't live to see the victory. We were told he was killed in a battle at Lake Ashangi in early April."

She took a deep breath. "He's buried somewhere in the desert. Mussolini wrote a letter to my mother. 'Thanks to your son, Fascist Italy has at last her empire . . .' *I hate them all,*" she said, her voice bitter despite the passage of time. "They have told us only lies."

CHAPTER 7

H oly Criminy!"
The words slipped out of the chief's clenched jaw like crushed pebbles. He was a religious man and rarely swore, but the temptation was strong. He stalked around from behind his desk and stood in front of Ferron, who was sitting in a plain metal chair without padding—one of the chief's schemes to avoid long visits. It was just after four in the morning.

"Two guys, *the* most important guy, the God almighty assault leader and what do you do? You stop to save a flipping coyote!" The old man, overweight for his height, looked like he was about to burst, his eyes like the buttons on a shirt five sizes too small. The red veins in his nose glistened with rage. "Over two years," he screamed. "You think you did everything? You think two months on the job and no one's done anything but you?"

"Hey, I didn't kill him," Ferron muttered. "Why don't you talk to the DEA? They supplied the fucking idiots."

He swore on purpose. The old man had already asked for his badge and gun. Disciplinary leave, without pay, while they investigated the case. The least he'd get was a written reprimand for his file. But they could fire him for all he cared. Big deal. He was fed up with the job, with the lack of control, with other people making decisions that affected his life. It had taken him five days sitting in an abandoned bunkhouse doing nothing to realize it, was all.

"Those idiots wouldn't have been there if it wasn't for you messin' up."

"The team was supposed to wait for us."

"What? A half hour? You think Aprico's going to sit there and not check in with his perimeter guards. They have a security system, you know. Every minute was precious."

Nick shrugged. "Hey, the bust went down."

"Yeah, and because of your screw up, Aprico destroyed half the goldarn book before they shot him. And then the DEA guy said you tried to pocket the thing."

"We had as much right to it as they did."

The chief ignored him. "And you know whose name was on the top page when they finally got it?"

He wanted to say, "Howdy Doody?" but thought better of it. He'd seen the names—a page with the heading "OSS/CIA"— and then his grandfather's name and current address, a guy named Theunis Kloos in Suriname, and several other names, with addresses in Washington, D.C.

The chief shook a stack of papers in his face. "They find your grandfather, is what they find. Thomas Gage, retired CIA officer. How's that look?"

"What do you mean, how's that look? You forget how we infiltrated the operation? You can thank my grandfather for that."

The chief sat down heavily and slammed his fist on the stack of papers. "And we can thank you for Aprico. We wanted him alive, not dead."

"Like I said. Talk to the DEA. They shot him."

"Ferron, I want you out of here. I'm recommending you see a counselor while internal affairs investigates this case."

"I don't need a counselor. Not for this at any rate."

"You got your head screwed on backwards, boy. Thinking a coyote was more important than the bust. When you come back, *if* you come back, you better have a different attitude or you know what's going to happen to you? You're going to make another stupid mistake and instead of costing the criminal's life it's going to cost you your own, or your partner's. Think about that while you're out there saving the world."

Yeah, yeah, yeah. An asshole, just like his dad.

• • •

Though the ten-year-old Volkswagen camper van was under-powered for its weight at 2000 cc's and needed a valve job, Ferron turned on the rear-vented air conditioning for Rowdy's sake. The Golden Retriever took the ride well, but not the heat. Two hours after his morning run around Himmel Park, he was still panting, his head lying on the damp carpet of the van where he'd slopped his drinking water.

"By tonight," Ferron told him, "we'll be in the mountains. Little cooler for you. Let you chase squirrels instead of cats."

That was a laugh. That morning, near the Sun Station post office on First Street, they'd passed a tabby who didn't take kindly to Rowdy's growl and his sideways prancing that was meant to frighten the cat into a run so the dog could give chase. Instead, the tabby arched his back and when Rowdy hesitated and then started to trot on by, the cat tore out after him, stomach low to the ground and tail uplifted. Rowdy never looked more shocked in his life, took off running as if a Pit Bull were after him. He was waiting for Ferron at the corner, a puzzled look on his face as if to say, *Was that a cat, or what?*

After the run, Ferron tried to call his sister Barbara again for news about their grandfather, but for the second time that morning there was no answer. Her husband Dick, a banker in Durango, was probably at work, but where was Barbara? Out with the kids apparently. She'd be surprised when he showed up at the door unannounced. But the house, a restored Victorian on historic Third Avenue, was large enough for the unexpected guest. And Gran Babbo's room would be empty—unless they'd brought him back from the mountains.

That was a long shot. They couldn't keep the old man in town. Every chance he got, he packed up his kit, drove out to the ranch where he quartered his horse Buck, loaded the animal with supplies, and hiked up to the cabin he'd built after he retired from the CIA and moved west to raise Nick and Barbara. The cabin, located in rugged country high in the San Juan mountains, was inaccessible even by Jeep.

Ferron had left Tucson at noon the day after the raid. He kept the van at top speed, which was five miles an hour under the posted limit, waiting all the while for the engine to overheat. The freeway, glimmering in heat waves, stretched out ahead of him like a column of mercury in a thermometer. His mind was as dazed as the sun-baked surface of the highway. He had tried to sleep after his morning confrontation with the police chief, but after tossing and turning on the bed for two hours, with Rowdy nervously pacing in the living room, he'd gotten up, showered and shaved, and then taken the dog for his walk.

The events of the past twelve hours were a jumble. Aprico dead and the chief blamed him. Shit! He wasn't even there. But that was the problem. The team hadn't waited for him. They'd gone busting into the place, firing like mad, and of course Aprico had fought back. Fought back until they killed him at least. How was he going to break that to his grandfather? Aprico was one of Thomas Gage's old war buddies. If it wasn't for their friendship he would never have gotten close to the man. And now? Now Aprico was a corpse lying in the morgue, riddled with bullet holes. He and his grandfather hadn't planned on that. Fucking DEA. Sending in two trigger-happy bastards. Couldn't wait to nail their first mobster. Now, he'd have to tell his grandfather that it was his fault. If he'd made it to the villa on time, Aprico would be in jail, not the morgue.

He wondered what the department was doing about Aprico's notebook—or what was left of it. The police chief blamed him for that, too. Hey, even if he'd been the first one in, Aprico would have torched a few pages. Too many doors between his henchmen and the master bedroom. What had the chief said? They caught the guy screwing the Columbian chick and he still had the presence of mind to destroy what he could.

The captain in charge of the raid had kept Ferron from taking part in the mop-up operations, but he knew they'd have a lot to go on. Before the police chief managed to order him to go home and not come back until they told him to, he'd seen some of the goodies they'd seized set up in a room for the TV crews, with Senator Sprague standing by to make a short speech, ready as always to take credit. It would take the department a long time to follow up all the leads from the raid, and Ferron would have liked to have been a part of that, perhaps tracking down some of the mafioso's underworld contacts. But not now. Now he might as well go out and track down the ruby-throated hummingbird.

• • •

It was dinner time of the second day, a Thursday evening, when he finally swung into Durango, happy to be off the freeway and back in a familiar environment. He saw some river rafters in yellow rain gear on the Animas River, paddling toward a bus that was waiting to pick them up. It didn't look like they were having much fun. He stopped at a phone booth to give Barbara a few minutes of warning before his arrival. She lived barely five minutes away.

"Nick," she said. "Where are you? I've been trying to get a hold of you all day. Gran Babbo's still missing. Dick's still out with the search party. The sheriff radioed in about an hour ago. They can't make it back in because of the storm. They'll stay in the cabin and start again tomorrow morning."

Damn! A knot of worry formed in Ferron's stomach. Gran Babbo could survive a snowstorm in the cabin, but outside, in the mountains, even a rainstorm might do him in at his age.

"Barbara, I've been on the road all day. I'm calling from the City Market here in town, near the Red Lion Inn. I brought Rowdy with me. If you've got any leftovers, I'll eat at your place and then try to make it up to the cabin tonight."

He sensed her surprise in the momentary silence. She'd thought he was calling from Tucson.

"I'm glad you came, Nick. There's plenty of food here. But you can't go up in this storm."

"Is Wolf still with you or did Dick take him?"

"He's here."

"Well, then he and Rowdy can keep me company. I know that route too well to get lost, even in the dark. I want to be there when they start the search in the morning." He paused. Would she know anything about the men she'd mentioned over the phone before the raid on Aprico's compound—the ones who claimed to be friends of his grandfather's former OSS comrades? That was a loose end he didn't like.

"Did those guys come back out?" he asked.

"Which guys? Oh, I don't know," she said quickly, remembering. "They wouldn't stop back here unless they couldn't find him, would they? I forgot to tell the sheriff about them. Does it matter?"

"Probably not," he said, covering his free ear. A truck was accelerating as it left a stop light on Camino Del Rio. "What did you say, Barbara?"

"I said, come on over, and after you eat we can stop by the police department and see if we can contact the sheriff by radio. Tell him about the men."

"Okay, and while we're at it, we can let him know I'm coming up."

At four in the morning on Friday, with the valley still dark, he rounded up the two dogs, threw a knapsack with two sandwiches, a pack of raisins, an apple, and a water bottle into the van and left Durango. He drove north, heading up along the Animas River toward Silverton. A light scent of wood smoke permeated the valley, but within fifteen minutes, he'd left the ranches behind and was slowly gaining in elevation. Just beyond Cascade Village, he took a left onto a gravel road near Cascade Creek and followed the creek upstream. Eventually, the ruts in the road were impassible, and he parked the van, slipped the pack over his shoulders, and set out on foot with the dogs sniffing out the way ahead of him. Twenty minutes later, he passed through a gate and was on Forest Service land. And soon after, he saw the San Juan County sheriff's Jeep Cherokee.

The storm that had provided cover for the raid on Beppe Aprico's compound had also swept across Southwestern Colorado. The ground was still wet, and rivulets crossed the road carrying the runoff toward the creek bed. Just before dawn, with the cloudless sky a pale blue, he reached a meadow where the nicker of two horses reached him. The dogs answered the neighing with barks, and one of the horses, a roan stallion with a bell on a neck harness, materialized out of the darkness, trotting toward them, his breath steaming in the cool mountain air, hoofs cutting into the soft soil. Ferron considered trying to ride the stallion, but without a bridle he figured the results wouldn't be worth the effort. He slapped the horse on the rump, called the dogs, their snouts deep in prairie dog holes, and set off across the creek and up a ridge that was lined with aspen.

The night before, after dinner with Barbara and the kids, his sister had convinced him he needed a few hours of sleep before beginning the arduous climb. The cabin itself was a good six-hour hike from Cascade Creek, all told about seven hours from the house in Durango.

When the two youngest kids had gone to bed and Jeffrey was watching TV, Ferron asked again about the two men who had come in search of their grandfather. He was drying dishes while Barbara washed. "Were they Americans or Italians?"

Barbara shrugged. "One was a black man, the other Italian, I think. They both spoke English, but the older one—the Italian—had an accent."

"You said they were friends of former OSS comrades."

"That's what the older fellow told me. He said he was a partisan from Bolzano. He met Gran Babbo once in the winter of 1944, when the OSS was coordinating the sabotage operations against the Wehrmacht supply lines coming from Austria."

Ferron tossed her an incredulous look. "He told you all that?"

"Nick, we did talk for a while. He thought he'd seen you and me in Verona when we were kids. He asked how you were doing."

He dried a pan and set it on the stove. "He asked about me by name?"

She paused, wringing the soap suds from her hands. "I think so—or maybe I mentioned it. I don't know, Nick. They seemed like nice people and they knew about Gran Babbo. Why so suspicious?"

"I'm just surprised anyone would come all this way to see him. Gran Babbo hasn't kept up with his men for years now."

Barbara set the last pan on the drainboard and pulled the sink plug. "We did go over once with Gran Babbo. To Verona."

"Yeah, about fifteen years ago." He paused. "You catch their names?"

She reddened. "The older one told me his, but I forgot. I think he called the black man Naveed. I remember because it sounded strange."

The name meant nothing to him, but then their grandfather had never been one to talk about his days in the OSS—or after. A twenty-year career with the CIA after the war had done nothing to loosen his tongue.

He hung the dishcloth on a rack to the side of the sink, then sat down at the kitchen table while Barbara poured herself a cup of coffee.

"Nothing for me," he said.

While she busied herself wiping the counter, he drummed his fingers on the table, lost in thought. Barbara sat down opposite him and reached for the sugar bowl, a squat ceramic hippopotamus. "What is it, Nick?"

He looked up and caught her eye. "You remember the cache?"

"The cache?" She tucked a loose strand of hair behind one ear. "Vaguely. But I haven't been up to the cabin in years. Not since the kids were born."

"What about Dick? He know about it?"

She shook her head. "I don't think so. Gran Babbo did take Dick hunting one year. They might have used it. Dick's never mentioned it to me. Why do you ask?"

"Just wondering if it was still there."

She stirred a spoonful of sugar into her coffee. "I don't think I could find it if I had to, could you?"

He was wondering the same thing. If Gran Babbo wasn't at the cabin, he might have gone to the cache for some reason. Years before, they had discovered a cave near the base of a cliff in a valley that was one ridge away from the cabin. Their grandfather had hauled some two-by-fours to the site, anchored them to each side of the opening, and built a gate against the face of the cliff, blocking the cave's entrance. Inside, they stored at least a month's supply of canned and dried food packed in sealed containers. On one trip, when he was still in high school, Nick had seen his grandfather leave a 30.06 rifle and a box of ammunition in the cave. But who knew what his grandfather had done in the intervening years?

Climbing the slope through the aspen, finding his way by landmarks that were engraved in his memory from countless trips as a kid, Ferron watched for signs of the others. The sheriff had taken a party of six men, guided by Dick Lowell, Barbara's husband. So far, he had seen no sign of the men and realized that Dick had chosen an easier slope, probably the one that his grandfather now took. In the old days, they used to head straight up the ridge, cutting over an hour off the length of the trip.

Higher up the mountain, the warm rays of the morning sun struck him on the back and he removed his jacket and tied it around his waist. He was already hungry—he'd skipped breakfast, even though Barbara had told him to help himself to the refrigerator. But he had been in too much of a hurry to eat. His knapsack had been packed the evening before. When he reached a narrow ledge, pockmarked with boulders and over-grown with Canadian thistle, he stopped for five minutes and ate a sandwich, giving each of the dogs a scrap.

The night before, after dinner and his conversation with Barbara, he had walked over to the police station on the corner of Second Avenue and Tenth Street to see if he could use one of their radios to contact the sheriff. A row of two-toned police cars, black on the bottom and white on top, with the town's new logo on the door, were parked diagonally in front of the building. Across the street loomed the brick mass of La Plata's County Courthouse.

Over the radio, the sheriff told him they'd been searching the mountainside where the cabin was located and the canyons between Coalbank Pass and the Molas Divide. No sign of their grandfather. "Tomorrow, when you get here, we'll be covering the ridges running east and west between Cascade Creek and Hermosa Creek. We wouldn't be out here," the sheriff added, "if the team didn't have a search-and-rescue training session planned. One of these days the Forest Service is going to order you to tear this cabin down."

No reason to tell the sheriff that wasn't very likely. The government had given his grandfather permission to build there years before; it was one of their ways of saying thank you for what he'd done in the war and after.

When he didn't say anything in response, the sheriff's voice had come back strong over the radio, the air waves crackling. "For all we know, your grandfather may be out on a hike. His pack's not in the cabin."

"What about his horse?"

"We found it tethered right outside. Stable's burnt to the ground. Looks like a recent fire."

How in hell had that happened? His grandfather didn't smoke. Wouldn't have started a fire anywhere near the stable. Unless sparks from the chimney in the cabin were at fault. The stable was really a lean-to, with one side open to the east and hay bales stacked at the back. At least, with Buck there, it meant his grandfather had made it to the cabin okay. Why had Wolf returned? Had he got lost on the way up, or had Gran Babbo gotten into trouble and sent him back?

The sheriff wouldn't know. Ferron told him he'd be there by morning and signed off.

Taking a sip of water from his canteen, he looked at the Australian Shepherd. Would he have obeyed a command to return home without Gran Babbo? Maybe. But in that case wouldn't Gran Babbo have tied a note to his collar—or an article of clothing, some sign that he needed help? The stable burning down wasn't really an emergency. At this season, Buck could do fine outside, and there was plenty of grass for grazing. "Hey, Wolf," he said, watching both dogs prick up their ears. "Where's Gran Babbo?" The dog cocked his head and then got to his feet. He trotted up the hill, then stopped to look back, wagging his tail. Rowdy, still panting from the altitude, lay spreadeagled in the shade of a boulder.

"Okay," Ferron said. "Let's get moving, Rowdy. Maybe Wolf can find grandpa."

CHAPTER 8

Friday, August 23, near Durango, Colorado

As they climbed through the trees, the sun rose higher in the sky. They moved at a steady pace along ridges and over crests, skirting the steep, narrow valleys, crossing small high-elevation meadows where wildflowers grew amidst the grass and leafy spurge, where orange butterflies hovered over the thistle blooms and small black ones rested on the rocks with wings steepled.

The names of many of the flowers came back from lessons taught long ago. His grandfather loved the mountains and knew every tree and plant that grew there—aspen, fir, spruce, pine, juniper, pinyon, evening primrose, Indian paintbrush, columbines, blue lupins, dandelion, wild strawberry, purple chiming bells, old man of the mountain. Gran Babbo would point them out, one after the other, as they chanced upon them during their mountain hikes.

Ferron looked at his watch. Close to ten o'clock. He'd be at the cabin within the hour. It was going to be a beautiful late summer day, the sun warm, the air cool enough to be a harbinger of the changing season. Fall came early at this elevation. The peaks nearby stretched as high as fourteen thousand feet and some of the trails ran above the tree line.

He stopped for a breather, his lungs aching with the strain. There was a faint hint of smoke in the air. They were in the middle of a small meadow, with Alpine tundra above and below.

For the last half-hour, Rowdy had followed along behind, no longer forging ahead with Wolf to scout out the terrain. The dogs had drunk from the creek earlier, but he poured a handful of water for both. When he straightened, he saw a sliver of smoke drifting out of pine trees from the direction of Siderock Ridge, a sign of life from the cabin.

"Come on, guys," he said. "Only another twenty minutes now."

Dick Lowell was waiting at the crest of the trail that descended to the cabin, hidden in the trees below. "Bad news, Nick," he said, before they'd even exchanged greetings.

"What is it?"

"One of the sheriff's men was kicking around in the ruins of the stable and found what they think might be human remains." He cleared his throat, looking away for a moment. "There's not much left of the body. They found what looks like part of your grandfather's rifle."

Ferron dropped his pack on the ground and squatted in the dirt of the trail leading down to the cabin. Around him, the stubby pine trees rustled in the wind and the strong scent of their resin filled the air. "What happened?"

"I'm not sure. I've been waiting here all morning for you. The sheriff and his men are searching the area. They radioed in about ten minutes ago. Something about finding a cache not far from the cabin."

He nodded. "That's Gran Babbo's." He picked up a stick and began to scratch in the dirt. "Any sign of anyone else having been up here?"

Dick shook his head. "I told the sheriff about the guys who talked to Barbara. There's no way to tell if they were here or not. Before his men found the remains, the sheriff thought maybe all three of them had left together. He said they were probably back in town, reminiscing over a beer."

"Not likely with Buck tied up here."

"No, that's what I tried to tell him."

He got to his feet. He could hear voices coming from the trees across the steep ravine. In a minute, the sheriff came into view and behind him three men carrying supplies, working their way down toward the cabin below.

"Come on," he said. "Let's get down there and see what they're doing."

"How long ago did it burn?" he asked, breaking the silence. The sheriff and his men were seated in the cabin eating lunch. They'd helped themselves to the supplies Gage had stashed in the cache. Ferron stood in the doorway, from where he could hear Dick laboring to saddle Buck. The sheriff would be using the horse to bring what remained of his grandfather's body off the mountain—almost nothing that was recognizable as human.

The sheriff wiped the soup from his lips. "Hard to say for sure. Over twenty-four hours probably. Ashes have cooled down. Course we had rain."

Ferron nodded. He could hear his brother-in-law knee the horse in the belly and then grunt and swear as he tried to tighten the cinch. Dick was accustomed to working in a bank, not on a dude ranch. It sounded like Buck was still one hell of a stubborn horse. The sheriff had already said they'd take the easier route back to Cascade Creek, where the coroner's station wagon would be waiting.

He leaned into the doorjamb. "What do you think he was doing with the rifle in the stable?" He tried to keep his voice even. That was the one thing that didn't fit with the idea of chimney sparks starting the fire.

"No idea. Hell, maybe he was shooting rats. Rifle might have ignited the hay and got him while he was trying to put it out. By the way, did you know he had a cache out there?"

"My grandfather set that up years ago. Kept supplies stashed for emergencies."

The sheriff took a bite from a tuna sandwich and spoke with his mouth full. "He left the door open. Must not have cared much about the supplies." He took a sip of coffee from a battered tin mug, wiped his lips carefully, and then said, "Did your grandpa ever talk about committing suicide?"

Ferron pushed himself away from the doorway, his voice hardening. "There's no way my grandfather would commit suicide."

"Maybe he started the shed on fire and then shot himself.

Tried to destroy his own body so you kids could get the insurance. He knew how that worked."

The men around the table were staring at him. "What about the guys who came looking for him? You ever thought he might have been killed?"

"Outsiders couldn't have found this place without a guide."

"My sister told them how to get here."

"Told them?" The sheriff laughed dryly. "Then they're out there wandering around lost. This ain't easy terrain."

"One of these guys was from northern Italy—a partisan. They know mountains."

"Not these mountains. And if the guy was that old . . ." He waved his arms. "Good luck."

"My grandfather's in his seventies and he made it up here."

"Yeah, with a horse." The sheriff shook his head and went back to eating.

"He didn't ride Buck. He used him to haul supplies. He was probably restocking the cache when they surprised him." The sheriff snorted. "Did you look around the cache or just take what you wanted to eat?"

The sheriff raised his head and stared at him. "You think I'm stupid?"

The tension was palpable.

"We didn't find anything unusual," one of the deputies said hurriedly. "Other than a box of ammunition with one shell missing. He must have kept the shells in the cave. Maybe the rifle was there too."

True, he thought, but that didn't mean Gran Babbo had committed suicide. And even if he had, there would have been no reason to start the stable on fire first. He tried to picture what might have happened, but nothing seemed to make sense. Had Gran Babbo heard the men coming, rushed to the cache, got his rifle, and then hid in the stable? If so, why not take all the ammunition? Or had they surprised him at the cache, killed him there, and taken the rifle and body to the stable, where they burned it? But there'd been no sign of violence near the cache, other than the door having been left open. That baffled him. A sign of haste or carelessness? What had Gran Babbo said to him on the telephone the last time they talked? If anything suspicious happened to him, he was to get in touch with a man named Harry Logan. Ferron had never heard of the man and Gage would only say, "If it comes to that, ask Janelle about him. She works at the luncheonette on Saturday and Harry's always hanging around there." Janelle. His old girlfriend. He hadn't planned on looking her up. It had been years since he'd seen her.

The sheriff interrupted his thoughts. "Nothing more for us to do here. I've already notified the town coroner and he said he'd call the state pathologist for a post-mortem. They may be able to come up with cause of death, but they don't have much to work with. My report'll say it's either a self-inflicted wound or an accident. You want to try to prove something else, go right ahead."

CHAPTER 9

Saturday, August 24, Durango, Colorado

W haddya mean you won't go swimming with me? Not even if I paid your salary for the day?"

Janelle Dutton laughed, her blond ponytail bobbing as she set a plate of cherry pie à la mode on the luncheonette's counter. "With someone who eats pie and ice cream for breakfast? I don't know about that, Harry." She pushed her sleeves up her arms and turned to get the coffee pot. A full-bodied woman with brown eyes that shone with cheerfulness, she lit up the luncheonette like a jukebox playing a hit tune. She was wearing a burgundy sweater over a cotton blouse, and a pair of gray corduroy pants. Her fingernail polish and lipstick matched the pale pink of her blouse.

Harry Logan, was seventy-six years old, a retired car dealer from Kentucky, who lived in Durango nine or ten months out of the year. She had met him one summer in a ceramics class at Fort Lewis College, and ever since then he'd gotten into the habit of stopping by the drugstore on Saturday morning, when she helped out a friend by working a half-day in the fountain area. A high school math teacher, Janelle, at thirty-one, was young enough to be his granddaughter, and never knew whether or not he was serious or joking when he flirted with her. What she did know was that she liked his wit, but then he'd had a lifetime of courting southern belles to refine it.

The old man winked at her. "Let's go down to Posner's Hole

today and go skinny dippin'."

"In this weather? Try me next summer."

"You may not be around then. Pretty girl like you might get snatched up any day."

She patted him on the arm and smiled ruefully. "Not likely, Harry. You ask me again next summer, in July when it's hot, and see what I say."

"Whaddya going to be doing all winter?" he asked. "Gotta keep warm."

She pushed a strand of hair behind her ear, a smile on her lips. "Hey, this isn't my only job," she said. "I earn enough teaching to buy a cord or two of pine for the fireplace."

"Still learnin' those high school kids how to count?"

She had moved from behind the counter to a booth a few feet away, where she began to stack a pile of dirty breakfast dishes. "Yep. Algebra this year."

"Hey," he shouted to her back as she moved toward the sink and dishwasher. "I was in Algebra once. During the war. African city. Let me show you around the Kasbah. Or through the cork forests of the Grande Kabylie."

She flashed a grin over her shoulder and then bent to fill the dishwasher, shaking her head. The cork forests of the Grande Kabylie! What a character. Always had something ready to make her laugh.

Saturday morning, Ferron was up early. Dick and Barbara and the kids, traumatized by the night before, were still asleep when he left the house at six. For an hour he walked around town, lost in thought, barely noticing that he was visiting familiar haunts, places his grandfather used to take him. What had Gran Babbo always said? The only thing that stands still and forever endures is death. Quoting Lorenzo de' Medici to him in Italian. Now, what remained of his grandfather—ashes and bone fragments—would be buried on the hill across the river, silent forever. Up there beside Grandma Olga. Twenty years she'd had to wait for him, while he kept up what he called a *corrispondenza di amorosi sensi*—a loving communication—between her spirit and his.

• • •

He took a deep breath and looked around. He was in front of the Public Library on Second Avenue, recalled the hours he used to spend in the reading room, devouring books that transported him into worlds of wonder, far from memories of the past and loneliness in the present, far from pain. From pictures of his father beating his mother. Better not to think of that. After she died, they hadn't let him see her body . . .

Too much time to think. The autopsy wasn't scheduled until ten.

He was wondering if he should find a restaurant for breakfast when he passed the Army-Navy store on Main Avenue. Across the street, on the corner of Main and 9th, he saw a red brick building and the familiar signboard—Parson's Drug Co. It had been years since he'd sat at the luncheonette at the back of the pharmacy. And, if his grandfather was right when they'd last talked on the phone, Janelle would be there. No need to call her later.

He crossed the street against the traffic light, only one car moving south down the block toward the train station, and entered the store. At the far end of the narrow shop, the fountain area lay unchanged by the years—booths to each side, in a black and white design that for its time must have seemed a shocking example of modern art, a series of tables down the middle, and a counter with stools at the back. The room was small, but mirrors to each side of the dining area helped ease the luncheonette's claustrophobic atmosphere. No waitress in sight, but one old man sat at the counter eating a piece of pie. Ferron took a seat in a booth facing out toward the pharmacy's racks and the street beyond.

"You look like someone who'd like a cherry shake," he heard someone say, coming up from behind him, the tone droll.

He looked up at the woman standing at his shoulder, at her smile that was like a cup of hot coffee in the morning. "Janelle, Gran Babbo said you'd be working here." She looked as good as ever. The last time he'd seen her they'd been toasting marshmallows in the fireplace of a cabin and eating them in bed. That was the night before he left Durango for good, heading for the University of Colorado in Boulder, and she'd promised she would follow a year later, after graduation from high school.

"It's been a while," she said. "I thought you'd miss those cherry shakes long before now." No recrimination, her voice full of pleasure at seeing him again.

"Thought of them every day," he said.

In high school, this was their favorite hangout. Every afternoon Nick would order a cherry shake and Janelle a rootbeer float. He hadn't seen her in fourteen years, but she still had those brown eyes that seemed to look deep within him, and round cheeks framing full lips quick to laugh. How did she manage to look so young and vibrant when he felt so old and tired?

He saw her own appraisive glance then and dropped his eyes. "I'm a little worse for wear," he said. "Gran Babbo died yesterday."

The smile disappeared from her face. She sank into the booth across the table from him. "What happened, Nick? I saw him just last week. He looked great."

"He was shot at his cabin in the mountains."

"Shot?" Her voice quavered.

"The sheriff thinks it was suicide—or an accident."

He paused, his eyes clouded, and she waited for a moment before speaking.

"And you don't?"

He looked up, surprised that she could read him that well. "It's not like my grandfather. He didn't live this long to commit suicide—and he was too careful to shoot himself."

Janelle stared at him. "Hikers? Someone who stumbled across the cabin?"

He shrugged. "I'm not sure. Barbara said a couple of guys were asking about him. She told them how to get to the cabin. One of them was a buddy from the war, she said. An old man from Italy. They haven't shown up."

"Nick, let me get you a cup of coffee and we can talk." She slid from the booth, then paused beside him, her hand on his shoulder. "It's still slow at this hour. Would you like me to call the owner? She can come down and start work early. I'm supposed to be here till noon. I only help on Saturdays, but I can take off early if you'd like."

He looked up at her, wondering what might have been if

things had worked out differently. "Thanks, Janelle. I'd like that."

They talked for an hour while Nick ate breakfast, avoiding the subject of his grandfather after he told her about the autopsy and inquest. He didn't mention the man his grandfather had said to look up if anything were to happen to him. Time for that later. He was pleased to learn Janelle had graduated from the University of Colorado. He'd lost touch with her when he went away, and when she followed, he was somewhere in Arizona, a dropout, caught up in his own problems and working for Southern Pacific as a crew dispatcher. It took him a year and a half before he decided to go back to school, this time to the University of Arizona.

"Graduating wasn't much easier for me," she said. "I started and then dropped out after a year kind of like you, but for different reasons. My mother had a stroke, so I came back to help dad. Eventually I went to the community college here in town and then finally returned to Boulder. I finished about four years ago now."

"What in?"

She smiled. "Management Information Systems. I thought I wanted to work in Denver, but I missed home too much. So now I'm teaching math at the high school. Remember that horse shed we had near the river? Dad turned it into a nice cabin for me. I'm close if they ever need help. And we still have the twenty acres when I need space."

He nodded, then looked at her left hand, resting on the table. She wore an emerald birth stone on her ring finger. "Ever married?"

She shook her head. "I thought I wanted a family, but it didn't work out. Most of the boys my age were already married or gone by the time I came back. I did come close once, but—" She pursed her lips and then shrugged. "What about you?"

Ferron grunted. "I came *too* close. I'm divorced. She's back in L.A. with her folks. I'm living in Tucson."

"I know about your job," Janelle said. "Your grandfather used to talk about you. Every time there was a bust that made the papers he'd come in proud as a pig who's just scaled a tree. He'd bring the clipping with him, showed it to everyone. He was an early bird like you. Always here at six in the morning."

"An early bird. Hell, I'm a night owl now. This is the earliest I've been out in months. I'm usually up till two or three and then sleep till noon." He rubbed his forehead. "Or lie in bed, I should say. I need ten hours anymore and I still wake up tired."

"Maybe you're depressed," she said, her eyes twinkling.

He snorted. "Maybe I'm an insomniac, you mean. I stay up until I'm exhausted, go to sleep, and wake up two and a half hours later. And that's it. The rest of the time I'm lying there half awake it seems." He waved his arms in a gesture of defeat. "That was one of the reasons my wife divorced me. The dreams. I woke up once with my hands around her neck. Thought it was my dad." He grinned. "About choked her to death. It didn't take her long to leave after that."

"I should send you to my therapist."

"Yeah, that's what the chief said when he fired me."

"You were fired?"

He played with the knife on the table. "More or less. Technically, I'm on disciplinary probation." He shrugged. "I've decided to quit before they kick me out. I've had enough."

She nodded without saying anything, her eyes watchful.

"My ex and I, we had to sell a house. We split the proceeds. If I watch it, I got enough to live five years if I have to."

"So you're not here asking for a job."

He grinned. "Not yet." It was nice to see her smile back, her eyes locked on his. "So tell me more about you," he said. "What was wrong with the one guy?"

"James?" She hesitated, her eyes flitting around the room. "Well, at first I thought he had a sense of humor, but he was sick." He raised his eyebrows at the harshness of her tone. "We'd watch a TV news report on a baby drowning in a toilet bowl and he'd get up to go to the bathroom and say, 'I have to go pee in the baby's swimming pool.'" Ferron laughed. "Yeah, well maybe that's funny now," she said, "but added to everything else it wasn't then. Every time he mentioned my therapist, he mispronounced the word as 'the rapist'. Things like that. He slapped me once when he was drunk and that did it. I left for good."

He leaned back into the booth, hands clasped in front of him. "Sounds like my wife," he said. "I don't guess you'd like being choked either—even if it was in my sleep."

When he reached the town morgue, he learned the medical examiner had already completed the autopsy. The inquest itself lasted barely an hour. Following the medical examiner's technical recitation of the manner of death, which was deemed to be a gunshot wound, Barbara testified as to their grandfather's recent actions, his good spirits and plans for the future, then mentioned the two men who had asked about Gage and who intended to look him up in the mountains. The sheriff noted that no indication of visitors had been found in or around the cabin or the cache. The weapon belonged to Thomas Gage. As far as he was concerned the probable cause of death was suicide.

Gage's doctor testified that despite his advanced years, he was in good health, both mentally and physically. He was a vigorous man, used to the outdoors, content with his life. In consideration of the family, and since no insurance claims were involved and no suicide note had been found, the medical examiner ruled that the cause of death was accidental. There was no need to bring the case to the attention of the county attorneys. The remains, at the family's request, were to be removed to the Hood Mortuary for burial in Greenmount Cemetery on Sunday morning. And with that, the case was closed. No one had said a word about Gran Babbo's past.

Outside, Ferron thought about that. After two years with the British Special Forces carrying out missions in Crete and Cyrenaica, after facing countless dangers underground in Cairo and Algiers, and then more time behind the lines with the OSS in Italy, after a twenty-year career with the CIA, how did Gran Babbo die?

Shot through the heart like a rabid dog.

It didn't seem right.

CHAPTER 10

Friday, March 19, 1943, the Lido between Ostia and Castel Fusano, Italy

A re you going to swim?" Carla asked.
Gage looked up in surprise. Holding a glass of Sambuca in one hand and a napkin in the other, he was standing in the drawing room of the Villa Delio, a sumptuous, beach-front edifice of vermiculate stone, situated along the Lido between Ostia and Castel Fusano. Earlier that evening, he and Carla had taken a crowded, thirty-minute ride on an electric train to reach the party. "Is that what you brought in the bag?" he asked. "A swimming suit?"

She laughed deeply. "No, I didn't bring a swimming suit. But in the sea at this hour . . ." She looked up into the moonless sky, its velvet darkness pearled with tiny droplets of shimmering white. "Who's to see? Didn't you notice the countess? Those ringlets of damp hair? She didn't get those at the beauty parlor. She and her lover—that nice young man you were talking to earlier—"

"You don't mean Dario?"

"Right. Once the sun set, they both went swimming. They undressed in one of the *cabine* and swam nude. We can do the same."

"But he's only sixteen. He's still in the *liceo*. My God, she's at least forty-five!"

She laughed at his surprise. "The countess picks them young . . . So, will you come?"

"Swimming?" He swallowed the last of his Sambuca. "I'd like to Carla, but Pavan is finally free from *la vecchietta*."

The *vecchietta* was the furrier's great aunt, a little old woman who spoke with a high cackle in a Piedmontese dialect. Gage, not having understood a word she uttered, had avoided the OVRA agent while the old woman had him in her clutches.

"Pavan just stepped out on the veranda to smoke," he said. "I need to talk to him."

Carla took his arm and stepped closer, her perfume reaching his nostrils, her breasts pressed firmly against him. At eighteen, she was in full flower and difficult to resist. For security reasons, he hadn't yet told her he had a wife in the States, with a daughter who would be three years old in less than a month. He would have to do so soon. Being eight years older than Carla, he hadn't expected her to be attracted to him—but the feeling, he suddenly realized, was mutual. And she had sensed his longing, despite his attempts to repress it. It would be necessary to let her know before either of them lost control.

Tell her about his family, he thought, and then try to put them out of mind. *He had to become Thomas Karl Ludwig. A bachelor. A playboy. He had to become an Austrian aristocrat if he wanted to survive.*

"Just remember," she said softly, "I've spoken to Pavan often—and last time I told him about you. He'll think you have German sympathies, so be careful how you approach him. He's very enigmatic. Sometimes I think he's about to say something that would show he is in favor with our cause and then . . ." She pursed her lips. "And then he gets an edge to his voice and what he says is the exact opposite of what one expects. You can't tell if he's being ironic or simply stating the truth as he sees it. Be careful, Tommaso."

Elio Pavan turned at the sound, his face dark and unsmiling as Gage slid a slatted deck chair near the balustrade and sat down heavily.

"A beautiful evening," Gage said, and then propped his feet on the top rail. The railing was of an ornate ironwork design, torsaded near the bottom, spiked at the top, and anchored by stone bollards set every three meters along the open porch facing the sea. At this hour, there was only darkness beyond. A faint breeze stirred, wafting the moist smell of the sea.

Without responding, Pavan knocked the dottle out of the bowl of his pipe, then refilled it from a pouch he carried in the side pocket of his gabardine suit. In a minute, his head was wreathed in lunt. He was not a man who looked easily approachable. Earlier, inside, Gage had taken stock of the man, noting his tight, sullen expression, the sardonic smile that punctuated his brief statements, the stubborn stance—arms crossed over his chest as he leaned against the wall. He had a blunt, almost belligerent jaw, an aquiline nose that made him look predatory, and eyes the color of galvanized nails. There was no light there; they absorbed everything and gave nothing back.

"I don't believe we've met," he said. "Ludwig, Thomas Karl. From Vienna. You may have known my uncle, Count Neumann."

Pavan turned to look at him, nodded once, almost imperceptibly, and resumed smoking.

Okay. The guy was not going to make it easy on him. He knew the type—the police agent who used silence as a method. But two could play that game. He settled down comfortably, letting the silence grow. Behind them, through closed French doors, he could hear music and laughter. Bright light cascaded out onto the veranda. At the railing's edge all was darkness. He heard the scrape of a wooden match, saw the flare of light between the man's hands, illuminating his hard face. A dangerous man to cross.

In a moment, the man's voice came out of the darkness like the flicker of a bat's wings. "Ever met Cavallero? A businessman like your—" The voice hardened, dissonant, like a taste of alum. "What did you say the count was, your uncle?"

Gage cleared his throat as if to speak, then merely nodded. He was familiar with the recent changes in the fascist ministries. The regime's press agency—the Agenzia Stefani—had seen to it that the newspapers were full of the Duce's personal directives, verification that his hands were still on the tiller of the ship of state. Marshall Ugo Cavallero had been replaced by General Vittorio Ambrosio as Chief of the General Staff in January and in early February the Duce, after firing his son-in-law Galeazzo Ciano, had assumed the portfolios, not only of Foreign Affairs, but of the Army, Navy, Air Force, and the Interior—and that meant that he was in charge, ostensibly at least, of the various fascist police forces, including the OVRA.

The Italian had turned to face him, leaning back against the railing, one leg crossed in front of the other, left hand under his right elbow. The fingers of his right hand curled around the bowl of the pipe, caressing it. He exhaled a plume of smoke. "Hear why he was fired?"

Gage nodded. "*Per le bustarelle.*" For bribes. Cavallero was no different than the other fascist party hierarchs with open hands. Fancy cars, dinner parties, wives and mistresses decked out in furs, while the people stood in line for their three-ounce weekly ration of beef and their monthly tenth of a kilo of butter—if they could find it. The hierarchs had private showings of the latest movie from Cinecittà, sipping Saccony & Speed port at their luxurious wing chairs in the drawing room of their villas. The poor sat on wooden benches in the neighborhood *Dopolavoro* club, drank coarse red wine, and read donated copies of ten-lire detective novels or paid six lire to watch scratchy, third-run propaganda films. No wonder the communists were doing so well at recruiting clandestine agents to work against the fascists.

He looked up and realized Pavan was staring at him intently. "What's that?" he said, afraid that he'd missed something.

"Not bribes. The real story."

He shrugged in apparent indifference. "The Duce does not like how the war is going."

Pavan stared at him. "Of course," he said coldly, "but the Duce always needs an excuse." He paused, shoulders hunched, then straightened and spoke quickly. "Benito and the Marshall were watching the troops on maneuver one day when Cavallero said he had to go *pipì.*" Pavan hacked out a single burst of laughter, the sound harsh and metallic. "And then, without another word, the Marshall walks over to a bush and starts to pee. He spits and he's so fat the spittle hits his belly and bounces off his uniform. Mussolini is staring at the man, thinking, this is my Chief of the General Staff? And then the Marshall, who notices the Duce watching him, looks down and says, 'If you see the little fellow, say "hi" for me; I haven't seen him in ten years.' And that did it. He was dismissed a week later."

"Very funny," Gage said, a tight smile on his face. "I'll have to share that with my uncle the next time we talk."

A moment of silence followed while Pavan lit his pipe again, his actions slow and careful. Between puffs on the pipe he asked, "How is the Count? The last I heard he was closing up shop in Vienna."

Too casual for his taste. He felt his stomach tighten. After all, this man belonged to an organization, the OVRA, whose goal it was to track down enemies of the state. The problem with attempting to recruit a police agent was that he might be after you.

"That's right," he said. "He's moved to Switzerland."

Pavan raised his eyebrows. "A neutral country. So he is not a good Nazi?"

Gage shrugged. "Even Mussolini tried to stop the Anschluss—back in '34, if I'm not mistaken. Of course, that was before Hitler endeared himself when the League of Nations had it in for Italy."

"Yes, in '34 we sent troops to the Austrian border and neither France nor Britain would help. Now they pay the price of not being our friends."

Gage, stretched out on the deck chair, clasped his hands on his chest. "Oh, I think they might still be your friends—the friends of the Italian people, that is. From what I've read, the British seem to believe there's a difference between what the people think and what their leaders do."

Between puffs on his pipe, Pavan said, "Perhaps."

"As an Austrian and an Italian, we both come from states that have been monarchies or empires, but I don't see what good it's done us. I, for one, have never been much in favor of totalitarian governments—they need too many policemen. The eye of the eagle and all that."

Pavan stroked the skin on his neck. "Information, my friend, is power. The only man as well informed as the Duce is the Pope—and he has only 480,000 square meters to protect—and thirty thousand priests scattered throughout Italy alone. Is that, too, not a totalitarian state?"

"The Pope is the head of a religion, not a tyrant. His men are priests, not agents."

"Ah, that must be why all our enemies keep ambassadors in the Vatican—for the salvation of their souls." Pavan spoke with a sneer in his voice, then gestured with the pipe, waving it in the direction of the city. "The Holy See has no airport, so these ambassadors travel through Rome with impunity. Even Roosevelt's special envoys pass through our capital unharmed."

"If I remember correctly, that's Mussolini's fault. He signed the Concordat." Gage smiled. "But as far as that goes, I haven't much liking for priests, either."

"So, you are a Lutheran—like so many of your countrymen."

"No, let me rephrase that. I don't much care for religion in general."

"You do not like dictators, you do not like priests, what do you like?"

Gage looked at the OVRA agent for a long moment. "How about freedom?"

Pavan's face cleared, his lips twisting into a tight smile. "And how, my Austrian friend, would you know what that is?"

"By it's lack."

"Yes, well . . ." Pavan shrugged and gestured with the pipe in his hand. "If it does you any good, I doubt Benito will last much longer—even the hierarchs are beginning to lose their patience."

"Who will your countrymen follow then? Another dictator? I hear his son-in-law thinks he can run things better."

Pavan was amused. "Ciano is a playboy . . . like you, no? All he does is play golf and talk."

Gage drummed his fingers on the arms of the deck chair. "I can do more than talk."

"And what are your resources?"

He shrugged. "My uncle is wealthy."

"And you work for your uncle?"

"My uncle's business interests have been hurt, particularly in Vienna. Here in Italy the situation is not much better. Your countrymen have gained a controlling interest in his shoe factory. Now, they are making mostly boots for the army."

"And in the old days they made shoes for the people."

Gage nodded. The man had spoken without sarcasm. "That's right, we made shoes for the people."

They stared at each other in silence. Pavan's pipe had gone

out and after a moment he turned around and knocked the upended bowl against the heel of one hand. Then, his voice low, he said, "Mussolini has made many changes these last few months . . . but I think it is too late now. The hierarchs have started a rumor. They are pressuring Mussolini for Senise's head." He turned around and faced Gage, both hands gripping the iron railing behind him. "Do you know who Carmine Senise is?" Gage shook his head. "He's the Chief of Police, a Neapolitan . . . like me. Recently we discovered that Senise's secretary, Pagnozzi, is a spy for *Colonello* Dollmann. Pagnozzi compiled a long report that went from Dollmann to Himmler. And Himmler has spoken to Hitler about Senise. He's too mild to suit the Germans. They will ask the Duce to dispose of him."

"And will he?"

Pavan pursed his cheeks. "Mussolini no longer trusts Senise. The chief told me it began when he changed our uniforms. He got rid of the lictorian fasces on the cap and shoulders."

"But not on the collar."

Pavan shrugged apologetically. "There was only so much he could do."

"And that was reason enough to distrust him, I suppose."

Pavan ignored his sarcasm. "Senise has established better relations with the Carabinieri, and naturally the Duce doesn't trust them. Their first allegiance is to the King."

Gage waved his hand as if to say, so what?

"Senise himself told me that the Duce is not happy with the information we are providing, so he has established his own intelligence service. *Il pericolo giallo*, the chief calls it."

The yellow danger? Gage shook his head, puzzled.

Pavan sneered. "They compile notes on yellow tissue paper."

Gage laughed, then grew serious. "And if your boss goes . . . what about you?"

"He is not my boss, he's my friend."

"I got the impression that you worked for the police. You said 'we' a moment ago."

The Italian frowned and then lifted his head and stared at Gage. "You know . . . the police in Italy are not like those in Germany; we have never been an organ of the Party. Yes, we have to say we are fascists, but we do so out of simple necessity.

The Chief of Police before Senise, Arturo Bocchini, he was considered a fascist, and some say Senise is an antifascist, but you know, they both had the same ideas about the police. The police do not judge the constitutionality of the law—or the legitimacy of the government. We exist to maintain public security."

"And public security," Gage said softly, "means repressing the left."

Pavan nodded curtly. "I have no sympathies with the communists. The Bolsheviks would have taken Spain if it weren't for Franco. Do you know how much they would like to establish themselves in the Mediterranean basin? I work in the office of the *Ispettorato Generale* under a man named Guido Leto, a Sicilian. One of my duties is to see that the Reds don't start an insurrection in Italy. Is that what you wanted to know?"

"I thought they changed the name of the General Inspectorate."

"Signor Ludwig, you know more than you let on. Yes, we call it the OVRA now—but we are not the monsters the public perceives us to be. It's the fascist militia that has exceeded the bounds; we adhere strictly to the law."

"Laws passed by the fascists."

"Some of them. As I said, my only interest is the security of the state."

"But the state is fascist. Your enemies are the parties of the left. You serve a dictatorship."

"I serve the head of the OVRA and through him my friend the Chief of Police."

"Is it true what they say? That the OVRA has files on everyone?"

Pavan stared at his shoes as if he hadn't heard. A woman opened the French doors behind them and began calling into the darkness for someone named Silvia. Pavan raised his voice. "*Non c'è,*" he said, repeating it when the woman persisted. "*Forse è andata a nuotare.*"

"*Mamma mia, a quest'ora?*"

When the glass door closed and the murmur of the party died away, the Italian turned back to him. "Since 1940, most Italians, including the fascists, have not been favorable to the war. Only

Achille Starace goes around saying, 'For me, war is like eating a plate of maccheroni.' For the rest of us . . ." He shook his head. "We have many friends and relatives in America."

"But Mussolini seems to hate the Americans."

Pavan laughed dryly. "You know what they say about Mussolini. He dislikes anyone who has thick hair or is taller than him."

"I guess he wouldn't take too kindly to either of us, then, would he?"

Because of curfew restrictions the party lasted till dawn. During the black-out, from ten at night until eight in the morning, taxis could be obtained only by calling through the Questura, police headquarters. Around three that morning, Carla fell asleep, leaning on Gage's shoulder as they sat on a love seat upholstered in tan suede.

Unable to sleep, Gage felt the first glimmering of a headache. The cigar smoke, the long night, the tension of playing a part in a play whose actions he had little control over, all added to the strain. He cracked his neck and tried to rotate his shoulders without waking Carla. Both her arms were wrapped around his left arm. She had removed her shoes, her legs bent beneath her on the love seat. For a moment, aware of the closeness of the sleeping girl, he felt a twinge of guilt. He thought of his wife in Washington, D.C., of his daughter Irene. She would be three on April 12. Once again he would miss her birthday . . . but war took no thought of the private lives of the men and women who served their countries.

And it was dangerous to think of Olga and Irene. How many times had his trainers told him? When you assume someone else's identity, you forget your own past. You construct a new life. To do otherwise brought the risk of exposure and death.

For a while, a French woman entertained the group by throwing the tarot, using the twenty-two Major Arcana cards in a ten-card spread. Between sips of Strega and deep drags on a thin Spanish cigar attached to an ivory cigarette holder, she interpreted the past, asked questions about the present, foretold the future. Gage was glad Carla awoke before they could get to him.

She stretched her arms and looked at him. "Is it morning already?" she asked, blinking her eyes in the light and then yawning noisily.

"Not long now," he said, shifting his position to look at her. "Would you like to take a walk on the beach before we leave?"

Carla rubbed her eyes and then shivered. "I'm cold, Tommaso." She yawned again and Gage found himself copying her. "You should have napped, too," she said. "You look tired."

He nodded. "We need fresh air. Let's get your coat and take a walk. I need to talk to you."

"*Va bene*, Tommaso." She stretched out her hand to touch him on the leg. "But I go only if you promise to keep me warm." And through her tiredness a beautiful smile lit up her face.

He found himself smiling in turn, his spirits lifting. Telling her about his wife, he realized, was not going to be easy.

CHAPTER 11

Sunday, March 21, 1943, Rome, Italy

On Sunday morning, Carla, fresh from mass at a small church on Largo San Rocco, asked how things had gone with Elio Pavan. They had been too exhausted to talk the Saturday after the party. She had returned home in a private car, having hitched a ride with an official in the Ministry of Popular Culture. He had spent Saturday evening alone, reading Goethe's *Sorrows of Young Werther* in the original, full of self-recrimination whenever he thought about Carla. He had not told her about his wife. Somehow the moment—Saturday morning, dawn on the beach, the sky hazy with light, the first, faint rays of the sun diffused by clouds coming off the Tyrrhenian—had not lent itself to confessions. They had walked in silence, hand-in-hand, enjoying the peace and solitude. On the return trip, they were greeted by the warbling of birds in the greenery near the beach. Neither had spoken.

In the apartment, Carla asked about Pavan a second time and Gage, brought back to the present and still angry at himself, spoke in a harsh tone. "Carla, would you forget Pavan, for Christ's sake. I didn't try to recruit him, okay. Let me get to know the guy first."

She was quiet for a moment. "I've been working on him for a long time," she said finally. "I think he's ready."

He nodded impatiently. They were seated in the drawing room of Count Neumann's apartment over tea and biscuits.

Antonio had just left with a coded message to be transmitted to General Clark's boys by radio. Gage had little to tell G-2; most of the message contained information compiled by Antonio's men on the number of German military units in Rome. Antonio's network, he was pleased to see, was actively at work and needed few instructions from him. Consequently, though Antonio continued to defer to him, he gave few orders to the Italian, preferring to let the man feel he was an equal. Ever since the incident at the bridge, when Antonio had been forced to abandon Gage, the agent had been subservient, bowing his head, beret clasped in both hands, as he made his reports, his tone almost apologetic.

Gage glanced at Carla. She was running her hand down a seam in the upholstered sofa, hiding the hurt in her eyes.

"You know what they say, Carla?" He had softened his tone, sorry for his earlier outburst. He was angry at himself not at her. He should have told her about his wife and he hadn't. "If you want someone's attention, you should whisper not shout. Let Pavan get used to my presence for a while. I've only talked to him once."

The first two weeks of April, Gage had no other opportunity to speak to Elio Pavan, but he did meet a man in Mussolini's private security force. The occasion was public—an evening at the Teatro dell'Opera, where a German troop was performing Richard Wagner's *Die Götterdämmerung*. He attended with Carla and another couple—Fabio, a slick, handsome playboy with wind-tangled locks and an easy grin, and his current lover, Rina, a tall, slim woman of twenty-five or so, with fair hair plaited in a French braid. Rina was the daughter of a Milanese businessman who'd grown wealthy as a result of the regime's African war, and Fabio had inherited his position in life from a family that claimed to be distantly related to the reigning Savoia family. Neither knew of Carla's work with the underground.

When Carla slipped out of her full-length wool coat at the *guardaroba*, Gage felt his heart pound. She was breathtaking in a lustrous, white silk gown. The full-length dress had a dropped waist on one side and soft shirring on the other. A close-fitting bodice, overlaid with metallic lace, was suspended from spaghetti straps, leaving her shoulders bare. "My mother's wedding dress," she whispered to him, her hand covering her chest. "I had a seamstress modify the cut."

"You look beautiful," he said, his voice suddenly hoarse. Her eyes sparkled in response and her cheeks flushed.

"So do you," she said, squeezing his hand.

Thanks to Count Neumann, he thought. With the aid of a penknife, he had helped himself to the Count's locked wardrobe, the formal evening wear redolent of camphor. After airing one of the outfits for two days, he had asked Carla if she knew someone who could lengthen the sleeves of the coat and the trousers, which otherwise fit rather well. Her mother had done the work. He now wore a studded white shirt with a standing collar, a white bow tie, which had taken him fifteen minutes to knot correctly, a white waistcoat, and a cutaway black coat with tails.

Before the curtain rose and following the orchestra's rendition of the fascist anthem *Giovinezza*, the audience gave a standing ovation to General Vittorio Ambrosio, Chief of the Italian General Staff, who occupied a box accompanied by several of his staff. The general had just returned from Salzburg, where Mussolini had met Hitler at Schloss Klessheim. The rumor currently circulating through the underground was that Mussolini had failed to distance himself from Hitler as hoped by his generals.

At the intermission, they joined the crowd that had stepped into the lobby where Blackshirt barmen were serving drinks. After chatting a few minutes with Fabio and Rina, with Carla carrying on their half of the conversation, he steered Carla away.

"Why so silent tonight?" she asked when they were alone.

He stepped closer to her and said, "Look to my left. See that short, bald man with thick glasses. He speaks German with an accent. He was discussing Mussolini's security with two of the German officers. He was bragging about how thorough they were. I'd like to talk to him if we can manage it."

She stepped to one side casually, her eyes sweeping the lobby. "That man with the greasy forehead and the receding chin? Makes his head look top-heavy?"

He smiled. "You have a way with words. Where is he now?"

"He just shook hands with one of the Germans." She paused.

"He's working his way in this direction."

"Okay. He's probably going back to the bar. Listen, Carla, I'm going to speak German to you. Nod your head anytime I stop. You don't have to respond."

"*Ja wohl, mein freund. Ich dich verstehe.*"

"I didn't know you spoke German," he said in surprise.

"Very little. I probably won't understand a word you say." She reached out and touched him on the arm and then laughed as if he'd said something humorous. He could see by her eyes that the man was approaching.

"That's true," he said, switching from Italian to German and raising his voice slightly. "We had only one anxious moment in Rome." He caught a glimpse of the bald man as he moved through the crowd to his right. "Our work really begins before the Führer travels. In '38, Schellenberg sent five hundred of us as tourists. We were the best linguists in the SD."

The bald man had slowed his pace, head turning to glance at them. Gage looked only at Carla, and then to his surprise she said, "*Was ist die SD?*"

"The *Sicherheitsdienst*," he said, happy she had given him the opportunity. "Himmler's security service. Schellenberg had us organized in cells of three—something he picked up from the Russians."

"What did you do in Italy?"

The bald man had stopped and stood two feet away, staring directly at the two. Gage continued to ignore him. "We were really just an information service—we reported on the feelings and attitudes of the people toward the fascist regime. Naturally, if we heard of anything suspicious in connection with Hitler's visit, we were to follow up on it."

"Excuse me," the bald fellow interjected, stepping closer. He spoke in halting German. "I don't believe we've met. Benelli, Sergio. Didn't I see you at German Embassy once. Several years ago, I believe."

Gage's heart skipped a beat. Had he just blown his cover? His knees were suddenly weak. The man's comment was not a ploy intended to insert himself into the discussion. Benelli *had* seen him before, and Gage knew when—the only time he'd been to the Embassy, the spring of 1937, at the reception given two weeks prior to his marriage to Olga. Her father, Frans Kraft, was an assistant Commercial Attaché in the German Embassy in Rome. Ambassador von Hassell had given Frans permission to throw a reception for his daughter in the Embassy itself, located on Via Conte Rosso. Gage had long feared meeting someone who'd been present. If Benelli placed him, he was in trouble.

He swallowed, said, "*Vielleicht*," hoping his noncommittal "perhaps" would settle the matter, and turned back to Carla. He opened his mouth to speak and then suddenly realized the words he wanted to say had been driven from his mind.

Carla, seeing the confusion in his eyes, came to the rescue, speaking quickly in Italian. "It's a pleasure to meet you, signor Benelli," she said, extending her hand and smiling. "My name is Carla Ceruti and this is Thomas Ludwig, the nephew of Count Neumann."

Benelli appeared unswayed by feminine beauty. He ignored Carla, his eyes locked on Gage. "I heard you talk about Hitler's visit to Italy," he said in his execrable German. "Which one was that? I was responsible in part for Italian preparations."

The man was a braggart and Gage wondered how he'd lasted as long as he had. If Mussolini knew how freely he spoke, Benelli would be in prison. But perhaps the man had nothing to do with Mussolini. Delusions of grandeur led to lies of the sort. He cleared his throat. "I was telling my companion about Hitler's visit to Rome after the *Wehrmacht* had taken Vienna."

"Ah yes, in May of '38. I remember the procession down the Via Triumphalis."

Gage nodded. He'd witnessed the event himself, working that spring as a part-time stringer for Reuter's, the international news agency. On the night of Hitler's arrival, the Via Triumphalis had been floodlit so brightly that the figures in the passing procession seemed delineated with a scalpel, and the tiers of the Colosseum rose into the tingling air as if about to be transported heavenward by a surge of colored flame. "I was telling my companion about the one anxious moment we had," he said, collecting his thoughts. Time to see if this guy was for real. "Remember when the crowd broke through the police cordon?"

Benelli cocked his head, the whites of his eyes bulging behind thick spectacles. "Are you sure? We had erected wooden posts moored in concrete along the entire route. The crowd was restrained behind heavy chains."

"Yes, but at a certain point, the Duce and Hitler got out of their car to look at a fountain. Remember? The crowd broke through the police and Hitler disappeared from sight. We had several anxious moments before the Carabinieri established control."

Benelli smiled, his forehead glistening with sweat. "The love of the Italian people . . ." He waved his hands expressively. "What can you do?"

"Yes, well, we did have our concerns because of all the attempts on Mussolini's life."

Benelli scoffed. "Those were years ago. A few deranged individuals. Today the Duce is not at risk."

"Perhaps we Germans could learn something from your security measures. I'm told that sometimes in the middle of his work the Duce jumps on his motorcycle with one of his kids sitting on the pillion and races off to Ostia."

Benelli tipped his head back, his receding chin lifting out of the folds of fat at his neck, and waved one finger in front of Gage. "Propaganda," he said, adding with an exaggerated smile, "but don't tell anyone I told you. The Duce goes nowhere without protection."

"How do you manage that?" he asked, doubt in his voice.

The lights in the foyer flashed—for a second time, he realized—and Benelli blinked his eyes and looked around the lobby in surprise. Most of the audience had already entered the theater. Among the stragglers, Gage saw Fabio Corsi, who was waving to Carla as Rina pulled on his arm.

"Listen," he said, reaching out to shake hands. "I'm having a small group over next Saturday night for a late dinner. Would you be free to attend? I'd like to talk to you about your methods. One can never learn too much."

Benelli beamed with pleasure. "Next Saturday? That would be the seventeenth, right?"

He nodded. The three of them had turned and were walking toward the *platea*.

"I'd be delighted," Benelli said. "And where are you

staying?"

Gage reached for his shirt pocket, then realized he had nothing with which to write. "Do you know the Via dell'Arancio—near the Ponte Cavour?"

Benelli nodded and asked for the number. He pointed to his glistening head when Gage told him and said, "No need to write it. I have a memory that forgets nothing."

The thought made Gage break out in instant sweat.

Book Two

The Hardening

"With 300,000 men fully armed, absolutely determined, and almost mystically eager to obey my command, I shall be able to punish all who have abused and attempted to besmirch Fascism."
—Benito Mussolini, 16 November 1922, announcing his dictatorship to the Chamber of Deputies

"Duce, you're too kindhearted. You'll never make a dictator."
—Adolf Hitler, 14 September 1943, at the *Wolfschanze* near Rastenburg, following the end of the Fascist Regime

CHAPTER 1

Sunday, August 25, Durango, Colorado

The funeral procession, with the Cadillac hearse leading the way, crossed the 9th Street bridge and began to rise up the slow curve of the highway that led to the Greenmount Cemetery on the hill overlooking Durango and the Animas River. Only six cars followed the hearse, all passing slowly under the wrought-iron arch. They proceeded on, turned left, and climbed higher, a wisp of blue exhaust seeping from the hearse's tailpipe as the driver accelerated to maintain his pace. Moving between shrubby juniper trees, they passed the Elk's Rest to the left of the road. The sculpture of the elk seemed somehow out of place, like a knickknack on the desk of a busy executive. And then they swung to the right, tires crunching on the gravel surface of an auxiliary road, and came to a stop near the tent where the sexton waited.

As Ferron stepped out of the Lowell's car, the incongruity of events overwhelmed him. The sun was too bright and yellow, the sapphire sky too transparent. Not a cloud in sight. No black umbrellas under lowering skies, no endless drizzle, no smell of rotting autumn leaves, no sere grass between the headstones, no time-worn inscriptions on crumbling vaults, no chill wind keening out of the north. The grass was neatly trimmed, the flowers cheerful, the granite slick and shiny. Even the graveside ceremony presided over by a Methodist minister seemed prosaic and mundane. And then the wind picked up, and the minister's words, like drifting leaves, were carried away by the breeze. The day's only appropriate moment, he thought. And then, as if to signal the moment's significance, there came from a distance the faint whistle of the Durango-Silverton narrow-gauge railroad, and finally that too died slowly away.

The site contained the grave of Ferron's grandmother Olga, dead now nearly twenty years. All he could remember of her was that she cooked big breakfasts and tried to teach him how to say *Salz und Pfeffer* in German. And his own mother, Irene, who'd died so violently four years before that? Where was she buried? Nick was only eight when she was killed and he couldn't remember a ceremony, had never visited her grave. He thought of the house in Grand Coulee. When he was six, two years before his mother died, he'd buried a dead sparrow near one corner of the garage, intending to dig it up years later with the hope of finding a perfect skeleton, like those of the giant dinosaurs in his science books. But then came the abrupt move, leaving behind his mother's grave, a father in prison, and memories he tried to forget. But some memories, like initials written in concrete, were buried too deeply to be washed away by time. And even if, over time, he forgot the details of his mother's death, he could never forget his hatred for the man who should have been his father. There were certain betrayals for which there was no forgiveness. What was that phrase that Gran Babbo was always quoting from one of the Medici? We are told to forgive our enemies, but no one said we had to forgive our friends. His father had betrayed his own family. Was there a worse crime?

As the mourners made their way to their separate cars following the ceremony, an elderly gentleman removed his fedora, and stepped in front of Janelle, who had her arm through Ferron's. Janelle nodded and said, "Hello, Mr. Logan. Nice of you to come. This is Mr. Gage's grandson, Nick Ferron."

The old man dipped his head toward Ferron. "Please call me Harry, Mr. Ferron. Janelle told me you wished to speak to me. May I have a word with you in private?"

"Now?"

Logan nodded, an apologetic smile creasing his ruddy cheeks. "Just for a moment."

Janelle squeezed Ferron's arm. "I'll wait for you in the car."

When the two men were alone, Logan clasped his felt hat in both hands and said, "I'm sorry to hear about your grandfather. I knew him for just a short time. We met at a Veteran's Day parade a few years ago and we used to get together occasionally at the American Legion hall. I was a prisoner of war in Germany." The old man paused, head bowed, as Ferron stared silently at the grizzled circle of thinning hair that wreathed the man's head like a horseshoe.

Logan stroked the bristle on his unshaved cheeks. "About three weeks ago, your grandfather left a trunk with me. For storage. I rent a house on 2nd Avenue, and Mr. Gage used to look after it for me when I went back to Kentucky to visit my kids." He raised his eyes and then hurried on. "You see, I didn't know him well, but I have a large attic that's empty and he asked if he could store the trunk there since he was living with your sister and the house was jammed. Of course I said yes. Mr. Gage refused to take any money for looking after my place and it was the least I could do." Logan twisted the brim of his fedora between both hands. "He did ask one thing, and that was to tell you about the trunk if anything happened to him. So it's there, anytime you want to come pick it up. Miss Dutton knows where I live."

Ferron looked off across the cemetery plot toward a van parked at the northern end. A tall, black man dressed in a tan smock opened the panel doors and removed a bundle of irises, which he proceeded to lay in front of a headstone. He cleared his throat. "Thank you, Mr. Logan. I'll bring Janelle along when I come." He paused. Barbara had never mentioned a trunk and he couldn't remember ever having seen one in the old house before Gran Babbo sold it and moved in with the Lowells. "I'm going to be returning to my sister's house for a few hours. Will you be home later this afternoon?"

Logan brushed his hand across his head and then replaced the hat. "Why don't you stop by between five and six? I'll expect you then."

The man with the irises returned to the panel truck and picked up the two-way radio. He pressed the talk switch three times and then waited. A moment later he heard Vasco Akkad's voice. "I'm in the clear. What is it?"

"The party's breaking up."

"Okay. I'm finished here anyway."

"Find anything?"

"Talk to you later. Pick me up in ten minutes."

Vasco Akkad had chosen the Elks Lodge on the northwest corner of 9th Street and East 2nd Avenue as the pickup point. The lodge was five minutes distant. It would take the cars at least ten minutes to get to the Lowell's house. He had a few more minutes before making his exit out the back. Both dogs had wagged their tails when he called to them, so he expected no problems in that area. He took one last look around the living room, at the photos on the mantel, the Bible on the coffee table with Richard Lowell's family tree inscribed on the flyleaf, the magazines on a rack by the recliner, the antique mirror that showed his own recently tinted gray hair. He would wash the gray out later that night. He hadn't needed the disguise.

Akkad had already searched the entire house—basement to attic, spending most of his time in the back room that served apparently as bedroom and den to Thomas Gage. Unlike the children's bedrooms, the room had an aseptic air to it, like that of a ward in a hospital. The narrow bed was made with precision. The drawers of the dresser in the corner were almost empty—a few pairs of socks, underwear, handkerchiefs, pants and shirts, with almost nothing hanging in the closet. The top of the desk was bare. He had rifled the drawers of the writing desk, searching for secret compartments, but found nothing significant. Envelopes, stationery, paper clips, a stapler, pens and pencils, a pair of old glasses—the usual paraphernalia that one acquires over time. Next to the desk stood a typewriter on a metal stand with a small bottle of white correction fluid and a dictionary. But no personal papers, no notes, no correspondence files, no passport or documents, nothing that would show who Thomas Gage was and what he'd been. But from what his pals in the DEA had told him by phone the man's name had been there in Beppe Aprico's address book—right next to Theunis Kloos. His boss in D.C. was right to be worried. The old man had told him to look for correspondence and personal papers, possibly memoirs or a diary. Akkad had found no trace of any of them. He'd even leafed through the volumes in the two bookcases, all to no avail. The same with the body in the mountains. After Naveed had killed the man, Akkad looked for a wallet, an identification card. But there was nothing on the man—and no papers in the cabin.

What next? Take care of the guy's grandson? Or follow him for a day or two first to see what he would do? If the kid gave up and went back to Tucson, fine. He would leave him alone. At this point, the more he thought about it, the fewer outsiders he and Naveed had to take care of the better. No reason to attract too much attention. Once Ferron was out of the picture, back in Tucson minding his own business, they could worry about Kloos in Suriname. Rent a two-engine plane, load it up with weapons, and hopscotch their way down through Mexico, to Belize City, and over to the capital city of Paramaribo. Then *pum!* A bullet to the head. He grinned. Finish ahead of schedule and take a little vacation in the Caribbean while they were at it. And if the boss wasn't happy they could always come back and do Ferron last. Save the kid for dessert.

CHAPTER 2

The trunk sat across two of the ceiling joists against a queen post to Ferron's right. It was a battered affair that looked, from the stenciled addresses and customs stamps, like it had been shipped across the Atlantic more than once. A sturdy padlock secured the center safety hasp. In the dim light that seeped in from a single window, he slid the trunk, which appeared to weigh about fifty pounds, toward the trapdoor. Holding the leather side strap, he lowered the trunk to Janelle, who caught it in both arms and handed it down to Harry Logan "Let me know if it's full of gold," Logan said.

Ferron had decided, at Janelle's invitation, to spend the night at her place outside town. Dick and Barbara had a full house, with Dick's two brothers and a sister and their seven children in from Denver for the funeral. Ferron was ready for a little peace and quiet. The trunk sat in Janelle's living room on a throw rug. He had used a hammer and chisel to break the latch. Without being asked, Janelle left the room to prepare a light dinner, while Nick examined the contents of the trunk. Inside, he found two stacks of books, all Italian works, some dating from the war years, some with inscriptions from Gage's parents dating to the 1920s. There was a leather-bound copy of Dante's comedy, with marginal annotations in English, in a young boy's hand, and other Italian classics. Alongside the books lay a stack of large manila envelopes and several file folders with rubber bands around them, and tucked in a corner was a packet of envelopes, some with airmail markings.

He opened the manila envelopes and found various records—a wedding certificate attesting to the marriage of Thomas Gage and Olga Kraft in Rome, Italy, on 1 May 1937, with one of the witnesses being a Frans Herbert Kraft, assistant Commercial Attaché, German Embassy; a degree in political science with a minor in history from Yale University, dated 1938; and other documents attesting to his grandfather's military service, including pay receipts, appointment and promotion letters, and several written commendations. Another envelope contained an odd assortment of decorations, ribbons, qualification badges, and insignia, including a major's gold oak leaves. Folded inside was a DD Form 362, a Statement of Charges for Government Property Lost, Damaged or Destroyed, with the handwritten note "Tom, I owe you for this one. Beppe." The item listed as missing was a two-ton lorry!

Along the back of the trunk, hidden by the stacks of books, was a case holding a pistol. A Mauser with two spare ten-round clips. The case itself was engraved in silver with the letters RFSS—and inside, on the satin lining of the case lid, the initials were written out in full—*Reichsführer der SS*. A Nazi weapon. One of the spoils of war?

He was about to get to the file folders when Janelle called out that dinner was ready. Over a plate of eggs and potatoes, with toast, sausage links and a rasher of bacon, he told her what he had found.

"Anything worth hiding?"

He shrugged. "Not particularly. At least nothing I've found yet." He took a drink of milk and wiped his lips. "There's one curious item—a government form accusing my grandfather of losing a two-ton lorry, with a handwritten note on it signed by someone named Beppe. That's probably Beppe Aprico."

"Who's he?"

"Someone my grandfather worked with in the war. He's a member of one of the New York Mafia families. He supposedly retired in Arizona about the same time Bonanno did. My grandfather introduced me to him last year."

"Police business?"

He nodded. "I was trying to infiltrate Aprico's organization. The DEA killed him in a raid this last week."

"Think there's any connection?"

"Between what?"

"Your grandfather's death and his?"

He thought about that for a moment. "Aprico might have found out I was with the police. I suppose his men could have hit Gran Babbo in revenge. A personal vendetta."

"But you don't think so."

"Well, I worried about it for a while, but I'd have expected them to come after me first, not him. I'm still not convinced my grandfather's dead. That corpse was burned too badly to identify. It was mostly bone fragments. It could have been anybody."

"Then where's your grandfather?"

He shrugged. "If someone's after him, he could be hiding out in the mountains. He could be in town—or out of the state. He's the type of man who prepared for all eventualities. And he had backup plans if something went bad with the original."

She placed her hand on his. "He was a nice man, Nick. For your sake, I hope you're right."

"The only problem is, there's no backup plan if you're dead."

After dinner, he returned to the trunk. The file folders held sheets of paper that had been torn from a notebook and stapled together. Janelle wanted to know what they were.

"Pages of a history of Fascism it looks like. See here, he starts writing in 1949 but makes notes on events as far back as 1922. And then—" He turned to another folder. "Here he has diary entries that date from the forties. Apparently he was using his diary and these old newspaper clippings to write the history."

Janelle looked at the stack of papers Ferron was removing from the folders. "He must have kept track of everything. That's a lot of material."

"He did mention once how he'd like to write a book about what happened during the war. Strange thing is, he never liked to talk about what he'd done in Italy."

"What's that?" She pointed to the stack of letters.

He removed the rubber band. "Correspondence." He frowned, looking at the stamps. "Some of this is recent. And look, Aprico wrote to him."

He flipped quickly through the envelopes. As he moved down the stack, the stamps changed, the amount of postage always smaller, until near the bottom the stamps cost only three cents. The last four envelopes had foreign stamps.

Janelle picked up one of the airmail envelopes. "This is really old, Nick. It's addressed to your grandfather in Washington, D.C., and came from Dutch Guiana." She turned the envelope over. "From someone named Theunis Kloos."

"Never heard of him. Wait—" He hesitated. "Kloos—that was one of the names in Aprico's address book. Along with my grandfather's. The don had connections with a lot of people in Washington." He picked up one of the recent letters from Aprico. "Let's see what he had to say." He began reading. "Listen to this," he said, a moment later. "Talk of the devil. Aprico mentions someone he calls 'our good friend Kloos' but he talks about Suriname. Where in hell is that?"

She shook her head. "Never heard of it."

"You have an atlas?"

"Let me get the dictionary."

Janelle left the living room and returned a few moments later. The sky had grown apricot-pink and she turned on a lamp and an overhead light. Her cabin lay to the north of town, where the valley began to narrow, and stood in a grove of immense oak trees that lined the Animas River. In the old days, the cabin had been a horse shed, but her father had remodeled the small rectangular structure, and added a loft bedroom. On the ground floor, she had a small living room with a stone fireplace in the corner, a bathroom under the loft ladder, and a kitchen with a dining nook. Outside the sliding glass doors, her father had built a deck that overlooked a garden, with the meandering course of the river just beyond, demarcating the eastern boundary of their twenty-acre ranch. The trees in the distance were slipping into shadow, merging with the mountain ridges farther east.

"They're the same thing," she said, surprise in her voice. "Suriname's an independent republic that used to be a Dutch colony."

"Dutch Guiana?"

"One and the same."

He looked at Aprico's letter again. "This was written on the twenty-ninth of July. Aprico warns my grandfather about Kloos. And then he says something about Kloos having figured out the puzzle. He has the clue they need."

The two stared at each other.

"The deaths are connected," she said. "This guy in Suriname was after both men for some reason."

"Maybe."

"Don't be so skeptical, Nick."

He rubbed his face tiredly, deep in thought. For a moment, he was angry with himself for walking around with his head up his ass. He was a cop. He wasn't supposed to have tunnel vision. He'd never stepped back to see the big picture. Hoping all this time that his grandfather hadn't died. That someone else was in the shed. "I'm going to have to talk to Kloos," he said, his eyes staring vacantly into the darkness outside the sliding glass doors.

"You can't talk to him now. It has to be the middle of the night there."

"I don't mean by phone. I want to look him in the eyes when he tells me what's going on."

"Get some rest and see what you can do tomorrow."

He looked around the room. Was she planning on them sleeping together? Her invitation had been to spend the night at her place, but he'd thought she meant the couch in the living room. He hadn't realized how small the place was. There was no couch, just a love seat and a comfortable recliner. If he slept in the living room, he'd be sleeping on the floor.

He tried to remember the last time he and Janelle had made love together . . . Fourteen long years ago. The night before he left for Boulder to go to the university. He cleared his throat. He wanted to look into her eyes but was afraid to.

"I'm too wired now, Janelle. I want to see what my grandfather wrote."

"That'll take all night," she said. "You need some rest."

He looked at the stack of material in front of him on the rug. "Janelle, I wouldn't sleep. And if I did I'd probably wake you."

Her lips pursed. "Wake me?"

He didn't smile. "With a nightmare." He could see she wanted to ask more, but didn't. "It's probably the job," he said, and then shrugged. "We see too much. Anyway, if it won't bother you, I'll just stay down here and read. We can talk more in the morning. What time do you get up?"

"Five-thirty," she said. "I help dad with a few chores before getting ready for school. We're supposed to be on duty by seven-thirty."

"Good. I'll see you in the morning, then." She moved toward the stairs to the loft. "Oh, Janelle." He cleared his throat as she looked back at him. "Would you mind keeping Rowdy while I'm gone? I'm going to make arrangements for a flight to Suriname. Gran Babbo deserves at least that much. It may take a week or two."

"I've always wanted a good watchdog," she said, tossing him a smile. "Good night, Nick."

CHAPTER 3

Saturday, April 17, 1943, Rome, Italy

W hat has Mussolini done for us now?" Gianni Traversa said. He was a jumpy man with a fleshless face, beady black eyes, a thin mustache, and an habitual offended look. At the moment the tendons in his neck were twitching in exasperation. "First we lost Italian East Africa, then the Germans took control of Libya."

"And they've lost it now," Ida Copetti said, exhaling a stream of smoke. She was a thin woman in her late forties with oversized hands and shoulders, thick, unplucked eyebrows that gave her forehead a perpetual frown, heavily made-up lips and cropped black hair. She had a mole on her cheek and she spoke with the hoarse voice of a heavy smoker. It was difficult to believe she'd been a former diva of the San Carlo opera company. She was sitting in Count Neumann's den in a Savonarola chair near a bookcase with leaded glass doors. Gage stood at her side, an awkward smile on his face. Sergio Benelli was in listening distance, his back to them, an open book in his hands.

Traversa, fascist pin in the lapel of his zoot suit, the baggy tight-cuffed trousers shiny with wear, took up the attack again. "Our invasion of Greece was a failure—it took the Germans to extricate us. Albania's going to slip through our fingers, and now we're going to lose Lampedusa and Pantelleria. Tunisia's a lost cause, our claims on Nice and Corsica are a chimaera, and who are our allies? The Japanese who we've never trusted and the

Germans who we've always hated." He looked at Gage, a false smile on his face. "With the exception of our host this evening."

Gage said nothing, but the smile had left his face. Benelli had turned around and was watching them.

Traversa turned back to the woman. "Do you think the people wanted war with America? Remember?" He raised his head, eyes veiled. "We cried when our American friends were forced to leave . . . And now these blessed *tedeschi* have taken control of the whole country."

Ida lit a cigarette and exhaled a stream of smoke. "Hitler learned his act from the Duce and now he tramples on the old man. We need to have coupons to buy clothes and the Germans walk in and take what they want." She shook her head, smoke curling around her hair, and then gestured toward the ceiling with the hand holding the cigarette. "I saw one of those Valkyries on the Via Condotti the other day—you know, blonde hair, one point eight meters tall, dress tight as a glove. She steps out of a two-seat cabriolet with a Nazi flag flying from the fender, flounces into Enzo's with her nose so high in the air her jacket rises off her butt, and buys the last twenty pairs of nylons. And we're lucky if we get one pair a year."

"And you can forget shoes," Traversa added.

Benelli's eyes, bulging behind his thick lenses, were focused on Gage. Somehow, as the host, he had to defuse the situation. Benelli, he could tell, was waiting for him to speak up in defense of the Germans. He cleared his throat. He would tell a joke, excuse himself to attend to his other guests, and then get Benelli by himself.

"I saw a cartoon in *Il Travaso* the other day," he said. *Il Travaso* was a comic magazine notorious for its earthy humor. "A man was bouncing along the street on his head. A curious friend asked him what he was doing and he said, 'What do you expect? The hat is old, the shoes are new.'" He chuckled dryly, but no one joined him. Ida Copetti's dark eyes looked at him with ill-concealed animosity. He shrugged, excused himself, and stepped over to Benelli, switching to German as if relieved to be speaking his native language. "May I offer you an after-dinner liquor, Herr Benelli? A Kirschwasser or a Courvoisier?"

Benelli reshelved the book he was holding, and Gage took the man's arm and led him into the drawing room. Benelli said, "It's fascists like those two who give us Italians a bad name with our German friends."

Gage shrugged. "Gas always vents itself out of the biggest hole," he said, a tight smile on his face.

Benelli chuckled. "*Das ist richtig*, Herr Ludwig. You have a way with words. Perhaps we should send them to Germany, *nicht wahr*? I hear the *Reichsführer*'s Mercedes runs on methane."

The two men laughed and Gage patted the Italian on the back as if they were old friends. "I think you and I would work well together, Herr Benelli."

"So how do you handle the crowds when *il Duce* mingles with the people?" Both men were holding brandy snifters.

Benelli stepped closer and lowered his voice as if to impart a confidence. "To you, Herr Ludwig, I tell the truth. The Mussolini you see in print and on the newsreels at the cinema—the one who confidently mixes with the crowd, the leader embraced by ex-soldiers, workers, farmers, prolific mothers, and all knowledgeable Italians—" he waved his arms expansively—"that man is a creation of the Minculpop."

"Certainly." Everyone knew the Ministry of Popular Culture was responsible for divulging the correct fascist image. "One understands the use of propaganda. But there are those times . . ."

"Let me tell you how we do it, Herr Ludwig." Benelli took a sip of brandy, then wiped his lips with the back of his hand. "We have divided the city of Rome into zones and the Duce's daily routes into numbered segments. Along his itinerary we station hundreds of OVRA agents in echelon, all in mufti but under the command of skilled police officials. The streets, the piazzas, the crossroads, the nerve centers—all are carefully surveilled. Sewer squads continuously inspect the route below the street. The Duce's car itself is escorted by another of equal power, filled with elite agents—members of our presidential protection group."

"Yes, I have heard of these men," Gage said, aware that Mussolini was technically the president of the Fascist Council. "They are well trained."

Benelli nodded. "Police motorcycles lead the way. They

inform the agents on the street that the Duce will pass in a few minutes. Vigilance becomes intense. Everyone in the area is scrutinized. If there is even minimal suspicion, the agents fall on you. You are sequestered in a doorway and searched. The risk to the Duce, as I said, is nonexistent."

"But what if one of your agents were to . . ."

"To shoot at the Duce? One man?" Benelli's voice was full of scorn. "It would be suicide—and for what? To dent the Duce's limousine?"

Later that evening, as he was leaving the apartment, Benelli said, "Herr Ludwig, you will have to be my guest at the Circolo della Caccia—the finest hunting club in Italy. But then perhaps you know it?"

He shook his head.

"I'm surprised. Count Neumann's apartment is only five minutes from Piazza Borghese."

Gage smiled to hide his awkwardness. "And we of the SD are hunters, correct?"

Benelli laughed. "Forgive me, Herr Ludwig. I forgot you have better things to do with your time." He reached out with his puffy hand and shook Gage's. "Perhaps the next time you are on a hunt, we will run across each other. Until then, *auf Wiedersehen.*"

When the guests were gone and Carla's mother was asleep in the bedroom, Carla said, "I don't like that one, Tommaso. It's too risky." The two of them were sitting on a love seat near a torchiere lamp with an upended glass shade that cast a soft glow on the ceiling.

"But he loves the Germans," Gage said.

"Two days after the opera, I thought someone was following me," she said. "I'm worried. Wouldn't he try to find out more about you?"

"Perhaps. My papers are the best the OSS could come up with. The Questura here would find nothing wrong with them."

"And if he tries to check with the Gestapo? I think we should stick with Elio Pavan. Benelli has nothing to do with the OVRA."

"I thought I might learn something about Mussolini's

security."

"The resistance has given up on assassination attempts, Tommaso. They are too risky and the Duce is too well protected." He yawned. "And Tommaso, you need more help. You're eyes are starting to look very tired."

She was right. There was too much for one man to do alone—even with Carla and Antonio's help. An hour earlier, after the guests left and while Carla made up the bedroom for her mother, he had sat at the Stipo desk across the room, encoding a message for Antonio to carry to the radioman at his wireless. It was all he could do to keep up with intelligence—organizing the reports, condensing them, encoding the messages, asking for follow-up reports—let alone attempt to recruit agents in the fascist or police hierarchies. He needed more time to work on his plan to gain access to the OVRA's files. Something had to be done. If he could come up with a list of informants, his mission would meet Bill Donovan's loftiest expectations.

"Shall I make up the sofa for you?" Carla was going to sleep with her mother in the matrimonial bed. "There are extra sheets in the bedroom."

He shook his head. "The blanket's fine, Carla." There was a quilt sitting on the floor near the love seat. "I'm going to work for a while."

She leaned over and kissed him on the cheek. "I could stay with you, Tommaso. This room is too cold at night."

He smiled. "With your mother in the other room?"

She snuggled up against him. "My mother is a deep sleeper."

He could smell her perfume—just the lightest fragrance of crushed gardenia—and the pleasant odor of her body. How long had it been since he and Olga had made love? Husband and wife. Too long. But that was a life he was supposed to forget. . . And if he made love to Carla, what then? She was a young girl with her whole life before her, a bud just waiting to blossom. He had no idea how many lovers she would take, perhaps none. Perhaps her first lover would be the man she would want to marry. And that couldn't be him.

Before he could think of something to say in response, something that wouldn't hurt her, she reached up and pulled his head down. Her lips were on his and when the kiss broke, he was surprised by the passion. In them both. He knew better—but knowledge against emotion was weak, especially when unprepared. And he felt particularly weak after the strain of the dinner party, a night spent talking to fascists who hated Germans and to fascists who loved them.

She reached for the button at the neck of her blouse, eyes dilating with desire as she stared at him, breath ragged.

"Carla—" She kissed him again and he felt the warmth of her breasts. His heart was pounding so hard his ears started to ring. "Carla, no . . . stop." He reached for her hand, which had slipped to the second button, and pulled it away. "This is not good for you."

"Why, Tommaso?" Her voice was husky with desire.

"When the war ends I will return home. You will stay in Rome and marry one of your countrymen."

She shook her head, her eyes soft with longing. "No, Tommaso. We do not know the future. Life is too uncertain. The war might end for us tomorrow."

He knew what she meant—capture . . . torture . . . death. And the war would go on without them.

"There are others we must think about—"

She freed her hand from his and raised it to his lips to stop him from speaking. "No, caro, we are alone and we have each other. When I am with you, no one else exists."

Why was it so difficult to tell her he was married? Was it because he had already waited too long? Because he was afraid he had led her on, even if only subconsciously, and telling her now would destroy the trust so essential to his survival?

"I don't want to hurt you, Carla. There's something you should—"

She put both arms around his neck and her lips sought his, cutting off the words he wanted to say. Her teeth bit him gently, and he could feel hot breath as her desire mounted.

"Carla, listen—"

With her lips caressing his, she dropped her hands from around his neck and loosened the remaining buttons on her blouse. She pulled away then, without shame, her breasts jutting as she leaned back. He was breathless, his own desire fighting against resistance, with all the weapons on the side of desire.

"Carla—"

"Tommaso, there is nothing you could do or say to hurt me." She pulled his shirt free and began to unbutton it from the bottom, while Gage struggled to find the words. Wouldn't *not* telling her hurt worse? She deserved to know while there was still time to say no.

"Carla, I'm married. I have a wife back in the states—and a young daughter." She ran her hands up his back, the touch of her flesh as she drew their bodies together sending a shiver through him. "Did you hear me, Carla?"

Her mouth closed over his, moist and soft, sweet as an oasis to a thirsty bedouin. His senses were stunned, his powers of rational thought overwhelmed by sensation—but, still, something held him back. And then, sensing perhaps his guilt, she drew away again. "Don't you understand, Tommaso? This is all that exists now for both of us. We may not be alive tomorrow. Tomorrow doesn't matter. Who you are, who am I—none of it matters. What matters is only what we feel for each other. I want to live while I have the chance. I don't want to die a virgin. I want to make love to the only man who matters to me."

My God, she was a virgin! What was he thinking? She had just turned eighteen, raised in a Catholic country, and until the war came along protected by a father who was no longer alive.

"Carla—"

"No more words, Tommaso."

She stood up and removed her skirt, and then stepped out of her panties, which were worn with age and frayed at the waist line. In the confusion of his senses, he felt a moment of compassion for what the war had done to everyone.

"Carla, you are very desirable . . ." He swallowed, hearing the shakiness of his voice. "But the first time—" He hesitated, his eyes rising to meet hers. "It should be with someone who loves you, someone who is free."

She smiled. "Tommaso, you don't understand, do you?" He looked at her with a question in his eyes. "You *do* love me. Don't you think a woman can tell? You just haven't admitted it—not even to yourself. You can love more than one person at the same time." She stepped closer to him, then put her hands behind his head. "Thomas, look at me. Can you tell me you have felt no love?"

She had called him Thomas rather than Tommaso, her tongue struggling with the first syllable, making her seem suddenly that much more vulnerable. He didn't know why it affected him as it did, but all resistance dropped away. He was not going to think, was not going to remember the past. He was going to live only for the moment. He was someone else now, another man. A bachelor, not a husband and father.

He knelt then and kissed her, taking in her essence, her pubic hair soft on his lips. She shuddered and whispered his name again and he ran his tongue between her legs, suddenly hungry to taste her. In a moment, he felt her legs quiver and he took her in his arms and laid her on the love seat. His mouth sought her breasts and he heard her gasp and saw the sudden flush of red on her chest.

"My God," she whispered. "Oh, Thomas, I want you in me."

He slid her to the edge of the love seat and when he placed himself at the entrance to her body, she pulled him in with a cry, and then her eyes opened wide and caught his and he could feel the love there as if it were palpable and heavy in the air. Their mouths and tongues touched and she pulled away gasping, startling by the intensity of sensation.

"Thomas, I want to feel all of you on top of me."

He tried to spread the quilt while still inside her and they both laughed at his ineptitude. With the first moment of fear and excitement behind her, she was giddy with pleasure. They slipped apart and she spread the quilt, doubling it back upon itself. On her hands and knees, with her back to him, she said, "Do you want me on top, Thomas, so you can see me?"

"Next time," he said, kissing her on the bottom and then turning her over on her back. He wanted the sensation of being between her legs, wanted to have her lift them and open herself to him again, wanted her to feel his weight as he pulled himself to her, wanted the sensation—which started where they were joined and spread through his body like warm clouds rolling over parched land—to last forever . . .

Later, with Carla asleep beside him, he thought about what he had done, about the excuses he had used. *Another man, a new identity.* Had he just been weak? He didn't like the thought and new excuses sprang quickly to mind, one after the other, crowding out recrimination. He even told himself that Olga would understand. He could heard her voice in his ear saying the same things he said, offering the same justification, mouthing the same rationalizations, and then, suddenly angry with himself, he knew this was no better than the tortured reasoning of a medieval logician twisted up in a false syllogism: Humans as a species have two feet. A chicken has two feet. Therefore, a chicken is human. His self-defense was as fallacious as that.

In the end, all he could do to assuage the guilt he felt was to tell himself that he was now living in a different world—a world far removed from the one he had known before the war. He *was* playing a role. He *was* living the life of someone else. Yes, they were excuses, but the old rules no longer applied. The man formerly known as Thomas Gage was now Thomas Karl Ludwig. And he had no choice but to accept what this man felt and what he said and what he did to ensure his survival . . . one day at a time.

CHAPTER 4

May 1943, Rome, Italy

Gage saw Elio Pavan two more times in May, once before the twelfth, when the Italian troops laid down their arms in Tunisia and Pantelleria was lost—the papers reported on the items with their usual praise of Italian valor, but the air of gloom was hard to disguise—once late in the month. Each time he led the conversation to politics, sounding out the police agent, skirting issues which seemed to antagonize the man, concentrating on those that allowed the OVRA agent to vent his frustration with the system. And every now and then he cast subtle hints as to his own persuasion. His sense of urgency was growing with each passing day.

When he casually broached the subject of the German police presence in Italy, Pavan talked about Himmler. The men were not alone. They were seated at a long table with eight other Italians, enjoying a banquet laid out by the former diva of the San Carlo opera company, Ida Copetti, whose husband, a dedicated fascist, was away on business.

"The first time I met Himmler," Pavan said, "was when he came for Bocchini's funeral. He visited Senise in his office after the ceremony." Pavan laid down his fork and gestured with his right hand. "When Himmler left, Senise told me what the *Reichsführer* had done. He'd taken out his pistol and showed it to the Chief. 'Each notch,' he said, 'is for someone I killed with my own hands.' And then he asked Senise how many he'd killed."

Pavan grunted. "The Chief said he waved his hands as if the number were too large to remember, and then you know what he told me? He said he'd never killed a fly. He called Himmler a *jena ridens*."

Ida Coppetti wiped her lips gracefully and then said, "My dear Elio, not all of us know Latin. What is a *jena ridens*?"

Before Pavan could open his mouth, Gage said, "A grinning hyena. He smiles and then calmly rips you to shreds."

Ida shuddered. "I've never met Himmler," she said. "Do bring him by sometime, won't you, Elio. He might be very entertaining."

In late May, after a Saturday morning visit to the Galleria Borghese with Pavan as guide, Gage and the police agent walked to the top of the Via Veneto, where they had arranged to met Carla and one of her friends, a young woman named Bianca, for coffee. A cool breeze swept across the city, a harbinger of afternoon showers, and high up in the sky a pale yellow sun poked its way with feeble fingers through the gathering clouds. It was sweater weather—unusual for this late in the spring. The two women had just finished shopping for clothes on the Via Ludovisi and were seated under a striped sun umbrella at an outdoor table of the Rosati bar. The two men joined them, introductions were made and when a waiter appeared each ordered coffee.

Like Carla, Bianca was active in the resistance, but did not work directly for Gage. She was a short, slim creature with milky blue eyes and a natural red tint to her hair, a Sicilian with Norman blood in her veins.

The bar served a *surrogato*, similar to the *miscela* Gage had drunk elsewhere, but made from roasted barley and peanuts. When the white-jacketed waiter sat the cups and saucers on the table, Carla took a sip from her *tazzina* and grimaced. "I bet this is not what the Duce drinks."

Pavan raised his eyebrows. "The Duce does not drink coffee," he said, a sardonic smile twisting the corners of his mouth. "He drinks only milk or camomile tea."

"Well, *he* has stomach problems," Carla retorted. "We don't."

"Yes," Bianca said dryly, "the vegetarian and the faithful

husband. Ask his wife Rachele. In Palazzo Venezia, they say he likes his women plump and with no perfume. The perfume gives him headaches."

Gage stared at her, surprised by the *non sequitur*, before he realized, when he heard Carla laugh, that the women were openly mocking the Duce's hypocrisy.

"Maybe his sensitivity extends to his temperament," Carla said, her tone arch. I've heard his wife say Benito never liked weapons either."

Pavan's smile tightened and his eyes hardened for a moment. Then, as if with great effort, he settled back in his chair, relaxed, and waved a hand expansively, his head tipped to one side. "The man is human. You do not know the Duce as he really is. I've seen him play with his children; he's quite charming in private."

Both women stared at Pavan, their mouths opening in amazement, and he hurried on before they could say anything, his blunt jaw thrust up at a belligerent angle. "I was invited to the Villa Torlonia once, years ago when I was being considered for the police. Senise took me on a visit. The Duce didn't pay attention when we first came in. He was playing in the salon with his children. They were pushing a wart on his neck with their index fingers and he would go *drin-drin* in a shrill voice—like a doorbell."

Bianca snorted. "Someday the people will turn his head into the hammer of a carillon. We can all play a pretty tune then."

Gage looked at Pavan, wondering if the policeman would take offense, but the man merely shrugged, his slate gray eyes showing no emotion. "It is the people who claim they serve him who deserve such a fate."

As usual, the man was ambiguous in his statements, sometimes leading Gage to think he was receptive to the ideals of the resistance, then suddenly speaking in support of the Duce. Every time Gage heard him speak, he was reminded of what Mussolini said when the Socialist party expelled him in 1914—"You hate me because you still love me!"

Displeased that the women had stung Pavan into defending Mussolini, he asked the Neapolitan about the relationship between the police and the Duce.

"The relationship is excellent," the Italian replied at once.

"Every day, the chief sends an officer with a mail pouch addressed to Mussolini. It contains decisions to be made, important reports coming from the OVRA's zones, from the Prefects, and from the Quaestors. The chief himself visits the palace at least once a week."

Gage was about to ask another question when he heard someone call him by name. A woman's voice. His heart skipped a beat and his stomach dropped. Please, God, let her say *ciao* and keep going.

No such luck. A woman in her late twenties rushed over to him.

For a moment he thought about denying who he was or pretending not to recognize her, but both were impossible. At least she'd used only his first name, but why did she have to see him when he was talking to Pavan, for Christ's sake? The name came to him then—Mila Stradino. He remembered her as an emaciated creature, a girl who ate like a bird, picking at her food and rearranging it on her plate in endless patterns; almost nothing touched her mouth. A model, that's what she wanted to be. The last time he'd seen her was at his own wedding.

"What are you doing in Rome?" she asked breathlessly.

"Business and pleasure," he said, wracking his brains for some way to get rid of her.

"Yes, I see," she said, glancing at the other women and raising her eyebrows. And then, with a puzzled look on her face, she said, "Where's Olga—or shouldn't I ask?" Coquettish again. Blast her.

"Olga's in Switzerland," he lied. "She wasn't able to come. And what about you, how's the modeling going?"

"With these fat cheeks?" she said, her voice rising girlishly. "No longer, Thomas. I tried it and didn't like it. I'm married now—with a boy and two girls. Can you believe it?" She patted her dark hair, cut in a page-boy style. Her eyes were still as deep-set as ever, black as a Stygian pebble, her cheekbones high, the face oval with lips painted a brilliant scarlet. Overdone, as usual, he thought, remembering the day of his wedding. Saturday, May 1st, 1937. Mila had caught the wedding bouquet after the ceremony, shrieking with pleasure and then joking about how unlucky she was. And now, six years later, she had three kids.

"Introduce me to your friends, Thomas."

He gritted his teeth, eyes hard, while Mila smiled at him. She was enjoying herself, sure that she had caught him with a lover. He made the introductions, his voice stiff, then said, "It was nice to see you again, Mila."

She refused to take the hint. "And nice to see you, Thomas. I miss my conversations with Olga. I never did learn German. And it would have been so useful, don't you think?"

He nodded, his smile tight-lipped, wondering when she would leave, when she would say something that would reveal the lie he was living. He and Pavan were still standing. And then Pavan, sensing his nervousness, said, "May I offer you my chair, signora."

Gage looked at Carla, hoping she would say something to free them—but what could she say?

"You're so kind," Mila said, "but unfortunately I must run." She stuck out her hand and both men shook it, Gage with a sense of sudden and unexpected relief.

"Some other time," Pavan said, and then she was gone.

It took a few minutes for Gage to regain his composure, and just when he did, Pavan asked who Olga was.

"A good friend of mine," he said, but sensed that Carla knew the truth. They had never talked about his wife after having made love the first time—and there was no reason for Pavan to know. "Olga Kraft. If I remember correctly, she was the daughter of a German diplomat."

He looked at Carla and thought, I should have told her more about Olga. It was better that she be a person for both of them. He'd been trying to protect Carla and himself by telling her as little as possible—at least, that had been his excuse. The guilt he sometimes felt was difficult to bear. To maintain his sanity, he had tried to forget his other life. And he had the rules behind him. To survive it was simply safer for all that he say nothing. Still, what he had done—and failed to do—continued to gnaw at him. She deserved better.

The ersatz coffee had soured in his stomach and when Pavan ordered a *supplì* for each of them, he was unable to do more than pick at his, his stomach churning at the first taste of the fat in which the rice ball had been deep-fried. He offered the rest to

Carla, and then listened with a distracted air while the two women carried on an animated conversation with Pavan.

Unnerved by the encounter with Mila, he returned to his apartment that afternoon without having broached the subject he'd intended to bring up—access to the OVRA files. Having laid the ground work over time, having hinted at his opposition to the regime, having tried to separate the fate of the fascist hierarchs from Mussolini's (to whom Pavan seemed devoted), he had intended to begin slowly—to ask first if Pavan would check a single file, that of a fascist businessman who, he would say, he suspected had been sabotaging his uncle's business interests. If the police agent agreed, if he broke regulations to secure the file, then the second request would come easier, and eventually he would ask for what he really wanted—lists of the regime's internal informants and of the double agents operating in and outside the country.

That night, for the first time since his arrival in Rome, he was sick. At home alone, nerves exacerbated by the close call with Mila, he wondered if he had made a mistake appearing as often as he did in public. Each time he stepped out onto the street, he was risking an encounter with someone who knew him. The private parties, the dinners, the socializing with fascists and *filotedeschi* alike—each carried its own danger, but at least he usually knew in advance the people he would be meeting. Irrespective of detection by old acquaintances, of the inadvertent disclosure, he risked arrest simply as a foreigner—even though bearing papers issued by authorities of the Greater German Reich and a police pass bearing the stamp of the appropriate Italian offices in Milan.

Twice that very day, in fact, after having left Pavan with Carla and Bianca, he had been stopped on the walk back to his apartment by uniformed military police agents, and the second time he almost broke from the strain. A young Carabinieri *tenente*, unfamiliar with Gage's German pass, had pulled him into a temporary military police post, set up in the lobby of a cinema in Piazza San Lorenzo in Lucina, barely two blocks from Count Neumann's apartment.

Present as a liaison officer and observer was an SS *Haupsturmführer*, a young man about Gage's age, with sandy-brown hair, pale-blue eyes, thin lips, and a crisp manner, who asked to see the papers issued in Vienna. While the German officer stared at the document, frowning and looking up from it to Gage as he scanned the lines, he could not take his eyes off the man's SS runes and the rank badges on his collar. The two men were nearly the same height, and he wavered, trying to decide if he should shrink down to emphasize his subservience or stand at rigid attention, proud to be a citizen of the Greater Reich.

"These papers—" the *Haupsturmführer* said finally, slapping them on the palm of his left hand, the silver threads of his RFSS cuff titles drawing Gage's eyes like a magnet. "I have never seen them done quite this way. Very unusual." The man spoke in German, the tone clipped.

Gage shrugged, teeth clenched to suppress the chatter he felt would break out if he relaxed his jaw. For a moment, his eyes dropped to the gold wound badge pinned to the SS Captain's left breast above the qualification badges. He considered asking the man where he'd received his wound and then thought better of it. The less he said, particularly in German, the better.

After staring at Gage for another long moment, the officer handed him his papers and turned to the Carabinieri lieutenant. In broken Italian, his lips barely smiling, he said, "Filled out perfectly for once. Whoever did this should be sent to Berlin to work."

On the street, a cold sweat broke out over his body and his mind refused to function; it was all he could do to swing one leg out in front of the other, his muscles contracting and relaxing mechanically, pulling him forward step after ragged step like an automaton. Not even his initial encounter with the fascist militia at the bridge on his arrival in Rome had frightened him as much. The encounter with Mila Stradino, the police scrutiny—both had pressed home the point: his life hung from a thread as thin and shiny as the silver of the *Haupsturmführer*'s cuff titles.

In the apartment he rushed to the bathroom, fell to his knees in front of the toilet and was physically sick. With no way to vent the anxiety that grew from living in continual tension in a city where he faced imminent exposure every time he appeared in public, his nerves were beginning to get the better of him. In the wrong crowd, in a gathering of fascists, with an agent of the

Gestapo or the SD present, one word of recognition—a reference to his nationality or the disclosure of his real name—and he was dead. The words, even if as innocent as those of a casual salutation, would be as effective as bullets. It was a thought he could no longer bear.

CHAPTER 5

May-June 1943, Rome, Italy

For the rest of the month, Gage cut back on his outings with Carla. From the relative security of the apartment, he continued to work with Antonio, organizing and encoding the data to be transmitted by Radio Fenice, and trying to forestall the city's resistance leaders who were pressing for drops of Allied weapons. As the days passed, the quality of incoming intelligence seemed to deteriorate. The partisan agents and other fifth columnists spread throughout the city and the surrounding countryside grew ever more reluctant to meet Antonio's contacts. When Gage finally asked why, Antonio stroked his mustache and said that a partisan known as Commander Vito was at fault. Gage had heard the name before but had never met the man, knew only that he beat new agents to test their loyalty and favored fake executions to see if any would break under the threat. Now it appeared he had been stealing their informants and spreading rumors that Gage was not to be trusted.

Gage ordered Antonio to set up a meeting with Vito at which he would settle the question once and for all. But despite Antonio's efforts, Vito would only agree to meet them on his own terrain. The contact point was the Lungotevere near the Ponte Sisto, where Vito was waiting with two of his men in a small, flat-bottomed skiff.

Once Gage had taken his place on the forward thwart, one of Vito's men poled the boat away from the bank while the other jumped out and restrained Antonio, who stood at the river's edge protesting the change in arrangements. Though seething inside at the turn of events, Gage said nothing, his face a mask, unwilling to give Vito the pleasure of knowing he'd been tricked.

Antonio was not so subtle. He scuffled with Vito's man and threw him to the ground, then stood over him and lit a cigarette with abrupt, angry movements, his bald head shining in the evening light. A good man to have as a friend, thought Gage, as he drew farther away.

The Tiber, in June, had lost its spring impetus and drifted between its walled banks with a quiet susurrus. The murky water purled in eddies that dipped and rose with the lazy rhythm of summer. A tawny sun was about to set behind the Gianicolo, and while it lingered, a warm haze hung over the water. The air was heavy with the perfume of lilac and jasmine, drifting down from the hills. The scene was one that made it hard for Gage to realize the world was at war.

In mid-river, with fishing poles angled downstream off the port side and with gnats buzzing in their ears, he and Vito faced each other and spoke for fifteen minutes. The Italian refused to accept any blame for what was happening with Antonio's agents, saying only that some of their contacts were coming over to him because they did not trust Antonio's security measures. Gage forced himself to contain his impatience, but near the end he let slip that he would notify the Allies of Vito's intransigence.

Vito shrugged his indifference. In the evening light reflecting off the Tiber, the scar that ran from his cheek to his ear stood out like a piece of gristle. "The British are very happy with what I'm doing," he said. "I have no fears in that regard. My men are well armed." His ferret-like eyes sharpened. "You have produced nothing during your months in the city. Perhaps that is why you are losing people."

Gage checked his anger. He wanted to tell the man that the only reason Fifth Army had failed to arrange a drop was because the Allies were planning for action on Sicily or Sardinia first. But anything he told Vito would be used by the man to aggrandize his own achievements. Instead, he hardened his voice and said, "Vito, I don't need excuses. If I hear of you or any of your comrades thwarting the efforts of Antonio and his men, *ti ucciderò io stesso*—I'm going to kill you myself."

Vito snorted but said nothing in response, his weaselly face twitching. His lips drew apart showing tobacco-stained teeth. He gestured with his head to the man standing in the stern and the Italian began to pole them toward the far shore where the current had slowly been tugging the skiff. As they neared a series of travertine steps laid into the embankment on the far side of the river, Vito leaned forward, his face contorted, skin stretched tight over his cheeks.

"Have you heard what the resistance leaders are saying? The Allies will soon put me in charge of all their intelligence operations in Italy. Then what will you do?"

Gage laughed in response, the sound tinny and harsh. He grabbed for a railing near the stairs and stepped out of the boat, the muddy water of the Tiber sliding by at his feet. On the stone walkway, struggling to compose himself, he turned and looked at the Italian. The distance between them was widening.

"Vito, let the rumormongers talk," he said, raising his voice, the tone patronizing. "They're just a bunch of *caccastecchi*— shitsticks. You need have no fear, my friend, since it's quite untrue." And with that and a big smile he turned and clambered up the steps, leaving Vito crouched in the boat, his face livid with rage.

One day in mid-June, Antonio burst into the apartment, danced a jig across the room while shouting "*Buone notizie*" over and over, before finally hugging Gage and planting a resounding kiss on both cheeks.

Antonio's glee was contagious. Gage stood there unable to repress a grin, staring down at his agent's bald head, at the man's thick black mustache which bobbed in excitement. "Calm down, Antonio. What is it?"

Antonio lowered his voice with difficulty. "Beppe received a message last night. Your Wild Bill just flew into Tunis and approved a drop for us—money, weapons, supplies, and—listen to this—two 'friends'. Thomas, I'm ecstatic."

A huge grin burst through Gage's attempt at self-restraint. "The bastards finally came through," he said.

"Yes, and your *colonello* Donovan is now a *generale di brigata*."

"Well I'll be. They finally promoted the old man."

"We have a code for the drop zone. The second series, site six."

That was a zone well north of the city but short of the Lago di Bracciano, in the rolling hills and farmland to the southwest of the Via Claudia Braccianese. After pinpointing the location's coordinates on a map, he asked Antonio if he still had agents in the area.

Antonio's smile disappeared and he shook his head morosely. "A few months ago, I could have driven there, but now . . ." He gestured in frustration. "We couldn't get a pass. The fascists have restricted travel. You have to be a big shot."

"Can't we forge a pass?

Antonio shrugged eloquently. "We haven't seen the latest changes. It would be a terrible risk—and even if we could, we don't have a car."

"What about the Ceruti's car?"

"Carla said it no longer runs. The parts for repair are not available."

The two men were silent for a moment.

"There is one source . . ." Antonio said hesitantly. "Vito."

Gage frowned. "Vito has access to a car?"

Antonio nodded. "And gas. He has a connection with an undersecretary in the Ministry of War."

"*Porca miseria!*" Gage turned his back and strode toward the kitchen, head dipped in thought. He drummed his fingers on the doorjamb and then swung around abruptly. "Would he loan us the car if we didn't tell him where we were going?"

Antonio pursed his lips. "I doubt it—but we can ask."

"I hate the thought of asking that *figlio di puttana* for anything."

Antonio rubbed his cheeks. "I will ask him," he said. "If he comes up with the car, what about the pass?"

Gage sighed. "Elio Pavan," he said. "He's our only chance. I don't know what it will be, but I'll manufacture some excuse. You see if you can get the car."

Two days later, Antonio gave him the bad news. They were seated in Count Neumann's den, where Gage had been encoding a dispatch for Radio Fenice with the latest items of intelligence. Antonio waved his hands and said Vito would provide a car, but only if three conditions were met. First, they had to tell him where the drop would take place; second, he would supply the driver but not the pass; and third, his men would receive a share of the booty. Gage swore vehemently, jumped to his feet, and raged up and down the den for several minutes. When he finally calmed down, Antonio asked him if he'd contacted Pavan about the pass. Gage shook his head in irritation. "I was waiting to see if we'd get a car. We don't need a pass if we have to get there in a donkey cart."

Antonio shrugged. "You couldn't slip a cart into the city if you tried. A car with a pass is easier. The fascists are checking everything coming in from the farms. Bootleggers are being shot on the spot." He grinned ruefully. "Did you read the joke in the paper last week? The militia stopped a man with a sack full of eggs under his shirt. 'Where did you get those?' they asked him. The man stared at them as if they were idiots and said, 'I laid them.'"

Gage nodded without smiling, an abstracted look on his face. His mind was too full of turmoil to appreciate the humor. After a moment he said, "Listen, Antonio. I'm going to invite Pavan to the apartment for a drink tonight. Do you think you could have some men in the streets?"

"After curfew?"

He nodded. "It'll be late. Pavan comes and goes as he wishes."

"Sure, he has a police pass and a motorcycle. Why do we need the men?"

"I'm going to tell Pavan the truth—that we need a pass to pick up supplies from a drop zone."

Antonio frowned. "I don't like it, Thomas." He scratched at his head. "Why don't we just say you've arranged to pick up some contraband. We can promise him a share—kill a pig and bring back the meat."

"We won't have room in the car."

"Make two trips."

Exasperated at the complications, Gage shook his head and strode to the fireplace, where he fingered a fire iron. "Pavan has to find out sometime. I need him to gain access to the OVRA's files. Sooner or later he's going to learn I'm working with the Allies. It's the only thing I can promise him. When the war ends, he'll have a letter guaranteeing him immunity from prosecution as a war criminal and attesting to the fact that he's materially aided the West. To a police agent that means the difference between life and death."

Antonio made a small deprecatory gesture. "What do we need the men in the streets for, Thomas? If Pavan decides to betray you, he's not going to tell you to your face."

"I know." Gage sighed tiredly, resting both arms on the mantelpiece, his back to the partisan. When he spoke, his voice was muffled. "If he decides to report what I've told him, there's a slight chance he'll go straight from the apartment to the Questura. That's the opposite direction from his home. If he does, kill him."

"He can always go home and call from there."

He straightened and turned to face Antonio, who looked at him with a pained expression. "That's enough, Antonio," he said firmly. "After I see Pavan tonight, I'll stay with Beppe. You can accompany me to the nest when the messages are ready for transmission. One of your men can watch this place. If Pavan's going to do something, he won't let much time pass. A raid anytime within the next few days and we know."

Antonio grimaced, his black eyes nearly disappearing. "I'm not so sure about that. All he has to do is come up with a pass, have the car followed, and he picks up two agents and everything else in the drop—and then us."

Gage brooded a moment, walking back and forth in front of the man. Finally he stopped and put his hand on Antonio's shoulder. "*Amico mio*," he said, his eyes weary, "at this stage that's a chance we'll have to take."

CHAPTER 6

Monday, August 26, Durango, Colorado

W hy's Rowdy barking so much," Janelle asked. She had slipped out of bed and stood on the staircase leading to her loft bedroom.

Her voice surprised him. Immersed in his grandfather's memoirs, he had heard neither the barking of the dog nor her footsteps. "Probably a possum," he said. "Shall I bring him in?"

"He's been barking for a long time, Nick."

He looked at his watch. Three-twenty in the morning. "Go back to bed," he said. "I'll take care of it."

He walked to the door of the cabin and stepped out on to the wood plank porch. Moving from light to darkness, he was momentarily blinded.

"Quiet, Rowdy! Be quiet! Come here, boy."

The Golden Retriever trotted to Ferron's side, turned around and growled into the darkness.

"What is it, boy?"

The dog refused to look up at him, his eyes trained on the darkness.

"Something scare you?"

He felt the dog lean into his side and squatted to pet him. "What was it, boy? A cat?"

The dog wagged his tail and looked up to lick his face.

"Okay," he said. "Good boy. Whatever it was you scared it away. Come on in with me now."

When he stepped back into the cabin, followed by the dog, Janelle had come down into the living room. "What was it?" she asked.

"Don't know," he said. "Sorry he woke you. You go back to bed. I'll keep him inside with me."

She walked over to the refrigerator, her eyes sleepy, and took out a carton of milk. "What's happening in the diary?" she said, pointing to the papers spread out in front of Nick.

"My grandfather's in Italy. He's been talking to an agent of Mussolini's political police. He's going to try to recruit him, I think."

"Any mention of the Mafia guy?"

"Not a word about Aprico. And nothing about the Dutchman either. Gran Babbo's working with an Italian girl named Carla Ceruti." He paused. "I hadn't realized he got married before the war. I was only twelve when my grandmother Olga died, and Gran Babbo never seemed to want to talk about the war days."

Janelle wiped the milk off her upper lip and put the carton back in the refrigerator. "You should get some sleep, Nick."

"I want to see what happens. I can sleep on the plane to Miami tomorrow."

"You're still set on going to Suriname?"

He shrugged. "Aprico's dead . . . my grandfather—what else can I do?"

"Do you want me to stay up a while with you? Read through the letters?"

"No, you have to teach tomorrow. Go on back to bed. I'll keep Rowdy quiet."

She walked over, petted the dog, and then kissed Ferron on the cheek. "See you in the morning, then."

"What the hell you trying to do?" Akkad swore as he pulled Naveed behind a tree and shoved him to the ground.

"Takin' a look around. You fell asleep. What are we going to do, wait here until dawn when they can see us?"

Akkad gripped his partner's arm and squeezed until the man grunted and pulled out of his grasp. "Listen," he said, his voice cold and full of menace. "I catch you again doing anything I haven't told you to do and I'm going to put a bullet through your head. You understand me?" Naveed grumbled something in what sounded like a foreign language. Akkad jerked the man's arm, thrusting his face an inch from his. He could smell the man's foul breath. "What the fuck are you trying to say?"

"This guy ain't the President. What's he going to do? Call out the National Guard? I pee on his shit."

"We already got one dog to deal with. We don't need you to be a second."

"Why don't we just go knock on the door and kill the fuckers?"

Akkad shook his head and snorted harshly. "Just shut the fuck up and stay where you are. I got other plans. You let me do the thinking."

CHAPTER 7

Wednesday, June 16, 1943, Rome, Italy

Carla wanted to be with him when he made the approach to Pavan, but Gage refused. They were standing in the kitchen of Count Neumann's apartment, washing the dishes from a light supper of coarse bread and a *minestra di riso e verdura*, which Carla had made using a wilted bunch of spinach and some rice left over from the day before. When she persisted, he closed his eyes for a moment, resting them from the reflected glare of the setting sun. He could feel the liminal traces of a headache caused by strong red wine and tension. "If something should go wrong, I don't want you implicated."

Carla slipped an arm around him. "Thomas," she said, smiling as if she were dealing with a child, "my being implicated is a foregone conclusion. He's almost never seen you without me in your company."

He paused and then softened his voice. "Not tonight, Carla. It's too dangerous. If something happens, Antonio will call your home. You'll have to go into hiding. I've asked him to take care of you."

"I want to be with you tonight."

He set the last pan on the drainboard. "Carla," he said patiently, "it's not possible. Ask me anything but that."

He saw the acceptance in her eyes finally, a moment of sadness, and then she brightened and stepped closer, moving inside his arms.

"We have two hours before curfew," she said, a mischievous grin appearing on her face. "You said ask you *anything*, right?"

"What?"

Gage sat upright in shock, staring at the placid face of Elio Pavan, who sat across from him in the den's wing chair. It was just after ten o'clock at night but the heat of a sweltering June day still lingered in the room. He could feel a stickiness under the arms and behind his knees.

"I wondered who you worked for," the OVRA agent said comfortably and then shrugged. "At first I thought you were with the Gestapo."

"But when did the British contact you?" Gage asked, still startled, the strain showing in his voice. How long had the policeman been playing with him?

"I contacted them." Pavan thrust his blunt jaw toward the ceiling, stretching the muscles in his neck. The sardonic smile he affected had disappeared. "Three years ago next month. After the Duce declared war, I asked a member of the British Legation in the Vatican to put me in touch with the British secret service. I met an SOE officer in Geneva later that summer.

"Three years." Gage shook his head, stunned by the rush of implications. "No one told me," he said.

"That's reassuring," Pavan said dryly. "I work for a man called Eagle Jack. He's the only one who knows my identity. I have a cousin who works on the Swiss desk in the Ministry of Foreign Affairs. I funnel intelligence to Geneva by diplomatic pouch."

"How do they pay you?"

"I have a private arrangement with Eagle Jack. I handle his financial and business interests in Rome."

Gage's eyes opened wider. He stared at Pavan as the man calmly took a drink of Strega and then licked his lips. "This Eagle Jack, he had business interests in Italy?" He found it impossible to contain his marvel.

"Did and still does," the Italian said. "Concealed holdings." For a moment an aloof smile flitted across his face. "Interests much favored by certain fascist hierarchs. With just ten percent of Eagle Jack's profits I will be a wealthy man when the war ends."

Gage stared at the policeman, breathing heavily, his mind growing numb as one revelation followed the other in rapid succession. What was going on? That the SOE would employ a spymaster with continuing business interests in a country with which they were at war was inconceivable to him. An agent, yes. A spymaster, no. "This Eagle Jack," he finally managed to ask, "who is he?"

Pavan's lips curled in derision. "Even if I could, you expect me to answer that? Eagle Jack is too smart to tell me his identity. I've only met the man once and he's never used any other name." The Italian shrugged. "After the war it will be a different matter. Maybe then I will learn *your* real name, right?"

Gage stared at the police agent without responding, aware that he would learn nothing more from the man—but that didn't mean G-2 couldn't come up with something on Eagle Jack. He'd put them on it with his next set of messages. And in the meantime? A dead end. He'd wasted months cultivating Pavan. He would have to back off now. The British shared intelligence but not their operations. They would want Pavan for themselves. His heart sank at the enormity of the loss. Who was he left with? Sergio Benelli—the fascist in Mussolini's private security force? He would never be able to recruit the man to the Allied cause, and even if he pretended to be with the Gestapo, what would he get? Gossip. Most likely not worth enough to justify the risk of discovery. No, his only recourse at the moment was to impose on Elio Pavan's friendship; the man worked for a British agent, they were allies. The granting of one favor, especially in an emergency, would not jeopardize that relationship.

But when he asked for help with the transportation pass, Pavan's face turned stubborn. "The risk of exposure is too great," he said. "I am involved only in intelligence, not in operations. And in any case only with the British."

"Eagle Jack," Gage said slowly.

"What about him?"

"The name—did you speak in English or Italian with the man?"

"What does it matter?"

"Did he have an accent? Are you sure he was British?"

"What are you trying to say?"

"The Eagle is an American symbol—not a British one. And Jack is just a common name."

Pavan snorted. "You work too hard, Signor Ludwig. Even I have heard of the Union Jack—the British flag in case you haven't heard."

"Okay, but what about the eagle. The man works for the Allies. He may not even be British."

"Do you think these things matter?" Pavan asked, a touch of incredulity entering his voice. "After all, the eagle is a fascist emblem as well."

Gage sat back in his chair and rubbed his forehead, his eyes bleak. "So you will not help us?" Pavan's dull gray eyes showed no expression. Gage leaned forward. "You could request permission from Eagle Jack if you wished."

"I don't need Eagle Jack's permission to secure a pass." The Italian paused for a moment. "What excuse do I use? The Lago Bracciano is a restricted area. We have a seaplane base there."

"We are relying on that. The soldiers are accustomed to planes flying overhead, even at night." Gage pulled at his ear in thought. Would it do any good to wound the man in his pride? "What about official business? Surely an agent of the OVRA is not restricted on where he travels."

Pavan shook his head. "I would have to file a report." He hesitated and then, as if he'd made up his mind, said, "Personal business is safer. I will try for a two-day pass to visit relatives. What vehicle will you be using?"

Gage told him.

"And you need it when?"

"The drop is scheduled for Friday, June 25th. We'll need Friday and Saturday to get there and back."

"You better hope the weather holds."

"True. We'll deal with that when the time comes."

"And if the vehicle is searched?"

"That's why we want a pass identifying the vehicle as that of an OVRA agent. They'll waive us through without questions."

"You are going to take part?"

Gage shrugged. "We'll have to see," he said.

• • •

But when the time came to pick the man to go with Commander Vito's driver, Antonio suggested one of his own agents, a young kid whose family lived on a farm near Manziana, a village to the west of the lake, just beyond the small town of Bracciano. Gage would have liked to have been present and wished he had time to train the men in drop procedure. Instead, he gave the men verbal instructions and sent them on their way.

Friday night, the 25th, he spent the time in his radioman's top-floor apartment on the Lungotevere dei Vallati, listening for the signal that would announce the departure of the plane from Tunis. The flight would skirt Sicily and Sardinia but faced detection from units of the Italian navy on patrol in the Tyrrhenian. Gage had no way of informing his men in the field if something should go wrong. If the drop was successful, Radio Fenice would be informed, but only after the plane left Italian-controlled waters. Beppe would respond only after the OSS agents arrived safely in Rome.

It was going to be a long night, followed by at least a day before the men returned. The car would be taken directly to a garage on Via delle Zoccolette, where Gage had arranged to meet Commander Vito for disposal of the supplies. The two OSS agents, Italian natives with papers identifying them as soldiers returning from the field, would be taken in by other families who had more space than Gage himself. Each would be carrying funds to replenish Gage's supply.

By Saturday morning, all was going well. Beppe had picked up both signals—the departure of the plane and the success of the drop itself. At eight that night, Gage went by himself to the address provided by Commander Vito. He was surprised to see that the garage was a business providing service to cars driven by fascist officials—the only vehicles, other than an occasional motorcycle, left on the city's streets. To the left of the garage doors, a narrow entryway—a light-trap, with a dark black-out curtain at both ends—protected the office where business was conducted. The men waited in a first-floor apartment, their tension growing as the hours dragged by. Gage was fed at a certain point, but kept to himself, refusing to join in the conversation. Near morning he fell asleep on a tattered sofa in the living room.

At midday, when no news had been received, he left the garage and walked back to Count Neumann's apartment where he met Antonio. He gave the Italian a message for Beppe to transmit and went to bed around four that afternoon.

Carla woke him just before curfew, arriving late so he would not be able to send her home. They ate together, talked for a while in the den, neither voicing the concern they felt, then took a bath, both managing to fit at the same time in the massive claw-legged tub. They made love, starting in the bathroom and progressing to the matrimonial bed, where Carla finally fell asleep. The edge had been taken off Gage's tiredness, so he returned to the study to read. He had to try hard not to think of Olga, not to feel sick with guilt.

Sunday dawned bright and clear with no word of the men. After morning mass, he and Carla walked to the *Galoppatoio* on the grounds of the Villa Borghese, where Pavan was accustomed to ride with other members of his circle. The OVRA agent frowned when he heard the vehicle had not returned. He claimed to have no knowledge of the situation.

That afternoon, Gage received a message from Antonio. Commander Vito had asked to meet him at a flower stall in the Campo dei Fiori near the statue of Giordano Bruno.

Five minutes after the meeting time, a young boy arrived and led Gage to a restaurant on a small street leading from the Campo to Piazza Farnese. Looking grim, Vito sat at an outdoor table, a glass of Campari and soda in front of him.

"What is it?" Gage asked, sitting down opposite the Italian.

Vito ran a finger down the scar that ran from his ear to his cheek, repeating the gesture several times before speaking, as if attempting to calm himself. "They are all dead," he said finally, his voice hoarse. "The driver was my brother."

Gage swore. "All of them?"

Vito nodded. "They were picked up less than an hour after the drop and shot as spies."

For a moment, he felt a whisper in his ear and the iron fingers of an ice-cold hand gripped his heart, squeezing, until the whisper in his ear turned into a roar. He took a deep breath, waiting until the roar in his blood subsided. "How did you get this information?"

"I have contacts with the militia."

"How did it happen?"

Vito's eyes shifted to one side, glancing beyond Gage at someone walking past the table. His mouth was tight-lipped.

Gage cleared his throat but said nothing. Turning his head casually, massaging his neck the while, he saw the object of concern—two black-shirted men, sauntering arm in arm, out for a *passeggiata*.

"I have men watching the square," Vito said, when the two fascists had moved on down the street. "We don't know if my brother or Antonio's man betrayed us before they were shot." He dropped his head, one hand picking at a thick, yellow thumbnail. "They were all tortured."

Gage swallowed the bile that rose in his throat. In war, you met death so often you thought one day it would become commonplace—but it never did. Each death hurt, even when you didn't know the men. It hurt because they were friends, friends you'd never met, soldiers who were coming to help you. Buddies . . .

Vito drained the Campari, then wiped his lips slowly, his ferret-like eyes refocusing on Gage's. "We may have been betrayed before the drop. How many people knew about it?"

Gage ran over the names in his mind. "You and anyone you told," he said first. "Antonio, of course." His stomach sank. "And Elio Pavan—the OVRA agent. We had to ask him for a pass."

"And your radioman, I imagine."

Gage nodded dully.

"Anyone else?"

He paused, breathing heavily. "A girl."

"Who?"

"She works with me."

"What's her name?"

Gage flared. "I'll take care of my own people, you worry about yours."

Vito rocked back and forth, his eyes taking the measure of the American. "If I were you, Major Tom, I'd be more than careful," he said. "This time it was my brother. The next time I'm going to make sure *you* pay."

"Vaffanculo," Gage said, shoving his chair away from the table and getting to his feet. "There won't be a next time."

CHAPTER 8

Friday, July 9, 1943, Rome

Less than two weeks later, early on a Friday morning, Gage woke to a loud knocking. He came to the door in his bathrobe and before opening it, asked, "*Chi è?*"

"*Polizia.*"

He looked quickly around the room, thankful that Carla had not stayed the night and that Antonio had not yet arrived with a new batch of reports to be encoded. When he opened the door, he saw a uniformed motorcycle policeman wearing black jackboots, a short man with upward jutting hair and a prominent Adam's apple, a kid no older than twenty-five, eyes nervous.

"What is it?" he said in German, drawing himself up.

The officer tried to speak in German, stuttered, and switched to Italian. "Are you Ludwig, Thomas Karl?"

He nodded curtly.

"I have a message for you." The officer handed him an envelope with no name or address on it.

He took the envelope, tore open the flap, and extracted a single sheet of paper, folded once. He opened the page and saw a brief message in German.

"Do you need transportation, Herr Ludwig?"

"What time is it now?"

Without looking at a watch the policeman said, "Ten o'clock."

"I'll get dressed and come on foot," he said. "Tell Signor

Benelli I will see him at noon."

Alone in the apartment he read the note again. The sheet of paper, bearing the letterhead of the Ministry of the Interior, was not a formal document, but a police summons nonetheless. What did the presidential protection service want with him? After inviting Benelli to Count Neumann's apartment for the dinner party, he had forgotten the man, agreeing with Carla that there was nothing to be gained and everything to be risked by cultivating his friendship. If the note had come from the secret police, even from Elio Pavan, whom he was now avoiding, he would have considered fleeing the apartment and going clandestine. Despite the assurances of G-2 that the incoming agents knew neither his cover name nor the address of the apartment, he had been tense ever since the failure of the drop. Commander Vito had said the militia shot the men as spies, but he had no proof. For all Gage knew, the militia was torturing the partisans and working backward up the lines of communication. Even Antonio failed to reassure him, despite the Italian's insistence that none of his agents, none of the men in the field, knew Thomas other than as an American major from the Office of Strategic Services living somewhere in Rome. So why was Benelli summoning him to a police post at an address that he recognized as being opposite Palazzo Venezia, Mussolini's headquarters? Were they hoping he would run? Had they staked out the building, waiting for him to betray himself? He took a deep breath and prepared himself for the worst.

Shaving, Gage thought of what Pavan had said when he confronted him after the failed drop. It was the last time the two men had spoken. They had met under an umbrella pine near the gallery of the Villa Borghese on a hot, windless Saturday afternoon, the first weekend in July.

Pavan, of course, denied responsibility, wiping his brow and the back of his neck with a handkerchief and suggesting instead that a foul-up at Gage's end had threatened to ruin *him*. "The OVRA has nothing to do with the militia," he added pointedly. "Until you came along things were going smoothly."

"If the militia traced the pass to you, if there was a personal threat, what would you do?" Gage replied. "You would throw us all to the dogs, right?" He was breathing heavily, oppressed by the sultry atmosphere.

Pavan's response had been an outburst worthy of the Neapolitan he was. He screamed and raged for five minutes, while Gage tried to placate him, glancing around nervously, afraid that Pavan's shouting would attract unwanted attention. Finally, in an effort to quiet the man and to part as friends rather than enemies (even if the relationship was only a façade, for he would never trust the policeman again), Gage apologized.

At that, Pavan quieted down but an uneasy tension hung in the air between them. A woman and two children took a seat on a nearby bench and Pavan gestured with his head toward a nearby path. The two men began walking toward the stone wall that ran along the Via Pinciana.

By way of excuse for his outburst, Pavan explained that things were not going well for him. "When Senise was our *capo,* I received everything I asked for. He was a fellow Neapolitan and a friend. There were no problems. Then the party pressured the Duce for his head and now we have General Renzo Chierici." The Italian shook his head. "He's been chief only two months but . . ." His voice trailed away.

"What's Chierici's background?" Gage asked, ever alert for information on fascist officials.

Pavan wiped his brow again, stuffing the handkerchief into the breast pocket of his gabardine suit coat. "A lieutenant-general in the militia. Since becoming chief of police, he's been collaborating closely with Himmler. The Nazis are happy; they never trusted Senise. And now they also have a friend directing the Duce's personal security."

Gage swung to face the police agent. "A new man?" he asked.

Pavan nodded. "The Prefect Stracca. A Germanophile. He wanted Senise's job but the Duce called him instead to Palazzo Venezia. The hyenas and jackals love him."

The news did not set well with Gage. "If you don't watch out," he observed, "before long the Nazis are going to be running this country."

Pavan snorted. "They already do. Every morning the German Ambassador visits Mussolini with a new list of demands. And to think—we taught them to eat pasta."

The two men resumed walking, each lost in thought. When they reached the street, they turned right toward the Porta Pinciana, dodging a woman whose bare-ribbed Cocker Spaniel was attempting, without success, to defecate on the sidewalk.

"I'm surprised they haven't eaten the creature," Pavan muttered, nodding toward the dog. "It doesn't look like they're feeding him."

Near the Porta Pinciana, Pavan broke the silence that had fallen anew between them. "I may not see you again, Thomas. It is dangerous for me to talk to you. Eagle Jack—" He pulled at his shirt, loosening the top button. "Well, perhaps it's best left unsaid."

Gage stopped short. "What does Eagle Jack have to do with this?"

Pavan shrugged. "If there's a risk to me, there's a risk to him. He has advised me to distance myself."

"You told him about me?"

Pavan stared at the American with a tight smile. "Of course. What did you expect?"

It was a question he had pondered ever since.

When Gage arrived at the piazza, a field-gray Opel with Nazi flags flying from the fenders was parked in front of the small police post across the street from Palazzo Venezia. He hesitated at the corner of Corso Umberto as a red Lati passenger bus crossed from north to south, heading toward the Guidonia airport in Ostia near the mouth of the Tiber. For a moment, he wished he was on the bus. From Guidonia, Lati, a transcontinental airline, flew seaplanes destined for Seville, Lisbon, Villa Cisneros, Pernambuco, and Rio de Janeiro. The safety of Lisbon beckoned like a beacon to a drowning sailor. Instead, he turned to his right and moved toward the Opel. Across the street squatted the heavy fortress of yellowish-brown stone where Mussolini ruled. Only two black-helmeted militiamen were visible, standing on guard in front of the great folding doors where vehicles could enter an inner courtyard.

For the first time, a block ahead of him, parked near the corner of Via degli Astalli, he saw two German troop carriers and behind them an armored car. As he watched, the vehicles pulled forward and stopped near the north entrance to Palazzo Venezia, directly opposite the Opel and the police post. He stopped, heart pounding, and turned his back to the street, scanning the brass name plates near a small entryway that led to a staircase in a building occupied by governmental offices. The temptation to run was strong, but he was afraid now to reverse direction. The two militiamen on guard at Palazzo Venezia had seen him approach.

To his left, he heard a voice shout in German. A woman in black walking behind him stopped, both hands laden with heavy net bags. She swayed with indecision, her eyes turning to him. "*Cos'è?*" she asked, wondering what was happening.

"*Non so, signora.*" Her guess was as good as his.

An SS *Hauptscharführer*, wearing a noncommissioned officer's field cap with the silver Death's Head badge, left the armored vehicle and crossed the street, where a higher-ranking German officer stood in front of the police post. Barely fifty feet away, the two men spoke for a moment, the officer, with a major's cockade on his hat, giving orders to the staff sergeant. In a minute the sergeant returned to the armored car, which pulled out ahead of the troop carriers and then waited for the driver of the Opel to make a U-turn. In the back seat of the car, head erect, the *Sturmbannführer* looked straight ahead as the Opel joined the convoy. When the car had cleared them, the woman with the bags hurried on past the police post and Gage breathed a sigh of relief.

As he approached the post, he saw that Benelli, dressed in a civilian suit, was standing in the doorway, watching the convoy disappear in the direction of Piazza Venezia. "Herr Ludwig, just in time," the Italian said in his heavily accented German. "How good of you to come." He straightened his thick spectacles and then tossed Gage the fascist salute.

About to shake hands, he forced a smile and responded in German. "It looks like I'm not the first of my countrymen to pay you a visit today."

Benelli nodded, and then one corner of his mouth dropped in regret. "Unfortunately the situation, I'm sorry to say, is quite different."

Gage looked at him with a question in his eyes.

"Come on in out of the sun," Benelli said, running a hand across his greasy forehead. "It's cooler inside."

Leading the way, Benelli took him to a small office, gestured to a chair, and sat behind a plain desk stacked high with papers. The Italian moved a pile to one side and grimaced. "We have over forty thousand border files, all known enemies of the regime—" he shook his head mournfully—"and half of them, it seems, come to my attention."

"You can't be too careful," Gage said firmly.

Benelli's eyes were fixed on a sheet of paper is his hands. "Yes," he said in an offhand manner. "Careful we are. You cannot cross a border into Italy without our knowing about it." He paused, then added casually. "But for you, somehow, we have no record."

Their eyes met, no expression passing between them, and Gage shrugged. "I crossed the frontier at Viggiù in early February."

"Coming from—?"

"Vienna by way of Bern."

"What day was that?"

He scratched his head. "A Monday. Do you have a calendar?"

Benelli turned and looked over his shoulder. On the back wall, appended from a nail, hung a small calendar beneath a placard reading *Qui non si parla di politica o alta strategia*—Here one does not speak of politics or high strategy.

Benelli handed him the calendar and he flipped back to February. He stabbed a finger at the date. "It had to have been the eighth."

"May I see your papers, please." Behind his thick eyeglasses Benelli's eyes were serious.

He reached into the inside breast pocket of his coat and handed Benelli the papers forged for him by the OSS.

"I'm going to leave the room for a moment," Benelli said, rising and stepping around the desk. "While I'm gone, why don't you have a look at this." He picked up a sheaf of papers on his desk and handed it to him. "This crossed my desk recently. I thought it might interest you," he added, one corner of his mouth lifting in a half-smile.

Gage swallowed when he saw the first page—a document

typed on official militia stationery. He did not look up, afraid his panic would show. Behind him, Benelli stepped into the hallway, leaving the door open. To control the shaking of his hands, he laid the documents in his lap, suspecting that he was under observation. In his initial shock, he found it hard to absorb the text and had to begin again from the start, his eyes straying to the heading.

Milizia Volontaria Sicurezza Nazionale
Comando I Legione—Ufficio Politico
U.P.I. - Pos. 934.1 / 4760 C.P.A.
Oggetto: Nominativo *Ludwig, Thomas Karl*

A lead weight settled in his stomach. What followed was a two-page report on his activities since arriving in Rome, with a sheaf of supporting documents attached. As far as he could tell, there were no conclusions made, just the observation of suspicious activity, including the fact that he spent little time at his uncle's factory or shoe outlets. The final paragraph noted that particulars had been requested on him and his uncle in Berlin and that secret agents in neutral Switzerland were also investigating. The names of the agents who'd filed the reports were blacked out. The document was dated at the end according to the fascist style: *Roma, 17 giugno 1943-XXII*, the twenty-second year of the Fascist Era.

He heard a voice behind him and Benelli entered the room. For a moment neither man spoke. "Thank you for showing me this," Gage said. "I'm sure there's some mistake."

Benelli nodded vigorously. "Yes, yes. I assumed as much. I have taken a photostat of your papers and we will find out who is responsible for the failure to report. The person will be disciplined of course."

"Perhaps the report was misfiled or lost. It's nothing serious, is it?"

Benelli clasped his hands on the desk and leaned forward, his eyes bulging behind the thick lenses. "Our German friends are not the only ones who strive to be efficient." He pointed to his jacket, hanging on an *attaccapanni* in the corner. A red stripe circled the left cuff, signifying that the owner had taken part in the March on Rome. "I was with the Duce in Milan before the March on Rome in '22. No one will forget his words to the train-master that evening. 'I wish to leave exactly on time,' the Duce said. 'From now on everything must work perfectly.' That, my friend, is what fascism is all about."

When he returned to Count Neumann's apartment, he saw that Antonio had come and gone, leaving a note with only the word *Emergenza!* and a number for Gage to call. He didn't recognize the number. The telephone in the apartment had been disconnected long before his arrival in Rome. He walked two blocks to a *Farmacia* on Via Tomacelli with a public phone and dialed the number.

The voice that answered at the second ring was unfamiliar. As always, he assumed all lines running through the Rome exchange were tapped by the police. He refused to identify himself. "Is Antonio there?"

"*Un momento, per favore.*"

In a minute Antonio was on the line. "Where are you, Thomas?"

"Near the apartment. Did you read my note? I had to see Sergio Benelli."

"Yes. I was afraid you'd been arrested. Carla's disappeared."

He clutched the phone tighter. "What?"

"She was supposed to meet a friend at the central post office. She left the Bar Zeppa at ten-fifteen. She was due at Piazza San Silvestro at eleven and didn't show up. I've called around for her and she's nowhere to be found. I'm afraid the police may have picked her up."

"What would she have been carrying?"

"News from our friends."

Agent reports. She could be shot as a spy. She would have had at least one packet with her—from the *cameriere* at the Bar Zeppa, a waiter who collected intelligence reports from other agents on that side of the city. "We need to talk, Antonio."

"I'll meet you in an hour at the cinema."

CHAPTER 9

Friday, July 9, 1943, Rome, Italy

When he arrived, by prearrangement, at the Cinema Imperiale in Piazza Barberini, he saw Antonio standing near one of the bollards that surrounded Bernini's *Fontana del Tritone* in the center of the square. The sea god blew a stream of water from his conch, pearl droplets falling into the granite shell and then splashing down into the pool at the fountain's base. Gage was sweating from his climb up the slope of the hill, and the mist that the breeze carried in his direction was refreshing.

"I came by way of Piazza San Silvestro," he said. "No sign of Carla."

Antonio nodded. "I've called her folks. She hasn't returned home." He lit a cigarette and then grimaced. "Not like the Chesterfields I smoked before the war," he said, waving the cigarette like a stick.

"Do you have someone who can ask for her at the Questura?"

Antonio took his arm. "Let's walk," he said, directing their steps across the piazza toward Via Barberini. "Her mother wanted to go there immediately. I told her to wait a day. If we go to police headquarters now, they will be suspicious, and if they do have her—" He shrugged his shoulders.

"There must be something we could do."

"Perhaps . . . if we find out where they're holding her."

"I'll contact Elio Pavan to see if the OVRA's picked her up."

"What happened this morning?" Antonio asked.

"I'm going to have to leave the apartment. Benelli said there's an investigation going on into my background."

Antonio tossed the stub of his cigarette into the street. "If the police have Carla, you would have to move anyway. She's a strong girl, but they'll make her talk."

A chill ran up his spine. "What if the Gestapo arrested her?"

Antonio shook his head. "Gestapo arrests have to be made through the Questura. Even if they want to arrest a German it's not that easy. The request has to be routed through the SS *Reichsführer Kanzlei* to Himmler himself, and then to the German Foreign Office, and from there back to Ambassador von Mackensen here in Rome. He contacts the Italian Foreign Office and then they get back to the police. When Ciano was Minister, he turned down many requests."

"But Mussolini's taken over that portfolio."

"His undersecretary Bastianini runs everything. He would not allow the Gestapo to arrest an Italian girl."

"Still, he's a Germanophile, too, isn't he?"

Antonio coughed and spat into the street. He walked for a while without speaking, then said, "Why don't you return to the apartment and pack up your things? I'll try to arrange a place for you to stay for a day or two, and then we can set you up in something more permanent. At the moment, we can't do anything for Carla."

Over the next week, despite his and Antonio's efforts, he heard nothing of Carla. Twenty-four hours after she disappeared, her family went to the Questura and reported her missing. Every day for the next week, they returned to the central police offices, until finally they were asked not to come back unless contacted first. Both civilian and military police claimed not to have anyone by her name in custody. Though unhappy at the contact, Pavan said the OVRA had not arrested Carla. Antonio sent women to all the major police posts to see if they had any record of her presence. None did. Gage and Antonio contacted every agent in their network and told them to spare no effort to learn what they could about Carla's disappearance—all to no avail. If they had a traitor inside, there was no way to figure out who it might be. Carla had met and talked to too many people. Finally, Gage humbled himself and called for a meeting with Commander Vito. But neither he nor his men had information.

"We lose people every day," Vito said to him in parting. "One of the hazards of living in our times. We all make sacrifices."

He had to clench his hands, fingernails digging into the palms, to keep from strangling the guy. It would have been a waste of time to suggest Vito might have a traitor in his ranks. He next made an appeal to as many of the resistance leaders as he could assemble at one time. Over the next several days all reported back with negative results.

Count Neumann's apartment had been abandoned after Gage removed his few possessions and the code books. Antonio arranged for him to stay in a small room in an apartment building on the Vicolo Scavolino near Trevi fountain. Without Carla, Gage found the lack of space unbearable.

He telephoned Carla's sister, Nina, from a public telephone at a bar on Via delle Muratte and arranged to meet her at the small church that overlooked the Piazza di Trevi. He remember her from Carla's birthday party as a cheerful girl with hazel eyes and round cheeks that shone with innocence. Back then, he'd talked to her for a moment, joking about how many boyfriends she must have at the *scuola media*, and Nina had said she hated them all, that they were all *Avanguardisti*—members of the fascist group for boys from age ten to fifteen. He and Nina had talked for a moment of the future, and the young girl, speaking idealistically of the innate goodness that she was sure would rise again to bring about a better world, had blinked back tears of conviction, lips quivering earnestly. When he saw her now, he was struck by the change. She was still a pretty girl, but she had lost her look of innocence; her eyes were now tired, her face pale, and she spoke in a voice that was flat and toneless. About her sister she could provide no information, and Gage, who had been thinking only of how he might track down Carla and not about Nina's feelings, was sorry he had asked her to come. Before she left, he hugged her and swore he would do all he could to find her sister, but the words had an empty sound.

What more could he say? That he would keep looking until

life itself ended? That was true, but what consolation was that? Life had never seemed more fragile. His last words were ones of advice, meant as much for himself as for her.

"Be careful, Nina. Even our friends might be enemies."

On July 18, he learned from one of Antonio's agents that Mussolini was leaving for a conference with Hitler at Feltre. Rumor had it that the Duce would pull out of the alliance and proclaim Italian neutrality. In failing health—on July 29 he would be sixty—the Duce had been badly shaken by the Allied success in Sicily. On July 12, the base at Augusta had surrendered without a fight. To the shock of the Germans, the Italian admirals had blown up all the coastal defenses before even sighting the enemy. Italian morale continued to sink.

Working distractedly, Gage encoded a message to G-2, Fifth Army, notifying them that the conference in Feltre was scheduled for the nineteenth. If the proper forces could be prepared immediately, the Allies, with partisan help, might strike a blow that would finish off both dictators at once. On the morning of the nineteenth, he was told that Feltre, eighty-two kilometers to the northwest of Venice, was too far from Sicily for Allied bombers. Nothing was said about other targets. At five minutes after eleven on that day, the first of four Allied waves of Flying Fortresses and Liberators bombed Rome, shattering the Holy City's aura of inviolability. Some of the planes flew low enough to machine-gun the streets. The anti-aircraft batteries emplaced around the city did not hit a single plane.

Five days later, on Saturday, July 24, 1943, the twenty-eight members of the Fascist Grand Council, attired in their black desert uniforms, met with Mussolini in Palazzo Venezia. When they left at 2:40 a.m., they had brought about the end of the régime. The next day, at five o'clock, Mussolini's chauffeur drove him to Villa Savoia to see the King. Following a twenty-minute conversation the Duce was arrested. Fascism had fallen.

The news reached Gage at 10:45 that evening, when a radio program was suddenly interrupted with the announcement that the King had accepted Mussolini's resignation as head of the government, prime minister, and secretary of state. Gage joined the crowds gathering in the streets, the curfew forgotten. In the darkness of the blackout, half-dressed people rushed through the streets shouting in glee. Fascist pins, derisively called *la cimice*—the bedbug—were stripped from lapels and flung into the streets. The glow of small bonfires broke the darkness as the people collected and burned portraits of the Duce. Marble busts of Mussolini were toppled and smashed, placards torn from the walls and ripped to shreds.

The fascist hierarchs had gone into hiding, many fleeing for protection to the German Embassy. Colonel Dollmann of the SS increased the number of guards on duty.

By the time Gage was able to contact Antonio, dawn had come streaking over the horizon, a flaming ball of sun igniting the city's hills, cupolas, and monuments.

"Where the hell are you?" the Italian shouted. "I tried to reach you at the apartment on the *vicolo*."

"I'm at a *caffè* near the Viminale," he shouted back. "On Via Palermo. The public phones are down in my area. I've been trying to get help to storm the palace, but everyone's afraid of the armed guards. There's a crowd demonstrating in the piazza, but whoever's in charge of the government called out the militia and it looks like some Germans have joined them. We lost our chance at the files, Antonio."

Antonio mumbled something in the background and then came back on the line. "A message came from Beppe last night. I just finished decoding it. You're being ordered back to Tunis."

"*What?*"

"The OSS wants you out of here. General Clark's going to be sending in another team."

He couldn't believe it. "But why now? This is when I can do them some good. I'm running out of operational funds—but that can be remedied."

"G-2 wants to take over. They know your cover's been blown."

"Goddamn those assholes! I can work underground as well as anyone else they send in." His anger, he realized, came from the realization that headquarters was suggesting he might have been responsible for Carla's disappearance, that anyone he knew was now in danger.

Antonio didn't respond.

"What about Carla? I told Nina I wouldn't give up until we found her."

Antonio sighed. "We can't do anything about Carla now. The police are rallying to the new government. Did you hear what Badoglio said on the radio?"

"What?"

"The war hasn't ended. Italy is fighting on, with Germany at her side."

"*Merda!*" He shook his head, his right hand pounding the wall near the telephone.

He'd just opened his mouth to ask another question when someone shoved him in the back and shouted, "Get off the phone." A heavy accent.

Before he could turn, the handset was knocked from his hand and a group of men grabbed and pulled at him. Gage jerked back to swing at the face nearest his, but someone grabbed his arm, and then an elbow from behind caught him in the kidneys. His legs collapsed in agony, but another man jerked him upright, hand twisted in his hair.

"We're clearing the area. Out!"

One of the men, in police uniform, kicked him out the door of the *caffè*. Gage rolled into the street, shielding his face from attack. German troops, arrayed in a phalanx, were preparing to sweep the streets around the Ministry. He heard a shot from across the square and joined the crowds running toward Via Milano. An elderly woman fell to the street in front of him. He held off the surging crowd until she could get to her feet, then took her by the arm and helped her along the way. To his left, the Ministry of the Interior loomed high above them, its gray walls and barred windows stark in the morning light.

Rather than returning to the small apartment Antonio had found for him, he headed straight toward the Tiber, angling in the direction of Beppe's radio nest near the Ponte Sisto. He had to find out what Fifth Army G-2 thought they were doing. With the successful Allied invasion of Sicily, the Germans were digging in on the peninsula; they were sure to send more troops now. General Clark's men would need a continual flow of military intelligence.

But headquarters responded to his demands to stay in Rome

with a direct order. He was to leave the city immediately, make his way to a point south of Pescara on the Adriatic, where he would be evacuated by a British motor torpedo boat and returned to AFHQ. He had served long enough under severe duress and was due some leave time while G-2, in conjunction with General Donovan, determined how best to use him again.

Gage left the city in the company of two partisans on Friday afternoon, July 30, lying under a pile of burlap bags in the bed of a three-wheeled Fiat truck. Two weeks later, after a successful evacuation from a beach south of Pescara, he sat by himself on a Douglas aircraft on his way to Tunis, saying his last words to Carla. *I haven't given up, Carla. I'm not done in Italy. They're withdrawing me now, but I'll come back and I will look for you until I find you, dead or alive.* He felt a shiver pass through him, a premonition he tried to ignore, but couldn't. *I will find you . . . and if you are dead, if they've already killed you, I'll make every last one of them pay.*

He owed Carla at least that much.

CHAPTER 10

Monday, August 26, Durango, Colorado

"What's happening in the diary, Nick?"
Ferron looked up. He was lying on the floor below the love seat, papers spread out in front of him. "Hi Janelle. I didn't hear you come down the stairs." Early morning light streamed through the eastward-facing windows, the room ablaze with a mote-mottled nimbus. He got to his feet and turned off the lamp. The clock on the wall in the kitchen read just after five-thirty.

"Shall I let Rowdy out?" she asked, moving toward the sliding glass doors.

He nodded. "I'm almost through with the file folders," he said.

"What's happening?" she asked again.

"Carla's just disappeared."

"I forget. Who's Carla?"

He massaged his forehead and yawned. "She's the young girl that worked with my grandfather in Rome. I think she's just been arrested by the secret police."

"Have you learned anything about Aprico?"

"He hasn't even mentioned the guy. I know they worked together in the war."

"Maybe it was later."

"That's possible. He's up to the summer of '43."

She was at the kitchen sink, filling a pot with water. "When did the war end?"

"Forty-five, wasn't it? I know Mussolini went north after his downfall. The Germans rescued him from the Italians and helped him set up a government in the north."

"So the diary doesn't help?"

He walked into the kitchen, open to the living room, and looked out the window. Oak trees rustled in the breeze. "I'm not really sure. There're so many names and different people he was involved with. I suppose any of them could have betrayed him."

"But why would they come back now? If they betrayed him, he should be going after them. Someone had a reason to kill him."

He shrugged. "I know he tried to track down somebody after the war—and even after he started working for the CIA. Maybe he was still doing something along those lines. Barbara said he spent a week in Washington, D.C., going over something in the National Archives."

Janelle raised her eyebrows. "After all these years?"

"Yeah, you're probably right. Maybe it all comes back to me. I used Gran Babbo to infiltrate Aprico's organization. He's dead, so I can't do anything about that. But there's still this guy Kloos— the Dutchman. He was in contact with both of them recently. Someone's going to pay for Gran Babbo's death."

"Is this just a vendetta for you, Nick?" Her voice was sad.

He placed both hands on the counter, his arms rigid. He stretched his back and neck muscles and then turned to her. She was spooning ground coffee into a filter. "Janelle, you know what he was to me. He was more than a father. I don't think I can ever pay him back. If this is a vendetta, then so be it. He deserves nothing less."

Over breakfast, after he had called several airlines and the Surinamese Consulate in Miami, she said, "Who's keeping your grandfather's dog?"

"Barbara. I'd ask her to keep Rowdy, but I figure one dog's enough."

"I was thinking they could both stay with me. I've got the room here. That dog's going to miss your grandfather. They went everywhere together. Maybe another dog around would help. He and Rowdy get along well."

"Yeah, but Wolf's used to the Lowell's place. Rowdy will mope around for a day or two, but after that he'll do fine here. I'll be back as soon as I can. You mind leaving him inside while you're gone in the daytime? I don't want him trekking back to Tucson."

"Sure, I'm only gone about six hours." She paused. "What about the rest of the diary—and the other papers and letters?"

"I'll take the final two file folders with me. I'm going to be stuck in Miami for at least a day or two. The Surinamese consulate tried to tell me it would take longer to get a visa. I told them this was government business and that the State Department would contact them to expedite the matter."

"Can you do that?"

"I have some friends in the FBI who can arrange for someone to call. Police business."

"So you're not just doing this for vengeance. You want the cops to get the bad guy."

He grinned. "They're going to kick me off the police force, Janelle. And if they don't, I've decided I'm resigning."

"But if you find out who killed your grandfather, you'll turn the matter over to the police, right?"

"We'll let the future decide that," he said.

Leaving the cabin at seven-thirty that morning, Janelle having volunteered to drive him to the airport in Durango, he said, "I left the letters in the trunk. If you want to read them, go ahead. I glanced at as many of them as I could; there doesn't seem to be much of significance. That Mauser I found in the trunk? I put it in the van with my own pistol. The keys to the van are on your kitchen counter."

"I hope this isn't a waste of your time, Nick."

"Kloos is the only one of the three still alive. I think he knew someone was coming after them or he wouldn't have warned the others. I have to get to him before someone else does."

She brushed back a strand of blonde hair that had slipped out of her barrette and then turned for a moment to look at him. "Are you taking any weapons with you?"

He scratched his cheek, then shook his head. "I can get what I need in the country. I don't want trouble with customs."

She nodded, her foot finding the brake. The car had reached the main highway leading into town. "I hope you're careful, Nick," she said, as the car swung out behind an old camper van with a rusty propane tank attached to the rear bumper. "It was good to see you again. I'm just sorry that what brought you back was your grandfather's death. I wish you didn't have to leave so soon."

There was nothing he could say to that.

On the crest of a ridge a scant half mile to the west of the highway where the foothills of the San Juan Mountains overlooked the valley, a man crouched on his haunches beneath tattered scrub oak and stared through a pair of binoculars at the two people in the car. He'd been watching Janelle Dutton's cabin since dawn. With a start, he recognized the man in the passenger seat. For a moment the long hair had thrown him—and then he nodded thoughtfully, understanding. It was because of the kid's undercover work.

As the car pulled away to the south, the man in the hills got to his feet, binoculars hanging from a strap around his neck. His eyes turned back to Janelle's cabin in the valley. Suddenly, sensing movement in the orchard just beyond the cabin, he brought his binoculars to bear on the fruit trees and adjusted the focus. There—approaching the cabin from the direction of the Animas River; they were moving quickly now, their faces turned toward him, coming into focus, the sun at their backs. A short white guy and a taller black man. They paused for a minute at the front door and then he saw them enter the cabin.

"Is that all the papers?" Akkad asked.

Naveed nodded. "Up the chimney. Letters, files, certificates of this and that. What about the medals? We take 'em?"

"We take nothing. Leave the fucking medals where you found them."

"Hey, man. It's not like they ain't going to know we was here."

Akkad moved toward the sliding glass doors. "Our orders are to burn all papers."

"If the fucking guy had fallen asleep, we could have torched him and the chick. Now that's one lucky bastard."

Akkad shrugged. "We get him on down the road if we meet again. My guess is he'll go back to Tucson now and we can forget the guy."

"So we did our job here. Where we going next?"

Akkad slid the door shut behind them, leaving the dog inside. The Golden Retriever had barked once, but wagged his tail the second he recognized Akkad's voice from the day before when he was casing the Lowell's place. "Well, we get someone to fly us down to the lovely Republic of Suriname."

Naveed grinned. He'd been briefed about the situation. "I always wanted to get me a Dutchman," he said. "Make the brothers down there happy."

"Yeah, I'm sure you'll fit right in," Akkad said. "Those Creoles and Bushmen or whatever they got down there are going to welcome you with open arms. Lawrence of Nigeria come to throw off the oppressors."

"You said it, man. It ain't original, but you said it right."

PART TWO

THE OVRA LEGACY

"A man who is good for anything ought not to calculate the chance of living or dying; he ought only to consider whether in doing anything he is doing right or wrong—acting the part of a good man or of a bad."
  —Socrates, quoted in Plato's *Apology*

Book One

Heart of Darkness

"Yu no kot' abra-watra, yu no de kos' kaiman mama."
"If you haven't crossed the stream, you don't curse the alligator's mother."
    —Taki-Taki proverb

CHAPTER 1

Friday, August 30, Parimaribo, Suriname

It started out all wrong.

First, the Suriname Airways flight out of Miami developed engine trouble and diverted to the international airport at Curaçao, where the passengers were delayed for three hours before the plane took off again. Then, in Zanderij terminal, there was no sign of the Embassy man who was supposed to pick him up. Ferron found a stuffy telephone booth, slammed the door shut with his flight bag stuffed beneath his feet, and dialed the Embassy. It was a Friday evening and the duty officer had no information. "If it's an official police matter, I suggest you contact either the People's Ministry of Internal Affairs on Independence Square or the Ministry of the Armed Forces and Police on Gravenstraat."

"Who's the local station chief?"

The duty officer laughed. "If there was such a thing, do you think I'd tell you over the telephone?"

"Then give me the number of the Ambassador." He was slowly losing his temper. Perspiration dripped off his forehead. After a week with little sleep—an hour snatched here and there— the humidity sapped his last residue of strength.

"I'm sorry, sir, but I'm not authorized to release that number."

"It's probably in the fucking public phone book."

"That you'll have to check for yourself."

Before he could answer, a dial tone was buzzing in his ear. He slammed the phone in its cradle and left the booth.

"Taxi, sir?" A shriveled up older man with dark skin and a deformed left foot opened the door on a battered Chevrolet. "Air-condition work very cool."

A rainstorm had just passed over the airport, great sheets of water thundering into the roof of the terminal and gushing out of the gutters in a broad stream. A momentary coolness, rapidly dissipating. The asphalt roadway had already begun to steam and the air felt heavy with humidity. Ferron slid into the back of the taxi, the plastic-covered seat moist to the touch. "I'm looking for a pension or guest house in the city," he said, after the driver moved behind the wheel. "Something inexpensive."

He had plenty of money, what with his credit cards and the funds his bank had wired from Tucson to Miami. He had over sixteen thousand in the bank, his share of what remained after the house was sold and the divorce lawyers paid off. Sharon didn't get alimony. She had her job, her own retirement fund, and no kids. So the money was his to spend. Still, it was better to be inconspicuous—and there was no reason to run through the cash just because he had it.

The driver looked over his shoulder. "I take you Johnny's Hotel on Keizerstraat. No cost you much."

Ferron sat back in exhaustion and stared out the grimy window to his right. Nearly a fifty kilometer drive to the center of Paramaribo. He would have preferred to open the window, but the driver had shaken his head and protested, pointing to the air conditioner that wheezed from below the dash. "It very cool," he said, but by the time the air reached Ferron it was warm and muggy.

The land, he saw, varied in terrain from wild jungle to cultivated garden plots. Stretches of tangled growth and more open savannah gave way to cocoa and palm trees, to citrus groves and banana plantations, to vegetable and rice fields. Lining the road were an assortment of ramshackle plank houses, thatched huts of the *bosnegers* and Amerindians, with jungle at their backs, and a few Florida-type bungalows on stilts. The telephone poles were square. Closer to city, the two-story clapboard houses had the sharply pitched roofs and gables typical of Holland.

Over breakfast his last day in Durango, Janelle had looked up Suriname in her encyclopedia and told him the country had been a possession of the Netherlands since 1667—the year the Dutch signed a peace treaty which ceded Neiuw Amsterdam, later to be known as New York, to the English in exchange for Suriname. The Dutch were elated at gaining a tropical paradise, five times the size of the Netherlands, in exchange for a barren city in the cold climate of North America.

Traffic thickened, the roadway jammed with donkey carts, bicycles, scooters, motorcycles, ten-passenger buses, pickup trucks loaded with men returning from work, and commercial vehicles. When they reached Lelydorp, an outlying area with numerous streets intersecting the roadway, he leaned forward. "Do you know where the central police station is?"

The driver swerved to the right around an oxcart. "We go Paramaribo—headquarters on same street as hotel. You find easy. Why you need police?"

"I'm looking for a man."

"One man hard to find."

"He's a big shot."

The driver shook his head. "I no know him."

Ferron grinned and gave up on the questions.

The Suriname river lay off to his right. He glanced at the map he'd picked up at the Consulate in Miami. After coming in from the southeast, the river curved to the right in a broad sweep before widening and then narrowing at its confluence with the Commewijne, after which both rivers debouched into the Atlantic. From the air, he'd seen the fluvial discoloration of the coastal waters followed by a band of swamps and what the pilot called *schelpritsen*—sand ridges—that ran parallel to the coastline.

He leaned forward again. "Do you know anyone who takes people up the river? Someone who knows the interior?"

The driver rubbed the wrinkled skin on his neck. "Good man with tugboat know everyone—name Martin Beam. He take you anywhere."

"Where can I find him?"

"He have office but never there. You go to river near old gas plant." The driver gestured over his shoulder. "Back there. He have tugboat *Flora* at wharf. You look for sign Drambranders *gracht*—mean water channel."

The taxi took a right on Maagdenstraat, an old street lined with two rows of immense palm trees. They were heading toward the commercial center, making their way in heavy traffic. At Jodenbreedstraat, a side street leading to the harbor, he could see wharves to his right. The waterfront was only a block away. And then he saw what he needed—a small sign for a guest house in the window of a two-story residence with a pillared veranda, set back from the road. He would let the driver take him to Johnny's Hotel and make his way back to the residence on foot. He knew he was being paranoid, but it never hurt to be safe.

Twilight. The Johnny Hotel. To cover himself, even though he wasn't going to stay there, he paid forty guilders for one night, about twenty-two dollars, then left through the inside exit to what the proprietor called the *bigi jari*—the big yard in back. The *pikin jari*, or smaller yard, fronted on Keizerstraat. To one side, between the detached buildings, there was what the man called a "Negro gate" leading to smaller clapboard houses hidden from view—the squalid dwellings of the ordinary working class.

Jogging in the heat, he'd made his way down a dirt lane between the shacks, simple wood structures set on pyramidal-shaped concrete pedestals, their roofs, most without gutters, steeply sloped. Metal drums and wooden water butts served as rain barrels, and warped planks were laid across ditches where the runoff drained away. The air was heavy with the smell of creosote and urine. Creole children, nude or wearing only shirts, stared at him in amazement as he passed. Not another white person in sight and from the looks the kids gave him not many ever came this way. A scrawny dog barked at him and tagged along for half a block before giving up and plopping down in the dirt. But no one followed him. That was what mattered.

The guest house had five rooms with two shared bathrooms. His room on the second floor looked out on a gable and a rain gutter that had to be a foot wide. In the middle of the room, there was a tester bed imported from Holland. On one side, against the wall, sat a table with a wash basin, a heavy delft pitcher covered with lace, and a frayed towel. The opposite side was occupied by a single, unpadded wood chair. Spartan but adequate; he didn't plan on being there long.

He showered and changed clothes before leaving the room, then walked along the harbor toward the city center, trying to orient himself. A last ray of evening sun glittered off the galvanized roofs of the warehouses and mercantile offices that fringed the quay. Soon, these dropped behind as the city opened up into its historical center. He passed an outdoor restaurant where the waiters had placed chunks of burning punk under the tables to drive away mosquitoes.

Alert for a tail, he sauntered through Independence Square by the old Palm Garden that led to the former Governor's Residence. Several kids tried to sell him gum or candy and he finally gave in, to save himself the annoyance. The sight of the outdoor eatery, he suddenly realized, had stimulated his appetite. He ate a meal at Njoek Sang's, a Chinese restaurant on Kleine Waterstraat beyond Fort Zeelandia, and then walked back in a roundabout fashion toward police headquarters. It was eight p.m. local time.

At the police station on Keizerstraat, he showed his American police identification and asked to speak to the highest ranking official in the building. He was led to an office with a bank of fluorescent lights overhead, where a light-skinned Creole in a business suit informed him that Hans Oostburg, the top police official in the country, had already returned to his home, a villa across the river on the outskirts of Meerzorg. He was surprised at the ease with which a meeting was arranged. The policeman telephoned Oostburg's villa and spoke at length in Dutch. Afterward, he told Ferron that the chief of police was having a dinner party that evening, but that he was welcome to come out to the villa later, say around eleven o'clock.

"Shall I have the chief's men send a car for you?" the man asked.

Ferron's eyes widened. He'd expected to use a taxi. "Do they have to cross the ferry both ways?"

The policeman nodded. "But there is also a police launch."

He didn't want to be that indebted to Oostburg, who he

gathered was just below ministerial level. "Why don't you have the car pick me up at the ferry landing on their side of the river?" he said. "I'll arrange to cross the ferry by myself. That will give me something to do this evening."

"Be careful about walking along the harbor at that hour," the policeman cautioned. "We have had troubles recently. A white man—" He paused and then shrugged eloquently. "For you, it is not safe."

"Thanks," Ferron said. "I'll keep my eyes open."

CHAPTER 2

Friday, August 30, Parimaribo, Suriname

Y ou watch," the old man said. "The guns will be junk."
"*Ai ba*! Indeed brother. Or another load of bad ammunition."

The *bosneger* guerrillas, dressed in western clothes but wearing Zoris—rubber Japanese sandals—were conversing in taki-taki when Kristine Kloos arrived at the abandoned tool shed in the old Beekhuizen railroad shops, near Dominee Creek on the southern outskirts of Paramaribo.

"*Yu prei nanga pikin dagu, a i leki yu mofo,*" Dosu said, shaking his head mournfully. He was a short, dark-skinned man with one blind eye, nearly sixty years old.

"You worry too much," Kristine told him in Sranan Tongo, the lingua franca of Suriname. She recognized the proverb: You play with a puppy and he'll lick your mouth. But she had no reason to distrust their suppliers. "The tugboat has already gone out to meet the freighter," she said. "They'll transfer all the weapons at sea and then the *Flora* will pull the freighter to its dock. Is the truck ready?"

The men had borrowed an old sixteen-foot, 2.1-ton Land Rover from the Paranam refinery. Half of the incoming shipment, which consisted of machine guns, rifles and automatic pistols of Czech manufacture, would be transported that night by truck across the river, where another group would continue on to remnants of the *bosneger* Jungle Commando in eastern Suriname.

The rest of the weapons would stay in the tugboat for the initial trip upriver. These men, loyal to Kristine, would accompany her on the tug and would carry the weapons the final leg of the journey in dugout canoes.

Moffi, the leader of the band, nodded, the expression on his face serious. He was a proud man, rarely given to smiling. In his early thirties, he had a powerful physique, with a long machete scar on his chest from a fight over a woman. He wore a T-shirt, cut low on the neck, and short pants. His men addressed him as *kabiteni*, signifying that he was a headman, ranking in authority just under the *granman*—the government-approved chief of his tribe. The forefinger on his right hand was a shriveled stick; a police agent, interrogating him concerning the murder of a government official, had once held Moffi's finger down a red-hot toaster, telling him he'd think twice before firing another gun.

"When do we leave?" he asked, speaking excellent Dutch.

Kristine looked at the man's wrist where a gold watch hung loosely. "An hour from now," she said, switching like him to Dutch. "I'll go first to make sure the *Flora* has returned to its wharf. The customs officials will be busy with the freighter, but you'll have to move quickly. I want you finished before dawn."

Dosu said, *"Hesi-hesi, bo', safri-safri bo', tu.* Haste is good, caution is good, too."

Kristine ignored the older man. "Moffi, once the truck is across the river, let Godjo's team take over. I want you men to go with me."

Moffi nodded. He reached into the pocket of a long-sleeved shirt lying on the bench beside him and withdrew a tobacco sack, after which he proceeded to roll a cigarette while he talked.

"The files came yesterday," he said between puffs. "None of us could read them."

"Did you bring them with you?" she asked.

He gestured toward Dosu and the old man pulled out a satchel.

Kristine opened the case, its lock having been broken by the guerrillas, and looked at a file. "Italian," she said. "My father could speak and read it well." She paused. "Any news of him?"

Moffi exhaled a stream of smoke and passed the cigarette to his younger brother Tano. "Heard a rumor he showed up in

Kwakoegron. A driver for Suralco said he offered a ride to a white man. The description fit your father."

She frowned. "A ride? Where?"

"To the airstrip near Gros."

Gros was a small village near Brownsweg, a mining town near the Afobaka dam. By now, her father would have flown to one of his plantations in the interior. What would he do next? The whole world knew his plane had been shot down, she had seen to that. The news would matter to very few—but to those few it would mean an end to the blackmail practiced so successfully against them. Still, even without his files, her father was a powerful man of immense wealth. There was only one thing left for her to do. Her father still trusted her; he had no idea of her role in this affair. She did not want him dead, if she could help it, but she did want one thing more from him—something he would not give up willingly: his wealth.

She looked around the tool shed at the men sitting on the work benches built into the wall and left there when the shed was abandoned. The men stared back at her expectantly. Manbote, the youngest of the group, spit nervously between his front teeth.

"Friends," she said, her face serious, "I have a riddle for you. *Te na mindri busi wan man sido' nanga wan kron na tap' en 'ede*. In the deep bush a man sits with a crown on his head."

Manbote grinned. He knew she was talking about her father. "*Ya, mati, dat' na wan ananasi*. Yes, friend, that's a pineapple."

The other men laughed.

"He's right," Kristine said. "Manbote knows his riddles well." She paused for a moment. "So now what do we do?"

Tano, who usually let his older brother Moffi speak for him, grunted. "Now we squeeze the juice from the pineapple."

Kristine nodded. "Okay, we understand each other." She knew that these men, despite their bravado, feared her father and his well-armed henchmen. "By tomorrow, we'll be better armed than our enemies. We must be ready to fight. For the first time we have a chance to win. It's up to us." She looked around the shed, catching each man's eye, and then said firmly, "For the people!"

"*Fo' ala suma!*" they shouted in response.

CHAPTER 3

Friday, August 30, the outskirts of Meerzorg, Suriname

Hans Oostburg, despite his name, was not from Holland. He was a Surinamese national of mixed ancestry, part Dutch, part Creole, educated in Amsterdam and trained in the United States by the FBI. A tall, handsome man with crinkly gray hair that hugged his scalp, a broad forehead, and strong chin and nose, he appeared in the uniform of a lieutenant colonel in the Surinamese Army.

"*Aangenaam kennis te maken, meneer Ferron,*" he said, extending his hand.

"I'm sorry I don't speak Dutch," Ferron replied.

"*Werkelijk?* We will speak in English then. I have been to your country often. It's a pleasure to meet you. Please come with me."

From the foyer of his heavily guarded villa, which was a large plantation house with green shutters and a colonnaded veranda running around the building on both stories and on all four sides, Oostburg led him into a first-floor sitting room tastefully decorated with Dutch antiques. A window air conditioner hummed in the background, but did little to cut the humidity. Catching Ferron's appraisive glance, Oostburg said, "The façade and most of the furnishings date from the early nineteenth century. We've done very little to change it. *Mag ik U jets te drinken?*"

"Pardon me?"

"May I offer you something to drink?"

"Gin and tonic, if you have it."

"*Gaat U zitten*," Oostburg said, pointing to an easy chair and then translating when Ferron didn't move. "Please sit down, Mr. Ferron." He smiled. "You must study Dutch someday."

"I never thought I'd need it in South America."

When Hans Oostburg returned with the drinks, he pointed to the chair and said, "That *bakstoelen*, by the way, came from Rotterdam in 1873."

"It's very beautiful." Ferron ran his hand along the teal-blue velvet.

After the pleasantries, an awkward silence extended itself between the two men. Ferron raised his glass when Oostburg said "To your health," and sipped his drink gratefully. After the dry heat of Arizona and the cool air of Colorado, he found it difficult to adapt to the tropical climate. The humidity hovered around eighty percent and the nighttime temperature, it seemed, varied little from that of the day.

Oostburg reached for a cigar box of Spanish cedar. "Will you have a good Dutch cigar?" he said, opening the box and extending it toward him.

"No, thank you. The drink is fine."

His host took a cigar and in silent concentration began to prepare it for smoking. He was enjoying the first puffs when Ferron broke the silence. "Why the special treatment?" he asked bluntly.

Oostburg glanced up sharply and then shrugged. "We like to help our American friends when possible. Our consular officials in Miami informed us that you were working with the FBI."

"Not really. I needed to speed up the visa process and just asked a favor of an old friend."

"We, too, have friends. They tell us you are a narcotics officer. Are you here on a drug case?"

He shook his head. "Personal business."

"Because if you are, we wish to cooperate. Of course, to operate in our country you need our permission and our help. I'll assign a man tomorrow to accompany you during your stay."

"My business here is private. It has nothing to do with your government."

Oostburg's eyebrows rose. "Then why have you come to

me?"

He cleared his throat. "I do need your help. I'm trying to locate a man. Theunis Kloos."

Oostburg frowned, running the hand with the cigar around an octagonal glass ashtray on a lamp stand beside his easy chair. He fidgeted with the ashtray until one edge was true to the coaster where his drink sat and the coaster was true to the edge of the stand. "You read about his plane being shot done by guerrillas?" he finally said. "The man may be dead."

"His plane was shot down?"

Oostburg's eyes narrowed. "You haven't heard? The Surinaams Nieuws Agentschap put out a bulletin just over a week ago."

"What happened?"

"The best we can determine there were two guerrilla units who shot down his plane—an old single-engine Norseman. We've found the wreckage. The guerrillas had one group in the jungle near the airport and another further south on a hill overlooking his flight path."

"What about Kloos?"

Oostburg shook his head and then rolled the cigar between his fingers. "We never found the body."

"Could he have survived?"

"It's possible." Oostburg tapped his cheek with one finger. "We know the guerrillas are still looking for him."

"Who are these guerrilla anyway?"

The official snorted. "Do you know anything about the history of our country?"

"Not really."

Oostburg settled back in his easy chair. "We gained our independence from the Netherlands in 1975. For a while we had a two-party parliamentary democracy." He shrugged. "Controlled by the right wing. In time, the 'have-nots' fomented nationalistic movements directed against the 'haves.' The military finally stepped in and took over in February of 1980." He snorted. "A coup led by only sixteen, poorly armed, non-commissioned officers. That is when your CIA became interested. Suriname is one of the world's major bauxite producers." Oostburg took a few puffs on his cigar in silence and then waved his hand in a dismissive gesture. "But really we are not so important anymore—still, after Grenada . . ." He paused, looking at Ferron intently. "You did not hear what happened with us?"

"I don't think much about Suriname makes our newspapers."

The man sighed. "You have to understand our history. Our revolution was led by sixteen sergeants with the support of two Marxist parties. The sergeants had no experience in running a country. Their leader was a maroon named Desi Bouterse—a lieutenant colonel now. The Dutch Military Mission did nothing to stop him. Bouterse walked a fine line for a while. Even the United States was reassured. But then the Cubans began to gain influence. They opened an office for their chargé d'affaires in Paramaribo in the summer of '81."

He rubbed his chin thoughtfully. "Bouterse needed the Cubans. A year later, in March, he had to put down a second coup attempt." He paused and took a sip of his drink. "After that, Bouterse became more autocratic. In December of '82, fifteen prominent critics of the regime were arrested, tortured, and executed while in military custody—trying to escape from the prison at Fort Zeelandia, we were told. Tass and Prensa Latina reported on the executions as the suppression of a 'counter-revolutionary conspiracy' and the Vietnamese party daily *Nhan Dan* called the action 'the crushing of an imperialist-abetted coup attempt.' So you see, the communists were increasing their presence here."

Oostburg tapped the ash from his cigar. "The situation continued to worsen. More deaths, more accusations of conspiracy . . ." He took several puffs and then squinted through the smoke. "In May of '83, your ABC network reported that Reagan had approved a CIA coup to topple the government."

"I assume they must have failed."

Oostburg shrugged eloquently. "The plan was shelved when your Congress opposed it." He tugged at one sleeve of his military coat. "Everyone became involved then. The Brazilians sent their top security adviser, General Venturini. He told Bouterse that Brazil would not countenance a Cuban influence on its borders. That's when Grenada was invaded. Maurice Bishop's death shocked the lieutenant colonel. He expelled the Cuban ambassador soon after—following a talk, I might note, with the American ambassador in Paramaribo."

"Did Kloos have anything to do with all this?"

Oostburg smiled thinly. "Let's just say he has his contacts with the Americans. But I'm sure things were not going quite the way he wanted them to. Bouterse visited Libya in March of '83, and the Libyans set up a People's Bureau in Paramaribo two years later." Oostburg laughed. "Your country warned Bouterse several times, including in January of '86, when you were bombing Libya. Very effective that. The Libyans were helping the guerrillas here."

"What about these guerrillas? What's Kloos done to antagonize them?"

"Kloos has always supported a return to a right-wing government. Bouterse came to an agreement with the old parties in 1986. A complete turnaround." The man cocked his head, an amused look in his eyes. "We are a small country, but very complicated, eh?"

Ferron nodded. "Do you have a file on Kloos? I'd like to know more about his background."

"What's the nature of your business with *meneer* Kloos?"

"I simply want to talk to him about a family matter?"

Oostburg raised his eyebrows. "A family matter?"

"I believe he may have some information about the death of my grandfather."

"Your grandfather died in Suriname?"

"No . . . he was murdered in Colorado—by someone Kloos knew."

Oostburg looked skeptical. "Are you sure of this?"

"I'm just following up a lead."

"I didn't know you were an investigative policeman."

"You wouldn't understand," Ferron said slowly. "I owe my life to my grandfather—and any iota of sanity left to me. He got me through a difficult childhood."

"Many of us have had difficult childhoods. That does not make us detectives." There was the faintest hint of rebuke in the man's measured tones.

Ferron took a deep breath. "His death may be related to a narcotics investigation. Have you heard of a man named Beppe Aprico—or of a Thomas Gage?"

Oostburg shook his head, lips pursed regretfully.

"And you have no file on Kloos?"

"I'm sorry, *meneer* Ferron, but I can't help you."

"Can you tell me how he acquired his wealth?"

"He's a *Nederlander*. His family had many plantations in Java before the war. I'm told he liquidated all his holdings in the East Indies before they gained their independence. He was wealthy when he first came to Suriname in the late forties—back when we were still Dutch Guiana." Oostburg shrugged. "And now he has a hand in everything."

Ferron nodded. The two men sat in silence for a moment. He could hear the measured footsteps of the guards as they patrolled the perimeter of the mansion. Oostburg pulled back the sleeve of his uniform and glanced at his watch. The hour was late.

"Where would Kloos go if he survived the plane crash?"

The official studied him for a moment. "Kloos has several plantations around the country, including some heavily fortified ones in the interior and along the Saramacca River. I would guess he might hole up in one of them or perhaps near Tafelberg. There's an airstrip there, and it's close to one of his residences in the mountains."

"How far is that from Paramaribo?"

Oostburg stroked his chin, hesitating, then said, "Do you know what the Bush Negroes say? If you stir up a hole, you'll find what's in it."

Ferron stared at the man, but said nothing in response, both hands clasped around the glass of gin, which was slowly warming to the touch.

Oostburg rolled the cigar between thumb and forefingers, his eyes contemplating the whisps of smoke that drifted toward the ceiling. He sighed. "Tafelberg is in the center of the country—about two hundred and some kilometers by air. Kloos's place is just southeast of the headwaters of the Saramacca River, near the boundary between the Saramacca and Brokopondo Districts. But as I said, he could be in any of the plantations."

Ferron nodded. There was one other item he needed to clarify before venturing into the interior. "You were talking about the guerrillas."

"Yes, we've had problems with several groups the last few

years. Have you heard of Ronnie Brunswijk? He's a Bush Negro or *bosneger* as we call them—one of Bouterse's former bodyguards. He leads a group called the Jungle Commando—the Surinamese National Liberation Army. They were active a few years ago in the eastern part of the country, along the border with French Guiana. The government negotiated a cease-fire in 1989." Oostburg smiled cynically. "So what do we have now? We have Amerindian groups, opposed to the government's agree-ment with the Jungle Commando, carrying out sabotage activities in the west. As I said, it's a very complicated picture." He stroked his chin for a moment and then gestured around the room with an open hand.

"We are a country of many religions and many nationalities. We must contend with four Muslim sects, with orthodox and modern Hindus—the *Sanatan Dharm* and the *Arya Samaj*, with Confucianists, Jews, African and Amerindian tribal religions, and nineteen Christian denominations including the *Evangelische Broedergemeente*. We have populations of Caribs, Arowaks, Wayana, and other native Indian tribes, six *bosneger* tribes including the Djuka and Saramacca, Creoles, Chinese, Hindustani, Indonesians, Dutch and other Europeans. Each has their own demands. It is very difficult to find stability."

Ferron swallowed the last of his gin and set the glass on a table to his left. "So who's in power today?"

A slow grin appeared on Hans Oostburg's face. "We have a president and an elected National Assembly now, but would you believe the prime minister is Henk Aaron?"

Ferron stared at him blankly. "Who's Henk Aaron?"

Oostburg's grin widened. "The same man in power before the first Army coup—a good old right-winger. And you wonder what the guerrillas have against Kloos? The country's right back where it started."

For the first five minutes of the return drive the moon was out between thick clouds, and from the back seat of the armored police car Ferron could see a silvery sheen to each side of the roadway. Rice polders, the uniformed bodyguard had said, tapping the window with the barrel of his submachine gun.

The effect of the moonlight on water was surreal, a landscape so strange that it seemed the work of a deranged artist who painted only in shades of black, gray, and silver—in broad swaths, broken here and there by clumps of palm trees or isolated buildings. Ferron cracked his window and sat back, breathing in the night air. Suddenly, the moon disappeared, slipping behind scudding clouds, and the night darkened—not a light visible except for the feeble yellow rays of the car's head-lamps. He felt a strange sense of absolute isolation, as if he were imprisoned in a cube dangling from a thread in a black and fathomless universe.

Was this what it was going to be like now that his grand-father was dead? He couldn't believe how much he missed the man. For a moment, he felt that he was once again a child—and that the night held only terror and murderous rage. He heard again his father's footsteps loud upon the stairs, each step a heartbeat that thudded in his chest. Somehow that dark night, before it happened, Nick knew his dad had meant to kill them all. An invisible force had lifted him from bed, had helped him wake Barbara and then open the window that gave out on the oak tree. They had heard the shots that killed their mother but had themselves been spared. And later, in the confusion of events that accompanied their father's trial, Gran Babbo had appeared to take them both away and to shelter them from what followed. And now he was gone for good.

It was then that the first bullets thudded into the car, shattering the silence. Ferron was aware of a momentary deceleration, the result of shock, followed by the realization of what was happening, and then the driver swore and jammed his foot on the pedal. Fifty meters down the road, another fusillade slammed into the car from the front. Ducking involuntarily, the driver hit the brakes and swung to the left, moving down a side road that ran along the river.

Ferron glanced out the window and saw more flashes of gunfire. The air was heavy with the smell of fertilizer from a nearby warehouse.

"Roll up your window!" the bodyguard shouted.

Before he could move, a stream of bullets whacked into the side of the car. The window glass cracked but did not shatter—the vehicle was reinforced for just such an eventuality—but the handle was jammed. The bodyguard leaned over from the front seat to help. Suddenly the man jerked spasmodically and collapsed with a sudden exhalation of breath, his body sliding into the back of the car. Hot blood spurted over Ferron's lap. He heard the driver swear again and looked up to see the roadway illumined ahead of them. A roadblock. Ten seconds at the most before they collided or were run off the road into the flooded rice fields on the left or the warehouses on the right.

The driver began to brake hard. Headlights from behind stabbed into the car's interior. They were sandwiched between a truck ahead of them and a car from behind. "Hang on," the driver yelled, taking his foot off the brake and tromping on the accelerator. Ferron fell back into the seat, his legs tangling with the bulky figure of the dead bodyguard. Twenty feet from the truck, headlights in his eyes, the driver jerked the wheel violently and the car left the paved road, plowed through a dirt bank and went airborne. A corrugated tin structure appeared before them and then the car hit the ground, bounced across a small parking lot and tore through the side of the warehouse, coming to a stop in a pile of machinery as the headlights exploded and the light died away.

CHAPTER 4

Saturday, August 31, the waterfront, Suriname River

In the sudden darkness, Ferron was momentarily disoriented. He could hear bullets pinging through the building's metal structure and whistling by overhead and then the hiss of the radiator. No sound came from the front seat. *Get out!* But the left door was jammed. He threw his shoulder into it and winced. The door wouldn't budge. He pushed the bodyguard to the floor, then slid to the passenger side and pulled on the door handle. The right door opened a few inches and then stopped with a shriek of metal on metal. A stray bullet smashed into the rear of the car. *Damn! He had to get out before he was killed!* He lay on his back and kicked at the door, his left hand struggling to gain purchase on the drive shaft. His fingers closed around the cold barrel of a gun. And then he was slipping through the narrow opening, his clothes tearing on the jagged metal. He stumbled over something in the darkness and fell to his knees. The bodyguard's submachine gun was still in his hands. He found the safety, flicked it off, and unleashed a stream of bullets toward the opening where the car had torn through the building. Slow them down while he found a way out.

Was that a lighter area ahead of him? He had to find a door or window and get to the river where he could hide. With only one clip, he wouldn't last long. Who in hell were they? Guerrillas who thought he was Oostburg, or Kloos's men? At the moment it didn't much matter. They wouldn't stop to ask questions.

He ran down an aisle between dark masses looming to each side of the warehouse, moving toward the lighter area, left hand stretched out in front of him for protection, right hand clutching the submachine gun to his belly. The door was locked and he had to waste another burst from the gun to get out of the warehouse. He could hear voices behind him—still distant and unintelligible.

The clouds had thinned out into a tattered sheet and were penetrated by thin shafts of silver that cast eerie shadows among the decrepit buildings and machinery clustered along the waterfront. He made his way over a stone wall eroded by the elements. He had to put some distance between himself and his pursuers before they realized he had escaped. He stumbled over a loose board and swore, hoping they couldn't hear the noise he was making. Ahead all was dark. He ran blindly into the night, his mind a jumble of sensations.

Beams of light appeared suddenly to his left. A car was approaching from behind, following the road that ran along the river, cutting the distance with the rapidity of a predator closing in for the kill. He saw a burned-out shack with a rusty Coca-Cola sign hanging at an angle and wanted to stop and rest, but there was no safety there. Would they see him if he lay down in the field and didn't move? *He wasn't going to take the chance.* He ran on. He heard shouts, realized that a second team was sweeping the field behind him. Thank God they didn't have dogs. Gulping in air, he glanced over his shoulder and saw flashlights and one large spotlight playing across the field as the car advanced. The spotlight didn't worry him; the men in the car would be blind to all but what the narrow band of light delineated. It was the others, spread out across the field, who were dangerous. Would it do any good to call out—to let them know he was an American? But maybe it was him they were after. The men had reached the burned-out shack. *Move!* He ran on, heart hammering in his chest like a pile driver gone painfully wild.

Unexpectedly the ground plummeted away and he stumbled, dropping into the void. He flew forward and slammed hard into the far wall of a ditch. A bolt of pain rocketed up his back. Stunned, he gasped for air and couldn't get any. Mud sucked at his hands and legs. A thin, wispy breath finally reached his lungs, starved for oxygen. A bullet whacked into the mud to his left. *They'd heard him fall! Had he cried out?* Desperately sucking in great lungfuls of air, he clambered up the side of the ditch and rolled over the top, his chest wheezing like an old pump. He'd lost the gun.

The men were shouting in excitement, their voices growing louder. He fought down his panic. *Forget the gun and get away from them.* Water—he could hear it rippling along the banks of the river. No other choice now. The car in pursuit had pulled ahead and cut him off. More men were approaching from directly ahead. He ran in the direction of the river, dread settling over his heart. He could swim, but the river was wide at this point. Far off across its black expanse he could see a thin twinkling of lights. Could he let the current carry him downstream and then swim back to shore—or would the men chasing him be watching at the ferry crossing?

He ran on toward the dark ribbon. Better to try and make it to the other side. Somewhere over there was his room—and safety. And then, ten feet away, the black void opened up . . . The river lay at the bottom of a steep embankment. In full stride, unable to tell what lay ahead, he went off the edge. He tumbled violently down the slope, all sense of direction lost, and hit the river with a loud splash. The current grabbed him immediately and sucked him down, carrying him away from shore. He fought his way to the surface, then twisted and pulled off his shoes.

The water was tepid and muddy. Behind him, as he swung around, he could see the flashlights grouped along the shore. The men emptied their guns into the river, shooting wildly, well behind him now. No one followed him into the water. He was surprised by the strength of the current, which bore him swiftly toward midstream and then apparently slowed down as the river approached its bend around Paramaribo. Struggling to keep his head above water so as not to lose sight of the lights on the far shore, he thought about the piranha. Their sharp jaws could devour a dog or a tapir in minutes. Would they come this far down river on its approach to the Atlantic? He hoped not. His guide book had said they preferred the brackish swamps upriver.

But what about the caimans—blood brother to the crocodile?

A dark shape was moving toward him from upstream, barely visible in the darkness. Heart in his throat, he tried to stroke quietly, swimming away from the shape, but its speed matched his. He was tiring rapidly, weighed down by his pants and the money belt around his waist. He didn't know now whether he'd be able to make it to shore. Surely the black shape would get him before then. He looked back and was hit hard in the side. His head slipped under water and he rolled, panicking. When he broke free at the surface again, the shape brushed against him and he felt the rough texture of bark.

A dead tree, branchless. Washed away from the water's edge somewhere upstream.

He grabbed for the log, heart thudding, and swung an arm over it, then cleared his lungs. The current was carrying the log into the inner sweep of the river, toward the warehouses that lined the waterfront near the center of Paramaribo. He rested then, gathering his strength, trying to recover from the adrenaline surges of the last fifteen minutes. Just before the river swept on around the bend, he would abandon the log and strike out for shore.

A moment of languor slipped over him—the exhaustion of too many sleepless nights and too many shocks to the system. Unable to resist the thought, he remembered the time when he was six years old and his father had taken him into the mountains of Washington state, to a bridge under construction near an abandoned air force base with an empty dome that once held a military radar. Stopping the car across the old wooden bridge, his father had walked with him to the middle of the new bridge, an unfinished structure, where rushing white water was visible between the sections of concrete. It was winter and Nick could hear the grumble and underwater crack of rocks being swept along by the raging current.

His father, despite Nick's terrified cries, had forced him to stand on the unprotected edge of the bridge, girders not yet in place, and lean out over the water, supported only by his father's hand—and then he had let go for a second, catching the boy at the last moment. Nick had screamed in terror, death a slip of his father's hand away—and his dad, angry that the boy didn't trust him, had beat him until he stopped crying, and then made him do it again.

Anger and hate rose in his gullet now at the memory, and when the moment came, he drove for the docks on the far shore, his mind oblivious to the pain in his arms and legs.

Twenty minutes later he pulled himself onto a rickety wood dock, floating at the water's edge below a larger concrete pier for ocean-going freighters. In the distance, he could see a snaky ladder leading up to the wharf. The bollards there were back-lit by two arc lamps at the end of a long warehouse. For a moment, lying on the dilapidated wood dock, the river visible through the cracked planks, he thought of his grandfather. Gran Babbo had always been like those bollards—a sign of strength and stability, strong enough to hold even the mightiest of ships. A sturdy presence in the dark. Cast a rope around him and you were safe. Now, someone had killed him and Ferron had never felt more alone.

CHAPTER 5

Saturday, August 31, Parimaribo, Suriname

He worked his way upriver, moving in shadows along the deserted wharfside streets and alleys, looking for the Drambranders channel and the tugboat *Flora*. He glanced at his wristwatch under a streetlight and had to wipe mud from the crystal to read the hour. Nearly two-thirty in the morning. His clothes were filthy and he was shoeless. The money belt around his waist chafed his hips. He pulled up his shirt, removed the belt, and wrung the water from it. The money inside was soaked and muddy, his passport wrinkled but legible, his credit cards unaffected. He felt a flutter near his head and looked up to see the flicker of bats in the streetlight. Insects hummed hungrily around his head. He stuffed the money back in the belt and hurried on.

The *Flora* looked like it had been decrepit fifty years earlier. It was a steam-driven, wood-built tug, with a rounded stern riding low in the water and a forward deck that swept slowly upward to the bow stem, where a single davit was mounted. The pilothouse was a two-story, square structure, the lower part enclosed—with three windows on each side and a door at the back. The upper level was surrounded by a low canvas rail open to the air. The forward mast and towing lights rose above the peaked roof. Behind the pilothouse stood an immense smokestack, next to the engine room, and then a long cabin with port holes and three doors—surmounted by an array of smaller masts and antennas.

On the rear deck lay cargo of some sort—stacks of boxes that ran toward the open stern with its cleats and towing hawser. Lights burned inside the cabin and the pilothouse, and an old truck was parked nearby.

The gun thrust into his neck from behind was cold. He stopped, his body tensing as he restrained the automatic reaction. Were he on a drug raid, the man with the gun would already have been disarmed and lying on the ground, in pain.

"*Wat wil jij haar?*" someone said quietly.

"I don't speak Dutch," he said, his body still. "I'm an American. I'm looking for Martin Beam."

A hand ran down both sides, searching for weapons.

"I'm here on business."

"*Wie is daar?*" he heard a woman call from the boat.

The pressure of the gun eased slightly. "*Een Amerikaan, Kristine. Hij wil Martin zien.*"

The woman appeared in the light near one of the old pudding fenders, a young Creole with long black hair tied up under a handkerchief folded in the native *tai-hede* fashion. "*Hoe heet jij?*" she asked him.

"My name's Nick Ferron. I'm looking for the owner of the *Flora.*"

"What do you want?" Her English had the crisp tones of Oxford English.

"I'd like to talk to him about a business proposition."

"At this hour?" She hesitated. "Come back tomorrow."

"I can't wait until tomorrow. It's very important I see him now."

A man listening from the darkness behind the pilothouse said, "It's okay, Kristine." His voice was harsh and guttural, the accent Dutch. A match flared, illuminating a whiskery face. The man lit his cigarette and then said, "Bring him on board, Tano."

Martin Beam was a crusty old waterfront rat, a short, wiry Dutchman who wore a grease-stained captain's hat, a tattered denim shirt with holes at the elbows, and jeans that were faded and worn. His shoes were canvas-soled sneakers. He hadn't shaved for several days and his whiskers had come in splotchy and grizzled. When he removed his hat to wipe his sweating forehead, he showed a close-cropped head of faded red bristles and a freckled forehead. His nose was swollen with veins and inflamed sebaceous glands and his cheeks were scarred from acne.

When Beam learned that Ferron wanted to go upriver to find Theunis Kloos, he squinted through a cloud of smoke but said nothing. The young woman, whose head had jerked up at the mention of Kloos, spoke instead, her tone sharp. "How do you know *meneer* Kloos?"

Ferron turned to look at her. They were seated in the master cabin, the woman on an unmade bunk, the two men in chairs. In the light of a globe lamp that hung from a gimbel overhead, he was surprised to see that her eyes were the color of cornflowers—a deep blue that lightened to flax when the light struck her just right. Set against her milky chocolate skin, the eyes stood out like jewels on brown velvet.

"Kloos was a friend of my grandfather's. They served together in Italy at the end of World War II. I need to ask him some questions. It's very important."

The woman looked at Beam and said something in Dutch, while Ferron cast an appreciative glance her way. She had an oval face, with the fine lines of a classic beauty—high cheekbones, a well-defined nose, and soft, delicate lips. She wore a patterned shirt open at the neck, where an amulet of black tourmaline—a *tapu* to ward off evil—was visible, and military fatigues tucked into a pair of jungle boots. As she leaned back, the swell of her breasts pushed against the soft fabric of her shirt.

When she finished speaking, Beam nodded. He took a final drag on his cigarette and then stubbed it out in an empty tin can that once held tuna. Ferron waited expectantly.

"Kloos is not an easy man to talk to," Beam said finally, in his rough voice. "If we find him, what makes you think he'll see you?"

"Someone is trying to kill the man. I may be able to help save him."

The young woman frowned. "A lot of people have tried to kill my father. What's one more?" Her voice was angry.

It took Ferron a moment to realize what she'd said. "You're his daughter?"

"I'm Kristine Kloos."

"But you're too young."

"I'm twenty-seven," she said brusquely. "My father was in his late forties when I was born. He divorced my mother when I was seven. I've seen him maybe five times since."

"Do you know where he is? I must see him."

She snorted. "The last I heard his plane was shot down in the jungle."

He was surprised at her lack of concern. "There are rumors he's still alive."

Kristine merely stared at him, no emotion in her eyes, which were now opaque. Ferron turned to Beam. "I'd like to hire the *Flora* to take me upriver to Kloos's plantation at Tafelberg."

Kristine said, "My father doesn't have a plantation at Tafelberg. He has a fortress in the mountains there and plantations along the river. You can fly to Tafelberg if you wish."

"Is that where you think he is?"

She shrugged. "My father could be anywhere. He can take care of himself."

He rubbed his cheeks tiredly. "Maybe so," he said, "but I need to see him about my grandfather—and about another man they both knew in the war—an Italian named Beppe Aprico. Aprico and my grandfather were murdered and I think your father knows who did it. I'd like to check his plantations along the river to see if he's hiding in one of them."

A Bush Negro stuck his head in the door, said "*D' u lai boto*," and left.

"Everything's loaded," Kristine said.

Beam nodded and turned back to Ferron, pointing at his bare feet. "What happened to your shoes?" A crooked grin creased his face. "You take a late night swim, buddy?"

"Someone tried to kill me tonight."

Beam tipped his head back, eyebrows rising under the bill of his captain's cap.

Ferron shrugged. "Either that or they thought I was Hans Oostburg."

Kristine Kloos looked at him sharply. "What does Oostburg have to do with you?"

"I'm a narcotics cop in the States. I stopped to see him for information on your father. On the trip back to the ferry, someone shot and killed the driver and a bodyguard. I managed to escape."

Her eyes were suspicious. "You swam across the river?"

He nodded.

Beam grinned hugely. "Well, I'll be a pissant's popsie," he said. "Not many people can lay claim to that. Buddy, you're lucky all you lost was your shoes."

"So, will you take me?"

Beam plucked at his lip where a piece of tobacco was stuck. "You're double lucky," he said. "We're headed in that direction. We got some supplies to deliver along the river. By dugout canoe higher up. If you're ready to leave now, buddy, I think we can find a pair of old canvas shoes around here somewhere that should fit you."

"I don't like it," Kristine said. Her eyes found the American's. "You're just asking for trouble, *meneer* Ferron."

"Call me Nick," he said cheerfully. "I don't mind trouble." He pointed to where she was sitting. "Okay if I crash on that bunk for an hour or two?"

In rising heat waves, fifteen minutes ahead of a torrential downpour, the pilot hired by Vasco Akkad, a man who called himself Wild Wiley Walker, brought the old Twinotter down hard on the narrow runway of the landing field at Zorg en Hoop just outside Paramaribo, last hop on the plane's journey from Tucson to Belize to Maracaibo. While Wild Wiley taxied to a Quonset hut hanger, Akkad unfastened his seat belt, turned to Naveed and said, "Hey, *neger, welkom in Suriname.*"

"Ah, come on, dude. Since when you know Dutch?"

Akkad grinned. "I read it on the sign out there."

"I suppose it said nigger, too."

"That's what they call them here," Akkad said. "*Bosnegers.*"

"Long as you don't say jungle bunnies I guess it's okay." Naveed stretched his stiff muscles. "Where's this woman live, anyway?"

"I got the address here somewhere. About the only thing the Company's good for down here. They said the cop's in town, but they haven't found him yet."

Using the old man's authority, Akkad had telephoned the CIA man in the Paramaribo embassy from the airfield in Maracaibo, Venezuela. The agent had given him an address for a Delphina Kloos, and then told him that Nick Ferron had showed up in town. The kid hadn't gone back to Tucson like Akkad thought he would.

Naveed flexed his chest muscles. "We should've burned the fucker in the cabin back in Durango, but that's okay. We find the woman and be there waitin' when the man arrive."

But the woman wasn't who they thought she was. They'd tortured her for over an hour before realizing she told the truth. "The friggin' Dutchman's ex-wife—not his daughter," Akkad said, flicking his cigarette lighter on and off. "How could the Company fuck up like that?"

Naveed spat on the floor. They were in a one-room shack on an alley in the western outskirts of Paramaribo. The creosoted walls were decorated with old Chinese calendars and pictures clipped from magazines. Several pieces of chipped crockery were stacked in racks in a small kitchen nook. The woman slept on a paillasse on the dirt floor. Akkad swore. "Stupid bitch. She don't even know where her old man is. I don't like wasting time." He shook his head. "Boss says the Dutchman's rich. Can you believe it? Leaving his ex-wife like this?"

Naveed looked dangerous. "She fuckin' put a hex on us, man. I don't like that black magic shit."

Akkad sneered. "You believe that crap?"

"Don't know, man," Naveed said, his eyes slitted. "All she say is *ogri ai*—the evil eye. You don't play around with that."

"Just shut the fuck up and kill the bitch," Akkad said. "We got other things to do."

CHAPTER 6

Saturday, August 31, Saramacca River, Suriname

Stripped to his shorts, Ferron slept while the tugboat left the Suriname river and moved through the Saramacca channel from Paramaribo to Uitkijk. At the Uitkijk landing, the Saramacca river, after its long drop from the granite and sandstone mountains and rugged rain forests of the interior, took a sharp turn to the west. Just before leaving the channel into the river, they passed a Failing 1500 rotary drill, operated by the Suriname Water Company, and several hours later, moving upstream on the Saramacca, an abandoned bucket-line gold dredge at the juncture of Haarlekijn *kreek*. Soon after, signs of civilization dropped away, and the only sounds were the cries of birds, the buzzing of insects, and the soft chugging of the tugboat.

Ferron woke in late afternoon, after nearly twelve hours of sleep, in time to help the crew load cordwood for the steam engine. The tug was drawn up at a mud bank near a *bosneger* village, the jungle closing in on both sides of the river. Several women, nude from the waist up, were cooking flat cassava cakes over primus stoves propped on the ground in front of their thatched huts. Nearby stood long, clay-smeared *obia* sticks with eyes carved into them to ward off evil spirits. The village children chattered animatedly with Kristine, offering her pieces of *karu-bojo*, a maize tart, while they told how a twelve-foot anaconda had eaten one of the village dogs the day before.

It was suffocatingly hot and the air smelled of decay. The

backwaters were thick with the rotting leaves of wallaba trees. Hummingbirds and blue morphos and an occasional white-capped tanager flitted through the sky. Clouds of insects drifted over the river.

That night, the men tied the tug to a large *katou* tree, its trunk anchored in the muddy bank by immense buttress roots. They were an hour beyond Kwakoegron and had already asked for Kloos at one of his plantations, where oil palms were harvested. The foreman hadn't heard from his boss. Over a dinner of fish, spiced rice, and canned green beans, accompanied by liberica coffee and topped off with *dram*, a white liquor that tasted like gin, Ferron tried to draw out Kristine, who seemed to have been avoiding him. Beam had returned to the pilothouse to check his charts, and the crew were outside on the stern deck, smoking hand-rolled cigarettes and trying to tune in a radio with an antenna strung to a mast at the back of the cabins.

At first, Kristine responded laconically to his questions and asked none in return. What finally drew her out was the question of politics. He was surprised at the vehemence with which she spoke against her father's activities. "My father has controlled the government of this country from behind the scenes for too long," she said. She'd removed the kerchief holding her hair and it now fell in luxuriant waves around her face. She brushed back a strand, and he saw she'd put on a pair of small sapphire earrings.

"And how's he managed that?"

"The same way it's always done. With money."

"How did your father make his money, anyway? Oostburg said something about family holdings in Java before the war."

"Does it matter? For all his bank accounts, my father is a miser. If he was hanging himself from a rafter and you rushed in and cut him down, he'd insist you pay for the rope."

He laughed, but she was not smiling.

"My father has not used his wealth to help the people—not even his own. My mother lives in poverty, on what she can make as a *wisi-woman*."

"A what?"

"She practices *winti*, a Creole religion." Kristine's gaze met his, her eyes disconcertingly direct. A note of disdain had crept into her voice. "My people go to them for black magic—hexes against enemies, protection from evil spirits."

"You don't seem to be a believer."

She shook her head and then closed her eyes for a moment. "It's not that . . . The spirits are very powerful—but these guides do nothing to help us in our struggle."

"And what struggle is that?"

"You talked to Hans Oostburg. Didn't he explain what's happening?"

"You're with the guerrillas, aren't you?"

"I'm with the people. In our struggle for freedom. For equality."

He stared at her thoughtfully. "Does your father know this?"

"I told you, my father has paid no attention to me."

"Where did you learn English so well?"

She hesitated. "That's the only thing my father has done for me. He paid for me to study in Holland, at Leiden—and at the university you must know English well." She paused again, her fingers tracing the rim of her coffee cup. "Before my father divorced my mother, I grew up speaking three languages—Dutch, English, and Sranan Tongo. I understand the Saramaccan dialect. My father also spoke some Italian. But he spoke the languages merely to use the people."

Ferron shifted uncomfortably. The muscles along his lower spine had stiffened, the aftereffects of his fall in the ditch the night before. "What are you going to do now?"

Kristine settled back and closed her eyes. She was sitting on the deck with her back to a bulkhead. He sat at an angle across the cabin, his head below a porthole. Outside it was pitch black. A kerosene lantern flared from somewhere on the stern. Earlier, the *bosneger* crewmen had said they were going hunting for what they called *gran metie*—large meat. Their word for tapir, she explained. And if they couldn't find that, they would look for *agouti*, a short-eared, large-eyed, rabbit-like rodent.

She opened her eyes after a moment and looked at him. "In your country you don't have to worry about these things."

He shrugged. "We have our own problems—drugs, murders, gangs . . ."

"We have them here, too."

Beam, muttering to himself, returned to the cabin, rummaged through a locker, found what he wanted, and left without looking at them. When the door closed behind him, Kristine said, "My father is planning to replace the current president with one more to his liking. He and I have the same idea—only my idea about who would be the best leader is the opposite of his."

"And how are you going to do this?"

"Through armed struggle if we have to. We'll use my father's money."

"I don't imagine he'll be too happy to learn that."

"You laugh at us? You think we are powerless?"

"No, I was just being realistic. If your father's the miser you say he is—and you want his money, I'd say you're going to have to fight for it."

"Will you help us?"

He was surprised by the sudden earnestness in her voice, at the intensity of her gaze. "With what?"

"We have many weapons—here on the boat. You said you were a policeman. The men need to be trained in their use. Like you, Nick, we are looking for my father."

"And when you find him, what then?"

She wrapped her arms around her legs, head bowed. "I don't want to hurt him," she said softly. She hesitated a moment and then lifted her head. "I mentioned his bank accounts, but my father doesn't trust banks. He has only two accounts—one in Switzerland and one in the Centrale Bank van Suriname. We won't touch either; we want only the gold and currency he keeps hidden in his villas. That is more than enough for our needs."

"Does he know what you want?"

She shook her head. "That's our only chance. I've left a message for him. He doesn't know I'm with the guerrillas. If he'll see me . . ."

She shrugged, her face unreadable, and he wondered what emotions she felt at the thought of her father. He could understand hate—and love for that matter, too, or perhaps a mixture of both. After a moment, he said, "Whatever happens, Kristine, I need to talk to your father before you do anything."

Suddenly, she was on her feet, brushing at her eyes. "I must go now," she said quickly. "Please, don't tell the men what we talked about." And then she turned away and rushed out of the cabin into the humid equatorial night. He followed her out the door and watched her move along the bulwark to the small end compartment where she slept alone. The door shut firmly behind her.

CHAPTER 7

Sunday, September 1, Saramacca River, Suriname

L ying on a canvas cot in Beam's cabin, he fell asleep to the soughing of the wind in the trees. A rainstorm came that night, even though the fall dry season had already begun, sheets of water cascading in torrents from the dark sky. The green canopy of the forest moaned and shrieked, whipped by a violent wind, and heavy branches crashed to the forest floor. He slept fitfully, his sleep punctured by nightmares, and woke early to a vaporous gray dawn. Mist hung over the muddy river, swollen with the storm's runoff.

"Rapids later today," Beam said over a breakfast of manioc-flour pancakes. "And by tomorrow you'll have to continue with dugout canoes."

At ten that morning, they stopped at another plantation, the workers' bungalows in sad disrepair. The stunted banana trees were losing out to the jungle. The few inhabitants still working for Kloos, Carib Indians under a Lebanese foreman, had given up their attempts at farming—Panama disease had wiped out the Gros Michel bananas introduced by Kloos, they said, and leaf spot disease had taken care of the Congo variety. With balata tapping in decline—golf ball covers were now made with balata gum from the Far East—the Indians were logging hardwood trees. The banak tree, possumwood, and Surinamese mahogany, which they floated down river to a sawmill at Kwakoegron.

Kloos had not visited the plantation in over a year.

By midday, a hot, brassy sun beat down on the tug. Fierce stabs of light glared off the river. The guerrillas were working their way along the banks, maneuvering the tug with poles through a narrow stretch and then pulling with tow ropes. They were afraid to enter the water because of the caimans. The *bosnegers* were quieter now, no longer trying to talk to Ferron in Taki-Taki or jabbering among themselves in dialect. The only sound came from flocks of iridescent parrots, squawking raucously in the dense treetops. In late afternoon, under the implacable fury of the sun, they talked to a chief at one of the small villages along the way. Rumors were being spread that Kloos was alive and that his men would soon take their revenge on the guerrillas responsible for shooting down his plane.

That night, after eating, Nick and Kristine found themselves alone again; Beam had gone off conveniently to tinker in the engine room. Ferron wondered for a moment if Kristine, earlier, had asked him to. The two globe lamps in the master cabin dimmed while they talked: Beam had shut down the old diesel generator and the lamps were running off batteries.

For over an hour, they talked about themselves, about their parents, about their lives growing up. He was surprised at the ease with which words poured out of both of them. Usually taciturn where his parents were concerned, he told her about his childhood—about his Italian father's violent temper, the beatings that made him hate the man, his feeble attempts to protect his younger sister Barbara when their father was drunk, and then about the murder of his mother and its aftermath—his dad stabbed to death in prison.

Kristine reached out and laid her hand on his arm. "Your father's gone. That makes it harder to reconcile the past. My father's alive at least. I have a chance to confront him for what he's done. To me, that's worth almost any cost."

She said it with conviction and he thought about that for a moment. "The past may have some answers," he said finally, "but I've got different questions than you. I'm not looking for my father. He was dead to me years ago. I wanted him dead as a child and I was happy when he died in prison. I was afraid somehow he'd get out and come back to finish the job, that he'd kill my sister Barbara and me." He shook his head, remembering the fear; it was only Gran Babbo's love that had finally washed the fear away. "It's my grandfather I care about. He was the one who raised us." He took a deep breath, letting himself feel the pain again. "Someone wanted my grandfather dead and I want to know why."

Later, he walked with her to her compartment where she hugged him before going in and he kissed her on the cheek. Her smile, in the dark night, was radiant. But before he fell asleep, he thought of Janelle. He had to keep some distance from Kristine, he told himself, or he would forget that her cause was different from his.

The next day before they set out again, the four men accompanying Kristine cracked open one of the wood crates at the back of the tug and removed several of the automatic weapons—an odd assortment of new and used submachine guns, semiautomatic carbines, most with Kalishnikov actions, and automatic pistols, all sold by a Czech arms dealer. For himself, to demonstrate their use, Ferron selected a short Valmet M76 Bullpup carbine, with a thirty-shot magazine, and a 9mm Llama double-action automatic, manufactured in Spain. With Kristine at his side, he took the guerrillas into the forest. Martin Beam stayed with the boat.

They followed a deer trail a short distance away from the river. Orchids and bromeliads and other parasitic growths bloomed in profusion. Rotting carcasses of trees added a scent of rich decay to the leaf-mold. There were ant trails everywhere. Along the banks of a tributary creek clusters of labaria sprouted, snake plant, with mottled stems and broad, arrow-shaped leaves. Blue and yellow butterflies fluttered through the air, making their way along the creek toward the Saramacca river.

The sullenness of the men lightened considerably at the sight of the weapons. The older men, Dosu and Moffi, owned single-shot hunting rifles, but had never fired a pistol—the government exercised strict control over handguns and prohibited automatic weapons. Their faces brightened yet more when they saw the devastating effect of the automatics. The youngest of the group, the kid they called Manbote, took to the submachine guns like an otter to water; his face split into a wide, gat-toothed grin as he emptied a thirty-two round magazine into the target, a handkerchief nailed to the trunk of a dead *mora* tree. "*Esi, esi,*" he yelped—"Quick, quick." The men began to dance excitedly, and Moffi clapped Ferron on the back. "Very good man," he tried to say in English.

Ferron, who didn't understand a word, grinned back happily.

The next day, Tuesday afternoon, they reached the Witiston rapids. Eight *bosneger* boatmen of the Matawai tribe, wearing only loin-cloths, helped them haul the crated weapons around the rapids and load them into four dugout canoes. Ferron was sorry to see Beam turn back with the tugboat. He would miss the florid-faced Dutchman and the tug's enclosed cabins, the canvas cot and electric lights, all representing a vestige of comfort and safety in unfamiliar terrain. Kristine, at least, carried a kit that held medical supplies—sulfa drugs, Halazone tablets to disinfect their drinking water, a tropical antiseptic called Furacin, and Paludrine tablets, an anti-malarial medication. The guerrillas shouldered several carryalls, two of them Kristine's, and an old leather satchel that seemed strangely out of place in the jungle.

The dugout canoes were larger than Ferron had imagined. Cut only from the straightest of *wana* trees and hacked out with an adz, heated and then wedged wide with crossboards, the canoes were powered by small outboard motors. In the middle sat a canvas-covered, makeshift cabin, where supplies were lashed down.

Before night fell, they had made the dangerous passage up the rapids at Grassdam without incident. They stopped at Wanati, ate a quick meal of spiced rice and meat, and slept under mosquito netting in the thatched huts of the villagers. At every village, the guerrillas left some of the weapons in the hands of the local *granman*.

A day without rain. An incandescent sun. Searing heat. The high-pitched whine of hungry insects. All morning, Ferron fought a queasy stomach. His forehead was feverish and he found it difficult to breath in the hot, moist air. The smell of gas exhaust nauseated him, and finally he had to ask to ride in the lead canoe, where a man named Wierai stood in the bow and pointed out the passage.

They did not make as much progress as expected. Once, after a particularly rough series of rapids, they had to stop for over two hours while the men cleared out the flooded gas lines of two of the outboard motors. Resting near the river in the shade of a *kuruballi* tree with mimosa-like leaves, he tried to nap to get rid of a headache that had grown steadily worse throughout the day. He dozed off for ten minutes and when he awoke, feeling better, he found Kristine, squatting on her heels in front of him, her hand holding a damp cloth to his forehead.

"Heat exhaustion," she said.

"How much longer, Kristine?"

"One more plantation today, then the fortress in the mountains."

"And if he's not there?"

"We look along the border with French Guiana, cover the Marowijne river from Stoelman's Island to the coast."

He couldn't keep the frustration out of his voice. "How much land does your father own, anyway?" This was a voyage into his own heart of darkness.

"He doesn't own it all," she said patiently. "Some plantations are run under government concession. These aren't all of them. Before you came, we looked for him along the Commewijne river. He has a residence at Destombesburg. We thought that was where he might go first."

"When we find him, do you think he'll see you?"

She leaned forward, resting on her knees in front of him. She looked as fresh as the first day he'd seen her, wearing khaki pants cuffed just above the knee and a white cotton blouse, lustrous black hair cascading off her shoulders, blue eyes that always startled him with their brightness.

"Our plans depend on where he is, Nick." She paused. "We need to overpower his guards. With me inside, we have an advantage."

"And if he doesn't meet you?"

"He'll meet me. I told you, he doesn't know what I'm doing.

And if he does and tries to stop us, I have something he wants."

"What's that?"

Kristine held his gaze for a moment before speaking. "The *bosnegers* have a saying, Nick. If strength doesn't get the cow into the barn, then try one small ripe banana." She smiled. "And that's exactly what I have."

They stopped for a meal in midafternoon at a small bush village. While they ate, squatting on their haunches, an old mongrel, ribs protruding like those of a long-beached whale, crossed the clearing one slow step at a time. Ferron grinned; he felt about as tired as the dog. Halfway across, exhausted by the heat and tormented by biting flies, the dog stopped and looked around, as if adjusting a heavy weight on its back. And then, resolutely, it plodded on until it reached a thin sliver of shade next to a thatched hut where it plopped down heavily, its head flat on the ground between two dusty paws. Ferron thought of Rowdy and wondered how Janelle was doing. He'd meant to call her from Paramaribo the day after his meeting with Oostburg. By now she would be worried. Nothing he could do about it but wait.

On the water again, in single file, they worked their way upriver until dusk, when Wierai gave the order to camp. Moving quickly in the twilight, the *bosnegers* cut straight poles, sharpened at one end, forked at the other, and then laid eave- and ridge-poles to form a shelter. For the roof, they cut fan-shaped leaves from a cluster of graceful manicole, a type of eta palm, secured everything with bush-ropes, and strung up hammocks and mosquito curtains. And then the humid night, the incessant itching, the clothes that chaffed, the sounds of night creatures scurrying over the ground and bats swooping through the air. On the forest floor, not a breath of wind stirred. Despite his exhaustion, Ferron could not sleep. His mind was on overdrive, running over the same images endlessly. Long, slow hours ticked by, each minute a restless eternity, each second a pounding of the heart. And then finally, near dawn, he fell into a state of fitful dozing.

• • •

Another day, another of Kloos's plantations. Kristine talked to the manager, while Ferron dozed under the canopy of one of the canoes. When she returned, he could see that she was agitated. "What is it, Kristine?"

"I know the manager," she said. "A man named Nahar. He's an old friend of my father's from his days in Java. He said news of our progress had been relayed to the plantation by radio."

He crossed his arms and thought about that. They were standing on the river bank, away from the men, their eyes on a caiman that lay on a sand ridge some distance away. "None of the other managers mentioned it."

She shrugged. "No, but apparently each one radioed ahead. My father has followed our progress from the moment we asked about him at the first plantation." She paused, her voice dropping. "He was here two days ago. He left a message for me."

Ferron felt a knot form in his stomach. "What'd he say?"

"He has a jeep with some of his men waiting for us near Tafelberg. They'll drive us to the fortress in the mountains—just you and me. He knows who you are, Nick."

He stared at her, his face tight. "But how—?"

"I don't know. I was just told he wants to see us both." She reached out and touched him on the arm. "Nick, wait for me in Wierai's canoe. I need to talk to the men."

He hesitated, about to ask if he could help, and then did what she asked. For ten minutes, the guerrillas listened to her intently. When she finished talking, the men nodded and went to work clearing out one of the canoes. They took the weapons, all but one of the carryalls and the leather satchel.

Kristine got into the nearly empty dugout and yanked on the throttle. "Come on, Nick," she said, as the motor churned the dark-stained water. "We're going ahead by ourselves."

CHAPTER 8

Thursday, September 5, Tafelberg, Suriname

They were met by four men in two vehicles, one an old military surplus truck—a Dodge 3/4 ton 4 x 4, with a Browning .50 caliber machine gun mounted on a pintle at the rear and a bren gun mounted to the right of the passenger seat; the other, a white, four-door Fiat sedan. The men carried sidearms in holsters strapped to webbed belts.

Before the armed escort arrived at the rendezvous, Kristine had changed into a skirt and blouse and combed her hair, leaving it down. Ferron, with no change of clothes, felt grimy and out of sorts. The day before, he'd tried to wash his clothes in the Saramacca river, but they felt gritty and smelled of mold. The big toe on his left foot poked through the tattered fabric of the old pair of sneakers Beam had given him. They were a size too small. The skin on his neck was irritated from a shave with one of Beam's dull razors.

As they climbed the winding road into the low forested mountains, the terrain changed. The red lateritic soil of the rain forests gave way to sandstone formations and large granite boulders that protruded in humps and ridges among the trees. The swamps disappeared. Rushing streams and falls carried silt and gravel down the narrow valleys. The air, however, was still hot and humid, with clouds building up to the southwest, signaling an afternoon storm. And then, rising out of the forest as they crested a ridge, Ferron saw a broad, table-like mountain.

Tafelberg. His heart picked up a beat and he took a deep breath to calm himself. Somewhere out there was a man with answers.

An hour later, in late afternoon, as they skirted the mountain to the south, the road deteriorated. They bounced through rocky stretches and over sharp ridges, the frame creaking with the twists and jolts, crossed great gullies and rushing streams, the tires digging for traction in the boulder-strewn creeks. A series of switchbacks cut up the side of an old worn-down mountain. The car's motor strained in low gear as they ascended. They traversed a narrow pass and climbed again, working their way along the base of an immense granite cliff that had sheared off and strewn its rubble below. For a moment, clutching an overhead handle to keep from banging his head on the roof, he wondered how Kristine's guerrillas expected to cover the distance. On foot, carrying heavy weapons, it would take them at least twenty-four hours.

Kloos's fortress was aptly named. Rounding a sharp bend, they passed beneath a series of pillbox fortifications linked by a rock wall that circled a ledge halfway up the steep western flank of the mountain. The road cut back twice before reaching the ledge and finally passed through an iron gate and came to an end near a grove of trees. At the back of the ledge, which was the size of a football field, sat a huge hunting lodge made of rough-hewn logs. Behind the lodge rose the steep face of the mountain and to one side a stream trickled out of a crevice, forming a pool before disappearing into the ground. With enough supplies trucked in, the place was a self-contained fortress, easy to defend, with access only from below.

The vehicles pulled to a stop in front of a long building to the east of the lodge—a new structure of steel beams and corrugated tin sheeting, with no windows. To one side stood a large tank for diesel fuel, next to a smaller shed holding a generator. When the doors of the larger building were opened and they drove inside, he was surprised to see a helicopter on wheels and several other vehicles, including military jeeps, one hooked up to a howitzer. From the looks of things, Kloos feared more than the *bosneger* guerrillas.

Kristine looked at him and he could see the tension in her

face. "It's been seven years since I've seen him," she said, as they stood by the car waiting for directions.

A door opened at one end of the warehouse and a tall man with a cane moved with stiff steps into the building. He stopped and squinted as if unable to see in the gloom. Behind him, bright light cascaded into the room, extending toward the car in a long, thin streak. Kristine took an awkward step forward, moving into the light, and then hesitated. Her body was suffused with radiance, a nimbus of liquid gold highlighting every feature. Ferron thought he'd never seen her look more beautiful—nor more vulnerable.

The tall man looked at them for a long moment, his eyes adjusting to the change in light, and then suddenly he seemed to totter. Ferron heard Kristine's quick gasp and saw her hands grip her skirt. The old man took two painful steps forward, then dropped his cane and raised both arms, and with a small cry Kristine rushed into her father's embrace.

As he watched them, the loss of his grandfather struck Ferron as never before.

Dinner was a sumptuous affair, a banquet for three. He and Kristine sat to each side of Kloos, at one end of a long refectory table imported from Italy. Their place settings were of silver, with delftware plates, and crystal goblets for the French wine. At one end of the room, an Italian tapestry hung from the wall. There were paintings of minor Dutch artists of the seventeenth century arrayed along another wall. Large pieces of dark-stained furniture completed the furnishings—a credenza and two bureaus for linens.

He had already seen the rest of the lodge—the sitting room and master den with library, the kitchen and pantry, the upper level with bedrooms to each side along a central corridor. The walls in the bedrooms were plastered and painted white; the ceilings had massive open beams that looked like they came from a nineteenth-century clipper. Eight-foot tall wardrobes with baroque arches and curlicues graced each room, along with large beds. There were tiled bathrooms with tubs and wood-stoked water heaters at each end of the upper level, and electric lights, powered by a diesel generator.

Over a first course of vegetable soup, served by a Carib Indian woman, Kloos turned to him and said, "You were smart to bring my daughter with you. I don't think I would have seen you otherwise. How did you find her anyway?"

Ferron wiped his lips with a cloth napkin. "You might say through Hans Oostburg."

Kloos nodded, and then, as if his mind had gone off on another track, said, "These are dangerous times in our country."

"Oostburg told me—but I'm not interested in your politics. I'm here because of letters you wrote to Beppe Aprico and to my grandfather, Thomas Gage."

Kloos reached for a piece of bread and tore it into chunks, dropping the pieces into his soup. "What did Oostburg tell you about me?"

"He said your family had plantations in Java before the war— that you had managed to liquidate your assets before the Indonesians gained their independence."

Kloos laughed and then grimaced, his body stiffening. Kristine looked at him with concern. "What is it, father?"

"My back—one of the effects of my plane being shot down. It hasn't quite healed." He pointed to the cane, which was leaning against his chair. "I don't normally need that, but I shouldn't complain. I'm lucky to be alive." He turned back to Ferron. "Is that all Oostburg had to say?"

"He said you were wealthy when you came to Suriname after the war."

Kloos snorted. "What he didn't tell you was what that wealth cost me." He waved at Kristine. "Kristine's mother was my second wife. I'd been married two years to a girl from Eindhoven when I had to go to Java in March of 1940. I left my wife and a young son behind me. My family ran two rubber plantations and a bauxite mine near Bandoeng. The government in The Hague had warned us that the Japanese were making plans to conquer the region. We knew we couldn't hold on much longer anyway; the people were agitating for independence." Kloos laid down his spoon, his soup untouched. "In May, while I was still in Java, the Nazis invaded Holland. My first wife Breechje and my son Thoden were living with my parents in Rotterdam. They were all killed."

A moment passed before Ferron spoke. "I'm sorry to hear that."

"Nothing I could do. If I'd have been there, I'd be dead, too. The flat where we lived was destroyed in a massive bombing raid." Kloos shoved his bowl aside, slopping soup on the table, and the Carib woman removed the bowl and wiped the table clean in the same motion. "When I heard the news, my life ended. The money didn't matter. The rubber plantations, the bauxite mine—" He waved his hand. "What did I care? I was ready to walk away. They only mattered because the Allies needed rubber and bauxite. But I soon found out that the émigré government in London wouldn't be able to help the colonies. I contacted a British officer in Singapore to offer my services to the Allies. The man worked for the Special Operations Executive. He sent me back to Java in an attempt to organize the natives against the Japanese." Kloos sighed. "It wasn't an easy matter," he said. "The Japanese played off the people's desire for independence. Most of the nationalists hoped for a Japanese victory; they wanted a quick collapse of the colonial regime."

"How long did you stay there?"

Kloos looked at the ceiling and thought for a moment, eyes squinting painfully, then went on as if he hadn't heard the question. "Despite the nationalists, I managed to put together a group of armed men—natives and Europeans. You met Nahar at the plantation yesterday. He was one of them. A good man." Kloos took a sip of wine, his hand shaking, and then continued: "I was still in Java when the Japs invaded in February. This was in '42. We fought for about three weeks until we were overcome by superior forces. Finally, I escaped, along with several of my best men, all natives. We made our way by boat to Sumatra. We had to listen on the wireless to news that the Japanese had released Sukarno from detention and allowed him to return to Java to fight the Allies. We lived in the jungles there for months— long, hard months . . . The Japs were tracking us down and slowly wiping us out. You wouldn't believe the atrocities committed— on both sides."

A distant look came over Kloos's eyes and he fell silent for a moment. The Carib maid was serving a main course of beefsteak, potatoes and gravy, and peas. She set another bottle of Mouton

Cadet burgundy on the table and brought out a fresh pitcher of iced water.

Kloos looked at the food. "It's hard to eat when I think about what they did to Sastro, one of my best men. Sastro smoked the cigarette they called *kretek*—made from tobacco and ground cloves rolled in a piece of corn leaf. He was addicted to it. Whenever I smelled it at night, I knew he was near. We found his head on a stake one day, with what was left of it stuffed with the cigarettes. They'd burnt his ears to a crisp, sliced off his nose, and cut his lips into thin strips. His eyes were pried open with bamboo shoots. My men responded in kind. I couldn't control their hatred . . . perhaps I shared it myself." He paused, his breath ragged. "We were betrayed once by a *tengkulaks*, what you would call a middleman or a broker, a man named Karta who bought tealeaf from the natives and sold it to the tea factories. When we found out, we came back and chased him down a road lined with tall damar trees. The man was too frightened to scream. Wongso caught him." Kloos's lips curled back from his teeth in a hideous grin, his eyes wild. "You would not want to meet Wongso. A very cruel man. Before Wongso was through, he died a horrible death."

Kloos stopped suddenly, breathing hard. He shoved his chair away from the table. "I'm sorry," he said. "I say I won't talk and then I do. After all this time, the memories . . ." He took a deep breath and sat without moving.

Ferron looked at Kristine. "I'm sorry," he said. "I shouldn't have asked."

Kristine's head barely moved in response. She looked sick.

Kloos stood without his cane, and moved to a sideboard. With trembling hands, he poured himself a tumbler of bourbon and drank it down in one swallow. After a moment, he turned around, one hand on the credenza for support, his face composed. "Forgive me, *meneer* Ferron. You were asking me about my letters to your grandfather and his friend." He cleared his throat, which had gone hoarse. "Have you talked to Beppe?"

"Not about your letters. Aprico's dead—and so is my grandfather. I think both of them were murdered. I thought you might know why it was done—or who's responsible."

Kloos said nothing for a moment, his face dark. "I didn't

know they were dead." He ran a hand across his face. "You want to know how I met your grandfather?"

"I've read a diary he wrote, but there was nothing in it about either you or Aprico."

Kloos set his empty whiskey glass on the credenza and returned to the table. The maid helped him into his seat. The man seemed to have aged in the last ten minutes, his face haggard and worn. "I don't have much energy after the plane crash," he said, his voice shaky. We can talk more tomorrow." He pointed to the food. "Eat," he said.

For the next fifteen minutes, they ate in silence, Kloos's eyes focused in an indeterminate distance, Ferron barely able to restrain his questions. The old man's mind seemed to have wandered far away, all animation gone from his face; he reacted like a robot, cutting the meat and eating it mechanically. And then, without warning, coming back from faraway, he said, "It took the British over a year before they pulled me out of Sumatra. They thought I was dead. The SOE had set up an intelligence network reporting from the Far East through the Vatican. I was sent there by my handlers. I wanted to go; I wanted to do anything I could to fight the Nazis; I wanted to kill the murders who took my wife and son." Kloos's voice had risen, becoming shrill. He straightened the silverware near his plate, aware that he had pounded the table. He shrugged. "Eventually, I was sent to northern Italy with your grandfather and Beppe."

"What did you do there?"

"We helped the partisans drive out the Germans."

"Why you?"

"Like your grandfather, I knew Italian."

"Did my grandfather ever mention a girl named Carla Ceruti?"

Kloos thought for a moment. "Thomas didn't talk much about women. It was Beppe who found a lover among the partisans."

"Do you remember her name?"

The Dutchman shook his head.

"Did my grandfather talk about someone betraying him in Rome, before you met him?"

"None of us talked about the past. We had too much in the

present to deal with."

"Such as?"

"Watching out for the *Nazifascisti*."

He felt a rising sense of frustration. Kloos was voluble about what didn't matter and laconic about what did. The maid was clearing the table. Kloos said something to her in a language Ferron didn't understand and the woman nodded. "We have chilled ice cream," Kloos announced proudly.

Kristine stood. "Will you excuse me, father? I'm going to my room." She walked over and kissed him on the brow. "It's been a long day." Moving behind her father, she turned to Ferron, her eyes trying to tell him something, but all she said was, "Good night, Nick. We'll talk again later."

He stared at her as she left the room, a puzzled look on his face. Kristine hadn't spoken once during the whole meal and he wondered why her father appeared not to have noticed. Did the old man think she came only to lead Ferron to him? Did he have nothing to say to his daughter? And what did Kristine plan to do now? He would have to speak to her before they fell asleep. It was already past eleven.

While he and Kloos waited for dessert, Ferron said, "My grandfather mentioned several people in his diary. May I see if you recognize any names?"

"Go ahead."

"What about a man named Elio Pavan? He worked with the OVRA."

Kloos shook his head. "Never heard of him."

"How about Sergio Benelli? He was a Germanophile who worked with Mussolini's protection service."

Kloos scratched his beard. "I don't recognize the name. As I said, we didn't talk about the past."

"What about a man called Eagle Jack? He worked with the British in Switzerland."

"Eagle Jack?" Kloos paused for a second. "Yes, he was a high-ranking officer in the SOE."

"Who was he? Did you know him?"

"Not really. He was pointed out to me once by Monsignor Montini in the corridors of the Vatican. I don't believe anyone knew his real name."

"He worked for the Vatican?"

"None of us worked for the Vatican. It was merely a safe haven. As I said, he worked for the British."

"Like you."

"Like me and many others."

Ferron pursed his lips in aggravation. The old man's faded blue eyes told him nothing. The Dutchman had to know more than he was letting on, and his reticence was baffling. He tried again. "I noticed from my grandfather's letters that you wrote to him several times right after the war and then nothing for what? Forty-some years? I don't understand that."

"Only a fool writes to someone who doesn't respond."

"My grandfather didn't respond?" He was surprised. Gran Babbo was a man who enjoyed writing.

"Your grandfather wasn't interested in old war buddies."

"I don't know about that. He took my sister and me to Italy several times when we were younger, to the OSS reunions. Did you ever attend?"

"For a while, but like all things, one loses interest in time."

"For some people interest grows with time."

The Dutchman smiled thinly. "Let's just say there was a misunderstanding between me and the others—and then I was too busy starting over in Suriname. Only Beppe bothered to keep in touch. That's how I learned about your father and mother. Did your grandfather ever tell you? It was Beppe who introduced the two of them at one of the reunions in Verona."

Ferron looked at Kloos in surprise. "My grandfather never talked about my parents."

"They would never have married if it wasn't for Beppe. That's why he was so eager to help when your father ended up in prison."

"Help with what? My father died in prison."

Kloos snorted. "Exactly. It was one of Beppe's boys who knifed him—as a favor to your grandfather, probably on Gage's orders."

He stared at Kloos, swallowed hard. "Impossible," he said, shaking his head.

"You didn't know?"

"Gran Babbo would never—" He stopped, overwhelmed by

the implications. His grandfather had ordered the death of the man who killed his daughter. His son-in-law. He'd taken his own vengeance for the murder of Nick's mother, doing what Nick had always wanted to do as a child . . . If that were true—and he was suddenly filled with certainty—were the deaths of Aprico and his grandfather simply another vendetta for an act that took place years before? It was possible. For the Italians, vengeance was a dish best tasted cold. He felt a shudder come over him. Would the past never cease to haunt him?

His mouth was dry. He took a drink of water, his hand shaking. "Is that why you warned them?" he asked. "Was someone from Italy out for vengeance? A relative of my father's?"

"My letters had nothing to do with your father. I don't know that Franco Ferroni had relatives who cared about him."

"Then why write to warn Aprico and my grandfather? Who was threatening the three of you?"

Kloos closed his eyes, the lines on his face deepening. "I'm very tired, *meneer* Ferron. Tomorrow—"

"Just answer me that. It should be simple. How did you know there was a threat? And why to all three of you?"

Kloos sighed. The ice cream in their bowls was melting. He took a bite and then sat back in his chair. "I have contacts throughout the world," he said. "Businessmen, government officials, people I met during the war—other men whose interests coincide with mine. Someone has been putting out feelers recently—asking about the three of us, trying to track us down." He shrugged. "Perhaps a former enemy agent bent on vengeance, an ex-fascist who has come to power in Italy and fears we might have information that could implicate him in crimes of the regime."

"After all this time? What information? My grandfather said nothing about this."

Kloos's head had sunk to his chest, his eyes tightly shut, and he was breathing heavily, almost as if he'd fallen asleep. Ferron could feel his own exhaustion settling over him. "What information are you talking about?" he asked again, his voice hoarse.

The Dutchman slowly lifted his head, breathed heavily

through his nose, then twisted his neck. There was an audible crack of cervical vertebrae. The old man thrust back his shoulders and grimaced. "Police files," he muttered. "Compiled by the OVRA during the war."

"And where are these files?"

Kloos shrugged. "Supposedly they were destroyed by the Germans . . ."

"But they weren't?"

"Someone fears otherwise. The three of us were trying to recover them at the end, but we were betrayed—" Kloos paused and pulled at his beard. "No one knew who was responsible. When things went bad at the end, we all got out on our own. That's all I can tell you." He slid his chair back from the table and gestured to the maid, who was standing just inside the door. "*Meneer* Ferron, I'm an old man and very tired. I'm going to bed now. I trust you can find your way to your room on your own. I'll see you in the morning. Until then, *Goede nacht.*"

CHAPTER 9

Friday, September 6, Tafelberg, Suriname

Ferron switched on a small bedside lamp and looked at his watch. It was just after one a.m. and the lodge was silent. He had knocked lightly on Kristine's door when he first came upstairs, but there'd been no response. Unable to sleep, his mind running over the day's events and the conversation with Kloos, he slipped out of bed and got dressed.

Kloos's guards, most of them Carib Indians, were not as ostentatious as the policemen at Hans Oostburg's villa. Ferron had seen them outside earlier, moving silently along the wall at the outer edge of the mountain ledge, and around the lodge and outlying buildings. They were well armed with automatic rifles and submachine guns. Inside the building, there was no overt sign of security. Kloos slept in a bedroom on the ground floor, off the master den and library. Whether his room was watched or not, Ferron had no way of knowing. He extinguished his lamp and when his eyes adjusted to the darkness left his room and moved silently down the corridor toward Kristine's room.

He knocked lightly and when there was no response, he tried the handle. The door opened in his hand. He stood on the threshold and stared at the bed, unable to tell if she was there. He felt for the light switch, found it, and flipped it on. The light overhead was dim. Kloos's generator ran at its slowest speed at night, providing just enough electricity to power a bulb of weak wattage. Kristine was not in her room. He slid his hand inside the sheets to see if they were still warm. He couldn't detect any heat—and that meant she was probably not in the bathroom at the end of the hall. What was she up to now? He knew she wanted her father's gold and currency, hidden somewhere in the fortress, but would she look for it on her own, without talking to her father first?

He heard a distant, muffled report. Recognized it as a single shot from an automatic rifle. He swore. If Kristine had stepped outside, the guards would kill her. Kloos had warned them about that earlier. A sudden burst of automatic fire punctured the night, clearer now. He moved quickly out of her room and toward the stairs leading to the ground floor. Halfway down the stairs, he heard shouts from below. A door was opened and men rushed out into the darkness. Bullets thudded into the wood logs of the lodge, and then came the sound of glass shattering in the den. There were windows there overlooking the valley below. At the bottom of the stairs, he saw the Carib maid, hurrying toward Kloos's bedroom. She said something he didn't understand, her voice raised in fear. He didn't wait to see what she wanted. He charged through the door leading outside and across the wood-railed porch, took the three steps to the ground and hit the dirt, rolling to his left in case someone had spotted him in the light of the arc lamp that illuminated a wide half-circle in front of the entrance.

There was no cover to either side. To his left and right, under the eaves of the building, a series of arc lamps cast wide cones of light along the lodge's façade. Someone had turned the generator to high speed, and the lights were so bright that beyond them he could see nothing. Gunfire erupted to the west, somewhere in the grove of trees behind the generator shed. Headlights stabbed across the rock ledge, racing toward the warehouse. Flashes of fire spouted from the vehicle.

He crawled toward the base of the lodge, looking for protection. The porch had an overhang and he crawled into the darkness below it, hoping there were no snakes. Until he could figure out what was happening, he was better off under cover, not out in the open. But where in hell was Kristine?

A terrible explosion lit up the night. He turned to see a ball of fire billow into the black sky—the diesel tank near the generator shed had gone up. The vehicle he'd seen a moment before—a jeep—had plowed straight into the tank. A man lay on the ground, writhing and screaming in pain as the flames devoured him. The shed housing the generator burst into flames. As Ferron watched, the lights along the building's façade went black. There'd be no power now.

Blackness—interrupted only by dying flames and the flashes of automatic weapons. Had the guerrillas made it to the fortress? But why attack before Kristine could talk to her father? Unless she'd never intended to talk to him in the first place. She was inside the walls where she could overpower the guards—a message on a two-way radio, a walk along the fortifications, maybe that was all it took. Knowing she was the Dutchman's daughter, what man locked in his pillbox would deny her entrance?

What would the old man do? There was no sign of activity in the lodge. He could see men advancing across the ledge's open plateau, firing into the building, but no one responded to the fire.

A light stabbed out of the darkness, blinding him. He ducked his head and rolled to the side. A stream of bullets tore up the ground ahead of him and then another burst thudded into the ground behind. He stopped, waiting for the shot that would finish him off. What in hell had he gotten into—coming into a country at war with itself? He was a fool to have thought he could uncover the truth. Were they going to kill him like a snake in its hole?

Men rushed past him and into the lodge, firing as they ran, their boots thundering over the wood floor of the porch. These guerrillas were not Kristine's *bosnegers*—not unless they'd all found boots. Moffi and his men had all either gone barefoot or worn Japanese sandals. He heard voices shouting at him, words he didn't understand. He looked up to see three black men, their rifles pointed at his head. One of the men gestured for him to come out. They led him away under guard, as firing in the lodge behind him stopped.

Was Kloos dead? The Dutchman had told him nothing of use, had furnished no names, provided no clues, pointed out no track to follow. Nothing except a rumor. And knowing that someone from the past was tracking down the three former agents didn't help. A dead end. He tried to steel his mind for what lay ahead. He was back where he started, with nothing to show for his labor—only now he was in the hands of the guerrillas.

CHAPTER 10

Friday-Sunday, September 6-8, Suriname

For two days he trudged through the jungle with the three *bosnegers*, a rifle prodding him in the back. None of the blacks spoke English. At night, they tied him to a tree, and he slept in fear that some poisonous creature would sting or bite him. Each morning he felt weaker and he knew the bats were sipping his blood while he slept. After the first night, he found nine bites and eleven after the second. Martin Beam had told him about the *Desmodus*, the vampire bat that fed only on blood, its gut too short to digest anything else, even an insect. Their front teeth were so sharp sleeping victims never felt the incision. As the anticoagulant in their saliva worked, they sucked up the drops of blood in their curved tongues.

At noon on the second day, they were joined by a larger group, several of the men carrying burlap sacks. None of the new men spoke English. That night, they reached a river and camped in the thatch huts of an abandoned village.

When he awoke on the third day, he heard the men shouting and singing. He stepped bleary-eyed from the hut to see Kristine standing in the morning sun before him, a grin on her face. He hesitated, overcome by conflicting emotions, happy to see her again yet distrustful of her actions. She was wearing a tan shirt, knotted at the waist, and short khaki pants. Her blue eyes sparkled and her teeth gleamed white against her brown face. In one hand, she held the leather satchel he'd seen with her earlier in the dugout canoes.

Seeing his hesitation, she said, "Nick, I was worried about you. I only learned where you were yesterday. I came immediately. These men didn't know who you were. They're from another tribe. I'm just glad you're alive." She stepped toward him but he didn't move. He was still angry that she hadn't told him her plans. He flinched when she reached out and touched him with her free hand. "I didn't kill my father, Nick. He escaped. But we have his money."

He stared at her, wondering if he should believe her. "Kloos escaped?"

"The lodge had a secret exit to an underground cavern. He got away by jeep, but we found where he stored the gold." She pointed to the burlap sacks in the clearing. "These bags are full of U.S. currency. The gold is already being shipped down river." He could see the exultation in her face. "Now we can fight my father and the men he supports with the same weapons he used for so long—money."

"And your father's alive?"

She nodded. "We destroyed everything—the lodge, the warehouse, the fortifications. We blew them up using his own explosives."

"But he'll just go to another of his plantations."

"Yes, but the plantations are not so impregnable. He'll never again have the money to build a fortress in the mountains."

Behind her, he caught a glimpse of Moffi's powerful physique, his right hand clutching a submachine gun. A rare smile appeared on the black man's proud face. He stepped forward and spoke quickly in taki-taki, gesturing with the gun.

"What'd he say?"

"He thanked you for your help. He said you left the front door open."

"I was looking for you." Her eyes were locked on his. "I'm glad you got what you wanted. For me—" He shrugged. "I have no answers. It was all a waste of time."

"Nick," she said, "I have the answers you want." She lifted the satchel in both hands. "I had them all along, I just didn't know it."

She showed him the ledger then, the names and addresses of

the men and women her father had blackmailed, dates and amounts of money paid next to each name. Along with the ledger, packed tightly in the leather satchel, were stacks of documents bound with sisal cord, each one a secret police file dating to the 1940s. The documents were not alphabetized and were clearly a very small part of a much larger group of files. Each document contained a series of cross-references and varied in length from one to three pages of closely packed text, written in a crabbed cursive that was difficult to decipher. From the number of digits in the cross-references, there had to have been thousands of files. This group appeared to be a collection that someone had hastily thrown together, following criteria that were not immediately evident.

"These files were compiled by the OVRA," Ferron said, squatting on his heels. "Mussolini's secret police. My grandfather spent months in Rome during the war, trying to gain access to things like this. But why did your father pick these people to blackmail?" He pointed to the names in the ledger.

"There's a dossier for every name, but I don't know enough Italian to read what crimes they committed."

He had skimmed a few lines of several of the documents at random. "No crimes," he said. "Or at least not obvious ones. Most of the files seem to deal not with enemies of the regime, but with fascist agents. Look." He pointed to one file. "It shows where this man worked and who he was following, and has cross-references to their files." He turned the document over. The crabbed handwriting continued on the back. "And there's a list of the people whose arrests he was directly responsible for and the disposition of the cases."

Kristine nodded abstractedly, her mind on the ledger. "Businessmen and politicians," she said.

"What?"

"The names in the ledger, they have to be prominent people, people with money. No one else would be bothered by blackmail."

Ferron nodded, his face darkening. Kloos had strung him along like a fool. "Your father lied to me—"

Kristine's eyes flashed. "I've heard tell the devil is evil."

He heard the sarcasm in her voice, even though gentle.

"You're saying I'm naive."

"The first time they meet him, my father strikes everyone as a good man. Perhaps you judged him by appearances. Like you, he's a handsome man." She shrugged. "He lied more by omission than by what he said."

He was conscious of the sun beating down on his body, but was too exhausted to seek shade. "I believed everything he told me," he said tiredly. "It could all have been a pack of lies."

"These names don't lie." She pointed to the ledger. Her forehead was beaded with sweat. "That's how my father acquired so much wealth so quickly." She paused. "There's one thing that bothers me. Look at the dates. He hasn't asked for money from any of these people for over a year."

"Perhaps he had all he needed."

She shook her head. "These are all Italian names. I know he's been blackmailing a businessman in the United States. A big man with contacts in the government of your country."

He was skeptical. He brushed absentmindedly at the flies swarming around his face. "Are you sure?"

"We have clerks in the Ministry of Foreign Affairs. My father used his influence to gain foreign aid and other concessions from the Americans. I think he bribed someone who's very powerful. I think *de Amerikaan* is the one behind all the attempts on my father's life. The Guerrilla Commando shot down my father's plane because we knew he was carrying important papers, but we've never attacked him in his plantations. Other men have."

He looked at her, trying to follow what she was saying, each breath he took slow and labored. The humidity was suffocating. He dropped his head, shut his eyes for a moment, squeezing the lids tightly, and then opened them. "If that's true, you're saying it's an American who killed my grandfather."

She nodded. "Someone who thinks your grandfather was working with my father."

"And Beppe Aprico," he added, blinking quickly. "They were all in northern Italy together."

Kristine riffled through a stack of documents. "Perhaps all three men had files like these. Men they were blackmailing . . ."

He considered the documents stacked on the satchel lying on the ground beside him. "I don't think so. I went through my grandfather's papers. There's no sign he knew about this."

"Nick—" Kristine paced back and forth in front of him. He lifted his head to look at her. "We have to find out who the American is." She squared around to face him. "He must be stopped."

He stared at her for a long moment, his eyes squinting against the sunlight. "Why are you so concerned about an American, Kristine? Your father's influence is worth nothing without these files."

"Not to the man he's been bribing. My father knows something about him—and that makes my father a threat. The American's fingers work the strings that make our government jump. He's helping to keep our current leader in power. I want him stopped—but you should want him, too, Nick. He has to be the man behind your grandfather's death."

He eased himself to the ground, stretching his stiff legs and then crossing them beneath him. Again he was conscious of the sun beating down, its glare unmerciful, of the stifling air. A weight pressed down on his chest, making each breath an effort. The *bosnegers* had divided up the burlap bags and were preparing to leave. They slid the dugouts from the bank into the muddy river. Moffi and his younger brother Tano waited by one of the empty canoes for Kristine and Nick.

"My grandfather's diary stopped after his first mission," Ferron said. "He never mentioned Aprico or your father. But there has to be more. I remember as a kid in Italy, at the OSS reunions, other agents used to ask Gran Babbo whether he had learned anything, if he'd found *il traditore*. I have friends in intelligence who've told me that during all the years my grandfather was in the CIA, he never gave up trying to learn the identity of someone who had betrayed him in the war. I used to think it might have been Beppe Aprico. The man was a drug boss, a criminal with tentacles everywhere. My grandfather helped me infiltrate his syndicate. I thought maybe Gran Babbo suspected Aprico all along. And then when I saw the letters from your father, I thought it might have been him."

Kristine knelt in front of him, listening intently, her face serious. "But you said my father warned the other two about a threat to their safety."

He nodded, tracing a circle in the dirt with his forefinger. "It's all very confusing. I feel like a cat chasing its tail." He paused and then went on angrily. "I come to Suriname and what happens? I find myself in the middle of a revolution. The man I'm looking for—your father—has everybody in the country against him."

"Not everybody, Nick." She placed a hand on his knee. "It's not that easy. He has all the people in power behind him—the military, the wealthy landowners, the multinational corporations, the leaders of a repressive government."

"It has nothing to do with me."

Kristine bit her lip and removed her hand. She looked away for a moment and then said, "Nick, we have a saying—even here in Suriname where everyone ignores us: We say the world is a horse's tail; it waves in all directions. What you do affects what I do. What your country does in mine affects me. We're all connected, but some are on top and some on the bottom. Big dogs do not bite each other. They bite the little dogs."

He shrugged. "So for protection the little dogs run in a pack."

"The *pikkie dagoes* are too scared, they hide under the porch."

He grinned, despite himself. He knew she was referring to him. "It didn't do me much good, did it?"

She smiled back. "But you're not really a *pikkie dagoe*. You're strong. You can help us while you help yourself."

"I need to talk to your father again."

"Nick, it may take months." She gestured around at the jungle. "We may never find him. He'll think both of us were behind the raid. Have you thought of that? You're his enemy now."

"Then what do you want me to do?"

"You know Italian. Talk to the people on this list. They were all spies and informers. They may know the American my father was blackmailing."

He snorted. "These fascists could just as easily be the people behind the killings. An Italian tried to find my grandfather before he was murdered. Like you said, the killer may think they're all involved in blackmail." He waved his hand in the direction of the ledger and then stopped, aware for the first time that he'd been thinking of Aprico as another victim just like his grandfather. But the man was killed by DEA agents on a government raid. It was hard to believe someone in Italy was responsible for that.

Kristine got to her feet and wiped the perspiration from her forehead. The *bosnegers* had removed their combat fatigues and wore only loin-cloths. Most of the dugouts were moving downstream, the sound of their outboard motors fading into the distance. The air vibrated with the shrill whine of cicadas. Ferron pushed himself off the ground and dusted the seat of his pants. She was right: there was nothing to do now but track down the names of the people Kloos had been blackmailing. See if there was a connection with an American. He would have to buy more clothes in Paramaribo. And new shoes and socks. He still had his money belt with his passport and credit cards and a wrinkled sheaf of water-stained twenty-dollar bills. A hefty bank account at home. All he'd paid for in Suriname was one night in the guest house. He owed Martin Beam for the trip upriver. He'd give the money to Kristine to pass along.

As they walked toward the dugout where Moffi and Tano waited patiently, he said, "And your father, Kristine, what about him?"

"We let him escape this time," she said softly, "but if we have to we'll kill him."

CHAPTER 11

Sunday, September 8, Zanderij airport, Suriname

He called Janelle Dutton at her cabin in Durango from a pay phone at Zanderij airport. Two weeks had passed since his departure. He missed the coolness of the mountains.

"How's Rowdy doing? he asked.

"Rowdy's fine, Nick, but someone broke into the cabin the day you left."

He paused. "What happened?"

"They didn't steal anything that I've noticed. They burned all the papers."

"What?"

"They burned what you left of your grandfather's diary in the fireplace. All the letters, too. The only thing I have is the last section you mailed back from Miami."

Damn. Someone was after more than just his grandfather. "I'm worried about you," he said.

"It's not me they want, Nick. They haven't been back since."

"I don't like it. You tell the sheriff?"

"I didn't know if you'd want me to."

He cleared his throat, thinking, wondering if that would have convinced the sheriff Gran Babbo was murdered. "It doesn't matter now, Janelle. Whoever did it is long gone."

"That's not all the news, Nick. Barbara called me last weekend. The police chief in Tucson got in touch with her. Said something about how you listed her as next of kin on your personnel form."

"What'd he want?"

"They fired you for insubordination. Were you supposed to stay in Tucson?"

"I didn't expect to be gone so long."

"Well, he said you didn't show up for your hearing—and that, along with what you did on the raid—were grounds for dismissal."

"Yeah, well, I was out the door anyway."

"Did you hear about the hiker that got lost here?"

"What hiker?"

"I just read about it in the paper today. Some guy's been missing in the mountains for two weeks. They just started looking for him."

"What took 'em so long?"

"He didn't tell anyone where he was going. Some retired guy with a wife in a nursing home in Telluride. His friends in Durango got a postcard, saying he'd be arriving last weekend. When he didn't show up, they called the police in Telluride. His car was parked in front of his house. The neighbors said he'd left on a hiking trip with a backpack. They finally figured out he'd planned to walk the whole route."

"Are you thinking what I'm thinking?"

"What?"

"Maybe Gran Babbo's alive."

Janelle was silent.

"I know I'm grasping at straws," he said, "but . . . I don't know, I just can't accept that Gran Babbo shot himself. And if he didn't, he sure as hell wouldn't let someone else sneak up on him like that. He was too smart—and too cautious. He'd never let himself be trapped like that."

"What are you saying, Nick?"

"I'm saying the body we found was not Gran Babbo's—it was some hiker he'd taken in."

"Shall I tell the Sheriff? When are you coming back?"

"The Sheriff already thinks I'm a lunatic. It won't do any good now." He paused. "Listen, Janelle. I hate to impose on you, but it's going to be a while before I get back. I'm leaving for Italy later today."

"What's going on?"

"I'm looking for someone."

She didn't respond for a moment. "What happened in Suriname?"

"I found Theunis Kloos." Ferron hesitated. No reason to mention Kristine. The details were too complicated to get into over the phone. "The old man didn't know it, but he sent me off on another track," he said. "I hope it doesn't take long."

"Well, if Rowdy can wait, I can, too," she said.

"The kid's on a KLM flight to Amsterdam," Vasco Akkad said into the phone. "With a connection on British Airways to Milan's Malpensa." Akkad was in the U.S. Embassy in Paramaribo, sitting in a chair opposite the desk of the CIA station chief. "He'll be leaving later this afternoon. Do you want us to tag along?"

The old man on the other end of the line cleared his throat. "No, stay where you are." He was in the Russell Building, one of the Senate's two office buildings to the north of the Capitol, standing alone at an assistant's desk in a small room overlooking Delaware Avenue. The phone was not secure. "I'll have someone pick up our friend in Italy." He paused, looking down at the traffic, halted by an accident at the intersection with D Street. Two cars heading toward Union Station had tried to fit side by side into the same lane. "What about your other objective—the Dutchman?"

"We're working on that."

"You're not on vacation."

"We're working hard. It shouldn't be long now. Someone else got there first and muddied the water."

"Well, remember what I told you." The old man's voice hardened. "I don't want you fooling around. You piss against the wind and you'll get your shirt wet."

"Hey, not to worry," Akkad said cheerfully, trying to repress a wide grin. "It's so fuckin' humid down here our shirts are already soaked. A little more pee won't hurt nobody."

Book Two

Embers of a Dying Fire

"The past really does belong to us. Good and evil, joy and sorrow—the past belongs to us, and according to Christian theology not even God can undo that which has been done."
—Benito Mussolini, *The Pontine Musings*, 12 August 1943

CHAPTER 1

Tuesday, September 10, Pavia, Italy

Patches of fog drifted off the flooded rice paddies of the Lombard plain. Ferron eased the Alfa Romeo 164 around a gentle curve on the narrow, provincial road running between Badile and the Certosa di Pavia, south of Milan. At five-thirty in the morning, the air was suffused with a pale blue light turning to gold at the horizon. Rising thin and narrow through the fog, rows of wispy cypresses and spirelike poplars delineated with columnar precision the boundaries between fields. Ahead of him, he could barely make out the taillights of a Piaggio "Ape," a three-wheeled truck called the "Bee," and then he was flashing his yellow lights in warning and sweeping around the vehicle. The sedan's tires whistled over the slick, black ribbon of deserted road that stretched into the hazy distance. It had rained most of the night and the road was still wet, but the car handled magnificently.

Monday afternoon, after his arrival in Milan, he had rented the powerful "S" version of the 3-litre Alfa Romeo sedan at an *Autonoleggio Maxicar* on Corso Buenos-Aires. The representative who handled the rental was a sleek, smooth-talking Italian in his early thirties, a sharp operator who wore a year's salary's worth of clothes—a gray, chalk-stripe wool suit with foulard square in the breast pocket, burgundy silk tie, hand-made leather shoes, and a Philippe Charriol twenty-four hour wristwatch, which he flashed when he offered Ferron a gold-plated Montblanc pen to sign the contract. Zebra and gazelle skins were tacked to the wall of his office.

Aware that the men he would be tracking down were undoubtedly rich, Ferron had acquired an equally flashy wardrobe, stopping at several of Milan's fancier men's stores on Corso Venezia and Corso Vittorio Emanuele and using his credit cards to buy what he needed. The Alfa-Romeo sedan was a final touch of luxury, meant to complete the picture of a prosperous businessman. At this rate, his credit card bill was going to put a big dent in his savings. Forget living in a cabin somewhere for five years without working. Sixteen thousand bucks no longer seemed like a huge chunk of money. Hell, it was all that was left from his marriage to Sharon. Perhaps he was better off spending it all and starting over from scratch.

In the car's trunk, he had one small suitcase with the casual clothes he'd bought before leaving Paramaribo, a change of dress clothes, and the secret police files that went with each of the twelve individuals he had selected before leaving Suriname. Lying on the seat beside him was a photocopy of the requisite pages of Kloos's ledger—Kristine had given the original to Martin Beam for safe-keeping—with names and addresses circled. He had concentrated on individuals with addresses in northern Italy, having determined he stood a better chance of finding an Italian who might know something about the three OSS agents in the area where they carried out their last mission.

For breakfast that morning, he'd had a sweet roll and a *caffè macchiato* at a small bar next to the hotel. He was twenty minutes out of Milan and the coffee had gone straight through him. He looked along the road for a clump of trees where he could stop the car and relieve himself, but there was only a verge of weeds, an irrigation ditch, and flat fields. Finally, unable to wait, he swerved to the side of the road near a deserted intersection and reached over to unlock the passenger door. In the silence, he could hear a muffled roar that quickly grew louder when he stepped from the car. A motorcycle appeared from behind, materializing out of the fog. Its throaty roar cut through the air like a sharp-bladed snow plow. As if in surprise, the cyclist straightened a moment, and the sound of the motor as it washed over Ferron changed in pitch, and then the man, wearing a black helmet and an army-green field jacket, roared on by. He tried to read the license plate, but couldn't make out the number, catching only the orange *MI* for Milano. Scowling, passenger door open as a screen, he urinated into the gravel at the side of the road. Earlier, after he'd left the city through Porta Ticinese, there'd been a cycle behind him on route 35, the long, straight road that followed the Naviglio di Pavia. The *naviglio* was a wide canal that ran from Milan to the Ticino River, which flowed through Pavia, forty-five kilometers to the south. There was a road to each side of the canal and he had crossed an arched bridge over the water to gas up at a *benzinaio* AGIP. When he returned to the highway, he was surprised to find what he thought was the same cycle, following behind at a discreet distance. Few other cars were on the road at that pre-dawn hour. He stepped on the brakes to see if the cyclist would pass him, but the rider left the road at that point, pulling into a complex of high-rise apartment buildings. Ferron put his foot down on the accelerator and pulled away, shrugging at his paranoia. It was unlikely that anyone would be following him already. He'd been expecting trouble—but only after he started contacting the men on his list. Victims of blackmail were sensitive—they had something to hide and wouldn't take kindly to his poking around.

His paranoia had surfaced Sunday afternoon on leaving Paramaribo, where there was some logic to it, at least. Zanderij airport was under heavy surveillance. But early Monday morning, in Amsterdam, between flights, he had made a systematic effort at Schipol airport to determine if he was being followed and had come up empty. No one seemed the least bit interested. And again in Milan he'd been careful, eying the people on the bus from Malpensa airport to the Stazione Centrale. From the station, after telephoning for accommodations—it was just after two-thirty Monday afternoon—he'd made his way on foot toward Piazza della Repubblica, lingering at the bookstalls under the trees along the avenue. And then he'd jumped on a tram, changed directions five minutes later, hurried down a deserted side street and caught a taxi to the Hotel Cavour on Via Fatebenefratelli, a section of the inner ring of streets that circled the Lombard capital's historical center. As far as he could tell, no one had followed him.

Now, after a good night's sleep to combat his jet lag, he was headed toward the residence of the second name on his list. His attempts the night before to contact the first man had proven a disaster. Part of the problem was he had no clue to the current occupations of the men on his list. He assumed they were wealthy—and thus probably either independent businessmen or industrialists, bankers or government officials, well-known personalities or the like. It was also possible that many had illegally acquired their wealth under Mussolini. The files, though difficult to read, showed that many had worked as secret agents for either the police or the fascist militia, or were connected in a variety of ways to the regime. Some had held offices in the fascist governments of their cities; others were informants. From cryptic notations, he knew that several were involved with German reprisals against the partisans, and possibly with civilian massacres. The third man on his list, for example, now living in Lucca under the name Vanni Cupo, had been a prison guard in Opicina, a village near Trieste. From among the *detenuti* held in the prison, he had personally selected thirty-seven of the seventy-two hostages who were shot by the *Nazifascisti* on April 3, 1944, in retaliation for the partisan bombing of a local cinema requisitioned by the Germans, an attack in which seven Wehrmacht officers had been killed.

He'd telephoned the home of the first man on his list from the Hotel Cavour at seven p.m. the night before. The man lived well to the north of the city, in the Brianza hills near the Lago di Pusiano, and Ferron was trying to save himself a trip. A mistake. The maid who responded to his call informed him that Signor Di Stefano was still at his office in the city.

"I'm an American businessman," Ferron said. "I have an appointment with him in a half-hour and I've lost the address. Can you tell me where I can find him?"

"You had an appointment at the bank?"

Was this a trick question? Better to play it safe. He didn't know if Di Stefano was a banker or not. "I've lost the address," he repeated.

He would have liked to have asked which bank; it seemed there was one on every block in the center. When he'd asked at the hotel desk earlier for a good bank to exchange a large sum of money, the clerk had smiled and told him that Milan province had over 812 bank branches, with 432 in the city alone. He could take his pick or exchange his money in the hotel, the implication being that the hotel, despite its less favorable rates, was easier for a foreigner. Ferron had smiled and found a bank on his own.

The maid hesitated. "What did you say your name was?"

He hadn't identified himself and he stumbled for a second before coming up with the name Marco Castello, adding, *"Sono italo-americano,"* as if that explained his delayed response.

"Please call back in ten minutes. I'll telephone Signor Di Stefano to see if he wants to give out his business address."

"Ma guardi, signora," a note of impatience had crept into his voice, "he gave me his *home* phone number and address, so why wouldn't he give me his business address. If I have to wait ten minutes, I'll be late."

The maid paused for a moment. He could sense her reluctance. She'd probably been warned to be careful of kidnapers. "What's your number?" she said. "I'll call you back as soon as I talk to Signor Di Stefano. It'll only take a minute."

"That's okay," he said quickly. He was calling from the hotel and didn't want to give out his number. "I'll call back in five minutes."

As soon as he got off the line, he swore at himself. He'd screwed it up with the lie about the appointment. Now the man would never speak to him. And what if there existed a network of former fascists? Would Di Stefano warn them there was an American asking questions? He tried to calm himself. All he'd done was tell a lie, but that didn't mean Di Stefano would suspect someone was tracking him down because of his past. As far as the Italian knew, the caller could be anybody. It would be worse not to call back. Then the alarm might go out.

Five minutes later when he telephoned again, the maid said, "Please hold the line, Signor Castello. He'll speak to you now. It will take me a moment to connect you."

The voice that came over the line was surprisingly firm. Without introducing himself the man said, "Who are you, Mr. Castello?" The tone was accusatory and Ferron could imagine the hand gesture that went with the question.

"I'm sorry to call this way," he replied. "I'm a computer salesman, working for IBM. Your name was given to me by a colleague of mine in Torino."

The voice interrupted him. "And who would that be?"

He paused, his eyes falling to the phone book near the telephone. He flipped it open and read the first name that struck his eyes. "Luisa Spagnoletti."

"I don't know the woman."

The man's voice was sharp, and Ferron hurried on, his tone apologetic. "Perhaps she heard of your name from someone else . . ."

"Isn't this an unusual way of doing business? What do you really want, Mr. Castello? You should know, I'm no longer in business for myself. When my father died, I retired to manage his estate. I still serve as a director on several boards, but that is the extent of my activity. I have nothing to do with the purchase of computers."

Nothing was going right, he realized. He should have prepared himself better before making the call. He was a cop, for Christ's sake. *Ex-cop.* He cleared his throat. "Do you know a Dutchman named Theunis Kloos?"

"No. Should I?"

"He's been blackmailing you for years."

There was a pause at the other end of the line. "Mr. Castello, maybe we should meet this evening—before I return to my home. Are you free at eight p.m.?"

"Yes." This was what he wanted—a direct confrontation, a chance to look the man in the eyes. Over the phone, if you didn't know a person's voice, it was harder to tell when someone was lying.

"Are you familiar with the Pirelli building?"

"Yes, I am." For years after it was built in 1959, the Pirelli building had been one of Europe's tallest skyscrapers, soaring to thirty-six stories. Coming out of the central station, one couldn't miss the steel-and-glass façade of the thin, rectangular structure, rising into the sky off to the right behind the rows of trees in the square.

"I'll meet you in the same square," Di Stefano said. "The piazza Duca d'Aosta. I'll be driving a dark blue Mercedes with

Lecco plates. Wait for me in front of the building, at the corner with Via Galbani."

And that was when the comedy of errors began. Ferron hadn't referred to Di Stefano by his first name when telephoning. The man who showed up was Luigi Di Stefano, not Giampietro. Giampietro had died two years earlier; his son knew of no attempts to blackmail his father, nor did he claim to have any knowledge of his father's activities during the war.

"But you must have been alive then," Ferron protested.

Di Stefano grinned. "Are you telling me I look old just because I'm formally retired and have gray hair? Mr. Castello, I was only five years old when the war began and ten when it ended. Do you remember what your father was doing when you were that age?"

The question had startled Ferron. He was ten when his father was killed in prison. Sure, he remembered it—and he remembered what it was like when he was eight and his mother was murdered. But he couldn't tell the man that, so the encounter had ended with him learning nothing about the first man on his list. The experience taught him only to be more cautious. He was determined not to repeat his mistakes.

Michele Bandini, the second man on his list, lived on a country estate to the north of Pavia, a city of 87,000 inhabitants on the banks of the Ticino River, former capital of the Longobard kingdom before the rise of Milan. In the Middle Ages, Pavia was a city of a hundred towers and, though it had lost most of them, it still boasted the twelfth-century Romanesque church of San Michele, where Charlemagne was once crowned; the Chiesa di San Pietro in Ceil d'Oro, mentioned by Dante; a Duomo with the third-largest cupola in Italy, to whose plans both Leonardo da Vinci and Bramante had contributed; and the fifteenth-century Visconti castle. Pavia was also the seat of the Necchi sewing machine company, a sign of the city's entry into the modern world. All this he'd learned from travel brochures picked up in Milan.

As he followed Bandini's car at six-thirty that morning, after staking out his villa for nearly an hour, he was struck by the decay of the industrial outskirts. Red-brick factories coated with soot alternated with squalid farmhouses with muddy yards and stickpole-anchored cones of rotting hay. Closer to the city, lay a few high-rise apartment buildings—bare, concrete edifices constructed in the fifties. A leaden sky added to the gloom.

Michele Bandini sat in the back seat of a Lancia sedan with tinted windows. Ferron had caught a glimpse of him as the car pulled from the long driveway onto the old highway leading into Pavia. Bandini was a short, bespectacled, scrawny man with cropped gray hair combed forward over a balding forehead and with the wrinkled features of a man sucking on a sour plum. Not the sort to draw out a smile in passing.

The Lancia traversed the city on Strada Nuova. Early morning traffic thickened in the narrow streets as the city came slowly to life. Near Corso Cavour, the driver stopped in front of a *caffè* and in a few seconds a waiter appeared at the curb, with a demitasse of espresso on a silver tray. The back window scrolled down, a thin hand reached out, took the cup and returned it a moment later with a folded Lire note of indeterminate denomination.

The Lancia pulled back into traffic and Ferron eased the Alfa Romeo into first gear. He left two vehicles between his car and Bandini's. The Lancia proceeded toward the Ponte Coperto, crossed the narrow bridge, and moved into the new city. Fifteen minutes later, the driver pulled up before a five-story building of new construction. The brass nameplate next to the double glass doors read S.E.D.I., with the name in full in French: *Société Européenne de Dévéloppement Industriel*. The driver escorted the older man into the building, then returned to the car by himself and drove away. Ferron followed him until he was sure the Lancia was heading to the estate. It appeared that Bandini would be in the office for the day. Fine, easier to do things at dusk, anyway.

Giving up the surveillance, Ferron doubled back, drove to the Palace Hotel overlooking Ponte Libertà, and checked into his room on the fourth floor. The lowering clouds had darkened, and he saw the first drops of rain sweeping across the river toward the hotel. In a moment, the windows were beaded. The wind gusted and then the downpour stopped as suddenly as it had started. He had a view of the river and through the mist he could see a couple in a rowboat, the woman holding a plastic raincoat over the two of them while the man rowed. A terrible day for an excursion. He watched, shaking his head in marvel, as the black-haired man beached the boat on a narrow lido and the couple stretched out on a blanket on the wet sand. They hadn't gone there for a picnic and apparently weren't going to let a shower deter them from their assignation.

After lunch in the hotel, he telephoned the switchboard at S.E.D.I. and inquired as to their hours. They were open from eight a.m. to one p.m. and then from four in the afternoon until seven at night. He decided he would go to the building in the afternoon to see about security. He wished he were armed. Bandini had no one riding shotgun in the Lancia, but the bulge in the driver's suit attested to the shoulder holster the man wore.

At five p.m., he left the Alfa Romeo in the Hotel Palace parking lot and took a taxi to the S.E.D.I. building. The entrance was overlooked by an Inelco security camera and the door itself opened into a curved glass cabin with a second, electronic door at the far end. A uniformed guard sat at a desk beside the glass cabin and asked for ID and the nature of one's business. Clearly, at his office, Bandini was well-protected.

Ferron flashed his passport and faking a strong American accent said, "I'm looking for the Banca Commerciale. I was told they have a branch in this building." He'd seen the bank's logo on another building nearby. The guard shook his head and then, without speaking, jerked it over his shoulder, in a gesture that meant not here, idiot, up the street. Asshole, thought Ferron. He'd spoken in Italian; the guy could've responded instead of acting like foreigners were *analfabeti* just because they didn't know the city.

He walked up the street, bought a *Corriere della Sera* at a corner kiosk, found a snack bar with a room in back separated from the front counter by a stringed-bead curtain, ordered a cappuccino and a brioche, and sat down in a comfortable padded booth to wait. An hour later, having finished the paper, he ordered a Branca Menta over ice (the crème-de-menthe made the harsh taste of the Branca Fernet palatable) and when that was finished a *supplì*—a croquette of rice stuffed with mozzarella and green peas—and a Coke. He used the small restroom off to one side and then left. It was six-fifty p.m.—ten minutes before S.E.D.I. would shut down for the night.

As he approached the building, he spotted the blue Lancia at the curb. The same driver waited, smoking a cigarette and flirting with two young women with books under their arms. Ferron stopped about fifteen feet away from the Lancia and stared at a window display under a sign reading *Giocattoli*—a toy store with all kinds of fantastic mechanical contraptions. The two girls said good-bye to the driver, a stocky man in his thirties with a pockmarked face and wavy black hair, and sauntered on down the street.

In a minute, Michele Bandini exited and was escorted to the Lancia. He walked with the feeble movements of an invalid and had to be helped into the back seat. He was carrying only a narrow-brimmed gray hat and wearing a dark wool topcoat that Ferron hadn't seen earlier. The door closed behind the old man and the driver, without looking around, straightened and stepped forward.

Ferron moved quickly then, coming up from behind. He waited until the driver opened the front door, jabbed a finger in his back, reached around in front for the gun in the man's shoulder holster, then in a gruff voice said, "*Va' via, o ti uccido*"— Keep walking, or I'll kill you—and slipped behind the wheel. He slammed the door, locked it while the driver stared at him in shock from five feet away, then pulled away from the curb with a grin on his face. The old man in the back seat had done nothing to stop him. "You should hire better help," Ferron told him in Italian. "If someone's close enough to stick a gun in your back, you should be able to put him down before he can open his mouth."

The old man said nothing and Ferron saw in the rearview mirror that his jaw was quivering. A drop of spittle appeared at the corner of his mouth as he nervously masticated air. He slipped the gray fedora on his head as if that provided a measure of security.

Ferron lay the chauffeur's gun on his lap and said, "*Non si preoccupi*. I won't hurt you unless you do something stupid. I just want to talk to you for a few minutes. You tell me what I want to know and I'll leave. You can drive yourself back to the office or call for help."

"What do you want?"

He took a right turn and headed west, searching for a side street where he could park in seclusion, in order to avoid the police patrols that the chauffeur would soon activate. The sky was rapidly growing dark as night fell. A blanket of dark clouds covered the moon.

"I'll tell you what I want in a minute."

He moved off the main street, turned on the headlights and the heater, then cut back toward the river, trying to find the sandy area he'd seen from his hotel window. Five minutes later, he found an unpaved road leading to the riverside park and pulled into a grove of willow trees, where he extinguished the headlights but left the motor and the heater running. Across the dark band of the Ticino river, he could see the lights of the Hotel Palace and the traffic on Ponte Libertà. His room was a short walk away. The hotel's lights dappled the water's surface with icy white pinnacles that rippled and thrust like flickering daggers.

He turned around and faced the old man. Bandini had shrunk into the corner as if trying to hide. "Shall we walk? Or do you prefer to talk in the car?"

The old man looked out the tinted window and shivered. The ground was still damp from the day's rain and a breeze was ruffling the willow trees. With a visible effort at controlling his fear, Bandini said, "You see what I've become. I'm a sick, old man. Why do you bother me this way?"

"The man who sends me is not as lucky as you," Ferron said gruffly. "You're sick, he's dead."

Bandini waved a trembling hand in front of his face. "I've been fighting for my health for five years. Now I've given up. I'm a walking dead man. I have nothing to fear."

"Except a guilty conscience."

He had deciphered enough of Bandini's file to know the man had been an agent of the notorious Banda Koch in Rome for three months in the spring of 1944. At the end of July he'd passed into one of the Italian SS police units established by Himmler. From there, he was posted to Milan on the recommendation of Peter Hansen Tschimpke, *SS-Brigadeführer und Generalmajor der*

Waffen-SS, where he was enrolled as a member of the *I°
Reggimento Waffen Miliz,* an Italian SS police unit trained in
Prague. Like the German SS units, the Italians swore an oath of
allegiance to Hitler and wore the silver death's-head emblem, the
only difference being that their insignia was red. Bandini had
taken part in the *rastrellamenti*—the roundups of men—in Val
Pellice and was personally implicated in the executions of six
partisans. Not many Italians would forget those deeds.

Bandini said, "I face death with a clear conscience. There is no
sin I have not confessed."

"And what about crimes? Perhaps confessed to a priest who
maintains a vow of silence, but not to the world."

"God does not require that we confess to the world. I have no
fear of dying."

"You must have feared something once. You paid extortion to
Theunis Kloos."

The black eyes blinked behind the thick spectacles. The
overhead convenience light, which Ferron had turned on,
reflected off the glass lenses. Bandini wiped his mouth. "I—I
never knew his name. He was an evil man who threatened to
destroy me and my family."

Ferron felt a rush of scorn and anger. "His evil pales in
comparison to yours," he said harshly. This man was a murderer,
pure and simple.

The shriveled head turned sharply toward him. The old
man's thin lips hardened. "What do you want? To stir up embers
on a fire that went out long ago?"

Ferron took a deep breath to calm himself. He hefted the
chauffeur's gun in his hand. It was a 9mm automatic, a Beretta 92
with a thin grip and a frame-mounted thumb safety. He was
familiar with the pistol; he'd fired other models in the same
series. He held the pistol where Bandini could see it and said, "If
I have to stir up the past, I will. You should have paid for your
crimes with your life. As I said, you're a lucky man. You tell me
what I need to know and everything stops here. You won't be
bothered again."

Bandini considered that, his manner subdued. "What's the
name of the man you say blackmailed me?"

"Theunis Kloos. A Dutchman. You never met him?"

Bandini looked out into the darkness, which had dropped down around the car like a black coffin. "I never knew who he was. I was contacted by letter and once by phone. I paid the money into an account in Switzerland. I was unable to learn the name of the person who opened the account."

"Did you ever go to the police?"

"I couldn't. I was assured by the man who contacted me that I would only have to pay a limited amount. Five hundred million lire."

Ferron raised his eyebrows and Bandini said, "In dollars that would be a little over four hundred thousand."

"Still, a tidy sum."

Bandini shrugged. "For some people. I had the choice of one lump sum or payments spread out over the years. I chose the latter. The man was very efficient."

"Do you know how Kloos got the file that made the squeeze possible?"

The old man's hard mouth twitched. "At the end, the Duce made many foolish mistakes. One of them was to ask Guido Leto to compile dossiers on the fascist hierarchs and other important men. Leto was head of the OVRA and vice-chief of police in the Republic of Salò. Mussolini thought the files would provide him with a bargaining tool if he gave himself up or was captured. The files were packed in several suitcases; they disappeared in the confusion of the final moments and none of us had the chance to find out who took them. It was only later that some of us who were police agents realized that we, too, were victims—that our personal files were part of the group. We were all running for our lives. I myself managed to scrape up a letter from one of the American agents in Milan, showing that I had helped the Allies." Bandini shrugged. "It was a lie, of course, but for certain sums of money, one tells many lies. The letter saved my life and allowed me to disappear into the masses—for a while, at least . . . until one day I received a telephone call." His voice died away.

"Were there any groups of ex-fascists you could turn to for help? Other people in the same predicament?"

The thick spectacles lifted and the old man stared at the overhead light for a long time before speaking. "The Germans were always better organized than we were. They were practical, we were artistic. I tried to contact friends for help, but by then everyone was working alone. No one trusted anyone else. We were all frightened by the work of the epuration commissions. Eventually I was afraid to contact even my old friends."

A moment of silence extended itself while Ferron stared at the shrunken wretch, trying to imagine the brutality of the man in his younger years. Finally, he broke the silence, his voice quiet. "What was the name of the American agent who gave you the letter?"

The cadaverous head turned toward him and then sank back into the seat. Bandini lifted a shaking hand. "I can't help you there. I believe the man was killed by the Germans before they surrendered in Italy."

"You're lying. Who are you trying to protect? You said you had nothing to fear." He waved the gun angrily. "You can't have it both ways."

The old man had closed his eyes and appeared not to hear. Ferron's jaw tightened. He leaned over the seat and gripped Bandini's arm with his left hand. There was no muscle to speak of beneath the coat—just a hard thin bone. "Tell me," he said, "did you ever hear of an American agent by the name of Thomas Gage?"

Bandini shook his head without opening his eyes.

"Perhaps under the nom de guerre of Major Tom?"

Bandini gestured helplessly.

"What about an Italian—a man named Beppe Aprico? Or a British agent—Eagle Jack? A girl named Carla Ceruti?"

Bandini's face was pale. His lips had lost all color. "I can't help you," he said weakly. "I've spent a lifetime intentionally trying to forget those years. Names—they drifted away like motes in a sunbeam, a shaft of light now here, now gone. For me, it is all blackness."

Ferron felt like strangling the man for trying to turn his bad memory into maudlin poetry. Kloos would have done better to have killed the stunted brute years ago, crushing him like an insignificant but odious bug—a cockroach feeding on the carrion of men who had fought for their country's freedom. He said nothing for a moment, his lips compressed, waiting for his frustration to lessen. Finally, he took a deep breath and exhaled slowly, as if attempting to expunge a vile odor. "Just one more question—" his voice had taken on a hard, sarcastic edge—"and you won't have to use your feeble memory on this one." He saw Bandini's eyelids flicker once. "Has anyone contacted you recently, asking about any of the people I've mentioned?"

A thin sigh eased out of Bandini's mouth. He placed a hand inside his topcoat and rubbed his chest. His mouth opened soundlessly.

"Just answer me, goddamn it, and you can go."

Bandini licked his lips. "I wish I could help you," he said in a feeble voice, "but I can't. Kill me if you must. I know nothing about those men. Please leave me alone." He started to cry.

Ferron shook his head, staring at the guy with mixed emotions. A waste of time. Nothing. Were they all going to be like this?

He took the chauffeur's gun when he left, moving swiftly into the darkness toward the Ponte Libertà.

CHAPTER 2

Wednesday, Sept 11, Lucca, Italy

On Wednesday morning, he rose early for the drive to Lucca, the only city in Tuscany that was on his list. He'd planned the first part of his itinerary with speed in mind, laying it out in a rough circle. When he was finished in Lucca, he would take the freeway to Florence and then move north through Bologna and Padua toward Vicenza and Verona. And if nothing turned up by then, he had addresses for men in both Trento and Bolzano farther north.

The sky was a compact mass of heavy, gray storm clouds that threatened rain. A cool wind blew from the west, sweeping down out of the Alps and across the Lombard plains. He turned on his parking lights and tuned the stereo to a rock station broadcasting out of Milan—Radio 105, or as the disk jockeys shouted, *Radio Centocinque*. Near Rapallo, the skies opened and a deluge thundered down, obscuring his vision. The Alfa Romeo's wiper blades whacked back and forth at full speed. Traffic was heavy and his progress slow. The road was encumbered with cars, their brake lights flashing intermittently, with trucks, tourist buses, and huge two- and three-trailer *autocarri*—lorries from the port of Genoa, all passing each other and throwing an oily spray into the air. Near Borghetta di Vana, there was a massive tie-up in both lanes. Traffic came to a standstill and didn't move for over an hour. A few drivers braved the weather and got out of their cars with umbrellas, moving forward in an attempt to learn what the problem was. They all returned shrugging their shoulders and answering questions with a curt *"Non so. Non si vede niente."* The line of cars and trucks stretched for miles with nothing in sight.

An hour and a half later, when traffic finally started moving again—though only at a snail's pace, Ferron drew abreast of the accident. A tractor-trailer rig had overturned, blocking both lanes. A tow truck had finally managed to clear enough of the wreckage for one lane to open. Triangular warning signs had been set up and red flares burned in the roadway. Two helmeted motorcycle cops were standing by and a police car had arrived, blue turret light flashing. The emergency vehicles had already left by the time he passed the rig and it was getting dark when he finally reached Lucca.

According to Kloos's ledger, Vanni Cupo, the third man on Ferron's list, had moved from a farm along the Serchio river below Monte S. Quirico into the city itself. His current address was on Via della Fratta, inside the walls and not far from the Via del Fosso, which ran along a grassy channel, once part of the moat, carrying water to the city. The building was a three-story *palazzo* with an electronically controlled door presided over by a uniformed guard in a small cubicle to one side of the entrance. Had he more time and a description of Vanni Cupo, he would have staked out the building, but as it was, he bent to the speaker and spoke in muffled English to the watchful doorman, who buzzed him in to the foyer.

The guard, a compact, efficient-looking man in his late forties, stepped from the glass cabin and inquired as to his business. The Italian cocked his ear as if that would help him understand, squinting in anticipation of a foreign accent.

"My name's Peter Cupo," he said, "from America." He spoke in English again, saying the name slowly and smiling broadly. "I came to see my grandfather, Vanni Cupo." He looked toward the marble steps. A red runner led from the foyer up the center of the steps as far as the first floor landing, then the steps narrowed and doubled back on each side of the building. A cage elevator with a grilled accordion-door stood at the top of the landing.

"Un momento," the guard said abruptly. "No speak English." He gestured to Ferron to follow and stepped into the cabin,

where he picked up a black phone. He dialed a number, said "*C'è qualcuno qui che vorrebbe parlare col Signor Cupo*," and handed him the phone.

He heard a woman say, "*Pronto, chi è?*" Voice querulous—not that of a maid, an old woman, probably the wife.

"Hello," he said. "I wonder if I might speak to your husband."

The woman said she didn't understand English and asked again who he was.

He gestured to the guard to step out. "I'd like to speak in private," he said, repeating the last word slowly. The man seemed startled by the request, but stepped out of the booth and closed the door behind him. Ferron turned his back and switched to Italian, speaking softly now.

"Signora, my name is Peter Cupo. From New York. I believe I'm related to your husband's family and I wonder if I might come up and speak to him."

"*Un momento.*"

He waited, turning around briefly to shrug his shoulders at the guard.

"Who are you?" Vanni Cupo's voice was ragged, the accent Triestine. "I have no relatives in America."

"Mr. Cupo, I need to speak to you about a very important matter. May I come up to the apartment?"

The man hesitated. "What's this about?"

"I'd like to ask you about some people you might have known in the war."

He could hear the man swallow. "I can't speak to you now," he said.

"Mr. Cupo, I came all the way from America to talk to you. If I have to, I'll contact the police." An empty bluff, but threats were sometimes effective when people were frightened or stubborn.

"I can't talk to you here. My wife . . ." Vanni Cupo stopped, his words draining away. When he continued, his voice was tired and raspy. "I can't take any more. He said it would end. That no one would bother me."

"Who did?"

Cupo did not respond.

"This'll be the last time," Ferron said.

"I can see you tonight . . . later."

"Tonight's fine. I'll come back whenever you wish."

"But not here—it would be inconvenient . . . for my wife, you understand." The old man thought for a moment and then cleared his throat. "My family owns a farmhouse on the road to Pescia. My son lives there, but he's in Rome for a *concorso statale*. Do you have a car?"

"I'll get there. How do I find it?"

"Take the road to Pescia. You'll pass Lunata in about seven kilometers. Keep going on the same road through Borgonuovo." He paused as if waiting for Ferron to catch up. "Two or three kilometers beyond Borgonuovo, turn left at the first crossroad. The road leads to Gragnano, a very small village with houses on both sides of the road. Just beyond the village, the road curves to the right and then sharply left. You'll see a stone farmhouse on the hill above the road after the second turn. There's a narrow lane you can take on the left."

"What time will you be there?"

"I can't leave until my wife falls asleep . . . Come around ten this evening—I should be there by then."

CHAPTER 3

Wednesday, September 11, Lucca, Italy

Ferron spent the next three hours wandering around Lucca, trying to enjoy the sights but with his thoughts returning to home. He'd telephoned Janelle Dutton in Durango late the night before after his encounter with Michele Bandini, catching her just as she was returning home from teaching at the high school. Classes had started a week earlier. Janelle was still worried about the break-in at her cabin and was anxious for his return.

"I get the feeling every night that someone's watching the place," she said. "I'm nervous. When are you coming home, Nick?"

Hearing her say *home* had a nice sound to it. He had an apartment in Tucson, but without a woman it didn't seem like a home. And now, with no job to tie him down, he felt cut-off and alone. He'd always enjoyed solitude . . . but with Gran Babbo gone—everything was different. Deep inside, he nourished a hard core of anger at the loss. Thomas Gage had been a good man.

When he didn't respond, Janelle said, "I'm keeping Rowdy inside at night. When he's outside, he barks, but if a stranger sweet-talks him, he wags his tail and licks the person's face."

There was a slight echo on the line, and in the background Ferron could hear a steady clicking as the *contatore* kept track of the time. The call was going to cost a fortune. "I'm not sure when

I'll be back," he told her. "I haven't had much luck so far. I may have to stir up a hornet's nest to get any results."

"Be careful, Nick. Your grandfather knew something that got him killed. I don't want the same thing to happen to you."

"*Uomo avvisato, mezzo salvato.*"

"What's that mean?"

"A man forewarned is a man forearmed." His tone was even. "My grandfather never knew what was coming."

"Sometimes knowledge isn't enough. They're going to be coming after you, Nick, and you don't know who they are."

He could hear the concern in her voice. "That's what I'm trying to find out—and when I do, I'll stop them."

"Nick, I know you like to do things alone, but I hope you get help when you need it." She hesitated. "I'm afraid of these people . . . They're not going to stop at killing your grandfather."

What could he say? For eight years, he'd been working with men who killed for a living—hoodlums *and* cops. No matter what side you were on, the killing would never stop; you just had to take your chances and use your wits and hope that justice triumphed over villainy, and whether it did or not, if you'd done your best, you accepted your fate with equanimity—at least, that's what the mind told you to do. The body did not always choose to go along.

She was waiting for him to speak. He shrugged and lifted the mouthpiece. "You know what they say, Janelle."

"What?"

"No one dies who wasn't born to die." He laughed, the sound sticking high in his throat.

"True," she said pointedly, and he could imagine her brown eyes flashing, "but most of us try to postpone it a while."

He grinned and said he'd do his best, then added casually, "Did they ever find that hiker you mentioned?"

"No. They're still looking."

He paused. "Would you do me a favor and call Barbara's husband? Ask Dick if he'll climb into the mountains this weekend and check Gran Babbo's cabin. Tell him to take a look at the cache and see if anyone's broken into it."

"Is it locked?"

"Yeah, I put the padlock back on when I was there."

"You're still thinking your grandfather's alive?"

"Anything's possible. That body was burned too bad to identify. The coroner and everyone else just assumed from the start it was Gran Babbo."

"If he's alive, Nick, wouldn't he have a key to the cache? What good does it do to see if anyone's broken in?"

"The cache was full when I looked. Dick can tell if any food is missing. If the lock's broken, it might be the hiker; if not and if things are missing, it has to be my grandfather."

"I'll call him tonight, Nick. And if he can't go, I'll take Rowdy and hike on up there myself."

"Do you remember the way to the cabin?"

She laughed. "You and I went there often enough."

They were both silent, thinking about the times they'd made love in the cabin.

"Thanks," he said. "Dick can tell you how to find the cache if he can't make it. It's not far from the cabin." He paused. "Take a gun if you go, okay? No telling who you'll meet in the mountains these days."

He left early for his appointment with Vanni Cupo, intending to case the farm and then return to Lucca for a dinner before going back out. He didn't want to be caught in an ambush. Threatening the man, while necessary, had consequences one could never determine in advance. The drive took twenty minutes. At six o'clock, there were few vehicles on the provincial road. Most of the through traffic—for cities like Montecatini, Pistoia, and Florence—took the E55/A11 *autostrada*. The clouds thinned out and though the sun was just below the horizon the sky lightened perceptibly as he approached Gragnano. A pale, nacreous haze hung over the hills, verdant with underbrush and stubby trees where they hadn't been cleared for pasture, terraced vineyards, or olive groves.

The farmhouse lay halfway up a hill that was wooded to each side but had been cleared for pasture in a broad swath up the middle. A narrow lane, marked by a low stone wall, twisted upward in a tight S-curve that was muddy and treacherous. At the first curve, he dropped into first gear, tires slipping for a moment and then catching hold. Tall grass grew at the verge of the road and was matted down in the center. From the top, there was a view of a narrow valley, given over to olive groves and small farms with orchards. At the back of the stone house, thick trees took over again, providing good cover to within fifteen feet. But unless one came on foot from over the hills, the approach was in the open and the road too narrow to turn around in until one reached the level spot where the house sat. The farmhouse itself was a low, ancient-looking stone structure with a hand-hewn beam for the lintel. The stone had been stuccoed at one time, but most of the plaster had fallen away. What remained—irregular splotches of color ranging in shade from a dull cream to pale orange—gave proof that the house had been often painted. The windows were heavily shuttered and the front door was made of massive oak planks, held together with metal straps and bolts. A low wall to one side enclosed a garden plot, choked with weeds and one old fig tree with dollops of darkening fruit. Behind the garden stood a low shed, open to the south, with a rusted Fiat 600 on cinder blocks and room for another car. A flagged walkway led from the shed to the house. There was no one in sight.

When he returned at ten that night, he almost missed the rutted lane beyond Gragnano. The sky was pitch black and the farmhouse unaccountably dark. It was only after he parked behind a late-model Fiat and got out of the rental car that he caught a glimmer of light behind one of the shuttered windows. The frogs and other night creatures had fallen silent upon his arrival, and he stood for a moment listening for activity inside or outside the house, but heard nothing. The night was calm, the trees still, not a breath of wind stirring. He slipped the Beretta automatic he'd taken from Bandini's driver out of his coat pocket and chambered a round. For a moment he wondered if he should have stopped at an *armeria* and bought another clip or two and extra ammunition.

When his night vision was as sharp as it was ever going to be, he moved along the flagstone path and stopped at the massive front door. He considered the boar's head knocker on the door, then quietly tried the heavy metal handle. The door was unlocked—and that surprised and worried him. No one, not even the *contadini* in the most isolated countryside, left their doors unlocked in Italy, not any more.

The hinges were well oiled and the door, for its size, swung with remarkable ease. Pushing gently, he stepped into the dark farmhouse and moved quickly out of the doorway, aware that for a moment he was silhouetted against the lighter expanse behind him. When nothing happened, he closed the door, found a bolt by touch, and slid it into its socket. He didn't want to be surprised from behind.

The room was darker than outside and he paused again, trying to pick out the main features. The walls to each side were cool to the touch, plastered and painted a light color, probably white. Dark squares marked framed paintings or photos, he couldn't tell which. The air smelled lightly of wood smoke, as if there had been a fire earlier, but the air was cold. The room appeared to be furnished with a sofa and chairs, a low cocktail table, a TV, and lamp stands. A tall *cassettone* that looked in the darkness like a highboy or a glass-enclosed hutch stood against the back wall.

He could feel cold sweat under his arms, the acrid smell of fear rising to his nostrils. There was a metallic taste at the back of his throat and in his sinuses. The taste brought back childhood sensations; he'd felt the same thing then, when his father was about to punish him. Like then, there was danger here, only he had no way of knowing when or where it might strike. He was familiar with this fear and considered it an ally, something that sharpened his reflexes and caused his senses to be in tune with the environment—with changes in light and shadow, with the slightest sound, the touch of a draft on his skin, the smell of another's perfume or aftershave or body odor, the taste of his own nerves.

He moved down the wall to his left, his belly tightening with each creak of the floor boards. From the size of the central room, he knew there had to be a door to each side. He found the first one and pushed down on the handle, swinging the door away from him.

Darkness—possibly a bed, a small writing desk, and a chair. "Signor Cupo," he called quietly. He did not expect an answer.

An open doorway at the back led into the kitchen. He checked it out and then moved across the main room to the far wall. As he drew near the door, he saw a thin sliver of weak light at the base, not enough to provide illumination but an indication that someone was in the room. He stepped to the side of the door, his back to the wall, Beretta ready for action. "Signor Cupo," he called again, louder this time.

No answer.

He reached around his body with his left hand and found the handle. He disengaged the latch and shoved the door open. The sudden exhalation—an odor of blood and feces—overwhelmed him and he reached for his handkerchief, gagging at the smell. The old man was behind the desk where he'd shot himself. He'd slid off the chair, his head coming to rest at a grotesque angle. A bullet through the mouth, it looked like. Ferron didn't move the body or touch the gun, a Rossi .38 Special with a well-worn stock of checkered wood. There was no note. Another dead end, literally this time.

He lay on his bed in the hotel room and stared at the ceiling. The shutters on his windows were still open and a streetlight from Viale Regina Margherita cast a sheen of pale light on the ceiling. He hadn't bothered to undress. In the morning, the man's wife would wake to an empty bed. Would the police check the farmhouse? He was sure the old man hadn't told his wife he was going out. Very likely she knew nothing of his past. What would she think? The son—or the police—would find the body first. There was no question that it was suicide. He had wiped the latches clean and worried only about the Alfa Romeo's tire tracks on the muddy lane. But whoever went up to check on the farmhouse would go by car, destroying most if not all of his tracks.

When had Vanni Cupo decided to kill himself? Before leaving the apartment or only when he reached the farmhouse? Had he sat there waiting for the man from America, intending to kill the inquisitor, and then decided he couldn't go through with it? Did it matter? He was dead and Ferron felt responsible. An executioner without judge or jury.

He thought again of the file on Vanni Cupo, the jailer of Opicina. Here was a man who picked thirty-seven prisoners to be executed for crimes they did not commit. If the partisans had gotten their hands on him, he would have suffered a horrible death. It was hard to imagine what these men Kloos had blackmailed had been like fifty years earlier. In old age, they were pathetic, no longer the hard young men who had made cruel choices, killing their countrymen in order to uphold a system that had long been abased in the eyes of the free world. What had made them so heartless? Was it pride of race? The desire once again to rule the world, to feel their chests swell with ancient Roman *virtù*? No, you could not call it virtue. Rather an insane drive for hegemony over their fellow citizens, a venal and egoistic passion that descended from il Duce and the party hierarchs at the top to the lowest fascist functionary at the bottom.

He wanted to, but he could not feel sorry for the man. Vanni Cupo should have paid for his crimes long ago.

CHAPTER 4

Thursday, September 12, Florence, Italy

On Thursday morning, rather than taking the *autostrada* to Florence, he decided to drive by the farmhouse to see if the *polizia* or Carabinieri were there yet. He had checked his map and saw that he could return to the freeway at Montecatini Terme. He was in no hurry since he'd called ahead and made reservations at the Hotel Cavour in Florence.

He got a late start, not having fallen asleep until three in the morning. The day was bright with a strong September sun and a sky that had been washed clean by the prior day's rain. He drove at a leisurely pace with the window down, enjoying the fresh air and the scent of pine. From the country road at the foot of the hill, the farmhouse seemed deserted, with no sign of activity in the environs. Apparently no one had found the body yet. All the better for him. He drove on without stopping, following narrow roads that wound in and out of the hills and sparse forests of the Apennines.

It was between San Gennaro and Pescia that he first heard the motorcycle. He was instantly alert, ears straining to pick up the sound. Was it the same cycle that had passed him on the road near Pavia? With the wind rushing into the car, he couldn't tell by sound alone. And then he saw the cyclist in his rearview mirror, leaning into the curves and overtaking him fast. It looked like the same guy. He rolled up the window and reached under the seat where he'd stashed the Beretta. *Okay, let's see what the bastard's up to.*

But the cyclist roared around him on a curve, bent low, moving to the inside and not looking over. Still, it was him, all right—the same army green jacket, the dark helmet, a Kawasaki racing bike with a contoured windscreen. No way was this a coincidence—the route too unusual for that. But where in hell had the guy picked him up again? The next time the occasion presented itself, he would stop him and find out who he was and who he worked for. For the moment, he pulled his foot off the accelerator and replaced the gun.

Straightening, he had almost no time to react. The first burst went low, slamming into the car's body, and he saw that the shooter had done it intentionally to let him know he was about to die. Automatic fire. The cyclist was standing behind his bike, off to the right of the road, firing in three-shot bursts. An Uzi. The second burst raked the front windshield, which shattered under the impact, cutting off his view of the road. One of the bullets—or maybe it was a piece of glass—had caught him in the neck. He had no choice then. If he accelerated and attempted to drive on past, he'd be cut to pieces. He jerked the wheel to the right and left the road, head bent over his fists. The guy was going to take him out—fine; he'd take the bastard with him.

The cyclist screamed and unleashed a final burst from the Uzi, the bullets passing overhead as he tumbled backward to get out of the way. A second later, there was a satisfying explosion of metal and glass—that would be the cycle, Ferron thought—and then a thud as the car and cycle en masse tore over the body of the hitman, and then the car went end over end and slid along on its roof while he watched mud and gravel fly. In what seemed slow motion, the car keeled on its side in a gully, the battered rear end finally coming to rest against a tree.

He hadn't lost consciousness—but the overabundance of sensation had stunned him. It took him several minutes to realize that the car was on its side and that he was strapped into the driver's seat and still alive. He looked down at his shirt and saw bright blood and was afraid for a moment that one of the slugs had caught an artery. He felt for his neck, where he'd been grazed, but the blood was already sticky and beginning to congeal.

My nose, he thought. I'm bleeding from my nose and I don't even feel it. He wiped at his nose. There was a funny smell—a vapor that made him dizzy. *Gas! Get out of the fucking car!* He unbuckled the seat belt and reached up to try the passenger door. It wouldn't budge. He could see the sun burning down from straight overhead. Have to go out that way. He found his suit coat on the floor and wrapped it around his fist and began to hammer at the shattered window. In a minute he was climbing out of the car.

Wait! What about the gun? He had to get rid of the Beretta or the police would cause him all kinds of trouble.

He couldn't find the gun in the front passenger compartment. He dropped back inside the sedan. For a moment, searching for the gun, he considered running. But the car would be traced to him within hours and then what? He'd be a fugitive with worse things to explain than an accident.

There it was—the gun, lodged under the dash. He climbed out of the car and tucked it into his waistband. He heard voices and saw a line of vehicles up on the road. A man and his two sons were working their way down the embankment. *Damn!* He stepped behind the car and tossed the gun into the underbrush. He watched it disappear with a feeling of regret. And then he thought of his suitcase with the files and the photocopied pages of the ledger. He had to get that out before the car went up in flames. The smell of gas was strong, but so far it didn't look like it was going to explode. If the wind kept the vapors away from the motor—

He walked to the back of the sedan. It was crumpled against a thick conifer that looked like a red cedar. He lay on the damp ground and reached into the opening at the bottom of the trunk and felt for his suitcase. If he could open it, he could salvage the papers.

He found the suitcase, but couldn't maneuver it well enough to get the latches open. He heard a voice calling him, asking if there was still someone inside. He stood and saw a middle-aged man and two boys in their teens. "I'm alone," he said. "Can you help me get my suitcase before the car burns."

"If it was going to burn, it'd have done so by now," the Italian said. You were down here ten minutes without moving."

"I didn't think I was even knocked out."

"We thought you were dead. There's a fellow on a motorcycle back there that didn't make it. He run into you? Passed us like a torpedo a while ago. I told the boys he was going to break his neck."

"Can you help me here? I think I can get the trunk open if we can roll the car away from this tree."

Working together, the four of them managed to tip the car in the direction of the slope, and he was able to retrieve his suitcase, which was relatively undamaged. Slipping in the wet soil, he clawed his way up to the highway where the line of cars at the side of the road was growing longer. A woman told him someone had gone ahead to Pescia to call an emergency vehicle. He turned to the man with two boys and asked him which way he was heading.

"Toward Florence," the man said. "I'm a salesman of stationery supplies in the city. Just picked up my boys from their grandparents in San Gennaro. We're in the *Ritmo*." He pointed to a small Fiat at the head of the line.

"Listen. I'm going to be held up quite some time when the police get here. I'm going to Florence, too. I know you can't wait, but I wonder if you'd do me a favor? I'm staying at the Hotel Cavour and I'm supposed to meet a colleague there to give her some papers. Would you be able to take my suitcase with you and leave it at the desk? She can pick it up there. I'd be happy to pay you for your trouble." He didn't want the files on him when the police started asking questions.

"*Ma cosa dice*? Pay me? Give me the case. It's the least we can do. I'm Carlo Becchi and if there's anything I can do for you in the city, you can contact me at the *cartoleria* on Via Ricasoli near the Duomo."

He thanked the man and looked back down the slope at the Alfa Romeo. The police would ask about his luggage, but he would tell them he was on a day trip and that his luggage was at his hotel in Florence. And the cyclist? The police would find the Uzi and when he told them about the shooting he would leave it up to them to decide why. He was a tourist, in Italy on vacation. The terrorist or kidnapper—he'd slip those words in right off— might have mistaken him for someone else or simply intended to rob him at gunpoint. But they would soon find out that he was a cop . . . Better to tell them that at the start. It might prove useful if he had to convince them he was telling the truth. He wouldn't mention that he'd just been kicked off the force.

"You knew the *americano*?"

Wouldn't you know it? The dead man had an American passport.

"No, I already told you that. I'd never seen him before. He had nothing to do with me. I'm in Italy as a tourist, nothing more."

"You are in Italy perhaps to undertake an investigation?"

All of them, even Ferron, knew that would be illegal. "I told you, I'm not carrying out *any* investigation. I'm on vacation, for Christ's sake. My family's Italian. I'm here to see the sights."

"Then why did the *americano* shoot at you?"

"Your guess is as good as mine."

"You are a narcotics cop, *vero*? Perhaps the drug dealers in America ordered the hit to embarrass us—to show we cannot stop attempts on the lives of the *polizia* here."

He shrugged. "I have no idea."

He was sitting in a wood-backed chair in a DIGOS office on the third floor of police headquarters in Florence. The Questura was located in a four-story, ivory-colored building built on the site of an eighteenth-century insane asylum that had been enlarged by the fascists in 1927 for government offices. The building, which occupied an entire block to the northeast of the historical center, had bars on most of the first- and second-floor windows and a flag that flew from a balcony on the third floor over the central entrance on Via Zara. On all four sides, they were surrounded by tall *palazzi*, with few stores in the vicinity.

From the start, the behavior of the Italian police alternated between friendly collegiality and hostility, the latter feigned in part. It was the only way they knew to ask questions. The DIGOS office where they held him, a large room with a high ceiling and bare walls, was not intimidating. Scattered around the room were six desks occupied by both men and women agents, all startlingly young. And between interrogation sessions, to break the boredom, he was taken on a tour of the building by a cheerful woman, a *Vice-Ispettore* named Laura.

The building's offices, she pointed out, were divided into two sections on all levels, with the ground floor holding the Foreigners' Office and the *Polizia Scientifica*. Half of the second floor was assigned to the *Polizia Giudiziaria*, responsible in part for car theft, security measures, and the coordination of police archives—the *Centro Elaborazioni Dati*, and half to the *Squadra Mobile* or *Volanti*. The mobile squad, with a side entrance on Via Duca d'Aosta and parking for some of their vehicles in a courtyard on the ground floor, dealt with narcotics, organized crime, homicide and other matters. On the third floor, the police chief and other administrative groups occupied the front of the building, while the Division of General Investigations and Special Operations had its offices in the back. The DIGOS agents dealt primarily with undercover work and terrorism. The upper level, finally, contained the *Polizia Amministrativa*, concerned with licenses and related matters, and *Criminalpol*, whose offices overlooked Via San Gallo.

As a former cop, he found the tour interesting, but the delay in releasing him chaffed on his nerves. He kept asking when he would be allowed to return to his hotel, but the investigators were apparently waiting on information. It was seven-thirty in the evening on the day of the attack and he'd been in the building for over five hours, with nothing to eat but a thin *panino imbottito* and a soft drink.

A boyish-looking agent, Giacomo Carbonati, entered the room and waved a sheet of paper. "We've found out who the *americano* was." The others gathered around as he perched on the metal desk closest to Ferron, one leg dangling, the other on the floor, a cigarette in his hand. Carbonati had short hair and intelligent eyes and wore a wool sport coat and slacks, in shades of gray. The collar of his white shirt was open, but he had a dark blue tie draped around his neck. "He's a member of the military intelligence unit at the air base in Avviano. You know where that is?" Ferron shook his head, frowning at the news. "It's outside Vicenza. The man's real name is Stephen Karmon. He was carrying a set of false papers, but he had a telephone number written in the back of his passport—651141. That's the main switchboard at the air base."

"You said military intelligence—does that mean Italian or American?"

"NATO," Carbonati said. "Under American control."

"What's the military say about him? What was he supposed to be doing?"

"So far, no one will tell us. They say he was on leave."

"What about the weapons?"

"The Uzi's not military issue. The .38 Special's a Czech weapon made by Zbrojovka-Brno and imported by F.A.S.S.A. in Milan."

Czechoslovakia—the source for the weapons used by Kristine Kloos's guerrillas. Probably no connection, but it made him think of her father. Theunis Kloos was alive and would want his revenge, would assume Ferron was behind the attack at the lodge near Tafelberg. Had he contacted his cronies in Italy? And if it wasn't him, well, maybe it was the man his grandfather had spent every spare moment of his career trying to track down. His pulse quickened at the thought. Was he getting close?

He cleared his throat. The eyes of everyone in the room were on him. They'd been talking about the gun. "Is that a common terrorist weapon?" he asked, to cover his excitement.

One of the women agents snorted. "All guns are common terrorist weapons. They use what they can get their hands on—and that usually means almost anything." She stubbed out a cigarette in a metal ashtray already jammed with butts. Like the other women, she wore a dark skirt and white blouse, but, in her case, under a burgundy-colored cashmere sweater. The others were wearing jackets. "What makes you think a NATO agent is a terrorist?"

The constant smoking had given him a headache, and his neck felt stiff from the accident. They'd taken him to the Hospital of Santa Maria Nuova near the Duomo, where his neck had been bandaged. The damage was minor, but his whole body ached from the jolting.

He said, "We infiltrate the terrorists, why shouldn't they infiltrate the intelligence community?" No one said anything in response, so he shrugged his shoulders. "You tell me what he was doing. I'm the victim here. How in hell should I know what he was doing?"

The woman exhaled a stream of smoke toward the ceiling and then looked at him, her eyes sharpening. "Why would NATO intelligence concern itself with you."

He could see several of them were suspicious. He didn't want to mention his real reason for being in Italy, but he had to say something. He thought back to Beppe Aprico. That was as likely an hypothesis as any.

"Before coming on vacation, I was working on an undercover operation against a crime boss in southern Arizona. I was close to proving his syndicate had ties to the CIA. He supplied them with money for their operations in Central America and they facilitated his shipments of drugs into the States. The man was killed before I could make my case." He paused. "The men who killed him were agents of the Drug Enforcement Administration."

The Italians were listening intently. Carbonati rubbed his cheeks thoughtfully. "You think the CIA ordered this?"

Ferron waved his hands in a gesture of uncertainty. "Or possibly certain elements connected to the agency. But as I said earlier it could just as easily have been a mistake. It might not have had anything to do with me." He could see that no one believed him.

They let him go then—with the promise that he would spend the night in the city in case something urgent broke, and would telephone Carbonati each day during the rest of his vacation. The police were in contact with NATO intelligence and TREVI—an EEC organization fighting terrorism and organized crime—and would see what they could learn about the dead hitman.

On his way to the Hotel Cavour that night, staring from his taxi at the foreign students and tourists clustered on the steps of the Duomo, Ferron breathed a sigh of relief. So far, fortunately, no one had made any connection between his visit to Lucca and Vanni Cupo's suicide. Hopefully, they hadn't found the body yet—but when they did, what then? It might not be too long before someone started asking some very hard questions, and when they did, he didn't want to be around to answer them.

CHAPTER 5

Tuesday, September 17, Vicenza, Italy

He headed north by train over the next three days, having dropped the problem of the wrecked Alfa Romeo in the lap of the insurance company. He continued to contact the other men on his list, varying the names he used for himself and the tactics. In Bologna and Padua, he pretended to be the grandson of a man being blackmailed by Theunis Kloos. He wanted to track the blackmailer down, he said, and he needed their help. Did they have any information on the Dutchman or any other British or American agents active in northern Italy during the last months of the war? The answer was always no.

The weather meanwhile had taken a turn for the better. The days were sunny and bright, with only an occasional white cloud adding a drop of insouciant color to the sky. The evenings were mild, turning crisp by dawn.

On Monday of the third week in September, he checked into the Albergo Milano, a small hotel in Vicenza. From a telephone call to a parish priest, he learned that the next man on his list, Giulio Borghesi, had a granddaughter named Nina, an unmarried woman. She was living by herself in Vicenza, the priest told him, where she worked for a local branch of a right-wing labor organization. Her grandfather was bedridden, having suffered a stroke two years earlier. Thanking the loquacious priest, Ferron rang off.

From Borghesi's OVRA file and Kloos's ledger, he knew that during the war the man had been a member of the MVSN—the Voluntary Militia for National Security. As a fascist agent, he was responsible for several atrocities during the massacres in Marzabotto, a *comune* of 4,200 inhabitants, located twenty-five kilometers from Bologna. Over the course of several months in 1944, Italian fascists wearing German uniforms guided two regiments of the "Adolf Hitler" SS Division under Walter Reder in their slaughter of partisans and innocent victims, including women and children. The children were told they were going to have their pictures taken and were then butchered by the SS with machine guns hidden in tents. When it was over, nearly two thousand people had been exterminated, including 226 partisans of the "Stella Rossa" Brigade. The operation was so successful that Marzabotto was listed as a model in the *Bandenbekämpfung in Oberitalien*, a manual distributed to Nazi troops conducting anti-partisan warfare.

With each man he tracked down, Ferron felt his anger grow. Kloos had picked out the worst cases as victims of his blackmail, but that he could have allowed these men to hide their pasts and go on living in freedom, taking advantage of wealth acquired through war crimes, was inexcusable. As he continued to decipher more and more of the material in the files, he was beginning to realize that he would have no choice before leaving Italy but to mail the documents to the appropriate government officials in Rome. At the same time, in juxtaposition to his anger, his respect for his grandfather grew. Gran Babbo had served against men like these listed in the ledger; he'd fought with his Italian comrades against the *Nazifascisti*, every day risking a horrible death behind enemy lines. If Kloos had shared his files forty or fifty years ago, perhaps Gran Babbo would have tracked down the man who betrayed Carla Ceruti.

Nina Borghesi lived on the third floor of a modern building of smooth, gray stucco in a residential area near the Palazzo Porto-Breganze. Her apartment was on the east side of a winding street called Contra Mure Pallamaio, and had a broad sheet of windows catching the westering sun in the late afternoon. The windows, inset six inches in white stone frames, were dressed with wooden *tendine* that were open despite the late hour. The woman had no one opposite to stare into her windows at night, and from the ground Ferron could see only the ceiling.

On Tuesday, he walked to the branch office of the labor union, said he was a journalist for a magazine in the United States, and asked to speak to Nina Borghesi. He was ushered into the office of an attractive woman in her late twenties perhaps, with chestnut-colored hair worn shoulder length and dark, expressive eyes behind large oval glasses. He told her he was in Italy compiling material for a book on his grandfather Marcello Ferroni, an Italian from Verona who had emigrated to the States following the war and who made it rich in California in the aerospace industry, working with Howard Hughes. When she asked why he wanted to speak to her in particular, he said his grandfather had mentioned Giulio Borghesi in his memoirs. The two had served together in the war. With Marcello Ferroni dead, he thought she might be able to get her grandfather to answer a few questions about their experiences in the war and about other people they both knew.

At his invitation, they continued their conversation over lunch in the underground room of the Trattoria Vecchia Guardia. They found a table against the wall, across from a refrigerated case holding bottles of mineral water, wine, and beer, and cans of Coke, Fanta, and Sprite. "Did your grandfather ever talk much about the war when you were growing up?" he wanted to know.

Nina fingered a CRODO ashtray on the table. "Do you smoke?" she asked, and then pushed the ashtray to the side when he said no. "Me neither. I quit over a year ago." She straightened her glasses. "My grandfather is not a big talker, signor Ferron," she said. "He married my grandmother because she was. It saved him from having to say much when they were courting. He did all his talking on the job."

"What was his work?"

"He was a union official, a very powerful man."

He looked around the room. "Were your grandparents married before or after the war?"

"After. My father was born in 1947."

"Where was your grandmother during the war?"

"The Borghesi family has lived in Vicenza for generations,"

she said, "but my grandmother came from a small village along the Lago Maggiore." Nina smiled. "She was a very spunky young woman. She fought with the partisans in the Val d'Ossola. They were very successful against the Germans."

Ferron hid his surprise. "Is she still alive?"

Nina shook her head. "She died three years ago. My *nonno* had his stroke not long after. He wants to join her, but his body won't let him go. Sometimes now he confuses me with her . . . he calls me Ida." She lifted her glasses with both hands and dabbed at her eyes. "I shouldn't cry. My *nonna* lived a very full life."

The waiter was at their table then, and he ordered first to give Nina time to compose herself. Most of the other Italians were eating pizza, cooked in a brick oven in the corner of the room, but he ordered a full meal, wanting the opportunity to talk at greater length. Nina had already recommended the *fettuccine alla zingara* for a *primo* and for the *secondo* he chose the *scaloppine al limone* with a mixed salad. She asked for the same.

While they waited for the pasta, he asked her again about her grandmother Ida, surprised that a woman who fought with the partisans would marry a former member of the fascist militia—or had she known? Giulio Borghesi had been active farther south, near Bologna. Could he have hid his past that easily, simply by returning to the city of his birth?

"Where did your grandparents meet?"

"In Luino," she said. "My grandmother hid *nonno* Giulio in her parents' house when he was fleeing from the Germans."

His mouth dropped open. He cleared his throat and reached for a glass, pouring some mineral water and taking a drink to cover his shock. "Your grandfather was fleeing from the Germans?" he asked, trying to mask his skepticism.

She nodded. "Field Marshal Kesselring had ordered two divisions to eliminate the resistance in the Val d'Ossola. My grandfather was wounded in the fighting and couldn't escape into the hills. My grandmother saved his life."

Ferron was nonplused. He had been prepared to say his grandfather Marcello (who didn't exist) was a fellow fascist militiaman during the war.

"My grandmother Ida led a very brave life," Nina went on. "She was only a young girl, but in the fall of 1944 she carried messages by ferry between partisan bands in the hills above Cannobio to those in Luino across the lake. When she walked through the village square, she had to look at boys who'd been taken prisoner by the SS. Do you know what the Germans did? They hung the partisans from meat hooks, with the points here." Nina pointed to her face. "Just inside the jawbones. They would hang there, writhing in pain—sometimes for hours, grandma Ida said, before the jawbone would snap and the steel prongs would penetrate into the brain." She paused. "I'm sorry. I shouldn't talk about this before we eat."

He was listening intently, his elbows on the table, hands clasped under his chin. "Your grandfather Giulio . . . you said he was from Vicenza. Why was he fighting so far from home?"

Nina raised her eyes. "So far from home?" She shrugged. "I don't know. The Germans were moving north I think. Why do you ask?"

"I was just wondering." He tapped his fingers absentmindedly on the base of his wine glass. "I never knew for sure what my grandfather Marcello did during the last years of the war. I think he started out a fascist, but he must have gone over to the partisans. He mentions a few by name, including some American agents."

"Maybe that's when he met my grandfather," she said.

"Maybe."

When the waiter brought the bill, Nina glanced at her watch and uttered an exclamation. "*Mamma mia, come sono volate le ore!* The hours have flown."

They'd been in the restaurant over two hours and most of the other customers had already left. Both had talked about themselves, he briefly, she at greater length. At a certain point, their waiter had disappeared into another room, where he was eating a pizza with the cook.

"I enjoyed talking to you," he said. "And watching you. It was a pleasure." She blushed. At least he didn't have to lie about that, he thought. She was a very beautiful young woman. "When do you have to be back at work?"

"I'm off until four," she said, brushing her hair behind her shoulders, "but I need to take care of some errands for my grandfather. What is it you wanted to ask him?"

"Can I see you for dinner again tonight?"

She leaned forward and placed her hand over his. "Nick, you're very persuasive." She said his name with a strong accent and he laughed. He'd already told her to use his first name.

"*Va bene*," she said then, "if you promise to talk more about yourself."

"I like to hear your voice," he said. "Will you see your grandfather this afternoon?"

She nodded. "I have to pay some of his utility bills at the post office and then I'll stop by his home for an hour."

"I have a list of names." He reached inside his jacket and withdrew a sheet of paper. "He may not know most of them—some were active in Rome in 1943, but I'm hoping he'll remember something. I wonder if it would help if you didn't mention me."

She looked at him, her eyes puzzled. "Why, Nick?"

He pursed his lips and rearranged the silverware on his plate. "In his memoirs, my grandfather said he and Giulio had had a falling out at the end of the war—over a girl, I think."

Nina's eyes widened. "Over my *nonna* Ida?"

"It's possible. He doesn't mention a name. Wait!" Ferron sat up and stared at the sheet of paper. "I've forgotten one name—and it's the same as yours!"

"As mine?" He could see she was curious. "Who is it?"

"Nina Ceruti. She's a girl my grandfather knew in Rome. I have her sister's name on the list, but not hers. Her sister Carla was active with the resistance. Nina was too young."

"Can I see the list?" He handed her the sheet of paper. She read over the names and frowned. "You didn't list your grandfather. You don't want me to mention him at all? How are you going to learn anything about him?"

"Find out if your *nonno* Giulio knows any of these other people first. If he can direct me to one of them, I think they'll be more willing to speak to me. And if he can't, then we can ask about my grandfather."

She rested her chin in one hand and stared at him, eyes thoughtful. "You think *nonno* Giulio would bear a grudge after all these years? Nick, he's on his deathbed."

"I know. But all the more reason not to awaken old wounds."

She considered that for a moment. "How do I explain this list?"

"You meet union leaders in your job, right?" She nodded. "Then tell your grandfather one of them asked about him. Someone he knew in the war."

"But who?"

"Do you have to use a name?"

"Nick, if this union leader gave me a list of names, wouldn't he tell me his own?"

"Pick one of your grandfather's friends then."

She shook her head. "I don't think he has any friends from the war years."

"What about your grandmother's friends? Make up a name if you have to. You can say it was someone who knew Ida in the war—a man trying to track down old friends."

"Okay, Nick, I'll try. But don't expect much. After his stroke, my grandfather is very hazy about the past. I'll have to be gentle."

He nodded. "That's another reason why I think it's better that you see him and not me. When he sees you, he sees a young girl. If he sometimes thinks you're Ida, the past may be closer to him than the present."

After trying to reach Janelle in Durango (he'd hoped to catch her before she left for the high school) and getting no response at her number, Ferron telephoned Giacomo Carbonati, the DIGOS agent in Florence. He made the call from a narrow, glass-doored *cabina* in the SIP office located on the corner of a *piazzetta* near the Duomo. Carbonati thanked him for checking in and said he had nothing to report. When Ferron asked what NATO intelligence had come up with, Carbonati said a resounding *niente*. Before hanging up, the DIGOS agent asked him where he was telephoning from, and he lied and told him Rome and added that he'd be in Naples the next day.

"Don't miss Capodimonte," the Italian said. "It's a great museum."

"Nick, he recognized a name!" Nina Borghesi waved the sheet of paper excitedly as she stepped from the building where she worked. "I've wanted to call you all afternoon. His memory was perfect." Her voice was jubilant, and his face broke into a grin.

It was seven o'clock in the evening and the outlines of things had grown fuzzy in the twilight. Behind him, cars jammed the Corso, brake lights flashing. At that hour, traffic proceeded fitfully, and impatient drivers revved their motors in frustration. Despite the inner-city restrictions on horn blowing, an occasional sharp blast cut through the air and echoed off the buildings. Pedestrians cluttered the sidewalks, some stepping into the street to pass others.

She stepped up to him and leaned forward and for a moment they both hesitated and then embraced. He kissed her on both cheeks, smelling her perfume, a hint of jasmine and violets. He could feel her excitement and the pounding of his own heart. "Who was it?"

"Beppe Aprico." She held both of his arms. "*Nonno* said he didn't know him personally, but he'd heard of him. He was an Italian agent parachuted into northern Italy by the Allies. *Nonno* said Aprico helped organize the strikes at FIAT-Mirafiore near Torino in March of '43." She paused, then tugged on his arm and said jokingly, "You know what they say, Nick, *labor omnia vincit*—labor conquers all."

He grinned. "I thought that was *amor* not *labor*." Impulsively, he hugged her, unable to restrain his gratitude. An old woman waiting for a bus beneath a *Fermata* sign, net bags clutched in both hands, stared at them with disapproval. Nina took his arm and they set off up Corso Andrea Palladio toward the Piazza dei Signori. They were going to eat at a restaurant with outdoor tables, with a view of the Basilica.

"*Nonno* Giulio said Aprico worked with the *gappisti*."

He frowned. "Aren't they terrorists?"

She laughed and shook her head. "You're thinking of the *nappisti*." She stressed the *n*. "The *Nuceli Armati Proletari*. That's a communist-inspired terrorist group. The GAP were the *Gruppi di Azione Patriottica*." She paused. "I was going to say they were very different, but actually they weren't. They both opposed fascism. The *gappisti* killed over thirty hierarchs and other fascist officials. It's just that in war you're a hero for doing that, in times of peace you're a terrorist—unless you win."

"Do I detect a note of sympathy for the enemy," he said. "I thought you worked for an organization to the right of center."

"I do," she said. "My grandfather helped me get the job. But things change." She smiled and pointed ahead of them. "Even this street. During the war, it was called Corso Principe Umberto, but now it's Corso Andrea Palladio."

"The consequences of defeat."

"My history teacher in the *liceo* used to tell us about the day the Americans rolled in as liberators. They freed Vicenza the same day Mussolini was executed and one day before the Germans in Italy surrendered. My teacher said everyone was glad it was the Americans and not the British who came. The Americans always threw candy and chewing gum to the kids; the British marched in singing 'Tipperary.'" They both laughed at that.

Over beer and a *pizza margherita*, Nina told him more. "I had trouble with some of the names," she said. "I didn't know whether to translate them or not. *Nonno* Giulio doesn't understand English, but how do you translate 'Eagle Jack'? I said *acquila* and then Giacomo, but he only looked quizzical."

"It was a code name of an American agent working for the British. He was stationed in Switzerland, so the partisans might not have heard of him. What about Major Tom?" No need to tell her that was his grandfather.

She shook her head. "The only other name that seemed to ring a bell was when I said the *Olandese*. He squinted and his face jerked, but then he said he didn't know any Dutchman."

"Did he recognize Theunis Kloos?"

"The name meant nothing to him."

"He's the Dutchman. I wasn't sure if he used another name or not when he was in Italy. Apparently Beppe Aprico didn't."

Nina had a remote look on her face. "That's strange, isn't it? I thought all the OSS agents used code names."

Ferron stared at her. He hadn't said any of the men were OSS. Or had he? He couldn't remember for sure. He'd said they were American—was that the same thing? "Did your grandfather talk about the OSS?"

"He just said their agents helped organize the partisan brigades. The Germans put a high price on their heads. When things started going bad for the Germans, Kesselring told his men to shoot any American found behind the lines—whether in uniform or not. *Nonno* said the partisans always had to worry about traitors betraying the Americans for money. The Nazis were paying huge sums."

He watched her cut a bite of her pizza, holding the fork in her left hand. "You have a very nice mouth," he said, marveling at the banality of his compliment, but she smiled with her lips closed, chewing the pizza. She had sensual lips that distracted him every time he looked at her, and her eyes were shining with repressed excitement. He didn't mean to be crass, but when you wanted information, it never hurt to use flattery. And, in this case, at least it was honest.

"Nick, I've been saving the best for last," she said finally, wiping at her lips with a napkin and then leaning forward earnestly. "You wanted to talk to someone, right? My grandfather gave me the name of a woman who knew Beppe Aprico in the war. Maybe she can tell you something about your grandfather. She worked with one of the partisan brigades north of Brescia. *Nonno* said she was arrested near the end of the war by Pavolini's *Brigate Nere*—the Black Brigades—but never shot because both the militia and the Black Brigades were falling apart. This was when Mussolini was fleeing north trying to reach the Valtellina—his Alpine Redoubt. Fascism was supposed to die heroically, but Pavolini's men stripped off their uniforms and scattered into the hills."

She took a deep breath and sat back in the chair, her face disappearing in shadows. Night had fallen and moths fluttered around the restaurant's external lights. Bare light bulbs hung from a cord strung on poles around the tables.

"It's funny," she said. "My grandfather's thoughts wandered for a while. He remembered some of the things Mussolini said to the people and some of the jokes they told about him. When Benito ordered his officers to stop the partisans, he said, 'The gun is a big mouth whose voice everyone understands.' *Nonno* said he never forgot that. And when he first met my grandmother, she had a drawing in the house that would have been enough for the fascists to kill her."

Ferron leaned forward, pushing his plate away from him. He hadn't finished his pizza, but he'd lost his appetite, his stomach churning with conflicting emotions. He liked this woman and he'd lied to her. But then her grandfather had lived a lie for forty-five years. What would her reaction be if she learned the truth? He finished the last of his beer and said, "What was the drawing of?"

She leaned toward him, her face coming back into the light. "It was a cartoon showing Hitler, Stalin, and Mussolini. Hitler was labeled *Baffino*, small mustache; Stalin, *Baffone*, large mustache; and Mussolini, *Buffone*, buffoon."

They both laughed.

After a moment, she opened her purse and handed him a slip of paper torn from a small *quadrato* notebook. "Nick, let me give you the name and address of the woman my grandfather mentioned. Her name is Silvia Pozzi and the last he knew she lived in Lugano."

He looked at the slip of paper. There was a street—Via Ciani— but no number. "Thanks," he said. He folded the paper and slipped it into the inside breast pocket of his suit coat. "If she's still there, this will be enough. Did he say how long ago it was?"

Nina shook her head. "This was all he remembered."

The two stared at each other in silence. He tried to think of something to say to let her know how grateful he was. He'd just met her that day, but it seemed he'd known her for a long time. And now he was going to have to say good-bye. That afternoon, they had both opened up to each other in a way that for him was unusual. Ever since the divorce from Sharon, he'd grown more and more sullen and less inclined to talk. Now, he realized, something had changed for him. And it didn't start with Nina Borghesi; it started with Kristine Kloos, when he told her about his father. Suddenly he thought he understood. He'd always wanted to kill his father for what Frank Ferron had done to the family. But someone else chopped off that avenue of escape when he was still a boy. Someone hired by his grandfather and employed by Beppe Aprico. And now? Now he was tracking down a man like his father, a man who'd destroyed the lives of other people, a traitor. The closer he got to the man, the closer he was to forgetting his father—no, not forgetting him, cauterizing the wound the man had left in his heart, cutting him out, once and for all. It was a complicated thought but it made sense to him.

"It's getting late," he said. "I want to get an early start for Lugano. Let me walk you home and then I'll stop by the station and see about a ticket for tomorrow morning."

"Where are you staying, Nick?"

"The Albergo Milano."

"The Milano! But Nick, that place is—it's nice, but it's small."

He grinned. Stuffed into his miniature room were a single bed, an *armadio*, a coat rack, a bed stand with a gray phone connecting him only to the front desk, a high-intensity gooseneck lamp with a flexible shaft, a sink with towel rack, a portable douche bowl, a shoeshine rack, and two mirrors. And almost no room to walk. "At least it's cheap," he said.

"Nick, the hotel's five minutes from here. Let's get your things and you can come with me. I have a large apartment, with a spare bedroom—and if you have to leave early, I'm closer to the train station."

He hesitated, then said, "Thanks. I'd like that. Let's go get my things from the hotel."

CHAPTER 6

Tuesday, September 16, Vicenza, Italy

At eleven p.m., four hours after the hotelier of the Albergo Milano reported the names and passport numbers of his guests as required by law, two men, one an Italian, the other German, showed up and stationed themselves at either end of the narrow Stradella dei Servi, where the hotel was located. The two men waited in the shadows until one a.m., when they quietly jimmied the front door of the hotel, locked for the night. Moving silently, one of the men used a penlight to look at the last entries in the registration book on the manager's desk, found the room number, and then both took the stairs to the right of the desk. They stopped on the third landing, where the Italian waited, standing in front of the door to the WC under a weak light bulb, while the German moved along the dimly lit hall to room fifteen. The German slipped a skeleton key into the simple lock and pushed the door open. A knife glinted in his hand as he moved into the room. A moment later, the German stepped back into the hallway and beckoned to the other man. "There's no one here," he whispered in Italian. "And his luggage is gone." He sheathed his knife.

The Italian swore. He stepped into the room and opened the *armadio*, then moved to the sink and felt the towel draped over the rack. It was still damp. "He was here earlier."

The German nodded. "He may be back. Wait here until dawn. I'll go to the train station and keep an eye out for him."

"It looks like he's already left the city."

The German's eyes glittered in the darkness. "Maybe."

"He's slipped through the net again."

"Shut up, will you?" The German's voice was low and hard. "Where can he go from here by train? Toward Milan or Mestre-Venezia, right? We have men watching both stations and all the major stopping points in between. He won't get far this time."

"What about the old man—Borghesi? You want me to go there tomorrow?"

"Don't worry about it," the German said. "He's already been taken care of."

CHAPTER 7

Wednesday, September 18, Lugano, Switzerland

In Lugano, a resort town just across the border in Switzerland at the base of the alpine massif overlooking Lake Lugano, Ferron checked into the Europa Grand Hotel au Lac, situated on the Riva Paradiso. He'd left Nina Borghesi's apartment before dawn, without saying good-bye. Now, from his room on the third floor, he had a view of Castagnola across the lake at the foot of Monte Brè. Two miles south rose the sugar-loaf, tree-clad San Salvatore. Both mountains, over three-thousand feet in altitude, were scaled by funiculars. In the curve of the lake between the two mountains, motorboats, one pulling a water skier, traced graceful swirls around the white sails of the wind-driven craft. A ferry and two tourist steamers also plied the waters.

Following his arrival and a telephone call to Silvia Pozzi, he ate a late lunch at the hotel restaurant. He had two hours to pass before meeting the woman, so he lingered over the meal and afterward took a walk along the lido. With the ice- and snow-covered peaks of the Alps a short drive to the north, Switzerland's Canton Ticino startled him with its subtropical climate and flora. Oranges and chestnuts ripened in the warm sun of late September, and palm and plane trees lined the promenades. It was as if summer had returned. The air was heavy with the scent of lemons and almond trees in flower, of bergamot and oleander, of laurel and camellia. And drifting down from the protective hills that surrounded the town like an amphitheater, came the aroma of pine.

At five, he walked to Silvia Pozzi's place on Via Ciani, took a rickety elevator to the fourth floor, and was ushered into the drawing room of a small, but elegantly furnished, apartment. Like his grandfather, Thomas Gage, Silvia Pozzi had aged well.

"But I'm nearly ten years younger than him," she exclaimed when Ferron complimented her. They'd been talking about their families for twenty minutes. "I *should* look younger. I was just a girl at the time. The men were all like older brothers to me—especially Beppe and your grandfather. Der Ned . . . he was like a distant cousin."

He raised his eyebrows. "Der Ned?"

"Short for *Der Nederlander*. Until you told me today, I never knew his real name. He was a Dutchman and he spoke four languages—Dutch, German, Italian, and English, along with a few Hindi dialects—all of them like a native."

He was intrigued by the distinction she'd made between the men. Most were like older brothers, Theunis Kloos like a distant cousin. "How well did you get to know Der Ned?"

"I worked with him, just like I did with the rest," she said. "But I liked your grandfather and fell in love with Beppe."

He was still puzzled. "What was so objectionable about Kloos?"

Signora Pozzi shifted in her seat and rearranged the lace antimacassars on the arms of the Queen Anne chair, upholstered in pale rose, like the ottoman at her feet. The two of them were sitting opposite each other, each with a glass of Martini vermouth. It was just after five in the evening, and the French doors were open to the balcony, which overlooked the Cassarate River two bridges before it debouched into the lake.

Just when he was wondering uncomfortably if she was going to ignore the question, she said, "Der Ned had an anger in him that was different from your grandfather's. Both men had lost women they loved, but with the Dutchman it went deeper. He'd spent a year in the jungles of Java and Sumatra and he'd seen the Japanese kill and torture his men. He kept it in, brooding over it, and it was hard to figure out what he was thinking. He never touched any of the girls."

"Did my grandfather?"

She laughed. "No, but you could tell he liked women. With Der Ned, you felt he hated everybody." She took a sip of the vermouth and leaned back in her chair. "Your grandfather was a man who loved the people he was working with. You know, Niccolò—" she'd instantly Italianized his name—"I met Nina Ceruti after the war once—at a reunion of some of the communist brigades in Rome. It was a beautiful *sfilata*; we paraded up the streets from Piazza Venezia to the Quirinale, red banners waving, and then met in a large hall at party headquarters. The Ceruti girl came, trying to find out if anyone knew what had happened to her sister. To Carla. She was such a pathetic thing, skinny as a wax match—a *cerino*—and just as fragile. The war had been over for three or four years, but she was still a very young girl—too young to have fought with the rest of us."

She set her glass of vermouth on a small stand, an antique like many of the other objects in the room. Coming in, he had passed in the hallway a walnut *sgabello* with an octagonal seat and a triangular, fan-shaped back; a dressing mirror of Venetian rococo; and an intarsia umbrella stand. To his left sat a lacquered *fin-de-siècle* bureau with a two-handled jug of Faenza majolica on top. On the wall hung two paintings by Giovanni Fattori, a nineteenth-century Tuscan artist, each worth more than all the furniture put together.

"Nina Ceruti's dead now, poor girl. I heard she died of meningitis before she was twenty-five. But that night we talked about Carla and your Major Tom for a long time. He'd already gone back to his wife in the States by then."

"Did anyone ever find out what happened to Carla?"

Signora Pozzi screwed up her eyes in thought, head tipped back. "I think I heard she was shipped by train to Austria, but I can't remember for sure. She might have died in a *campo di concentramento*. You know, dear, we had concentration camps in Italy, also. Near Trieste. Not many Italians know about that, but it's true." The older woman licked her lips, head bobbing. She had rosy cheeks and her gray hair clung to her head in tight curls. Her face still carried traces of youthful beauty.

He leaned forward on the *art nouveau* sofa, arms resting on his knees, both hands clasped around the glass of vermouth. "I don't understand why Aprico left you after the war. You said you were lovers."

She nodded, but said nothing for a moment. When she spoke, it was with a slow, serious voice. "Caro Niccolò, I have outlived two husbands—and now Beppe—and I must confess, I still don't understand men. Whoever can explain them to women would do the world an inestimable favor."

He smiled and made a small deprecatory gesture. "When men understand themselves, then perhaps they can clue in women. It's like Mark Twain said, the more books the experts write the more darkness they cast on the subject and if they keep going, pretty soon we'll all be ignorant."

Signora Pozzi looked amused.

"How did you meet Aprico?" he asked.

The signora chuckled. "Beppe was always interested in money. British Special Forces recruited him in one of their field prisons in Blida. He'd been arrested in Algiers for getting into a bar fight with a group of British officers. He spent several long hot months locked up. One of the conditions of his release was that he parachute behind the lines into northern Italy. He would have preferred to go to Sicily, his homeland. Did you know? He was the one who suggested they spread the rumor about the oranges before the Allies invaded the island."

"About oranges?"

She nodded. "Beppe was good at black propaganda. He told them to tell the farmers that the *tedeschi* in Sicily all had syringes to suck the juice out of the oranges on trees." She laughed. "To be collected and sent back to Germany for vitamins. The peasants actually believed it. They thought they'd be left with dry oranges."

"What was his mission in northern Italy?"

"He worked in Torino at first, directing sabotage efforts against industrial *impianti*. He instigated several very successful strikes at the FIAT plant there. The plant was turning out fifty trucks a day, and the Germans were taking all of them. "

"You mentioned money. What did that have to do with it?"

Signora Pozzi plucked at her skirt. "After his success in Torino, Beppe came to Lake Garda. He'd heard that the Germans had removed ninety-five tons of gold from the Bank of Italy's reserves in Rome." She looked at Ferron with an ironic half-smile. "After the war, we learned Beppe was five months too late. The gold had already been shipped to Germany. I always remember what General Graziani said—'The Germans are stripping Italy and won't even leave us our eyes to cry with.'"

"So that's when you met Aprico?"

She nodded, her eyes remote for a moment. "I was a member of the communist armed resistance, running messages between cells in the Val Trompia, north of Brescia. In April, the leader of my squad sent me to Salò, to try to find work as a clerk in one of the fascist ministries. The ministries were spread out along the western shore of the lake, in villas. The Germans had sealed off the whole region and SS patrols controlled the roads. Beppe showed up one day in the mountains and said he wanted to work with the local dagoes and 'eye-ties,' as he called us."

Ferron looked at her in disbelief. He leaned forward, hunching his shoulders. "He was Italian, too."

"Italian-American, you mean. And he considered himself more Sicilian than Italian. Beppe's father was one of the *fuorusciti*—the émigrés. He left for America in the early thirties." Her face grew pensive. "Beppe told me he was sixteen at the time and didn't speak English. It was hard on him in New York. He got into fights with the other boys and stopped going to school, then got into worse and worse trouble, until finally the only way out was to become a GI. He joined the Army and took part in the landings in North Africa. Right after that was when he was arrested by British MPs and locked away for the duration. He almost killed one of their officers." She shook her head and chuckled dryly. "He said it was five against one, so he had no choice . . . but that was Beppe." She pursed her cheeks. "He had a violent nature with other men, but he was very gentle with me."

That wasn't hard to believe. Aprico had always been a lady's man. "Did you get a job in one of the ministries?"

She nodded, her fingers touching the pearls around her neck. "Beppe asked me to try for the Ministry of the Interior. Their spies knew what everyone else was doing. Beppe was operating a radio transmitter and was worried about the danger of enemy detection-finders. He wanted me to find out how many they had and how they were used. We were setting up drop zones and we needed to know where the patrols would be. The Germans were lighting decoy fires to confuse the pilots, and he thought if we could find out ahead of time where they were going to do it, it would make it easier to select a site farther away.

"At that time, both the Party Secretariat and the Interior Ministry were located in Maderno. Buffarini-Guidi had been forced out as Interior Minister just a few months earlier, but he was still working with Alessandro Pavolini, the party secretary. I made sure they saw me in a local restaurant and used my feminine charms on them. A week later, Pavolini put me to work in his personal secretariat. With my help, Beppe and the others carried out a series of surprise attacks against crack SS units and the fascist militia."

There was a note of pride in her voice. "We helped Allied PWs escape. We sabotaged bridges and railroads and communication lines and ammunition dumps all over the north, and bombed the offices of the *Militärverwaltung*—the Germans' military administration. They were conscripting young Italian boys—rounding them up on the streets and in their homes, and sending them off to Germany to work in Hitler's factories. Beppe was a master of guerrilla warfare."

"How long did this go on?"

She sighed and closed her eyes for a moment. "It seemed forever but it was only nine or ten months—maybe a year. It was very dangerous for all of us."

He nodded, then set his empty glass on a cork coaster on a three-legged pedestal table to his right. He leaned back and crossed his legs, straightening the crease on his slacks. "How did Aprico meet my grandfather?"

Silvia Pozzi folded her hands in her lap, head bobbing up and down in thought. "Beppe was in radio contact with the British and he kept asking the Special Operations Executive for help. I had gained access to the ministry's secret files and we needed to know what the Allies wanted us to get. Finally, his contact in Siena told him two men would be coming in on a joint OSS\SOE mission."

"And that was my grandfather and Theunis Kloos."

She nodded. "Major Tom and Der Ned."

"When did they arrive?"

"Sometime in the spring of '45. The Allies were advancing

north and the situation was beginning to decay. The Germans and fascists were preparing for their final retreat. Beppe wanted to organize a squad—ten or twelve men—to steal the gold he was sure they would take with them. Major Tom wanted to go after the hierarchs, who were trying to escape to Switzerland." She paused. "By the way, did you know that Lugano was one of the centers of antifascism in the early years of the dictatorship?"

He pretended interest and then went on impatiently. "What happened at the end in Italy?"

Signora Pozzi stared at the floor, as if lost in thought. After a moment, she said, "Der Ned was the mission's liaison officer. He was in contact with an SOE agent in Milan, someone Beppe didn't know. We had discovered that the OVRA files were at Valdagno. The SOE agent was running the operation from Milan."

"Do you know the man's name?"

She paused, squinting, and then wagged her head. "I can't remember his code name." She looked around the room vacantly and then her eyes suddenly brightened. "I called him *l'uccello.*"

"The bird? Why?"

She scratched at her cheek, frowning. "It had something to do with his name—some kind of bird perhaps."

"An eagle?"

"Yes." She nodded quickly. "How did you know? *Acquila Giacomo*—Eagle Jack, that was it. A strange name. It was easier for me to say *l'uccello.* I don't speak English you see."

Ferron's hands were clasped, one thumb tracing the lifeline in the other palm. "What did Eagle Jack tell Kloos to do?"

"Der Ned was told to pursue the documents."

His head snapped up. "What documents?"

"A special group of OVRA files. A month earlier, Mussolini had asked one of his henchmen to go through the files and pull out certain documents. The man had to go through our office for formal approval. He had a long list of names—agents provocateurs, double agents, partisan infiltrators, German spies, fascist profiteers and administrators Mussolini knew were corrupt. There was a separate list of foreign leaders—Roosevelt, Stalin, Churchill, Hitler, and a few other men I've forgotten. The files were boxed up and moved to the Villa Orsolina in

Gargnano, where Mussolini was staying."

"What happened to them after that?"

"After the war, some of them went back to Rome. The police let the people sack the building where they were stored and a lot of them were destroyed."

"And the others?"

"Some stayed near Lake Garda." She paused, pointing to a light switch near the door. "It's getting dark. Would you mind turning on the lights?"

The room, still warm from the day's sun, had grown dusky with twilight. A breeze ruffled the damask curtains near the French doors. Outside, swallows were sweeping over the river, their wings beating erratically as they dashed after insects, and traffic on the bridge was thinning. Overhead, a wispy layer of clouds was fading from rose to gray.

When he returned to the sofa, the signora continued. "I remember reading Rachele Mussolini's biography of her husband. After her husband's death, Churchill came to northern Italy to paint. But why to the shores of Lake Garda? She claimed his real purpose was to recover his letters to the Duce. Churchill supported fascism for a time in its struggle against communism."

"Are you sure that's not just communist propaganda?"

Signor Pozzi said sternly, "Rachele Mussolini was *not* a communist. When he tried to escape, the Duce was carrying a portfolio of documents that disappeared—just like his treasure. After the war, they blamed the communists. There was a trial in Padua. The 'treasure of Dongo' they called it—from the village where we stopped Mussolini's convoy. Supposedly ninety million in gold bullion and foreign currency. Someone said that the 52nd Garibaldi Brigade turned the treasure over to a communist leader in Como and that it had gone to enrich the coffers of the party. And then they found out that the men who personally knew about the affair had been killed in mysterious circumstances."

"You said there was a trial in Padua—how did the trial end?"

"There were thirty-five defendants and almost four hundred witnesses. One of the partisans said he'd loaded five suitcases of gold in one truck and three large sacks of foreign currency, mostly English sterlings and American dollars, in another. The man they were alleged to have gone to denied ever having received them. Near the end of the trial, one of the jurors committed suicide and a mistrial was declared."

"What happened to Der Ned and the others?"

"I never saw Beppe again. The last days were very confusing. He was in the hills and I was ordered to stay in Salò until the Allies arrived. Before they left, Beppe and the others got into a big fight. They were speaking in English so I couldn't understand, but it was very violent. I know they didn't trust each other. Beppe stormed out on his own. Eventually I heard he'd fled to Switzerland and disappeared."

"Fled? Why would he have to flee?"

"Why?" She hesitated, staring at her sturdy black shoes. "After we executed Mussolini and recovered the treasure, I think Beppe made sure he was in one of the trucks with the money. That was what he had come for—the treasure. I always thought he loved me—we had a very passionate affair—but with him what always mattered most was getting rich. I was told there were four men in each truck, but for Beppe that would have been nothing. A few bodies among all the rest would never be noticed."

Ferron let her words hang for a moment, thinking about how Aprico had gained his wealth with a criminal act, and had then gone on to use it for more of the same. He took a deep breath, repressing his anger, then asked. "What happened to Kloos and my grandfather?"

Silvia Pozzi lifted her head, her thoughts coming back from far away. She looked around the room as if to reassure herself of where she was. "Major Tom is the only one I ever saw after the war—at one of the OSS reunions. He didn't want to talk about himself. All I know is he was picked up by the Germans but escaped the same day and made his way back to Milan, trying to hook up with *l'uccello*. No one knew what happened to Der Ned. I always assumed he'd gone back to Holland."

The old woman looked at a gilt bronze and porcelain clock on the mantel over the apartment's gas-jet fireplace. It was getting late. "Would you stay for a light dinner, Niccolò? *Una minestra di spinaci?*"

"I'd be happy to stay."

"It does me good to talk to you," she said in a quiet voice. "I never had any children . . ." Her face grew pensive. "I sometimes think about how different life would have been had Beppe stayed with me. I don't think I've ever loved anyone as much as I loved him." Her voice died away and she bit her lip. "So long ago and yet I still feel it as if it happened yesterday." She stopped to compose herself, shaking her head as if surprised by her emotions. After a moment she said, "Maybe that's hard for you to understand. You knew a different man." She stopped short and got to her feet, her eyes moist.

A moment of uncanny silence followed, and then he rose, feeling awkward that he hadn't responded. "We all change," he said belatedly, but she was already turning to go to the kitchen and seemed not to hear.

Do we all change? he wondered. He wasn't so sure about Aprico. Beppe had started out as a schemer—a lover of women and a deceiver of men—and he'd ended up the same way.

CHAPTER 8

Wednesday, September 17, Lugano, Switzerland

It was dark when he left Silvia Pozzi's apartment and took Via Casserate along the river toward the lido. Isolated streetlights cast a harsh artificial light that delineated the night like a scalpel. The only shadows were in the recessed doorways of the apartment houses. Cars were parked bumper to bumper at the curb, but the streets were deserted. The stillness was broken only by the sound of his heels on the sidewalk.

As he approached Via S. Balestra, a Renault sedan swung around the corner and went by in the opposite direction, windows open, radio on full volume, two couples inside—boisterous tourists, he thought. He recognized the song on the radio—"Bello e impossibile." Gianna Nannini was singing about dark eyes, a kissable mouth, and a deadly game. *Un gioco micidiale.* Was that all it had become? He had made up his mind what he was going to do next. Theunis Kloos—*Der Ned*—had lied to him. He was the liaison officer with Eagle Jack, the man he claimed to know only by name. And who was Eagle Jack? The Dutchman had some questions to answer and this time he was going to make him tell the truth.

Thursday, September 19, Milan, Italy

Janelle said, "I had to have the Sheriff out last night."

"What happened?" He was telephoning from Malpensa airport. It was seven o'clock on Thursday morning in Milan, ten p.m. Wednesday night in Durango. He had twenty minutes before his flight to Amsterdam.

"Rowdy's been acting up at night. Like I said, I think someone's been coming around. I've been nervous ever since they broke in and burned your grandfather's papers. They're looking for something."

"What'd the Sheriff do?"

"Poked around, couldn't find anything and left."

"Can't he leave an officer in a car out there for a night or two?"

"He says he can't spare any men. I'm too far off the beaten track, Nick."

"You have your gun?"

"I've been carrying it around the cabin. At night, I leave a string across the stairs. It's tied to a can, so if anyone gets in and comes up after me, I should hear them."

He paused, absorbing what she'd said, the slight undertone of anxiety in her voice. "I shouldn't have brought Gran Babbo's trunk out there. Why don't you stay with your folks for a few days?"

"Are you coming back now?"

He looked out the door of the glassed-in cabin, a wave of exhaustion washing over him. Two other passengers were waiting to use the phone, twitching impatiently. "Janelle, I have to return to Suriname."

"To Suriname? Why?"

"Kloos has something else to tell me. I'm getting close, Janelle. I can smell it. And there's someone who doesn't like it." He turned his back on the people waiting outside. "Did Dick go up to Gran Babbo's cabin?"

"Last Sunday. He said it didn't look like anybody had been there." There was a moment of silence on the line, and then she continued, "They're downgrading the search on the missing hiker. The Sheriff said no one really knew if he was even in the mountains."

"Okay, thank Dick for me, will you? I appreciate the help." He didn't know what he had expected his brother-in-law to find.

With Gran Babbo dead, the cabin meant nothing to Ferron. "I have to go now, Janelle. Take care of yourself. I'll call you again from Suriname."

He hung up the phone and took a deep breath. Tracking down Kloos wouldn't be so easy this time. But if he's there, I'll find him, he thought. He's got some questions to answer and this time stories aren't going to be enough.

BOOK THREE

IN THE HANDS OF FATE

"All say, 'How hard it is that we have to die'—a strange complaint to come from the mouths of people who have had to live."
—Mark Twain

Chapter 1

Friday, September 20, Parimaribo

"Buddy, it's all gone bad," Martin Beam said, looking at the deck. He was sitting on a bunk in his tug, the master's quarters lit only by a candle. His face looked ghastly in the dim light, like a burnt-out hotel with busted windows. His eyes were dull, his pimple-scarred face ravaged by exhaustion. There was a smell of putrefaction in the cabin, of rotting food left out to spoil. A swarm of cockroaches had tumbled off the table at Ferron's arrival. The *Flora* had an air of neglect about her. The steam engine and the auxiliary generator were silent.

Ferron eased into a more comfortable position. It was a Friday, just after midnight, and the only good rest he'd gotten in the last two days were four hours in the hotel in Lugano. He'd been unable to sleep on the KLM flight from Amsterdam, keyed up by events and worried the Jungle Commando might kill Kloos before he could track him down again. "Where is everybody?" he asked. He'd found Beam alone in the boat, tied up at the Drambranders wharf in Paramaribo.

"Gone," Beam said, his eyes blinking rapidly. He reached for a bottle of whisky and tossed down enough to stun a normal man. "Dosu and Manbote are in prison. In Fort Zeelandia. Kristine's mother's been tortured and murdered. Kristine's in hiding."

"What happened?"

Beam stood up and waved his arms, swaying like a pine tree

on fire. "The whole country's up in arms. Kloos showed up at his Tempati Creek plantation, up the Commewijne river. He's ordered Kristine arrested on sight—and shot if she resists. He's scorched the butts off every bureaucrat from the president and the prime minister on down." Beam sat down hard. "The Army's got three thousand men in the field and a paramilitary force of nine hundred charging around in Armored Personnel Carriers. You got the Air Force crisscrossing the interior. The Navy has nine patrol boats, half of them with cannon, working their way up the rivers and creeks. And you know what the Jungle Commando has, buddy?" He looked up wildly. "Shit running down their legs, that's what—if they have any legs to stand on." He gestured around the cabin. "They're running like these cockroaches for any dark spot they can find."

"Who killed Kristine's mother?"

Beam shook his head. "Don't know. Maybe somebody looking for Kristine. They arrested the leader of the eastern Commando a week after you left. Army's cracking down hard. They'll shoot them all, once they get what they want."

Ferron reached for the whisky bottle and took a swallow. "Can anybody get to Kloos?"

"To kill him?" Beam snorted and shook his head in disgust. "Kristine's men are too frightened to attack him now."

"What happened to all the weapons?"

"Half of the local *bosnegers* tossed them in the river the minute they heard the government was coming down hard."

He examined the man, his hunched shoulders and bent head, the air of dejection. "Isn't anybody going to fight back? There's got to be something they can do."

"Yeah," Beam shot back, his voice sarcastic, "give up or kill themselves."

The man's shadow wavered on the wall and then grew dim as the candle flickered and guttered. In a minute, they would be sitting in darkness. Ferron leaned forward and took a deep breath. "Martin, I need to see Theunis Kloos."

The old man erupted in a high-pitched cackle that sent shivers up Ferron's spine. He waited a moment, then said, "Martin, I need your help. Can you take me there in the tug?"

Beam tossed back another snort of whiskey, then swallowed

and licked his lips like a sick dog. "Army's reinforcing the place now with SKM troops. Thank God for Colonel Pindu at least. Last I heard his guerrillas had surrounded the plantation. But if they don't act fast, they'll be cut to shreds." He got to his feet and fumbled in a locker for another candle.

Ferron leaned back into a bulkhead, dismayed by what he'd heard. "Who's this Colonel Pindu?"

"A Creole officer. Left the Army about a month ago. The only guy with any guts. He took over the eastern command after Godjo was arrested."

The new candle flickered into life.

"Can you take me to him? I need to see Kloos."

Beam shook his head mournfully. "That's a war zone, now, buddy. The Navy'd blow us out of the water." He moved back to his bunk. "They've stopped all commercial traffic on the river."

"Can I fly in?"

"No travel allowed in the interior. Hell, buddy, you're lucky they even let you back in the country." Beam stroked his rough cheeks. "You watch, in a day or two, they'll be shutting off the borders. They'll round up the foreigners and fly them out of the country."

Ferron's expression turned grim. "Then I hire a motorboat and go up the river by myself."

"You'll never make it out alive." He shook his head. "You don't know the Commewijne."

"It's a river, right? Pretty hard to get lost."

Beam snorted harshly. "With a thousand creeks flowing into it. You get back in the interior and you'll—hell, buddy, it's suicide. You'll never find Tempati Creek. It's like an old woman's varicose veins up there."

"I don't have any choice, Martin."

Beam muttered something to himself and then swore out loud. "Damn it all. You're just like Kristine. You're going to get us all killed."

"If you don't help, I'm going to the police. I'll ask Hans Oostburg for help."

"He'll kick your ass out of the country for meddling in political affairs."

"Or better yet, I'll go to the military."

"What?" Beam jumped up like spit on a hot griddle. "Are you crazy?"

"Suriname needs American support, right? The country's fighting to put down a revolution. The military won't want an international incident on top of it. They'll get me in to see Kloos."

Beam considered that, blinking his rheumy eyes. It didn't look like he'd shaved or bathed for several days; his body gave off the odor of a sour drunk. "Nick, ol' buddy," he said finally, "whose side are you on?"

Ferron's temper flared. He was tired of the guy calling him buddy. "I don't see you doing much. I thought you were a friend of Kristine's."

Beam's head bobbed up. He stared at Ferron and then nodded wearily. "She's like a daughter to me."

"And you're doing nothing to help."

Beam sighed. "We'll have to get a smaller boat," he said. "We can't go in the tug."

CHAPTER 2

Saturday, September 21, Zorg en Hoop, Suriname

Saturday morning, Moffi, the *bosneger kabiteni*, and his younger brother Tano drove Ferron to the house of a man named Sastro Karta, an Indonesian plaiter of chairs, who lived in the suburb of Zorg en Hoop and had a telephone. Sastro's house was of clapboard, with a sharply pitched roof, a railed balcony on the second story, and porches running along the dirt street. Ferron lay down on a narrow bed in a windowless room while the men left to contact Kristine and work out the details of the trip.

He hadn't slept during the night and had passed beyond exhaustion into a nervous state where sleep seemed impossible. In the outer room, he could hear the muffled sounds of Radio KBC. Their commercials were in one of the local languages, with an occasional item in English. He couldn't quite make out the words. Finally, he drifted off into troubled sleep, his head weighed down by a mass of atmospheric pressure that seemed twice what it should be.

Later that afternoon, Moffi and Tano returned with Martin Beam. Ferron joined them in the kitchen, feeling sullen and groggy. The house lacked air conditioning and the muggy air was oppressive. They sat around a kitchen table on wood chairs with rattan seats and backs, while the Indonesian served tea, *asogri* cakes, and sliced melon. The cakes were made of ground corn, sugar, and raisins, and were too sweet for Ferron. He sipped his tea and ate the melon.

When they'd finished, Beam wiped his lips and looked across the table. "Okay, buddy" he said. "This is how it works. We leave Sunday night, but it's going to be tricky. Kristine will meet us on the river."

"Why not tonight? If Colonel Pindu's men attack the plantation, Kloos may be dead before we get there."

"These things take time," Beam said. He pointed toward the Indonesian. "You'll be staying here with Sastro. My tug is under surveillance. There's nothing you can do until we're ready."

"Where's Kristine?"

"Kristine's going to be busy."

"Doing what?"

"We can't make it up the Commewijne river and through those creeks in the tug. First of all, it's too large; second, I'd never get a permit for that. The tug's going to be out in the Atlantic where the Air Force and Navy can spot it any time they want— only thing is, thanks to Kristine, we won't be on it."

Ferron looked puzzled. "I don't understand."

Beam grinned. His mood seemed to have changed completely from the night before. "A switch," he said. "Wait and see the boat Kristine's on. We're going to be riding in a Navy patrol boat and a few sailors are going to be fishing off the side of the tug."

"How's Kristine going to get a Navy patrol boat?"

"You leave that up to her."

The encounter was to take place in the middle of the Suriname river just off Leonsberg, located in sand flats to the north of the capital. The river narrowed and then took a sharp turn to the west at that point, joining up with the Commewijne river, which flowed from farther east, before emptying into the Atlantic. The plan was to make the switch in midriver, then for the patrol boat—under guerrilla control with Ferron, Beam and Kristine on board—to run for the Atlantic, bearing toward the floating *lichtschip* off Warrapabank. At that point, they would cut their running lights and double back up the Commewijne river, moving at night as far into the interior as possible despite the danger of colliding with stray logs and other debris or of running aground.

Beam had called a friend at Goddodrai, a village in the interior, where they would lay up in a boatshed until the following night. At Java, where the Kleine Commewijne joined Tempati Creek, they would head east up the creek and then south toward Nassau Gebergte, transferring to dugout canoes, if necessary, after Poitehede. They expected to reach Kloos's plantation, east of Hok-a-Hing Gebergte, some time before dawn on Tuesday.

The success of the operation depended on Kristine. She had gone to the harbormaster's office late that evening with an involved story about a Jungle Commando plot to smuggle drugs to a trawler at sea, where they would be exchanged for weapons. The Navy had a patrol boat on harbor duty, and the plan called for her to talk her way aboard. She would be needed to direct them to the rendezvous.

With the end of the rainy season, the days had grown hotter, but at night a cooling trade wind swept along the coast. Ferron was dressed in black—a pullover shirt and cotton pants, with thick-soled sneakers. Beam and Moffi had managed to find weapons for all of them. Ferron carried the short version of a Soviet AKM assault rifle. They had picked up four other rebels, all heavily armed. On the way out the central channel at midnight, their passage was uncontested. No Navy ship appeared in the darkness to hail them. No one seemed to notice their running lights. There was no patrol boat where the river narrowed. They couldn't drop anchor in the middle of the channel, so Beam headed toward the Atlantic, looking at his watch and swearing.

"She didn't convince them in time."

Or they'd simply arrested her, Ferron thought. "What do we do now?"

"Go out to sea, turn around, and come back in again. Make them think we're the ship with the weapons."

Ferron didn't like it. He'd been expecting things to go bad ever since he'd learned the plan. When he'd asked Beam why they didn't just attack the men at the dock if they were going to take the patrol boat by force, Beam had claimed it was too risky. If they jumped the Navy in mid-river, it might give them an hour or two before anyone found out something had gone wrong. "But we'd have the element of surprise if we attacked on land," Ferron had argued, adding, "If they see us in the river, they're going to be expecting trouble."

Beam had refused to listen. He'd told Ferron this was Kristine's plan and they'd do it her way. She was the one risking her life.

And they weren't? Ferron thought.

In the Atlantic, they ran for a half-hour at slow speed toward Trinidad, then swung about and headed back. They reached the Vissersbank an hour after midnight and began to move upstream, eyes peering into the darkness. Tano and another man stayed in the master cabin as a back-up, but the other three rebels took up positions lying on deck, flat up against the gunwale. In the darkness, they were invisible. Moffi and Ferron stood on deck, with Beam in the pilothouse at the wheel. The warm air smelled faintly of sewage.

As they drew abreast of Nieuw Amsterdam off the port side, Beam cut the running lights—if they were smugglers, they had to look like it—and they moved upriver in darkness, the only illumination provided by the lights along the waterfront in Paramaribo ahead of them. Ferron saw the patrol boat then, dead ahead, a dark shape in the water moving slowly toward them with a white light at the bow, and green and red running lights on the starboard and port sides. Before he could speak, a powerful searchlight stabbed out of the darkness and bathed the tug in a blinding glare. A voice, amplified by a loudspeaker, shouted something in Dutch.

Beam reversed his engines, throwing the stern in, and the pilot of the patrol boat cut the throttle and turned the rudder hard right. The bow swung in that direction and the patrol boat began to drift slowly toward them with the current. Shouted commands rang out. Moffi dropped his weapon, raised his hands, and stepped away from the gunwale and Ferron followed suit. As the patrol boat approached, it looked like there was a sailor at the wheel and several other men standing in the stern, but no sign of Kristine. Had something gone wrong?

The two boats bumped gently and one of the sailors threw a line to Moffi, who secured it to a stern cleat. In a moment, they were boarded by two sailors, who slapped Moffi and Ferron up against the side of the master's quarters. And then, before they knew what had happened to them, the two sailors were knocked cold, the rebels rising like phantoms from the scuppers, and the three others on board the patrol boat were staring down the barrels of assault rifles.

Ferron picked up his rifle and stepped quickly to the gunwale. Moffi had already disappeared over the side. "She's here," Moffi called over his shoulder. Ferron heard Beam grunt behind him and then disappear down an engine hatch into the bowels of the tug.

He saw Kristine then, lying on the deck of the patrol boat, her hands cuffed behind her back. "Is she okay?"

Moffi tore a strip of tape from her mouth.

"I'm fine," Kristine said, her voice hoarse. "Tano, get the key for the handcuffs."

Tano pivoted toward the sailors and said something Ferron didn't understand. One of them handed a key to Tano, and he jumped into the boat and bent to uncuff Kristine. The engines of the tugboat suddenly churned to a stop. Beam had sabotaged them, along with the radio, as directed earlier by Kristine.

"Moffi, it's time," Ferron said. "Tell the sailors to get up here. We're switching boats."

The sailor behind the wheel resisted until he saw Ferron aim the assault rifle at his head. "If he's not out of there in thirty seconds, his head gets blown off."

Moffi started to translate, but the sailor understood. He left the wheel and followed the other men on board the tug. At a sign from Ferron, the four rebels jumped into the patrol boat, one by one. He tossed a knapsack in after them. Kristine tried to speak and then began coughing.

Ferron said, "Take the wheel, Martin. Let's get out of here."

He clambered into the patrol boat after Beam and then turned back to the Navy men marooned on the tug. "Do any of you guys understand English?"

One of the men nodded, shielding his eyes from the glare of the patrol boat's spotlight.

"We're meeting another ship off the coast," Ferron said. This was the lie the men had agreed to. "Near Guyana. When you're rescued, you can tell the Navy they'll find their patrol boat between here and Georgetown. We'll drop the anchor and set her adrift. They should find it before it gets carried too far."

One of the sailors had moved into the pilothouse, where they could hear the harsh sound of the tug's starter grinding away with no result, followed by swearing.

The sailor who spoke English said, "What about us? We're going to be swept into the Atlantic."

"They're some fishing poles in the cabin," Ferron said. "Take a little vacation. The Navy'll find you soon enough."

CHAPTER 3

Sunday, September 22, Commewijne River, Suriname

Kristine stared at him wide-eyed in the darkness. "Nick, you came back." A note of marvel in her voice. "I thought I'd never see you again."

He bent forward to speak. "You okay, Kristine? What'd they do to you?"

She sat with her back to the gunwale, her knees drawn up to her chest. She was wearing a dark skirt and blouse, and sandals on her feet. Long strands of hair swirled around her face as the patrol boat gained speed. "Nothing—compared to what my mother suffered. They beat me." Her voice was rough, her lips puffy from the salt they'd given her to make her thirsty. They had tortured her for over an hour before accepting her subterfuge as the truth. She rubbed her wrists where the handcuffs had chaffed the skin.

He reached out and found her arm, skin hot to the touch; she was burning up with a fever. "Martin told me about your mother. I'm sorry, Kristine."

When she looked up, her eyes glittered in the dark like those of a wild beast. She nodded, but said nothing for a moment.

"Let me get you some water," he said.

She reached out and grabbed his arm before he could move. "Nick, if they find you with me now, you'll be shot on sight. Let us go on without you. Get out of the country while you can."

"I'm not leaving, Kristine. Not yet." He turned away from

her, looking for the knapsack he'd thrown on board. Beam was pushing the boat at full throttle toward the mouth of the Commewijne river, running lights extinguished. Behind them, the drifting tugboat had disappeared from sight.

"Throttle down when you reach the confluence," Kristine shouted, her voice rasping. "I don't want anyone to hear the route we take."

Behind them, from the direction of Paramaribo, they could hear the muffled beating of a chopper on patrol. Would the helicopter spot the disabled tug? Ferron hoped not. He was banking on several hours before the patrol boat was missed or the tug discovered. They needed the delay to give them time to escape. Once the tug was discovered, the Air Force and the Navy would launch a search of the nearby Atlantic and the coastal shelf, and all the rivers in the vicinity. The guerrillas had to move fast during the first hour or two, dodging the searchlights of the choppers on patrol and avoiding any other patrol boats that might be waiting upstream. If they met the Navy along the Commewijne, they'd be in trouble; the patrol boat they'd confiscated had no cannon.

He found the knapsack and removed a canteen. "Here, Kristine." She'd fallen over on her side, her head on a life preserver. He helped her sit up and unscrewed the cap. "Drink this. You hungry?"

"I'm too battered to feel like eating," she said. "They beat me for a long time." She took a long draw on the canteen. "Don't you have anything stronger than water?"

He grinned. Her voice sounded better already. "Martin," he shouted. "Pass us that flask in your back pocket."

Later, she said, "You didn't come back for me, did you, Nick?"

He stared at her a moment in the dim light of the console, wondering how much showed in his own eyes. He'd heard the hurt in her voice. They were moving through a rough stretch around a bend in the river near Slootwijk, and Beam had gone forward to watch for rocks. Ferron stood at the wheel and Kristine sat to the side, facing him. A pale sheen, cast by a gibbous moon waxing toward full, illuminated the darker masses in the water. Beam had wanted to use the searchlight, but Ferron was still wary of detection.

"No, Kristine," he said softly, so Beam couldn't hear. "I came to see your father—but I'm happy you're with us."

Kristine took that in and then said, "Thanks for helping, Nick. Martin was ready to give up. He told me how you badgered him. I'm glad it was you."

By the time they reached the boatshed at Goddodrai an hour before dawn, they were exhausted. Beam's friend was a Creole named Petrus Lambertzen, a balding, smooth-faced man who ran a bedraggled chandlery and boat service for tourist excursions into the interior. As the sun bounced into the limpid sky and arched upward with stunning speed, Lambertzen guided them along a weed-choked path to a dilapidated shack with half-inch cracks between the wall planks. *Baboenefi* surrounded the shack on three sides, the razor grass named for a Hindustani knife. The smell of leaf-mold was strong and the air so hot it was hard to breathe. Stretched out on worn paillasses, with straw poking through the frayed linen covers, the nine of them tried to sleep away the daylight hours, awakening in late afternoon for a cold meal of cassava cakes and yams, baked the day before, and dried fish with chilies.

"After tonight," Tano said, "we get more men—the Djuka. Good fighters."

"What are they armed with?" Ferron asked. "Spears?" The heat had made him short-tempered.

The young man snorted. "No spears. Guns. Before he was captured, *kabiteni* Godjo sent many weapons to the Djuka."

Moffi said, "You should no worry about guns, Nick. My people say, *Fesi ben de bifosi spikri.*"

He looked at the older man, who was squatting on his haunches and sucking the pulp from the purple skin of a wrinkled yam. "What's that mean?"

Moffi's serious face broke into one of his rare grins. He tapped his chest, where the long machete scar glistened. "Faces been there before mirrors."

Ferron turned to Kristine. She had finished eating and was combing her hair, which she'd washed outside with rain water collected in a barrel. "I don't get it," he said.

She looked at him, her face somber. "In the old days, the whites had astonishing mechanical devices, but in the bush, for the escaped slaves, the gods were still powerful—they made faces before men made mirrors." She paused, water dripping from her hair to her shoulders. "I told you my mother was a *wisi-woman*, a sorceress. My friends think her powers have passed to me."

Before he could ask more, Beam cleared his throat and said, "We need to get moving. We have a long, dangerous haul tonight." He spoke in a quiet voice but his sunburned face seemed unnaturally taut as he got to his feet and adjusted the bill of his faded cap. "Once Kloos learns about the patrol boat, his men will be waiting for us—and I don't think the power of the gods is going to stop their bullets. Kloos has his own black magic or he'd have been dead long before now. And you know what they say." He looked around the room for a moment, his eyes hooded. "When you eat with the devil, you need a long fork."

Just before dawn, the dugout canoes slipped out of Tempati Creek and were drawn up on a muddy bank downstream from the plantation. The patrol boat, which had followed behind during the last stretch, pulled at times by tow ropes, was tied fore and aft to trees along the bank. The guerrillas hacked a clearing in the tangled lianas and set up camp, pitching lean-tos in a large circle. The Djuka boatmen who'd been awake all night fell immediately asleep in their hammocks. At Kristine's request, a runner left to contact the area's tribal chiefs and the local units of the Jungle Commando. She'd been told that Colonel Pindu had called for a final meeting to go over the plan for the attack, and she wanted to be included, knowing that her presence would inspire the guerrillas.

While the others set up camp, posting guards to watch for government troops, Ferron worked his way upstream with Tano and Chaku, a Djuka who had once worked for Kloos on the Tempati Creek plantation. Away from the creek, which was wide and deep enough near the plantation to be called a river, the jungle floor was clear of vegetation, the tall canopy of trees cutting off all light, but tangled vines impeded their progress.

The only sound, other than their labored breathing, was the high drone of cicadas, the incessant buzzing of insects, and an occasional bird call. An hour later, as they approached the plantation, which lay on the other side of the creek, Ferron noticed the smells of cooking in the hot, stale air—the spicy odors of Indonesian food. For three days, the workers had not left the compound, Chaku told him. Ferron knew what that meant— Kloos was preparing for the guerrilla attack.

Kristine had told him what would happen if forces of the Jungle Commando captured or killed her father. "The military is afraid this time," she said. "With my father out of the picture— with the Americans standing by doing nothing, the people will unite and overthrow the government. Many of the soldiers will come over to us then. Without my father behind the scenes, the government will collapse. They need to protect him."

The government had clearly recognized the danger. SKM troops were visible in the compound, and one of their helicopters was on the ground in an open space behind the plantation house. The Commando would have to make sure the chopper didn't leave with Kloos, or the attack would be for nothing. He would check to see that Colonel Pindu had assigned a squad to shoot down the bird if it took off during the attack.

With the help of dangling bush ropes, he and Chaku climbed one of the taller *baramalli* trees, and Chaku identified the various buildings in the compound for him. The plantation was a village laid out on a large plot of land shaped like half of a stop sign with the flat side facing the wide creek, which ran north toward the Commewijne river and the Atlantic. Kloos's engineers had dug a half-mile ditch around the compound, diverting part of the creek to form a swampy moat, originally intended to control the invasion of voracious ants and now serving for defense against guerrilla attacks. Around the inner side of the moat, his workers had constructed a packed-dirt rampart, with a wood-stake fence along the top. Chaku said there were caimans in the swampy water and pointed stakes below the surface. The rebels would have to cross with makeshift bridges or at one of the two wooden bridges at the north and south end of the island, both heavily fortified. The bridges led to fields behind the island where groves of palm trees stretched for miles. The Tempati plantation was one of the country's largest producers of palm oil.

Inside the fence, along the island's curving eastern side lay the worker's houses, lined up like rows of military barracks. To the south, next to a watchtower overlooking the creek, sat a laundry room and supply store, and behind them a large provision garden leading to the plantation house, which faced the creek in the middle of the island. A heavy gate opened to a boat landing and a shed, patrolled by guards.

The plantation house, a two-story building with attic and double verandas on all four sides, was surrounded by the bright cerise of bougainvillea. The wooden louvers over the windows were tightly closed, and from the outside there were no signs of life within the house. At the back of the building, just beyond the helicopter, they could see a rectangular, cement-block-and-stucco clinic, painted white. And to the north, near the gate leading to one of the bridges, perched a small chapel with a steeple and cross. At the far north, an L-shaped building housed a tool shed and mechanic's shop. Most of the trucks and harvesting equipment were stored off the island in a large warehouse lying about two hundred and fifty feet into one of the palm groves.

The compound presented a complex objective, difficult to attack from several directions at once, and Ferron wondered what Colonel Pindu had planned. Even if the guerrillas made it across the moat undetected, climbed the rampart and breached the fence, they would face heavy resistance from a variety of points, with numerous obstacles and good cover for Kloos's men. The first objective, he imagined, was to gain access undetected. If they could silence the watchtower and take out the guards at both bridge gates, they might be able to infiltrate a large number of guerrillas before the workers and soldiers were aware of their presence. The workers would be armed and thus needed to be neutralized before attempting to take the plantation house itself. No matter how they attacked, Kloos would have plenty of advance warning. If the Jungle Commando could successfully push from the east, routing the workers from their houses, Kloos might be inclined to attempt an escape via the boat landing to the west. But if he did, the Commando would take him with ease. The Djuka could block both ends of the creek with guerrillas in dugouts, and should Kloos's guards fight their way through the first line of men, Beam had the patrol boat to chase him down.

"Okay," Ferron said. "I've seen enough. Let's get back to the camp."

Several of the Jungle Commando's leaders were experienced military men, and many of the guerrillas had been trained by the Army. Colonel Pindu listened to Ferron's questions, nodding his assurances, and then laid out the plan of attack. The guerrillas had amassed a force of nearly two hundred well-armed men. The attack was scheduled to begin Tuesday at four in the morning, when the compound's guards would be at their sleepiest. Fifteen minutes after the guerrillas attacked from the east, a squad of eight men, in two dugouts, would cross the creek to take the boat landing. Ferron had asked to be included and Colonel Pindu had acquiesced. He'd told them to take only the landing, but Ferron had other ideas. Somehow, he had to get into the house before Kloos escaped or the others killed him. The guerrillas had been told to try to capture him alive, but most doubted that Kloos would let himself be taken.

When night fell and the darkness closed around them like a suffocating pillow, the others drifted off to sleep while Ferron lay in his hammock and listened to Kristine's unsettled breathing. She was lying next to him in the lean-to Tano had built, and he could reach out and touch her if he wished. He heard her moan and wanted to whisper that it was okay, that she was only dreaming, but something held him back. Perhaps a dream—even a nightmare—was better than the reality that faced her in the morning. Though tired, he was seized with a restless anxiety; he felt like a kid with matches about to set fire to a spider, overcome by a desire for vengeance, even though his mind told him it was wrong. His nerves jangled with repressed emotions and confused memories: memories of his mother and her violent death . . . hatred for his father . . . love and sorrow for his grandfather. He wished Gran Babbo were alive to confront Kloos, to learn the name of the man who had betrayed him so long ago. Gran Babbo had deserved to see justice done—deserved, before dying, a chance to reconcile his past and find peace. It was too late for him now—but not too late for Ferron:

Gran Babbo had taken care of the traitor in Nick's life, his own father; now it was time to return the favor.

Aware that he wouldn't fall asleep if he stayed where he was, he rolled out of the hammock, found his sneakers and slipped them on after making sure they were empty—he'd seen enough insects to last a lifetime. Orienting himself in the dark, he felt a hand on his arm and froze.

"It's me," Kristine said. "Where are you going?"

He let his breath out, heart pounding from the influx of adrenaline. "To the creek," he said. "Want to come with me?"

Chapter 4

Beam was on duty watching the patrol boat, which earlier in the day they had managed to work through the narrow rocky stretches using ropes and the expertise of the Djukas. There had been no rapids to match those on the Saramacca river. One of the guerrillas had sold Beam a jug of brandy and Ferron found him sitting on the deck with his back against the gunwale. Beam perked up like a radar blip, happy to have company. He popped the cork stopper and offered the jug to Ferron. "Home-brewed," he said. "Careful, buddy, not to snort too much. This'll turn up your nose like a bull sniffing cow pee."

Ferron took a swallow, coughed as the fumes seemed to rise through the top of his skull, and handed the jug to Kristine. She wet her lips cautiously and returned the jug to Beam. They settled down then, talking quietly for a while and then sitting in companionable silence, each lost in thought.

After midnight, the moon rose over the creek, clearing the jungle growth to each side and casting an eerie sheen over the glistening black ribbon of water. The moon was moving toward full and in the cloudless sky, it seemed a large cold lozenge, riding high above the hot, still air of the jungle. For a moment, seeing the shiny disk, Ferron recalled the time his father had caught him stealing a quarter off the kitchen counter in their home in Grand Coulee. Frank Ferron had heated the quarter with a match and then dropped it in the boy's palm. Nick still had a faded scar from the burn.

Beam muttered a few words, his head lolling to the side, and Ferron realized the older man had fallen asleep. The jug of brandy was gripped loosely in his grease-stained fingers.

"Better cork the jug," Kristine whispered.

"You want to head back to the camp?"

She shook her head, then moved across the boat and sat close to him, sliding under his left arm. "Hold me for a while, Nick."

She shivered as if having seen a ghost, and he brushed the hair away from her face. "Where will you be tomorrow?" he asked. Colonel Pindu had divided them up into different platoons.

"I go in with the squad taking out the watchtower," she said. "We have one of the radios. We'll let the others know what's going on inside the compound."

"Do you think we're doing this right? Saving the plantation house till the last?" He was worried about what her father would do.

"We couldn't take the house from the creek. Not enough boats and too easy to be detected. We'd never make it over the walls or through the gate there. You'll have a hard enough time just trying to secure the boat landing. With the SKM troops here, my father's men will be armed with M-16s and shoulder-fired grenade launchers."

"I talked to the men earlier. We're going to carry one of the dugouts upstream through the jungle. We'll drift down from the south. If we're lucky, they won't see us until it's too late."

"You'll have to get by the watchtower first."

"But you'll have taken it, right?"

"Taken it or burned it down. If we have to burn it, the men at the landing will be waiting for you."

"It won't be the first time I've done this." He thought of the coyote pups he'd saved and how he'd missed out on the attack on Beppe Aprico, how he'd angered the chief and cost Senator Sprague the photo-op—but there'd been plenty of other raids where he'd gone in against superior fire power and succeeded.

"You don't have to risk your life, Nick. This isn't your cause."

"Kloos is my cause. If I don't get there first—" His voice fell away, and then came back with hard determination. "This time, your father's going to tell me what I want to know."

Kristine slumped forward. "He's no longer my father, Nick. For me, he's already dead." She hugged her knees to her chest. "The Navy men knew I was his daughter—and still they tortured me. He gave his permission to have me shot on sight, Nick. They would have killed me sooner or later. I'm nothing to him—a mosquito he'd slap against the wall with his slipper."

He listened without reply, his arm resting lightly on her back. Another one, he thought, another victim of neglect and abuse. They were denied even the right to grieve.

CHAPTER 5

Tuesday, September 24, Tempati Creek, Suriname

The first sounds of rifle fire crackled through the compound at four-fifteen that morning—an isolated burst near one of the bridges. And then, as the dugout slipped downstream, Ferron heard the harsh staccato of answering fire and the battle's crescendo swept over the compound with the sudden and unexpected fury of a desert thunderstorm. Had the guerrillas secured the bridges or were they going to be cut down as they tried to cross the moat? He couldn't tell if the explosions were inside or outside the compound. Among the first infiltrators, Colonel Pindu had assigned several men to take the helicopter. The guerrillas wanted to seize it before it was damaged or shot down. Ferron listened for the thunder of its blades, aware that Kloos might attempt to escape before the battle approached the plantation house. His pulse was pounding as he bent over in the dugout, his left hand gripping the sling of the AKM assault rifle riding on his back. He had an unsheathed, eight-inch combat knife in his right hand.

Gliding down the dark creek, he wished he knew what was happening inside the compound. From the sounds of the weapons, a war had broken out—but that's just what this was, he thought, the first full-scale battle of the revolution. And it was men like those inside the compound who had tortured Kristine—the enemy. Remember your objective, he told himself. He wasn't here to avenge Kristine. He couldn't afford to get carried away by the impetus of the battle or by emotion.

Two hundred yards beyond the watchtower, the dugout bumped around a rock hidden below the surface of the water and swung sideways, catching the full force of the current. The Djuka dipped their paddles in, attempting to regain control, but the rush of water tipped the boat downstream. Ferron leaned the other way, and then felt a sudden swoop as the dugout swung free and increased its speed. And then came a tremendous jarring collision with another submerged rock, and he heard a splash as the guerrilla crouched in the bow lost his balance and tumbled into the water. *Damn!* He dropped his knife and reached for the man's shirt as the dugout swept by. Behind him, the steersman dropped his paddle and leaned over to help. By the time they pulled the man into the canoe, they were in midstream, moving fast, with the boat landing barely fifty yards away. A rickety dock extended twenty feet into the wide creek, its rail glinting in the light of a single bulb under a tin shade appended over the door of the boatshed.

They were going to miss the landing. He had wanted to hug the shoreline, not approach from midstream. The guards would spot the dugout.

"Into the water," he hissed.

The guerrillas stared at him in amazement. They'd just pulled a man *out* of the water. "No swim," one of the Djuka hissed back. "No swim."

"I'm going in." There was no time to waste. "Row ashore when you're past the landing and come back." He hoped they understood him. He'd asked Colonel Pindu for men who knew some English.

His knife. He dropped to his knees, his hands sweeping the bottom of the dugout. He couldn't find it. They were almost opposite the landing. No time to look. He swore silently, sat on the edge and rolled backwards over the side, feeling the water close instantly over his head as the dugout shot away from him. He stroked quickly for the surface and watched the dugout disappear downstream, gliding like a black water snake toward the shore. A dark object rose beside him and sputtered. Ferron raised a fist, ready to strike, and then saw white teeth appear. It was a man, not a beast—the guerrilla called Agbe, the one he'd pulled from the water, a big grin on his face.

"Me wet," Agbe gasped. "Come with you, but no swim." His arms were flailing madly underwater as he struggled to keep his head above the waves. An automatic rifle was strapped to his back.

"Grab my rifle," Ferron said, afraid the sound of the man's frantic paddling would alert the guards at the boatshed. He turned his back and sank below the surface as Agbe did what he was told. When Ferron surfaced again, glad he'd worn sneakers and not combat boots, he got his bearings and began to swim toward shore, towing Agbe behind him. The gun's sling was pulled tight across his chest.

Had they been detected? Men were moving at the boatshed near the landing. He could hear shouts. But their attention seemed to be directed toward the plantation house. In the distance, gun fire rippled and crackled like lightning. As he swam toward shore, fighting the current which weakened as he left midstream, he counted six men outside the shed, with one squatting on the end of the dock, peering into the darkness. And there would be more at the gate behind the boatshed.

The water was warmer near shore, more sluggish and muddy. Were there caimans waiting on shore or in the water? He'd seen them the day before. His feet struck mud and slipped. He pushed forward, moving on his hands and knees through the water. The sludge squeezed through his fingers like thick pudding. He reached around and pulled Agbe beside him.

"Give me your knife," he whispered. "And stay here until I come back. Don't use your rifle."

He could tell Agbe was frightened, knew what the man was thinking. The guerrilla's head jerked as he watched for movement along the shore. Everyone knew how quickly a caiman could move if it scented prey. If he gave his knife to Ferron, unable to use his rifle for fear of alerting the guards at the boatshed, he was sentenced to death if attacked by one of the creatures.

"No," Agbe said, as the American tried to pry the knife from his fingers. "I go. You stay."

"You can't swim," Ferron said, his voice hushed but urgent. "There's a guard at the end of the dock. Stay here. No one will see you."

Agbe shook his head. "I go," he said. "Walk underwater."

"It's too damn far."

"I kill him. No one hear. You watch."

He released the man's hand and sighed. He didn't have all night to argue. "We'll go together," he said. "Hang on to my shoulder."

Despite his sympathy with Kristine's cause, he did not like killing men he didn't know. He'd seen the first man die quietly, blood gurgling from his neck while Agbe held his head underwater as the body jerked and spasmed. The guard had been squatting on the end of the dock, peering out at the creek, rifle held alertly. But he was too stupid to put out his cigarette, a thick, hand-rolled smoke with the smell of cloves. The red glow had stabbed out of the night like a beacon, illuminating the round face of a Carib Indian. The second the Carib's hand left the trigger guard to remove the cigarette, Agbe had taken him from straight on, rising out of the water like a hungry caiman, his knife slashing across the man's throat before he could get beyond the moment of shock. Ferron had grasped the man's rifle, jerking him forward and wrenching the weapon from his hands. The cigarette rolled across the end of the dock and dropped into the water. The Carib died soon after.

When the body drifted away, Ferron grabbed Agbe's arm and stuck his head next to the guerrilla's ear. The water came up to the shorter man's chest. "Take his place," he said. "Only face inward. Be ready to shoot, but watch for me. I'm going to see what's in the boatshed."

"You no speak Djuka language," Agbe said. "You too tall. Me go."

A minute later, after another fruitless argument, Ferron was squatting where the Carib had been, facing inward, his eyes piercing through the gloom at the side of the boatshed. He'd seen movement there, and wondered if Agbe was walking into a trap. With each step the guerrilla took, Ferron could hear water dripping onto the dock. A shaft of the setting moon pierced the trees on the far shore and glinted off the tin roof, leaving the dock hidden in shadow. In a half-hour, the sky would lighten. Ferron wanted to be inside the walls before then.

He wiped the water from his eyes. Movement again. Dark shapes in the shadows. He pointed his rifle at the shadows and waited. The door to the boatshed opened and a guard stepped out and then stopped, silhouetted in the open door. Ferron heard a surprised voice and Agbe said something in response. The guard stepped back and reached for a sidearm. Before Agbe could fire, a long burst shattered the doorjamb and ripped across the guard's chest. Someone had fired from the shadows at the side of the boatshed. Ferron rolled to the side and dropped into the water, coming up ready to fire.

Agbe stood on the landing and emptied his rifle into the walls of the boatshed. From the shadows at the side, two other rifles spat fire. It looked like the rest of the team had made it back from wherever they had landed. An answering hail of bullets came from the direction of the gate and for a moment the guerrillas ceased fire as they dove for cover. The boatshed burst into flames and Ferron went underwater.

He surfaced downstream, making his way to shore and into the brush at the base of the wall's ramparts. Light from the fire flickered over the walls, casting weird shadows, and he could smell the odor of kerosine as if drifted on the light wind. If Kloos had kept a fast boat in the shed, it was destroyed now. There wasn't much reason to hold the landing any longer. The guerrillas there could take care of themselves.

He wished he were better equipped. A rope now would do the trick. He needed to get over the wall in a hurry, while the guards at the gate were still occupied at the boatshed. He moved farther away from the fire, into the shadows, then crawled up the slanting rampart and got to his feet. He tried to wedge his fingers in the chinks and cracks between the half-shaved planks that made up the wall, but could find no true handholds. The planks rose a good twelve feet into the air. The wall, it seemed, was insurmountable. He dropped to his knees. If you can't go over, go under. He dug at the base of the fence with his hands. The ground was stony. Hell, if he couldn't get inside, the rifle did him no good. He upended it and began to stab at the ground with the barrel, using it as a crude pick.

As he worked, Ferron could hear the battle waging on the

other side of the wall. Explosions echoed in the distance. The fight inside was going down hard. He hoped Kristine was still alive—and her father, too, for that matter. *Please, God,* he thought, *don't let it come down to nothing.*

Fifteen minutes later, with sporadic flames still puncturing the night from the direction of the boatshed, which had nearly burned to the ground, and heavy fighting continuing inside, he reached the bottom of the planks. He cleared the rubble away and gripped one of the planks, planting his feet on the wall and pulling until it felt like the veins in his forehead would pop. The plank wouldn't give. He dug for more leeway and tried again, this time hearing the first squeak of sixteenpenny nails losing their grip. He pulled again. The base of the plank came free and he moved to the next one.

Five minutes later, he squeezed under the wall, the rough edge of the plank scraping across his skin. From what he could see in the darkness, there were no guards covering the wall. The rifle was worthless, the barrel jammed with rock and dirt. He dropped the gun and began to run in a crouch toward a line of palm trees that stretched between the tool shed and the plantation house. Most of the fighting seemed to be centered behind the plantation and to the south, although he could see flashes of gunfire on a line between the tool shed and the chapel. An orange haze lightened the sky from the direction of the workers' barracks.

Bullets raked the area between the palm trees and the house, and a heavy machine gun answered with a throaty roar from the upper balcony. The guerrillas had surrounded Kloos's headquarters on three sides, cutting his men off from the workers' barracks. The rattle of submachine guns and rifles was deafening, and chips and splinters of wood flew from the louvered windows and clapboard siding of the plantation. The colonnaded veranda was in shambles and the balcony rail on the upper level had already disintegrated under the heavy fire, hanging in chunks from shattered posts. Higher up, the ornate brackets and decorative frieze running below the cornice had been cut to shreds. Kloos's men had gone upward during the course of the battle, and most of their firepower seemed to pour down from the parapet.

For a moment, aware of how he'd worked his way inside the compound, he worried about a tunnel. While all the attention was focused on the men fighting from the roof, Kloos might have already slipped away down below. How could anyone live through the fusillade of bullets pounding into the house?

He slithered forward, stopping at the palm tree nearest the house. Five feet away lay a dead soldier, an Uzi lying just beyond his grasp. Ferron scampered forward, retrieved the submachine gun and rolled back behind the tree. There was a momentary lull in the fighting, and he could make out the dark shape of guerrillas as they approached the plantation house, running in erratic spurts like a drunk trying to make his way across a crowded parking lot. Suddenly, a white sheet waved from one of the windows, and several men on the roof tossed their weapons over the side and stood up, their hands raised.

A shouted command rang out. Ferron got to his feet, watching intently. He suddenly realized that most of the guerrillas would not have been told of his presence. A white man among Creoles and Blacks, with a weapon in his hands, would be considered an enemy. He leaned the Uzi against the palm tree and waited, weighing the advisability of stepping out into the open. Why not let the guerrillas capture him? he thought. They'd put him with the other whites—with the Dutchman. What did it matter? Kristine would soon be there to identify him. But what if they were executing Kloos's men on the spot? He looked toward the main gate leading to the boat landing. The guerrillas there would know him. But the gate, though abandoned, was still locked. He swore to himself. Kloos's fate was out of his hands. The guerrillas had beaten him to the prize.

CHAPTER 6

Tuesday, September 24, Tempati Creek Plantation, Suriname

Kloos's face, once darkly mottled, had the pallor of a corpse. Blood stained his white shirt, soaking through a towel that had been wrapped around his chest. He'd been shot more than once, and grenade fragments had torn through his left arm, now heavily bandaged. A Creole doctor had tried to patch his wounds and then shook her head at the futility of the task. There was nothing more she could do. Kloos was now sleeping.

Kristine stood in the hallway with Ferron, her back to the open door. The sun had risen two hours earlier and the heat swarmed in through the shattered windows at the end of the hallway. Her father was in one of the plantation house's inner bedrooms, a room with no windows. He would die with a vision of emptiness—a white wall devoid of pictures. A fitting end for a man who had lost everything.

Colonel Pindu had got what he wanted from Kloos—the names of his contacts in the U.S. Embassy, CIA agents all. The helicopter had been captured undamaged and the colonel was flying back to Paramaribo where other troops had stormed the capital at dawn. The President and Prime Minister had fled the country for Holland, leaving on the same plane that had brought in a crowd of foreign journalists.

"The day is ours," Colonel Pindu had told them. "We'll have a new government in place by nightfall."

Pindu had wanted to take Kristine with him in the chopper, but she asked to stay at the plantation, promising to return to Paramaribo as soon as her father died. They had all seen there was no hope for him. "I'll stay to help Nick," she told the colonel. "He needs to talk to my father while there's still time."

Ferron had been brought to the house under gunpoint, but had been quickly recognized by several of the guerrillas. Kristine had arrived from the watchtower soon after. Her squad had taken it without casualties, directing the ground attack by radio for the duration of the battle. The scene between father and daughter had been full of tension. Kristine had refused at first to see her father, but the old man had asked for her, aware that he was dying.

"I am not a man who can change his life on his deathbed," he told her, his voice rasping with the effort to speak, but his mind still lucid. "I fought for what I believed in—just as you have . . . and that's already a lot. But victory—" He shook his head and lapsed into silence for a moment. "Victory is in the hands of fate. *Fate*, not God." He coughed. The sputum at the corners of his lips and in his beard was streaked with rosy threads of blood. "I lost my faith when the Nazis killed Leota and our baby boy. Now I want only to die in peace."

Kristine stared at him with hard eyes, her lips compressed. She thought of her mother—Kloos's second wife—and how she'd died. "My mother was tortured—I was tortured. The people your money supported were just like the Nazis." Her words were thin and strained. "I was your daughter, too, but as far as you were concerned, I never existed."

Kloos looked up at her with haunted eyes. He was sitting in a large bed with a brass headboard, pillows propped behind his back. His cheeks were sunken and two dots of white cartilage stood out at the end of his nose. His face had lost all color and his faded blue eyes had dulled. He licked his lips and tried to swallow. His eyes strayed to a glass of water on a white wicker lamp stand beside the bed. "Your mother—it wasn't my people who killed her." He tried to raise his right hand, and then dropped it tiredly on the bed. "Can you forget the past?"

Kristine said nothing.

"The past—" He closed his eyes as pain flowed through him,

the wrinkles in his face deepening. His chest rose and fell with the effort of each breath. "The past is behind us . . . We can't change what's happened. But if you can forgive me for how you were raised—" he waved his hand in a feeble motion as if to encompass the past—"I can forgive you for anything you might have done to hurt me." He gasped for air. "We've both suffered."

Kristine nodded dully, but words of forgiveness would not come to her lips. She took a deep breath and brushed the hair out of her eyes. "You can do one thing to change how you've lived," she said. "You can tell Nick Ferron the truth about his grandfather. If you do that, you and I will part in peace with each other."

He was afraid that Kloos would lapse into a coma, but the Dutchman woke just before noon. The doctor had stopped the external bleeding, but Kloos's life was slowly hemorrhaging away deep inside his body. Ferron had found a chair in the kitchen and sat at the head of the bed, the room lit only by the light seeping through the open door to the hallway.

"You returned," Kloos said, recognizing him. "What'd you learn?"

"I learned you didn't tell me the truth. You said you didn't know Eagle Jack, but you were the liaison with him at the end of the war."

Kloos nodded weakly. "It no longer matters. Perhaps the vengeance you want will avenge us both."

"I don't want vengeance. I want the truth. If you commit a crime, you pay. I want the man who ordered my grandfather killed."

"You want Eagle Jack," Kloos said. "He betrayed us all in the war and he's done it again. I thought I could use him—that his money, his influence with your government, would keep my men in power. He's turned against me, because I threatened to expose him for the traitor he is. He tried to cut his ties with me. Sure, he speaks against the rebels, but he protects himself. He rubs both sides of the coin."

The old man stopped and gasped for breath, tears appearing at the corners of his eyes. He'd spoken in a rush. "Water," he said, his eyes fluttering.

Ferron reached for the glass. "Hang on." He lifted the glass to Kloos's mouth and poured slowly. Water ran down the man's beard and onto his shirt.

With his eyes shut, the old man said, "And now he wants to run for President."

"President of what?"

Kloos tried to smile. "Of your own country."

That set him back for a moment, but he wanted answers. He didn't care what the guy was running for. "Who *is* he? I need a name. No one in Italy knew who he was."

The Dutchman struggled to take a deep breath, his face wrenched in pain. "The man is a traitor . . . the Senator from Virginia—Earl Sprague."

Ferron's eyes widened. "Senator Sprague? He's Eagle Jack?" He found it hard to believe. The Senator was well known in Arizona, where the conservatives had often quoted his anticommunist views. He was a vocal force on the Senate Intelligence Oversight Committee, constantly warning about the threat of Cuban influence in the southern hemisphere. These days he was hot for drug interdiction. He was always there for the photo-op when a major bust went down. He'd been waiting in the wings to take credit for Beppe Aprico's arrest. Or had he wanted him dead all along? The implications were too much to consider at once and Kloos was clearing his throat to speak.

"I found Eagle Jack's OVRA file," the old man said, the words coming in a rush between gasps of air. "A double agent. The dossier didn't give his real name . . . but he was a U.S. businessman. With steel and aluminum companies. He worked to see that his companies benefitted from the war effort . . . and that their products helped the fascist cause. To hide his activities, he let himself be recruited by the British. They wanted to use his business connections in Europe. He asked only that his civilian identity be kept hidden. That he be known as Eagle Jack."

Kloos voice died away and he struggled to breathe, taking quick short breaths that seemed to tire him. He closed his eyes in exhaustion, his head tipped to the side. After a moment, he coughed, drool tinged with blood seeping out of his mouth, then grimaced, as if trying to hold his insides together. When he spoke again, his voice had tightened with the strain.

"The British stationed Eagle Jack in Switzerland . . . one of their top officers. He collaborated with Mussolini—trying to protect his holdings in Italy and Germany. He was afraid the Reds would take everything." Kloos paused, his breathing ragged. "He manipulated and betrayed American and British agents. He was the man behind the arrest of Carla Ceruti."

"But how did you identify him?"

There was no answer. Kloos had slumped forward and passed out.

Ferron leaned the limp body back into the pillow and bent over to see if the Dutchman was still breathing. A light waft of air brushed his cheek. The man was a strong old buzzard. He looked over his shoulder for Kristine. She'd stepped into the hall, unable to watch her father's labored breathing. "Get the doctor, Kristine."

The Creole doctor fastened a blood pressure cuff to Kloos's right arm. "We'll leave this on," she said. "His blood pressure's dropping."

"Don't you have anything you can give him," he asked. "Intravenous fluids or plasma?"

The doctor shook her head. "Not out here. The clinic was destroyed in the attack."

"What will happen? Is he unconscious?"

"Not yet. He's sleeping. But he'll lose consciousness eventually. He's bleeding internally. It seems to have slowed down, but—" She shook her head in resignation.

"Can I wake him? I need to ask more."

"Let him rest five minutes."

Kristine came up the stairs from the first floor, where she had been at the radio speaking with Colonel Pindu in Paramaribo. "The sailors were picked up, Nick."

"What?" He found it hard to come back to his thoughts on Senator Sprague.

"I just talked to Colonel Pindu. Martin's boat was found by troops loyal to us. Other than what Martin did to the engines, there's no damage to the men or the boat."

"Good." He tried to pay attention to what she was saying.

"Nick—" Kristine had taken hold of his arm. "The colonel

talked to the American ambassador. The Americans have agreed not to interfere with the new government." She grinned. "The colonel threatened to expose several CIA operations."

"Your father's fading, Kristine. He's a tough old guy to get this far."

She took a deep breath and nodded. "Have you got what you needed?"

He shrugged and then leaned into the wall along the corridor, facing her. His tiredness was beginning to catch up to him. He found it hard to organize his thoughts. "I'm not sure I believe what he's told me," he said finally. "The man who betrayed my grandfather in the war is a U.S. Senator now, a man who's going to run for the Presidency. I asked him how he identified the man and he passed out before he could say." Ferron hesitated. "Your father's dying anyway, but this is killing him."

She touched him on the arm. "Nick, he wants to do this. Telling you the truth is washing away his past. He wants to die in peace with the world."

She slipped inside his arms and he hugged her for a moment. "Let's go in, Kristine. I think you should be with me now. It's almost time. He needs to know you're there at the end."

CHAPTER 7

Tuesday, September 24, Tempati Creek Plantation, Suriname

Kristine held her father's hand while he talked. The old man had drunk more water, coughing up blood between swallows.

"Didn't I tell you before?" He had come back stronger than before, his innate resilience refusing to buckle under. His mind seemed determined to ignore the fact that he was dying. "Before I went north, I saw the man in the corridors of the Vatican. He was pointed out to me as Eagle Jack. This was before the last campaign. In Milan he worked through intermediaries; I never met him face to face. I didn't know he was working both sides. Over thirty years passed before I saw him again—only this time he was known as Earl Sprague, and he came to my country because of business interests. His companies wanted our bauxite mines. I recognized him immediately. And by then I knew from the OVRA files that he was a traitor."

Ferron was standing beside Kristine. "Why didn't you tell me?"

Kloos tried to find him in the darkness, his eyes unfocused. "I didn't trust you. I thought you would come after me if you knew what happened."

"What about Eagle Jack's OVRA file? Is it here in the house?"

"I destroyed it." His voice fell to a whisper. "It was too dangerous to carry. It was all in my head. I didn't need proof."

"What happened in northern Italy in '45?"

The old man closed his eyes and took a long, slow breath as if trying to draw himself into the past. "I met your grandfather in Caserta that spring," he said. His voice had come back with renewed vigor, like the last flicker of a dying candle. "We were assigned to work together with Beppe Aprico and the partisans in the hills around Mussolini's Republic in Northern Italy. Our mission was to see that the files of the secret police didn't disappear. Police headquarters were in Verona, not far from Salò and the other ministries." He took another deep breath, the lines around his eyes deepening at the effort. "I was working with the SOE and your grandfather with the OSS. The British told me my liaison was Eagle Jack. I was to tell no one of this arrangement. Eagle Jack never met his agents face to face; messages were passed by couriers. Through them, Eagle Jack said the British were concerned about secret police documents relating to Churchill—his dealings with Mussolini. If I came across any OVRA files having to do with secret agents, I was to seize them and turn them over to Eagle Jack in Milan. He also asked for his own file."

Kloos stopped talking. The words had tumbled from him in a rush, propelled by the wind in his lungs. He took several quick breaths, his body twitching as if nerve impulses were firing erratically. A moan escaping from his lips.

Ferron bent over him. "More water?"

Kloos's eyes were closed again. "Let me rest," he said weakly, and then seemed to slip away again.

The doctor took another reading of Kloos's blood pressure. "It's dropping," she said. "Not much longer now."

Ferron looked at Kristine. "He may not wake up."

"Give him a moment," she said. "He's not ready to give up yet."

The Dutchman wet his lips and said, "No time to tell it all." He paused, as if each sentence was an arrow pulled from his body. "At the end, we all split up . . . The war was breaking out around us. Germans deserting. Tearing off their uniforms and escaping into the hills. The partisans were looking for Mussolini . . . Then we heard they had captured him near Dongo." He sucked in a wheezy breath that made Ferron flinch and then went on, his voice growing weaker with each word. Ferron was bent over the bed, head cocked to listen, his eyes focused on a spot to the right of Kloos's pillow.

"Major Tom—your grandfather—he was supposed to meet me near Maderno. Eagle Jack arranged the rendezvous . . . I was returning from Milan. Then I heard Major Tom had been detained by the Waffen SS. In Maderno." He stopped for a minute, eyes closed. "At the time, I had no reason to suspect Eagle Jack . . . too much confusion . . . later, your grandfather blamed me." He opened his eyes, the pupils rolling wildly, and struggled to sit up. "But I had nothing to do with it."

And with that, he fell back into his pillow and seemed to calm down, his breathing growing more regular. He rested for a few moments, then opened his eyes. His fingers closed around Ferron's arm with surprising strength. "I was with the partisans who attacked the Germans and allowed Major Tom to escape. The *Standartenführer* holding your grandfather let him go to save his own life . . . he even gave Major Tom a gift—a box with an SS Mauser."

So that's where the gun in his grandfather's trunk came from, Ferron thought. A man trying to save his own life.

"Water," Kloos said.

Ferron reached for the glass and poured a few drops into the Dutchman's mouth. Kloos swallowed twice, then turned his head to the side, water dribbling onto the pillow. After a moment, he said, "We helped the partisans. We seized several German trucks loaded with fascist documents. At first, it didn't look like any were secret police files. Major Tom rushed back to Verona, to OVRA headquarters, while I sifted through the files with the partisans. And then I found a case with special dossiers. I didn't tell anyone. I made sure they were loaded into the car I was driving, a car provided by Eagle Jack. The partisans went one way and I went another. I never saw your grandfather again."

"What about Aprico?"

Kloos thought for a moment, eyes squeezed tight. "They said Aprico disappeared—headed toward Switzerland in a three tonner." He tried to smile, his lips twisting into a grimace. "With part of the regime's treasure. No one could prove anything after the war."

"Did you give the special files to Eagle Jack?"

Kloos tried to shake his head. "I set fire to the car. I left a message for Eagle Jack that everything had been destroyed." A harsh laugh shook the dying man. "The only one who didn't get away with something valuable was your grandfather—all he got was a stack of medals."

Kloos died two hours later, and Kristine, dry-eyed, left instructions for him to be buried in a small cemetery behind the chapel. Ferron could not tell how she was taking his death. "Are you staying for the ceremony?" he asked.

She shook her head, showing no emotion. "There's no one there, now," she said. "My father's life has been erased like chalk from a slate. I'm needed in the capital."

He said nothing in response. You could erase the chalk, he thought, but the marks remained forever.

A day later, in Paramaribo, prior to his noon departure on a Suriname Airways flight to Miami, he was asked to come to the United States Embassy on Dr. Sophie Redmondstraat. It was not the ambassador who wanted to see him, as he'd expected, but a lower ranking Foreign Service official, who introduced herself as Sarah Byram. Byram informed him that the Embassy had received several telephone calls of an emergency nature from a Janelle Dutton in Durango, Colorado, who was trying to contact him. "You may use the phone in my office to make the call," she said, "but we'll have to receive payment before you leave."

When she left the room, he picked up the phone and placed his call through the embassy operator, who routed it through the Surinamese telephone office on Valliantplein. To one side of the desk, a black and white television set was tuned to the *Surinaamse Televisie Stichting*, with the volume turned off. A news program, it looked like, with the Chyrons and other graphics in Dutch. Five minutes later, Janelle was on the line. It was nine o'clock in the morning in Suriname, six a.m. in Colorado.

"Nick," she shouted, before he could say anything, her voice gleeful. "I've been trying to reach you for two days. Your grandfather's alive! He called me from Washington, D.C. He said he thinks he knows who tried to have him killed."

"Gran Babbo?" He couldn't believe how hard his heart was pounding. "He's alive?" He slammed his fist on the desk in exultation. "I can't believe it." And then, unable to restrain himself, he leaped and whooped until his vocal cords hurt. He was so excited he began to hyperventilate and had to ask Janelle to wait a moment. His ears rang and he felt dizzy. He sat down on the floor, his back against the desk, taking deep breaths to calm himself.

When he could talk, he put the phone to his ear. "I can't believe it, Janelle." His voice sounded strange inside his head, as if he were speaking in a tunnel, an echo on the line. "But what happened at the cabin then? How is he?"

"He's fine, Nick. He hid in the hills for a while. He sounded tired and said he was a little weak from not eating much, but he's doing great. I asked him about the body burned in the hay shed, too. He said it was a hiker he'd taken in—that retired guy that went missing, just like you thought. Your grandfather wasn't there when the guy was killed, but he got back before the sheriff showed up. He found a matchbook with a telephone number written inside."

Ferron exhaled a deep breath. He still felt shaky. "But why didn't he come down? And how'd he find out who was after him?"

"He didn't come to town because he didn't want Barbara's kids to be in jeopardy. It took him a while to figure things out. He traced the phone number to an office in the Capitol."

"Did he say who was behind it all?"

"He's not sure, Nick. I told him what you were doing and he said he wants to talk to you before he does anything."

"Listen, Janelle. Tell him I know who betrayed Carla Ceruti in the war. I know who set him up in Italy. It may be the same guy. It has to be."

"Was it Kloos?"

"I can't talk over the phone. I'm in the embassy in Paramaribo. This line is probably monitored. I need you to do me a favor, Janelle. Can you call Gran Babbo and tell him I'm coming? I'm supposed to arrive in Miami at 4:05 this afternoon and I have a connecting flight with American Airlines two hours later." He suddenly realized the grin on his face was so wide his cheeks hurt. *My God, Gran Babbo was alive!* It was incredible.

"To Durango?"

He laughed, feeling giddy with happiness. "No, to Washington, D.C. I was going there anyway."

"I'd like to come there, too, Nick. I've missed you."

He tried to clear his head, his mind so full of jumbled thoughts it was hard to concentrate. "What about your classes?"

"There's a substitute teacher who's always happy to replace me. If I'm back by next Monday, I'll only miss three days. I've never seen the capital—and Barbara can take Rowdy. He'll have Wolf for company. You wouldn't believe how happy Wolf was when we said "Gran Babbo's coming." His ears pricked right up. We should have waited. The dog won't leave the door now—but he was so down before, moping around and not eating."

He felt like he'd finally caught his breath. "How's Rowdy doing?"

"Great. He loves romping through the fields here. Eats like a horse."

He laughed. "Yeah, never even missed me. Rowdy's so laid back, he probably wont even get up off the floor when I get back."

"I will," she said, and he laughed again.

"Listen, Janelle. I'll call the Grand Hyatt and make reservations for a suite. Gran Babbo can join us there. You may not get much sightseeing done, but it'll be nice to see you both." He couldn't believe how happy he was. He was glad she wanted to come, too. His grandfather could probably use her company; Ferron didn't want him in the way when he tracked down the Senator. No telling what might happen, but he sure as hell was going to make sure Gran Babbo wasn't hurt.

He could feel renewed energy coursing through him. "This has cost me a fortune, Janelle, but it sure as hell is worth it now. There's one thing I want you to do. I found a Mauser in Gran Babbo's trunk along with his papers and medals. Could you pack that up when you come? Don't carry it on board. Check it through. And when you call Gran Babbo tell him I said he finally has an appointment with his past. He's been waiting a long time for this."

When he hung up, he broke into another huge grin, the smile

so enormous he felt nothing could wipe it away.

BOOK FOUR

NETHER GROUND

"Hung on a rock—the traitor; and, around
the Furies hissing from the nether ground."
        —Virgil

Chapter 1

Friday, September 27, Washington, D.C.

Rain beaded the windows as the dark blue Chevy van with D.C. plates and an Alamo rental sticker left the Capital Beltway and took state highway 50 through Fairfax, Virginia. The driver was not familiar with the area and pulled over at a gas station to ask for directions. Five minutes later, after backtracking a half-mile and stopping at a grocery store, the van turned south on an undivided road and then, twelve miles later, took a right turn on a smaller unmarked side road that curved gently to the west. At ten o'clock in the morning, under a lowering sky, traffic was sparse. A tanker truck, with Stuart-AGIP painted on its side in yellow and black, passed the van going in the opposite direction, and then the Chevy was the only vehicle on the road. The tires whistled plaintively on the rain-slickened pavement and the driver turned on the wiper blades as heavy rain started to fall. In a minute, the windshield began to cloud up.

"Do you know how to work this defroster?" Janelle Dutton asked, her right hand fumbling with the heater controls, left hand on the steering wheel.

Thomas Gage leaned over from the passenger side and flipped a switch. Air began to blow, but the windows only grew more opaque.

Janelle took her foot off the accelerator and leaned forward, trying to clear the condensation with her hand.

"Pull over," Gage said. "I'll check the manual to see how this works."

Janelle eased the van to a stop on the grassy verge of the road, where a ditch was beginning to fill with muddy water. Her hands were slippery on the wheel and she dried them on her skirt, then wound down the window just far enough so the rain wouldn't blow in. She glanced at Nick's grandfather as he flipped through the manual, glove box open in front of him. His cheeks had reddened and his eyes were bright. A handsome man, thin and smooth-featured. More like a college professor than a man of action. But now he burned with the zeal of a bloodhound after the fox's scent.

In a few minutes, if they could find the place, they'd be outside the estate of the man he'd spent a lifetime trying to track down. Nick had tried to convince him to stay in the hotel room while he took care of things, but Gran Babbo would have none of it. This was his battle and he was going to fight it himself. Nick could go to the Capitol and see what he could find out, but Thomas Gage was going to case the Senator's countryside estate. That's where they would confront the man. Where the Senator felt the safest. Nick had agreed, but only if his grandfather came back and they planned the infiltration together. In the meantime, he would try to learn what he could about the Senator's schedule.

In the silence of the countryside, the sound of the wiper blades thumping back and forth grated on Janelle's nerves and she shut them off. What limited visibility there was instantly diminished to nothing. Broad sheets of water flowed down the windshield, as the clouds opened up and emptied themselves in a furious deluge. A horrible day for what they had to do.

A few moments later, back on the road with the defroster hard at work, Janelle drove at a reduced speed as she tried to keep her eyes on both the road and the odometer. Gusts of wind buffeted the van. The tall grass in the fields to each side flattened out under the onslaught. Perhaps the weather would keep others inside and make their task safer.

"That's it," Gage said, pointing off to the left where a high perimeter wall surrounded a wooded area. Behind the scattered trees rose a knoll on which sat an impressive Victorian manor house with a mansard roof and dormer windows.

She took a quick look. "Where's the main entrance?"

"Around the bend probably. See that driveway beyond the line of spruce? There's a rose garden just to the other side."

"Shall I stop?"

"Not here," he said. "Too conspicuous." He unfastened his seat belt and leaned around, finding a grocery bag in the back of the van near the ten-foot step ladder. Inside the bag, they had dumped two packages of mushrooms bought at the grocery store in Fairfax. "Once I'm in the woods, I'll wipe some mud on these," he said. "Just a harmless old man looking for fungi." He slung a pair of binoculars around his neck.

"What if they don't have mushrooms growing around here?"

Gage laughed. "I'll plant a few."

As they drove by the entrance to the estate, he looked across the road at the guard house. "How many did you see?"

"One man. Looked like a security service." A moment later, Janelle glanced in the outside rearview mirror. The van itself had no side windows in back. "The guard house is out of sight. Shall I stop?"

"Let's follow the perimeter wall as long as we can. When the road curves away, I'll get out."

Gage was going to scout the perimeter on foot. At the moment, that was the only thing Nick had agreed to, and even then reluctantly. Janelle didn't know what all Nick had planned but she could tell there was going to be a fight with his grandfather each step of the way. Gran Babbo simply wasn't going to stand by and let Nick take care of his business. She looked over at Gage, concerned about the bad weather. "It may take you longer than you thought."

He nodded. "Give me an hour. By then, I'll be back at the far end—in that grass by the side of the road. It looked deep enough to hide in. If I'm not there, keep going." He looked at his watch. "Try again a second time about twelve-thirty. That'll give me two hours. Don't drive by more than twice. If I'm not there, go on back to the hotel. I'll get in touch later."

"We should have brought an umbrella. You'll catch a cold."

"I'm not worried about a cold; just pray I don't catch a bullet. I've hiked the San Juans in worse weather than this." He pulled out a broad-brimmed fisherman's hat and clamped it on his head, then found the clear plastic raincoat and slipped it over his jacket and the binoculars. "This'll keep me dry. Pull over here." The perimeter wall angled sharply uphill and the road curved to the right and dropped into a low stretch, more swale than valley, interlaced with meandering runnels.

"I still think you should've brought the gun." She eased the van to a stop in the middle of the right lane. The dirt at the side of the road sloped into a ditch. This was not the time to get stuck.

He said, "If they find me out there, I'm better off without it. Let Nick take care of that. Besides, that Mauser's so old it'd probably blow up in my face." He opened the door and stepped out into the rain, which had diminished to a steady drizzle. "I'll be okay. See you later, Janelle."

Ferron's first stop that morning was at the Capitol, where he found the Senator's outer office, said he was a constituent by the name of Fred Jensen, and wondered if he could make an appointment to see the Senator. The receptionist, a young woman in a wool business suit, with short black hair and an efficient manner, adjusted the red cloth flower pinned at her throat and said she was sorry, but the Senator was unable to fix any appointments due to his heavy work schedule that week. "He has a major speech on the floor of the Senate this morning, and an important announcement to make to the press later today. I'm afraid he'll be very busy for quite some time. May I ask the nature of your business?"

"Just wanted to greet an old friend." He smiled pleasantly, then glanced around the reception area. "Any chance to see what the Senator's office looks like while I'm here? This is the first time I've actually taken the trouble to come on in. It'd be something to tell the kids."

"There's really nothing to see." She forced a half-smile that signified further conversation was pointless.

"Well, I'll come back another time. Thanks for the information."

He'd seen the security arrangements. If what he'd heard from Kloos was true and Sprague announced his candidacy for President, his protection would increase. It wouldn't necessarily be that difficult to see the man as long as one came unarmed, but to do so in private and unnoticed was the hard part. The Senate Office Building was not the place.

From the Capitol, he walked over to Constitution Avenue and flagged down a cab. He'd wanted to walk to his destination, but the midmorning sprinkles were beginning to thicken into sullen rain. A cold mist swept across the city from the Potomac.

In the cab, his stomach growled and he thought about stopping for a snack before lunch. He'd skipped breakfast that morning, rising before dawn and taking a brisk walk over to the Vietnam Vets Memorial, where he'd found one Ferron and five Gages in the directory, none of whom he recognized. When he returned to the hotel, his grandfather and Janelle had already eaten and both were anxious to get started on the surveillance they'd discussed the night before.

At the moment, Ferron's next stop was the J. Edgar Hoover Building. The night before, he'd telephoned an old FBI buddy at home, requesting a meeting, and the agent, a man named Curtis Woods, whom he'd met a few years earlier at the FBI Training Academy in Quantico, and once on a case in Arizona, had asked him to stop by at eleven on Friday morning. He checked his watch. Ten minutes to spare.

The taxi dropped him off at the corner of E Street and Tenth. He walked up E Street, crossing from the FBI building to the other side of the street, where he waited in front of The Lunch Box, a hot food/salad bar joint, located between a Penn Camera store and a McDonald's restaurant. Overhead, lowering clouds threatened to unleash a downpour. At five after the hour, Curtis Woods swung out of the underground garage and picked him up on the sidewalk. Woods was wearing a gray suit and had lost most of his hair since Ferron had last seen him. The skin on the top of his head glistened like a pair of well-shined black shoes. A former fullback at Penn State, now in his early thirties, he was of medium height, with a thick neck, broad shoulders and powerful thighs. He was driving a white Ford sedan with government plates.

"Let's go to Georgetown," Woods said. "I need to meet someone at Olsson's Books after lunch.

Ferron grinned. "I didn't know you met informants in bookstores."

"He's an accountant," Woods said. "Works at a bank on M Street and thinks he's found a case of major fraud by the bank's management. Might be drug connected."

They stopped at Garrett's on M Street and sat at a table opposite the bar, where a lamb-sized leather rhinoceros hung from the roof on green ribbons. Over beer, minestrone soup and a plate of fettuccine, he told Woods about his work on the Beppe Aprico case, without, however, mentioning its aftermath. Outside, sudden gusts of wind and the ping of pelting rain on the restaurant's windows announced a deluge. While they ate, the curbside gutters filled with rushing storm water and traffic backed up in the street in both directions. Horns blared, and the sudden red bursts of brake lights flattened out against the windowpanes, now opaque, like fireworks blossoming under-water. A nice change from jungle heat.

When they'd finished the meal and Woods looked at him expectantly, Ferron got down to business. "I've just come back from South America," he said. "Left my gun in Tucson. I need to borrow a pistol for a day or two."

Woods raised his eyebrows. "What for?"

"Nothing criminal."

They both laughed.

"Is this something I'm going to regret? You going to get me in trouble?"

"You don't have a toss-away?"

The FBI man pursed his cheeks, his eyeballs rolling up as he looked at the corner of the room and scratched his neck. "I suppose I could get you something. You want a hide-away?"

"It doesn't matter."

"I got a Smith & Wesson 469, but it can be traced to me."

"Anything else that can't be?"

Woods eyed him, bobbing his head knowingly. "Nothing criminal, yeah, right. You said 'borrow.' Am I going to get this back?"

"Come on, Curtis. Next you'll be asking me to write you into my will."

"When you need this?"

"Now."

"Shit." Woods sat back in his chair, both hands on the table.

He wore a large college ring on his right hand. He thought for a moment, drumming his fingers on the table. "Where you staying?"

"At the Grand Hyatt—over by the Convention Center."

"I know where it is." Woods sighed. "Let me meet my man at Olsson's first. I got a Colt .45 I can let you have, but I have to stop by the house. You can wait in the car and come with me. That soon enough?"

"Thanks, Curtis. Guess I'll have to send you a Christmas card this year, won't I?"

CHAPTER 2

Friday, September 27, Washington, D.C.

From Wood's house later that evening—it had taken the FBI agent longer than he thought to finish his business—Ferron took a Yellow Cab back to the hotel. The rain had ceased, but a cool wind whipped the flags and banners hanging in front of the buildings along the way. On the ride, he thought about what his grandfather had told him the night before. Gran Babbo had talked about the documents in the National Archives—a microfilm collection of Mussolini's private papers, acquired by the Psychological Warfare Branch at the end of World War II.

"I've spent long hours pouring over them" his grandfather had said. "I never could find the connection I needed. No references to any of the people I met in Rome during the war."

"What about the Italian authorities? Couldn't they help?"

Gage had shrugged eloquently. "They were trying to forget. Who wouldn't?" He snorted. "When I last checked, which had to be sometime around 1960, out of sixty-four postwar prefects, sixty-two had been functionaries of the Ministry of the Interior under the dictatorship."

"You're kidding," Ferron said.

His grandfather had studied him cynically for a moment. "That's not all," he said dryly. "There were 241 vice-prefects and every single one had been part of the state during the fascist era. And it continued at the lower ranks. Of the 135 quaestors—" he turned to Janelle—"that's a position equivalent to our police chiefs, 120 were members of the fascist police, and the other fifteen had joined before fascism but remained in the service throughout the period."

"The postwar government let that happen?" Janelle asked, her brow furrowed.

Gage opened his hands in a gesture of resignation. He was sitting in a cane-panel tub chair facing the room's sofa, with a desk and telephone across the room. Janelle was on the sofa, Nick near the desk in a straight-backed chair.

"Right after the war, everyone was trying to contribute to what the Italians called 'the pacification of minds.' If the new government had dismissed everyone who served the state under fascism, there'd have been no civilian police force. The Italians figured out that only five of the 139 vice-quaestors had contributed to the liberation by collaborating with the Resistance."

Ferron grunted. "You have to admit, the police aren't your ideal collaborators. We're trained to uphold the law, not ask questions about its constitutionality."

Gage looked at him with disapproval. "Have you already forgotten the lessons of Nuremberg?"

Ferron grinned. "The Nazis had a madman issuing orders. They should've known they were committing crimes."

"Well, if *they* should have known what was right and wrong in a time of war—and I agree that they should have—then *you* should be accountable in a time of peace, when the situation is clearer. As far as I'm concerned, the judgment of the individual cop forms the cornerstone of the administration of justice."

"I don't think too many judges would agree with you," Ferron said. He stroked his chin, a thoughtful look coming over his face. "I always wondered why the Italian government didn't bring more of the fascist officials to trial for crimes against the people."

Gage said, "First of all, you don't know what they did." Ferron grinned at the reprimand. "The situation was very different in Italy. And there were trials." Gage paused. "Of course, the outcome wasn't always what one would have wanted. Guido Leto, the guy who headed the OVRA for ten years right up to the collapse of the Republic of Salò, was absolved of all crimes after the war. He became the director of the Italian police schools, and then retired to private life in 1952. I interviewed him once, trying to find out if he knew anything about Carla Ceruti. He claimed he didn't recognize the name."

"But how could he get off scot-free?" Janelle said, her eyes flashing with quick anger. "If he was the head of the regime's secret police . . ." She stopped and waved her hand in frustration.

Gage nodded. "There were others who deserved to be punished and got away. The Italians proclaimed an amnesty in the summer of '46—the *Amnistia Togliatti*. The only people not included were the highest ranking fascist officials—men who'd directed civil, political, or military commands." He laughed. "Hell, most of those had already been shot by the partisans. No, it wasn't just." He shook his head. "All the presidents of the fascist Special Tribunals got off."

And then they had talked about Eagle Jack and Gran Babbo had grown pensive.

"I suspected Eagle Jack at the time, but couldn't prove anything. No one would tell me who he was. I don't know if you remember in my diary, Nick, but Elio Pavan, the agent who was working with the British? He'd contacted Eagle Jack about my operation in Rome. It wasn't just at the end when Eagle Jack set me up for the Gestapo that he turned bad. If what Kloos told you is true about him ordering Carla Ceruti's arrest, I'd have disappeared before too long also. That's the type of trade-off he'd have made throughout the war if he wanted the fascists to protect his business interests."

Gage thought about that for a moment. "After the war, Kloos was the man he had to worry about—and it sounds like Sprague was using Kloos as much as Kloos was using him." He shook his head ruefully. "That situation in Suriname is going to make the Senator look like a prophet. That'll help his campaign. He may ride it all the way to the nomination."

"Maybe," Ferron said. "But sending his boys to eliminate you is going to make him look like a killer, even if we can't prove it— and so far, the people of this country haven't taken kindly to electing killers to office. Besides," he added, his face darkening, "Eagle Jack has a score to settle with you first."

CHAPTER 3

Friday, September 27, Washington, D.C.

It was late when Ferron reached the hotel. A pianist in a tuxedo was playing the white grand piano in the middle of the atrium's lagoon. He wondered what Janelle and his grandfather had learned about Senator Sprague's estate in the Virginia countryside.

Ferron took the elevator to the second floor and then the hallway to the right. Stepping into the room, he was pleased to see that the lamps were lit.

Janelle bounced up from the sofa, where she'd been watching TV in the suite's main room. "How'd it go, Nick?" She looked over his shoulder, while he removed his jacket. "Where's Gran Babbo? Those two men you sent picked him up at four."

Ferron felt a lead weight plummet into his stomach. "What men?"

Janelle stared at him. "Oh, no." Her lips quivered. "There was a message from you at the front desk when we got back. Your grandfather didn't question it."

Ferron sat down on the bed, his whole body suddenly exhausted. The magnitude of his stupidity hit him then, hard—the phone call from the embassy in Paramaribo, the CIA's interests in the country, Sprague's connection to the intelligence community, and then his arrival at the Senator's office, acting like an empty-headed hayseed. His photo was probably on the Senator's desk before he'd touched down in Miami the afternoon before. He'd underestimated the Senator's resources. Did he have his men everywhere?

He put his head between his hands, too overwhelmed to ask questions. What good did it do to know what the men who picked up his grandfather looked like? There was only one thing that mattered. After all his work, before the battle had even begun, he'd lost the war.

Earl Sprague had won.

He raised his head tiredly, aware that Janelle was standing beside him with her hand on his shoulder.

"Earl Sprague—" he said. "He's got Gran Babbo."

CHAPTER 4

Friday, September 27, the countryside near Washington, D.C.

The Senator received his house guest in his den, a half-hour after a late dinner alone. His television interviews had been taped from the Capitol earlier in the afternoon, after which he had managed to leave undetected in his chauffeured Lincoln. A fire crackled in the fireplace, and the French doors were closed, their external shutters battened down. Though expecting his guest, he was dressed in a blue robe with white piping, and dark brown slippers. The letters WC were embroidered in a florid red script on the tongue of each slipper.

"What's the WC stand for?" his guest said, when Vasco Akkad, the man who had brought him there, left the room. "Waste containers?"

The Senator smiled thinly. Though the old man in front of him could barely stand and spoke through bloodied lips, he sounded like every other old spy the Senator had ever met. They never could repress their cutting wit. That wouldn't save him now. Before midnight, the man would be dead.

He looked down at his slippers; the red letters were initials. "Winston Churchill," he said.

The old man tried to laugh. "Those belonged to Winnie?"

"Hardly."

The Senator sat in a teal-blue wing chair and crossed his legs. A Mauser pistol, in an open case embroidered with the initials *RFSS*, lay on the lamp stand to his right, next to a tumbler of whiskey. His fingers caressed the gun. "Awful nice of you to bring this with you." He paused, looked again at his slippers. "I should have married Gracie Allen," he said. "I saw a photo of Churchill in slippers like these and told my wife I'd like some just like them. She didn't think to get the initials right. Poor woman." His lips curled in a wicked grin that sullied his patrician features. "I misspelled her name on her tombstone."

He pointed to his left in the direction of the fire, to a recliner upholstered in dark velvet. "Have a chair. It's a cold, wet night out there. Would you care for a whiskey?"

The old man snorted. "Not yours."

"Then you'll excuse me if I drink alone," the Senator said. "Make yourself comfortable. We have a lot to discuss—although I must say, you don't have a lot of sand left in your hourglass."

The old man shrugged. "One makes the best of what's in one's power and takes the rest as it comes."

"Yes, I suppose so." The Senator picked up the Mauser. "So, this is your sign of triumph. You got the better of one man, but that was it, wasn't it? I'll have to put it with my *Eiserne Kreuz*." He pointed to a small open safe, hidden under one of the outer hearth's stone panels, and smiled. "Of course, it's not just an Iron Cross; it's a Knight's Cross with oak leaves. I don't imagine you've seen many of those. I take it out for special occasions such as this."

The old man's smile was scornful. "What's so special about this?"

The Senator shrugged. "It's not often I get to kill one of my former agents."

"I wouldn't know about that," the old man said. "You did it often enough in the war."

CHAPTER 5

Friday, September 27, Washington, D.C.

T hat's him," Ferron said, pointing to the TV. The anchor-
woman on the early edition of News 7, broadcast by the
local ABC affiliate, had just turned to another camera, her
eyes finding the TelePrompTer. "At a press conference this
afternoon, Senator Earl Sprague, Chairman of the Senate
Intelligence Oversight Committee, announced his candidacy for
the office of President of the United States."

Ferron said, "The bastard. I'd like to shoot him." He aimed
the Colt at the TV screen, then hit the mute button on the remote
control with his left hand. He turned to Janelle. "What did Gran
Babbo do with that Mauser?"

"He had it with him when he left." She stopped talking and
pointed to the television. "Look, they're covering the revolution
in Suriname."

He turned up the volume and listened intently. Following a
brief clip from a reporter in Paramaribo and another from an
analyst at the State Department that spoke of U.S. warships
standing offshore, Senator Sprague appeared again on camera,
his right hand raised like that of a prophet threatening eternal
damnation. He warned of the threat of a reign of terror for law-
abiding citizens in Suriname and spoke in dire tones of the
revolutionaries as a band of terrorists, supported by Cuban
agents and armed by the Libyans.

"Bullshit," Ferron said. He picked up the remote control and clicked off the television. "Let's get going, Janelle. We don't have time to listen to him blather."

"Tell me again what Gran Babbo said about the estate?"

Janelle looked at him as he maneuvered the van into the right lane of the expressway. They had just crossed the Theodore Roosevelt Bridge and were trying to make the connection with Arlington Boulevard, State Highway 50. Despite the late hour, traffic was heavy. A semi-trailer truck loomed in the rearview mirror, then swung out beside them and pulled ahead, cutting off their view of the signs overhead.

Janelle cleared her throat. "Inside the brick perimeter wall, there's an electrified barbed-wire fence. Your grandfather said it looked new, so he wasn't sure if it was hooked up yet, but the best assumption was that it is. If you cut it, an alarm will probably go off in the guard house."

"How close to the perimeter wall is it?"

"About five feet."

"Did he say whether he thought there were sensors between the wall and the fence?"

"He didn't say." She put her hand on the dash as he braked for a BMW that had cut in front of them and then signaled for an exit. "Your grandfather did say something about ELTE cameras along the perimeter wall and floodlights. He said that might mean some type of pressure-sensitive alarm buried in the ground."

Ferron exhaled sharply. "Damn. They'll have video covering the entire perimeter."

"There's a wooded area at the back of the property and your grandfather saw some fawns, so he didn't think there'd be any sensors inside the wire—at least not in the woods. But about 100 feet from the manor house he detected several infrared posts. From the receptors, it looked like beams spaced a foot apart from about one foot off the ground to six feet."

"Great." He shook his head in disgust. "Guess I should've parachuted in." He paused, racking his brain for solutions. "I wonder if the deer trip the infrared alarms?"

"Your grandfather didn't think they'd go that close to the house." She turned to look at him. "I didn't know you'd learned to parachute."

He snorted. "Never have. Closest I've come is rappelling down from a helicopter. But if we'd had time . . ." His voice trailed away.

He felt a growing sense of frustration, caused in part by what he was hearing from Janelle, in part from trying to concentrate on his driving and formulate a plan of attack at the same time. It wouldn't do to get in a wreck before they even left the city. Everyone was driving like an idiot. The rain had stopped falling and the road was starting to dry, but the thick traffic threw up an oily spray. Except for the broad arc cleaned by the wipers, the front windshield was grimy with grease and dirt.

He rubbed his right eye. The beginnings of a headache. "Anything else, Janelle?"

She hesitated. "Your grandfather said the wall is patrolled by at least two guards, each with a team of Doberman Pinschers."

He swore and hit the steering wheel. "How often?"

"Every fifteen to twenty minutes."

He tried to fight down his anger and frustration, clenching his teeth until his jaws ached. What he needed was an assault squad. Earl Sprague was ready and waiting. After a moment he said, "I wonder if they patrol at night."

She didn't say anything.

"Yeah, stupid question." He touched the Colt .45, riding in the pocket of his jacket. Thank God Curtis Woods had come through. "I may have to shoot the dogs."

"There's some pepper in the box in back," she said. "Your grandfather had me buy it before we went out there the first time. There's an ax, a step ladder, a flashlight, some duct tape."

"None of that'll do much good with guards around. If I go over the wall, they're going to know I'm coming a mile away. Probably have me on camera the whole time."

"The guards were armed with submachine guns. Your grandfather said something about one having a TEC-9 and the other a MAC-11."

He swore again. He knew the weapons well. "Thirty-two- and thirty-six-shot magazines," he growled. "Drug dealers love 'em." He tried to steel himself for what lay ahead. Was it hopeless?

They passed under a gantry announcing Glebe Road, highway 120, and he slowed.

"That's not it," Janelle said. "Keep going. We'll be in Fairfax County before long."

He nodded absentmindedly. Forget the wall, he thought. "What about the front gate?"

"There's a glassed-in cabin with at least one guard on duty. Your grandfather said the gate looked too strong to crash—and it's electronically controlled from inside the cabin."

"Anyone go inside or out while you were there?"

"Not that we saw. I wasn't there very long." She tugged on her sweater. The van was starting to get hot. "I still wish you'd called the police, Nick."

"And tell them what? Two men stopped by the hotel and picked up my grandfather?"

"Tell them about Sprague."

He laughed harshly. "The man just announced his candidacy to be President. The first thing they'll think is we're wackos. Especially without evidence."

"But you're a cop."

"Was a cop, you mean."

"That shouldn't matter."

He shrugged. After a minute he said, "If Sprague hadn't been so paranoid, he could've denied everything. All I have is a dying man's words. Kloos destroyed the dossier."

"Sprague doesn't know that."

"True. He probably thinks we have his OVRA file."

"Except you haven't gone to the newspapers."

"He'd be expecting us to come to him first. He knows if my grandfather suspected him of betraying Carla Ceruti, he'd kill him." Ferron shook his head. "Sprague has a lot to pay for. He's not getting away this time. If he's hurt Gran Babbo, I'll hunt him down if it's the last thing I do.

Janelle bit her lower lip. "So how do we get in?"

"Damned if I know."

CHAPTER 6

Friday, September 27, Washington, D.C.

Twenty minutes later, they left Fairfax and turned south. Janelle looked at him. "You have a plan, Nick?"

He glanced over at her briefly, hearing the anxiety in her voice. "I guess I just have to walk up and tell them who I am."

In the darkness of the country road, dash lights casting dim shadows, he said, "I should have left you back at that convenience store in Fairfax, by the phone booths. I could have told Sprague we'd trade the dossier on him for my grandfather."

"But then what?"

"At least you'd be able to call the police if I didn't show up."

"We're back where we started."

"Not quite. The police would have your word that I went in and didn't come out."

"Can't we say the same about your grandfather? Where else would they take him?"

He could think of a lot of places. Gran Babbo could be at the bottom of the river by now. "Sure," he said, "we could lie. We could say they took him by force—that he was brought to the estate. But he might not be there. Even if the cops believed us, it'd take them all night to get a search warrant. If Sprague's goons kidnaped Gran Babbo, they're not going to keep him sitting around in the basement." His voice grew cold, all emotion suppressed. "He may already be dead, Janelle. You have to prepare yourself for that." Was he speaking to himself? he wondered. He took a deep breath. "If he is, Earl Sprague is going to suffer before he dies."

Night swept over the hills like a spreading pool of black ink, obliterating every feature of the land and erasing the boundaries between earth and cloud-covered sky. The darkness moved swiftly and unimpeded, like a wave at sea, until it hit the brick wall of the estate, where it was suddenly shattered, driven back by the intense glare of the wall's perimeter lights. Sitting on a knoll in the middle of the estate, visible through the trees along the western side, the manor house glowed like a phosphorescent sea anemone in a black-lit aquarium.

Five hundred feet from the wall, Ferron eased the van to a stop and looked at Janelle. "I'm going to let you out here. Take Gran Babbo's rain gear and hide in the grass. If I'm not back by dawn, flag down a car and call the police."

"You drive up to the gate and they'll find your gun," she protested.

"No they won't." He pulled the Colt .45 from his belt and handed it to her. "You're keeping it. Ever shot one like this?"

In answer, she chambered a round expertly and sighted down the barrel. The gun was aimed at Sprague's mansion. "I can protect myself, Nick. It's you I'm worried about. What are you going to do?"

"I don't know," he said. "I'll just have to see what happens."

Janelle shivered and stared at the van's taillights as it moved slowly away from her, following the gentle curve of the road. The darkness closed in around her. She thought of Nick sitting inside, one hand on the steering wheel, the other on the gear shift. She felt his solitude then—the fragility of human life. He was going in alone against Sprague and his men, no weapons to help.

Despite his exhaustion, perhaps because of it, she and Nick had made love the night before, after Gran Babbo had gone to sleep in one of the suite's bedrooms. It had been fourteen years since they were high school sweethearts, since they said good-bye when Nick went off to college, not knowing that circumstances would cause them to drift apart. Their first deep kiss was like a long-awaited homecoming, a sense of restoration. Yet, his hand on her breast, the merging of their bodies, had felt as natural as if it was only yesterday that they'd last made love. They'd laughed, then, at their passion, at the eagerness with which they devoured each other. Like young lovers making love for the first time.

She couldn't lose him now. She wasn't going to say good-bye again.

When the taillights winked out, she dropped the rain gear at the side of the road and began running.

CHAPTER 7

Blinking in the harsh glare of the floodlights, Ferron rolled down his window and leaned out to speak into the microphone grille mounted at the side of the entryway. Just beyond, he could see the glassed-in cabin and a panel of video screens.

The guard straightened, his eyes widening in surprise. A young kid in uniform. He punched two buttons on the console and stared expectantly.

Had an alarm gone out already? Ferron wondered. He identified himself and then said, "Please let the Senator know I'm here to see him."

The guard ran his tongue over his front teeth before speaking. "I'm sorry, sir, but the Senator's not expecting anyone this evening."

"He left a credit card at the Pussycat Nightclub, and I need to know what to do with it."

The kid tried to restrain a grin. "Very funny, sir. The Senator asked not to be disturbed. He doesn't frequent nightclubs."

"Look, just tell him I'm Thomas Gage's grandson. Tell him I've come from the OVRA."

"The what?"

"The O-V-R-A. He'll know what I mean."

The guard turned his back, picked up a telephone, and spoke into it. After listening for a moment, he swivelled around and said, "Someone'll be down for you in a minute."

Ferron took his foot off the clutch and moved the nose of the van up to the gate. He waited ten seconds and said, "How about opening the gate so I can wait inside."

The guard shook his head. He pointed through the glass. "Back up and pull over to the side. If you're going up, it'll be in one of our vehicles."

He glared at the kid, but did as he was told. Five minutes later, a Jeep Cherokee Laredo pulled up and a tall black man stepped out. He looked to be about six-five and 280 pounds. He sported Nike tennis shoes, blue jeans, and a light poplin jacket emblazoned with the name of the Washington Redskins. The jacket was unzipped and Ferron caught a glimpse of a shoulder holster. A diamond stud glinted in the man's left ear.

"Step inside," the man said, gesturing to a small gate at the side of the guard post.

Ferron heard the latch click as the guard inside the cabin pressed another button. He stepped through the gate and a hand snagged out, grabbed his jacket and pulled him forward, off balance. The black man slipped behind him, caught him in a half nelson and threw him up against the Jeep.

"Spread 'em," the man said, kicking at his feet.

"I'm unarmed. Is this how you treat your guests?" He spread his feet and gripped the top of the Jeep with both hands.

"You ain't no guest," the man said.

"Check with your boss and you might find out differently."

The search for weapons was quick and effective.

"Hands behind your back."

He heard the clink of handcuffs.

Damn. Have to act now in front of the other guard. He couldn't go up to the house with his hands cuffed. He'd have no chance.

He dropped his left hand with studied ease, then gripped the man's wrist and spun around, pulling the wrist across the other man's body and throwing a hard right at his jaw at the same time. The blow glanced off the man's cheek and Ferron felt the wrist come loose as the man twisted his powerful arm. An elbow slammed back into his midsection and he doubled over, gasping for breath. He heard the door of the guard post bang in its frame and caught a glimpse of the uniformed guard with a shotgun in his hands. A hand grabbed him behind the neck, the grip like that of an eagle with iron talons. Fingernails cut through his flesh. He moaned and collapsed to his knees, pain rocketing down his back. A fist slammed into the base of his spine and he fell face forward in the gravel. The sciatic nerve in both legs tingled and his arms went numb.

From behind, he heard the sharp report of gunfire—a pistol, not the shotgun. The uniformed guard screamed and pitched to the side, his shotgun skidding across the graveled roadway. Ferron stared at the gun, which had come to rest with the barrel aimed at his head. The grip on his neck loosened as the black man pivoted and reached for the pistol in his shoulder holster.

Ferron tried to yell, but no sound came from his throat. His mind told him to roll into the man—throw off his aim—but the body would not respond.

He heard another sharp report, then two more.

He jerked his eyes around, twisting to see who was shooting, expecting a bullet in the back of the head. A heavy body fell, thudding into the ground two feet away, shuddering like a massive tree chopped down in the forest. *The black man.*

"Are you okay, Nick?"

Janelle!

He tried to swallow, a long, dry capsule of fear stuck sideways in his throat. He rotated his neck, hearing the vertebra crack. His body ached as if he'd been in a head-on collision with a Mack truck.

"Get up, Nick. I'm locked out."

A few minutes later, both men were bound with duct tape. Ferron dragged them into the guard post.

Janelle looked worried. "Did I kill them?"

He straightened with a grimace, then shook his head. He rubbed his back at the base of the spine. "They'll live," he said. "But they aren't going to be too happy about it for a while." He tried to grin. "Good shooting."

She was too preoccupied to respond.

He looked around the glassed-in booth. No sign of activity on any of the video screens, but none of them showed the interior of the house. "Get in the Jeep," he told Janelle. "You can drive."

"You want the Colt?"

"Keep it."

Outside, he picked up the shotgun, gritting his teeth at the pain in his lower back, then found the black man's pistol—a 9mm Ruger with a fifteen-round magazine. There had been no extra clips in the man's jacket. In the distance, he heard a dog bark.

Janelle had turned the Jeep around and threw open the front passenger door. "Hurry, Nick," she said. "We've been here twenty minutes now. I can hear the dogs."

CHAPTER 8

Friday, September 27, Washington, D.C.

They'll know we're coming, won't they?"

Janelle clenched the steering wheel as the Jeep negotiated the sweeping drive that led to the mansion at the hill's crest. The Colt rested in her lap. Ferron was holding the shotgun in his left hand; his right gripped the Ruger automatic.

"They might. The uniformed guard punched a couple of buttons when I first drove up." He paused. "When we get to the house, I want you to stay in the Jeep. Turn it around and keep the motor running."

"You might need help, Nick. Who knows how many—"

A hail of bullets from up ahead and to the right cut off her words, stitching a path across the side of the Jeep. The windows on Ferron's side shattered. Shards of glass blew through the interior and he felt sudden, sharp pain as the fragments shredded his clothes and laced their way down the side of his face. His finger jerked in shock and the Ruger automatic coughed and spit fire as a bullet plowed forward into the dash. The vehicle left the road and jolted to a stop, radiator hissing. For a second, they both sat there stunned, and then another burst raked the vehicle and he screamed, "*Get out!*"

She opened her door and fell to the ground, her head pressed into the wet earth. Ferron scrambled after her, tumbling from the car and falling on top of the shotgun.

"You okay?" Twisting away from the Jeep.

"I think so." Her voice was choked.

"Get behind the tire. Here." He handed her the shotgun. "It's only got two shells."

"I've lost the Colt."

He crawled to the door and reached inside, his free hand sweeping the floor board. "Found it."

He sensed movement at the back of the Jeep and turned to look, heard Janelle gasp. A dark shape hit the ground and went into a roll. Before the man came to a stop, a fulminous blast blew by Ferron's ear, deafening him. Janelle had emptied both barrels of the shotgun in panic, the shells plowing into the ground near the shadowy figure. Ferron tracked the rolling shadow, unleashed three well-spaced shots.

The gunman did not shoot back.

Ferron slapped the Colt into Janelle's hands. He still had the Ruger. His ears were ringing, but he could hear a shout from the direction of the mansion. He scurried down the slope and found the dead man's submachine gun.

When he returned, Janelle was leaning against the front tire, breathing hard. "Are you okay?" he asked again.

She didn't respond.

"They're going to be coming from the house," he said. "I've got to leave you." He held out the submachine gun and she stared at it a moment before reaching up to take it. "I'm going to circle around and try to get in from the back," he said. "Can you hold them for a while?"

"I'll try."

"No telling how many bullets are left in the magazine. When it's empty, start running. Keep the Colt with you. It's dark out here, they might not find you. If they do, use the Colt."

CHAPTER 9

Friday, September 27, Washington, D.C.

The manor house was bathed in soft light as Ferron skirted the southern exposure and cut up the hill along a line of cypress trees that led from an ornamental shrub garden toward a garage at the back of the mansion, hidden from the road below. He could hear no sounds from the direction of the Jeep. An undercurrent of worry washed through him, and for a moment he wondered if someone might attempt to sneak up on Janelle. Maybe he shouldn't have left her. He might already have lost Gran Babbo; he didn't want to lose Janelle, too. She'd seemed in a daze, and he wasn't sure if her silence was from shell shock or grim determination.

Take care of yourself, Janelle. Nothing more he could do for her now. He had to worry about what lay ahead.

"What is it?" Sprague asked, upset that his top security man had returned to the den. "I told you not to disturb us."

"I need to talk to you in private," Akkad said, his face flushed, heavy Italian accent forgotten.

Sprague picked up the Mauser his men had taken from Gage and followed Akkad into the hall outside the den.

When the door closed behind them, Akkad said, "The kid showed up."

Sprague's eyes brightened. "Where is he?"

Akkad hesitated. "Don't know for sure. Randall called

Naveed down to pick the kid up in the Jeep. Somehow the cop overpowered 'em both." He hurried on when he saw the scowl on the Senator's face. "We think we have him pinned down behind the Jeep. Want to talk to him before we kill him?"

"Just take care of it and get back here for the old man. I'll be done with him by then."

"I'll give the order to hit the Jeep hard. I got three men on it. I had to send two down to the guard house. Naveed's scalp's peeled back like the lid on a sardine tin and Randall's got a bullet in his shoulder. We're not going to be able to cover this up."

"What do the guards know?"

"Nothing. I told them it's an assassination attempt."

"Okay. After you kill Ferron and we get rid of Gage, we'll call it in that way—a rogue cop gone wild."

The Senator put his hand on the door knob and turned to go in. Akkad reached out and stopped him. "That Mauser," he said. "I wouldn't trust it."

Sprague sneered and patted the pocket of his robe. "Unlike you, I don't screw up. I have my own gun. You worry about Ferron."

The Senator swung the door open and stepped into the den. Gage was staring at him from his seat by the fire, a question in his eye.

"It's nothing." Sprague had a sardonic smile on his face. "We just killed your grandson."

Downstairs, the double doors leading to the kitchen shattered under the force of a heavy blow.

Vasco Akkad was running. As he passed the light switch controlling the lamps in the second-floor corridor, he flicked them off, took the stairs three steps at a time. When he reached the first floor landing, he heard a maid scream in the kitchen and then fall silent. He lifted the two-way radio from his belt and spoke into it. "He's in the house," he said. "Get up here now."

Before he could turn off the radio, he heard a desperate call. "Vasco, this is Trell. Keith's been shot. There's still someone in the Jeep."

Akkad froze. He was sure Ferron was in the house, so who was in the jeep? Had the guy contacted a friend in D.C.? Another cop?

Shit! The girl in the hotel. Keith had been shot by a girl! He depressed the panel on the radio and whispered. "Trell, that's a fucking girl you're shooting at. Get the hell down there and kill the bitch, and then get back up here. We got an assassin in the house. I'm shutting off now."

Ferron tied the maid's hands behind her back with a dish towel. He'd hit her hard and she was lying on the kitchen floor. Unconscious but breathing. He stood, saw an eight-inch knife with a serrated blade on the counter and stuck it in the left pocket of the jacket, the blade running through the seam. He found the light switches near a door leading down a corridor to a pantry and extinguished them, pausing a moment while his eyes adjusted to the darkness.

Two pilot lights on the old gas stove cast a feeble glimmer from one corner of the room. He could smell onions in the air and a faint hint of a fragrant spice, vaguely familiar—tarragon or rosemary, maybe—something his ex-wife Sharon used to cook with. He didn't know the layout of the manor house and didn't know where to go next, but he knew he had to move fast. If he hadn't done it already, Sprague would not hesitate to kill Gran Babbo. Before shutting out the lights, Ferron had seen a narrow staircase descending at the back of the pantry. He'd have to search for the staircase for the second floor.

Go up or down?

Up, he decided, knew immediately why. He didn't like basements. A quick vision of a coal bin. A naked five-year-old boy locked inside by his dad. Stale air, pitch black and cold, with hard lumps of coal to sit on. Another of Frank Ferron's punishments. There were some things you never forgot.

Gran Babbo, where are you?

He listened for sounds, heard only water dripping from a leaky faucet—then the light hiss of a gas water heater in a closet near the pantry. Sight gone but other senses sharp. Still no sound of footsteps, no scuffle in another room, no cries for help. Where in hell did they have him?

He heard gunfire in the distance—outside. The faint echo of sharp percussion. They were attacking the Jeep.

Janelle!

Don't let them get you!

And what about himself? He couldn't stand there all night. Had to find the staircase.

Move!

He felt his way along the wall, found and went through the swinging door that led down a corridor to the dining room. He paused again while his eyes tried to pick out the objects in the dark room. Was it empty? Was someone waiting for him to make a mistake?

Have to chance it.

He ran across the room diagonally, dodging between the long, refectory table and a wheeled trolley with cut-glass containers, angled toward a door that was outlined on three sides by a thin gleam of light from beyond. He flattened himself against the wall next to a tall cabinet with a domed shell, listened again, heart pounding. He took several deep breaths to calm himself, then laid his ear against the door.

The house was as dead as a tomb. He turned the beveled glass knob, and pushed the door open. A lighted hall led to the front door, surmounted by a semi-circular leaded-glass arch. To his left, against the wall, a staircase with a polished wood balustrade led to the second floor. *Good. He'd found it.*

Cut the lights. Otherwise, he'd be moving up the stairs like a duck in a shooting gallery.

When the hallway was dark, he made his way to the foot of the stairs and paused at the newel post, his left hand on the cool, slick banister. The wood gave off a smell of lemon-scented furniture polish. Suddenly the hair on the back of his neck stood up. A quick vision—the cross-hairs of a telescopic sight focusing in on his head, a physical pressure as if a bullet were boring a hole through his skull. He abandoned all caution then, running up the stairs in a forward crouch, the Ruger automatic in his right hand.

A shot rang out and slammed him into the wall, the force of the concussion jarring his body. The gun started to slip from his fingers before they contracted reflexively and closed around the grip. He could hear other bullets then as time seemed to slow down. He tumbled backward down the stairs, felt another bullet slam into him, screamed and caromed off the wall and through the rail, dropping the last three feet to the floor. He landed on his side, and his head slapped into the floor. He lay there for a moment, stunned by the blow, aware that he needed to move or he'd die with a bullet in his brain. He sensed a presence descending the stairs, saw a flash of gunfire, raised his pistol and fired.

The shot caught Vasco Akkad at the bottom of his right mandible. The jaw shattered and the 9mm slug flattened out and carried onward, exploding through the parietal lobe and out the top of his skull along with fragments of bone and brain tissue. Ferron heard another shot from overhead, the sounds of a scuffle.

"Nick," his grandfather yelled. "I'm up here."

He came up off the floor like a man on fire, the pain in his side and arm merging in one mad impulse for vengeance. He pounded up the stairs, stumbled over Akkad's dead body, his eyes desperately searching for Earl Sprague. The door to the den was open and a blaze of light spilled out into the corridor. As he reached the landing, he heard another shot in the room, the sounds of a scuffle, glass breaking, and then the lights went out.

Suddenly, from down below, he heard his name called. He stopped for a moment and turned, the pain flooding back into him.

"Nick," she screamed. "It's Janelle. Where are you?"

"Stay where you are," he heard himself roar, the sound loud in his ears, reverberating like thunder.

He tried to move up the hall and felt suddenly weak. His left arm hung limp. He could feel the blood running down into his shoe. His side burned—a sharp sting that started small and radiated out in ever expanding waves of pain. The knife he'd stuck through the seam in his jacket pocket was gone.

Shadows flickered on the opposite wall of the corridor as the log fire crackled inside the den. Before he could get there, the door slammed shut and he heard a body fall. Another shot rang out, slashing through the door and into the corridor.

Get down the hall and get in there!

He stumbled toward the door, the left side of his body scrapping the wall and leaving a trail of blood. A hazy feeling swept over him and he started to fall.

Can't loose it now!

Deep breaths. Clear the haze.

Each gulp of air seared through his body like a branding iron.

He was at the door then, not remembering how he got there or how much time had passed. Time and space had ceased to exist. A black cloud swirled around him. From deep inside came the words: *Kick it in and kill the bastard!* A vision of his father—dark hair . . . dark eyes . . . thick, shaggy eyebrows and hairy arms. Arms raised to hit him.

He screamed and kicked at the door, shattering the hinges. And then he was inside the room. Without knowing how he did it, unable to feel, his left hand found the light switch while he raised his right hand and sighted in on the target in front of him. The man was on the floor, Mauser in hand, head raised to look as Ferron fired the bullet.

The face in front of him was that of Thomas Gage.

CHAPTER 10

L ife and death.
Two sides of the same door.
Life was the only illness that was one hundred percent fatal.

You didn't ask to be born, you didn't ask to die; you had no choice in the matter. Your only choice was how you lived in the short or long span allotted to you. And when the end came, you only hoped it came fast.

Ferron didn't know when the thoughts passed through his mind, but it felt like they scrolled by while the bullet he'd fired tracked its path across the room. At the last second, with his grandfather staring down the barrel of the gun, he'd twisted his wrist, deflecting the bullet, which tore through the back of Sprague's wing chair and smacked into the mantel of the fireplace. Ferron dropped to his knees, mouth opening in shock. In his blind fury, he'd almost killed the only man he'd ever loved.

"Gran Babbo," he said. "It's you."

And then he pitched forward and passed out.

Sprague rolled to his side, his eyes wildly searching for the gun that had slipped from the pocket of his robe during the scuffle with Gage. And then, on his hands and knees, he saw it on the floor beside the sofa. Slobbering from the exertion, his eyes frantic, he lunged for the gun and came up with it. He was about to turn to fire, when he felt the cold barrel of a gun at the base of his neck and a woman's voice said, "Drop it, asshole."

Ferron stood with his right arm around Janelle. His grandfather had pocketed the Senator's pistol and held the Mauser pointed at the man's chest. Sprague sat on the floor, his face ashen. For once, he looked his age—an old man staring death in the face.

Ferron cleared his throat, fighting the pain that made it hard to talk. "Janelle and I are going for the van, Gran Babbo. You've waited a long time for this. He's all yours."

When they reached the front porch, Janelle said, "Sit here, Nick. I'll bring the van up."

He obeyed her command, feeling dizzy. A heavy weight of blackness pressed down on him. They'd already called a doctor in Fairfax, who was waiting at a clinic. "What about the others?" he managed to ask.

"Dead or wounded," she said. "After you left, another guy attacked the Jeep. He killed the last two guards by mistake. They were coming up behind me. He shot at everything that moved." She looked haggard for a moment, and then added, "I got him."

She paused. "Just hang on, Nick. You're going to make it."

Thomas Gage looked at the man known as Eagle Jack. All sign of life had gone out of the traitor. The man stared numbly at the floor, his eyes hooded. Gage crossed the room, walked by the Senator, and stripped the medals from above the mantelpiece— a British Military Cross, the French *Croix de Guerre* with Palms and Star, the U.S. Distinguished Service Cross, and the Legion of Merit with oak-leaf clusters—then tossed them into the fire.

On the way back, he stopped at the cocktail table and bent over to retrieve the Knight's Cross that Sprague had laid there while he boasted about his exploits in the war. Himmler had personally awarded him the medal and Sprague had wanted the former OSS agent to see it while they talked.

Gage walked back to where the man sat on the floor and looked down at him.

The Senator glanced up tiredly and said, "Get it over with."

Gage raised the Mauser, paused a moment, then shook his head. "Shooting you is too easy," he said. "You deserve to die— a horrible death. But that would make me a killer just like you . . . There'll be others who lack my compunction, those who lost more than I did, those who can't forget. You can try to run, you can try to protect yourself, but they'll hunt you down." He lowered the gun and waited until Sprague looked up again. "You haven't suffered enough, Senator. Tomorrow, on the steps of the Capitol, statements will be released detailing your activities in the war—the agents you betrayed, the lives you took, the wealth you accumulated with the help of the fascists. And from what my grandson tells me, the revolutionaries in Suriname have their own documents. You illegally subverted funds to the right-wing regime there. All you ever cared about were your own business interests."

He paused and the scorn in his voice grew stronger. "You're no patriot, Eagle Jack. Patriotism is no more than a feeling—and you don't even have that. Sacrifice makes it a virtue—and that's something you could never do. Those, by the way, are Mussolini's words, Senator. But you always were a coward. You thought only of yourself. It took a long time, Eagle Jack, but the world is going to know it all. Before I'm through with you, I'll see that you have neither wealth nor power."

Gage took a deep breath and exhaled slowly. His body was trembling. "I'm only sorry that public disgrace and prison—and fear of the men who'll try to kill you—are not enough." He dropped the Knight's Cross at Sprague's feet, then waved the Mauser. "Here," he said. "I've been saving this for you." He tossed the German gun on the wing chair nearby. "Another trophy. Add it to your collection."

And with that he turned and left the den. It was time to take his grandson home.

Before he reached the bottom of the stairs, he heard the single gunshot from up above. The faintest trace of a smile showed on his face and then disappeared. He thought of Carla Ceruti . . . saw her face as it first appeared to him so many years ago in Rome across the outdoor table at the caffè near Piazza Colonna, a young girl in full bloom . . . cut off before her time. He saw her raising her arms to bunch her dark tresses, stray wisps of hair escaping from between her fingers like the notes of a near-forgotten memory. He said good-bye to her as he'd said good-bye to his daughter Irene, a mother bird shot out of the sky with two fledglings in the nest, and as, years later, long after the war was over, brought down by one of Nature's villains, he'd said good-bye to his wife Olga, before she was laid to rest. *Requiem aeternam dona eis, domine, et lux perpetua luceat eis.* Eternal rest grant unto them, O Lord, and let perpetual light shine round about them.

Not long now before I see you once again . . .

He straightened then, took in a deep breath and let it out slowly.

It was finally over.

Eagle Jack's last campaign had ended in defeat.

ACKNOWLEDGMENTS

I am indebted to many individuals for background material and items of fact. Some people provided answers to questions without realizing why they were asked; all were generous in their responses. Any errors or changes in historical fact are, of course, my own responsibility.

For their help with specific details, I thank Lise Leibacher, the late John Gesell, Jonathan Beck, Gianni Spera, and Jean-Jacques Demorest; for comments on the plot, Peter Rubie and Stephen Mertz; for encouragement, Ronald Argo; for instruction in Dutch, Rex Torres, and in German, Roland Richter and Beate Gilliar; for their aid with software, Claire Lauer, Mark Bryant, and Jim Austin; and for information on Suriname, the Consulate of the Republic of Suriname in Miami.

Among the individuals who were of aid as published sources of information, let me cite the following, using their titles at the time: for SWAT team tactics and equipment, Dave Bartram and Tim Bourgoine; for MANTIS and narcotics trafficking, Pima County Sheriff Clarence Dupnik and Sheriff's Lt. Paul Pederson, Tucson Police Chief Peter Ronstadt and Captain James Koch, Assistant U.S. Border Patrol Agent Tom Wacker and Tucson Chief Ron Dowdy, and Agent-in-Charge, U.S. Customs Service Tucson office, Thomas A. McDermott.

Numerous authors provided useful background information: for *North Africa*, Carleton S. Coon, Donald Downs, Roy Farran, and the Great Britain Naval Intelligence Division; *for the OSS and SOE*, William Stevenson, R. Harris Smith, Harry Howe Ransom, Hilary St. George Saunders, John Gooch, Stewart Alsop, Thomas Braden, MacGregor Knox, Corey Ford, and Thomas F. Troy; *for Allied military operations*, Charles R. S. Harris, Norman

Kogan, Chester G. Starr, and Mark W. Clark; *for Mussolini and Italy in the Fascist Era*, Peter Tompkins, Reynolds and Eleanor Packard, S.K., Giuseppe Antonio Borghese, Benito Mussolini, Rachele Mussolini, Galeazzo Ciano, Edda Ciano, Albert Kesselring, Emil Ludwig, F. W. Deakin, Howard McGaw Smyth, Charles F. Delzell, Max Gallo, and two reference works—the *Enciclopedia dell'Antifascismo e della Resistenza* and the *Historical Dictionary of Fascist Italy; for Indonesia and the Dutch*, Leslie H. Palmier and J. D. Legge; *and for the Republic of Suriname*, J. Warren Nystrom, R. W. G. Hingston, Richard Price, John Walsh, Robert Gannon, Charles J. Wooding, Willem F. L. Buschkens, Henk E. Chin, and Hans Buddingh', as well as publications of the following groups: The Ministry of Foreign Affairs (Suriname), the Geological and Mining Service (Suriname), the International Bank for Reconstruction and Development (head of mission, Richard H. Demuth), and The Economist Intelligence Unit (London).

I refer those who read Italian and wish to know more about the OVRA to three invaluable sources: Guido Leto, *OVRA. Fascismo—Antifascismo* (Rocca San Casciano, 1951), Carmine Senise, *Quando ero Capo della Polizia, 1940-1943* (Rome, 1946), and Ernesto Rossi, *La pupilla del Duce. L'O.V.R.A.* (Parma, 1956). The first two authors were members of the Fascist police, the latter one of the OVRA's victims.

ABOUT THE AUTHOR

Born in Bellingham, Washington, Ron Terpening attended grade schools in Ferndale, Warden, Wenatchee, and Seattle, after which his family moved to Portland and then Gresham, Oregon. He received his Bachelor's degree from the University of Oregon in Eugene and his Master's and Ph.D. from the University of California at Berkeley. He has lived in Mexico City and in Pavia and Florence, Italy. He taught for four years at Loyola University of Chicago, and is currently a professor of Italian at the University of Arizona.

He and his wife, Vicki, and their five Golden Retrievers live in the foothills of the Tucson mountains.